# UNSEEN CITY

"If Amy Shearn's fiction is as much fun to write as it is to read, that's welcome news because it's impossible to read her novels without wanting more, more, more. In true Shearn style, *Unseen City* is whip-smart, hilarious, and also deeply touching, and this story about mismatched New Yorkers finding common ground in a city they've decided—come hell or higher rent—to adore, will delight and charm you long after the last page."

—COURTNEY MAUM, author of *I Am Having So Much Fun Here Without You* and *Touch*

"In *Unseen City* Amy Shearn has written a sad and funny and profound book. This is a novel about grief and human connection, about today and yesterday. And it is damn hard to put down."

—DARIN STRAUSS, bestselling author of *Half a Life* and *More Than It Hurts You*

"I wish I had written this book. . . . It's smart, funny, and gorgeously written. I am in awe."

—JULIA FIERRO, author of *The Gypsy Moth Summer*

"Atmospheric, poignant, well-observed, and sneakily funny, Amy Shearn's *Unseen City* is one from the heart, an absorbing read for all those who love Brooklyn, great writing, and the human spirit."

—KEVIN BAKER, bestselling author of *The Big Crowd* and *America the Ingenious*

# UNSEEN CITY

*A NOVEL*

*AMY SHEARN*

 Red Hen Press | *Pasadena, CA*

Book design by Mark E. Cull

Library of Congress Cataloging-in-Publication Data

Names: Shearn, Amy, author.
Title: Unseen city : a novel / Amy Shearn.
Description: First edition. | Pasadena, CA : Red Hen Press, [2020]
Identifiers: LCCN 2020025806 (print) | LCCN 2020025807 (ebook) | ISBN
   9781597093675 (trade paperback) | ISBN 9781597094320 (epub)
Subjects: LCSH: Paranormal fiction. | Domestic fiction.
Classification: LCC PS3619.H434 U57 2020 (print) | LCC PS3619.H434
   (ebook) | DDC 813/.6—dc23
LC record available at https://lccn.loc.gov/2020025806

Publication of this book has been made possible in part through the financial support of Bianca Richards and Linda Horioka.

The National Endowment for the Arts, the Los Angeles County Arts Commission, the Ahmanson Foundation, the Dwight Stuart Youth Fund, the Max Factor Family Foundation, the Pasadena Tournament of Roses Foundation, the Pasadena Arts & Culture Commission and the City of Pasadena Cultural Affairs Division, the City of Los Angeles Department of Cultural Affairs, the Audrey & Sydney Irmas Charitable Foundation, the Kinder Morgan Foundation, the Meta & George Rosenberg Foundation, the Albert and Elaine Borchard Foundation, the Adams Family Foundation, the Riordan Foundation, Amazon Literary Partnership, and the Mara W. Breech Foundation partially support Red Hen Press.

First Edition
Published by Red Hen Press
www.redhen.org

## ACKNOWLEDGMENTS

This book has been a long time coming, and over the years, I'm sure I've been helped by innumerable people, places, and forces of nature I'm forgetting.

Thanks are due to:

My tenacious agent, Julie Stevenson; wise editor, Kate Gale; and all the good people at Red Hen Press, for believing in this book.

My first readers, Lauren Haldeman and Siobhan Adcock, far better writers than I, who have now, many times over, made my writing much, much better.

Anita Romero Warren, who gave me a behind-the-scenes peek at the Weeksville Heritage Center; Ben and Ivy Gocker, who walked me through the research process and gave me the scoop on librarian life and the Brooklyn Collection (and, for that matter, to all the Brooklyn Public Library librarians, who make our city so much more livable); Annie Polland for lending me an insider's look at the Tenement Museum; Catherine Newman, Joshua Mack, and Luisa Colón, for sharing their memories of NYC in the '70s and '80s and fact-checking my pizza parlors; John K. Cox for answering my biomedical engineering questions; and Penina Roth and Rich Jean for helping me to keep it real when writing about Crown Heights, religion, and race. Miranda Beverly-Whittemore and Julia Fierro: our conversations about writing are so nourishing. All my witches: you know who you are and you know how you've helped.

The many writers and texts that informed the historical aspects of this story include but are not limited to: Judith Wellman's indispensible reference on Weeksville, *Brooklyn's Promised Land: The Free Black Community of Weeksville, New York*; Kevin Baker's meticulously researched novel *Paradise Alley* (shout-out to Lynn McKee at my coffice Steeplechase Coffee, who pointed me in the right direction); Zetta Elliot's YA novel about Weeksville, *A Wish After Midnight*; Luc Sante's *Low Life*; and the Weeksville contemporary works of Walt Whitman, Herman Melville, and William Wells Brown. The *Bowery Boys* historical podcasts and Ken Burns's documentaries on the Civil War were also immeasurably helpful.

Caroline and Tony Grant of the Sustainable Arts Foundation, for funding some of the babysitting hours that allowed me to plow through the first draft of this book. Though spaces are so important in this book, I was often writing it in spaces not my own; without Rachel Sherman and the Founders Workspace,

Elsie Kagan and the Interlude Artists Residency, and kind friends and neighbors who lent me their empty apartments, the final draft would have never seen the light of day.

My parents, Peggy and Don Shearn, whose story of coming together as two lost souls provided the initial spark of this book. My little brother Ben Shearn: you're all right too.

Harper and Alton, my everythings.

*For my parents*

# UNSEEN CITY

The dead are constant in
The white lips of the sea.
Over and over, through clenched teeth, they tell
Their story, the story each knows by heart:
*Remember me, speak my name.*
—Charles Wright,
  "Homage to Paul Cézanne"


*we are in the midst of strange and terrible times—*
—Walt Whitman,
  in a letter to his mother, July 15, 1863

# 1

**IT ISN'T EASY**, you know, being a ghost. Watching the world go on without you. Watching your city expand and contract, shuddering through municipal labor pains. A bridge, another bridge. A veining of trains. Appendectomies of buildings that once seemed solid as the earth itself. To see your home reclaimed by people who note the walls and floors and quality of light but never once consider that it all belonged to you. That it should belong to you. People who think that the past is dead, that the dead are done. Watching your things sifted through and disposed of. To have lost your hope of ever leaving a mark on the world. To see what a small corner of it you ever inhabited.

You love this city, this stupid, beautiful world. You believe in it. Of course you do. But does it believe in you?

Here is what I want to tell you.

# 2

**THERE ONCE WAS A WOMAN** named Meg Rhys. Haunted houses became a particular problem for Meg Rhys just after she turned forty, at the exact moment when, though it was true that she lived with only a fickle housecat and towers of books for company, it no longer seemed funny to go on calling herself a spinster librarian. Not that anyone said "spinster" in twenty-first century New York City except for Meg herself, and she said it *ironically*, the same way she *ironically* cultivated the silver streak in her hair, which she felt lent her the air of an otherworldly eccentric until the aforementioned birthday at which point the loss of pigment promptly ceased to seem intentional. Above all, Meg wanted the map of her life to be intentionally plotted, a course charted by her and her alone.

But at forty it was too late to turn back—a hairstyle change would only attract the attention of nosy relatives certain it signaled love or other retrograde "improvements"—and so she kept the piebald bun coiled around a Number 2 pencil that recalled to her the quiet pleasures of standardized tests. Equally symbolic was her bicycle with its Wicked-Witch-of-the-West basket, the bicycle itself a rickety second-hand number Meg had gotten good at riding while wearing the ankle-length skirts she wore not in an Orthodox or even Amish way but mostly for the swishy acoustics, weaving in and out of traffic entirely without imagining her body crushed by a box truck—she almost never thought about that at all anymore.

The librarian in her knew that no story was only one story.

Yes, it was true that her cat was named Virginia Wolf, and yes, she knew that "Woolf" was misspelled; it was meant to be a joke, and it was actually, when you thought about it, quite witty—not that anyone ever did seem to think about it much. July's chess master had critiqued the name in a fit of postcoital persnicketiness—a tendency augured by his precise sexual gambits—positing that since wolves were canines, it would be a funnier name for a dog. But Meg Rhys didn't like dogs. Nor did she lead a life conducive to needy creatures (and thus hadn't seen the chess master since). Her younger brother James, on the other hand, owned a beagle that took Prozac, which was all anyone needed to know about that.

Yes, Meg knew that she didn't *have* to be a spinster. This was how it was often said by her mother or her mother's friends or by frustrated men when she shooed them along—the chess master, the bankish guy before him (he'd been great at buying wine but loved a particular movie in a way she found unforgivable). Meg wasn't unattractive! They knew of *much* less desirable women who had married and even had children! It could still all turn out okay for her! Her! A smart lady with a good job, decent interpersonal skills, an appealing if snaggletoothed smile, a passable figure she knew how to flatter, a bookish intelligence that surely someone found appealing. Couldn't she find a husband? They usually forgot to ask the question, Did she want to be a wife? Because the answers were, of course—to the former, yes, to the latter, no. All her heroes had resisted wifehood: Jane Austen, Emily Dickinson, Lolly Willowes. Okay, so Lolly Willowes was a fictional character and eventually became a witch, but still, Meg reasoned, better a witch than a wife. Just look what had happened to Sylvia Plath, to Dorothea Brooke.

You couldn't say that, though. It rankled. It offended married people because you were implying that their own carefully constructed lives had snags woven into them. That they might have chosen another way and turned out perfectly as satisfied, or more so—no one wanted to hear this. So she had a stock response: "If I ever married, I would lose my Spinster Librarian card." She'd said it so many times she'd begun to imagine the card was an actual object, providing access to books no one else knew existed, which, she felt, would be a much more useful resource than a spouse any day.

Meg Rhys—it was pronounced "Reese," yes, like the pieces, no, that was not funny to point out to her, and no, it hadn't been her idea to call her column in the library newsletter "Rhys's Pieces," a name she in fact found repellent—was the almost-head librarian of the Brooklyn Collection, a glassed-in suite populated by beleaguered trolleys and swaybacked shelves that groaned beneath leather-bound volumes, an informational ghetto on the second floor of the Brooklyn Central Library, crammed into three rooms approximating the floor-through layout of a typical brownstone tenement, a place whose flat files of annotated maps had given Meg a shudder of longing the first time she saw them. If Meg's brain—or soul, or whatever you wanted to call it—had been a building, it would have been the Brooklyn Collection. So she was happy—or content, that was grown-up for "happy," wasn't it?—to spend her days there, usually alone, often in silence.

Every evening at a quarter after five, once the custodial staff had absolved the featherweight garbage bags of their penciled paper and seltzer cans, after lights had been dimmed and the Brooklyn Collection doors locked, Meg Rhys said goodnight to Gil and Helen and made her way downstairs—the actual stairs, never the escalator—stopping to check for what was new on the Hold shelf for her. Generally she would take home whatever book she found there and read it immediately, swallowing it whole like a snake digesting a cow. Today there was the first volume of an epic novel written by an African American wife and mother, which was being universally touted for its candidness about female lives; there was also an illustrated biography-in-verse about Emily Warren Roebling and the construction of the Brooklyn Bridge. Meg shared forced pleasantries with the dead-eyed circulation clerk who checked them out for her. (The self-checkout lanes were empty, but Meg didn't believe in them; she already did enough things by herself.) Then she made her way out of the employees-only exit, holding the books to her chest like a shield.

Meg walked through the lengthening shadows in the Bookmobile parking lot, past the wall she loved, her favorite wall in the whole city, the one place where you could still see the library's original Beaux-Arts façade—a secret spot she wished she had someone to show—to the rack where she locked her bike. As on every night, the books went into the basket, the witchy bike was mounted, and, though sometimes a friend was met for drinks or else Meg headed into the city for a concert or art opening, tonight she rode home because she needed to think, pedaling faster and faster as she went, weaving through bus lanes with what might have appeared to be youthful abandon but was actually more like self-immolation. Sometimes, when your sister was killed in a bicycle accident, the only thing to do was to take up biking yourself (or so Meg had found), wedging your skull into expensive helmets molded from spacecraft materials, studying bike lanes like a palm reader learns life lines, leaving your own virtual trail of 311 calls to report lane violations: proving, in other words, that it could be done. That she, Meg, could do it. That she could survive. That the city would not pulverize *her*, no matter how hard it tried.

The bike ride home was hard—Brooklyn was hillier than nonbikers imagined—but Meg welcomed the cleansing sweat, the clarifying breathlessness. It helped prepare her for her after-work ritual of sitting in her studio apartment with a cup of strong tea and, as she did more often than she liked to admit to anyone (even her brother James, who frowned at her when she spoke of it), talking to said dead sister.

"Oh, Kate," muttered Meg as soon as she'd locked the door and barricaded her bike against it. The cat walked by indifferently swishing her tail, which was about the kind of greeting Meg was used to at this point in her life. Meg dropped her bag, started the kettle for tea, and washed her hands in the kitchen sink with expensive, pretty hand soap. Now that she was letting herself think about Kate, she acknowledged that in her final iteration Kate had been relentlessly health-conscious, piously eco-friendly, had always refilled her all-natural hand soap at the health food store. Kate had once picked up an empty plastic bottle on Avenue A, looked at the mandala on the label and teared up, saying, "How *could* they?", meaning a supposedly spiritual-y company should have known better than to contribute to the island of plastic in the Pacific. That very afternoon Meg had accompanied her—as Kate carried the empty bottle the entire way in order to safely deposit it into her own meticulously kept recycling bin—to Kate's new apartment, a walk-up hovel only an optimist could love, with the Craigslist roommate who would insist they pay the next month's rent when Kate died.

That afternoon when Kate was still alive and would be for a little while longer, she wanted Meg to meet the mangy cat she'd rescued from a bag lady's cart on the Q train, which she had planned to keep but hadn't yet named. "That's very *Breakfast at Tiffany's* of you," Meg had observed, and Kate had laughed and said, "What?" And Meg had tried to explain how in Capote's novella there was a cat called Cat, but apparently Kate hadn't read it, though, when pressed, she recalled that she had actually once seen the movie, which Meg (a fan of the film but used to scolding her little sister as a matter of course) scolded was not the same thing, not the same thing at all. Meg had watched her beautiful sister clutch the disease-ball of an animal to her chest and had wanted to protect her. The cat eerily resembled a subway rat Meg had nearly stepped on a few hours earlier.

"You can't keep that thing," Meg had said. "You realize that, right? It has mange. Not like, 'you mangy old cat' as a turn of phrase, but like, it literally has a disease called mange." Sometimes Meg remembered Googling "mange" on her phone to prove her point but couldn't have because there hadn't been phones like that, not then. In the end, she couldn't protect Kate from anything.

Not that Kate ever wanted protecting, and in the moment had only laughed at her. Meg could see her laugh, but it had been robbed of sound, impoverished into a silent movie, and she could no longer remember its wind chime tinkle, or who knew?—maybe it had been a horsey guffaw. She saw Kate throwing back her head, showing rows of orthodontically tended teeth, voice redacted. (How stupid the world was, Meg thought, that technology had been devoted to pointless things like virtual reality and space travel, that millions were invested in restoring famous movie props or preserving museum dioramas but not to preserving what really mattered, i.e., the sounds and smells of the dead.) Kate had handed her the cat then, and Meg had flinched, feeling her skin crawl with mange and fleas and AIDS and sadness and whatever else street animals were afflicted with. "I'm taking her to the vet tomorrow," Kate had said, "if I have time." Of course she would have time. She was only twenty-five years old. Kate had had plans for the next day and the next day and the day after that, and plenty of time for all of them. The days belonged to her, like rooms in a house she had purchased. "And I *am* going to give her a name. I just haven't decided on what."

When Kate was killed a few days later, Meg took the cat. She named it Virginia Wolf, which was a name that had more to do with her own bookishness and labored sense of humor than with Kate, who would surely have named it something earnest like Journey or Krishnamurti, and let it run free. Meg took the animal to an overpriced vet who pumped it full of vaccines, washed and dried the matted fur, and sold her a steel-toothed comb. Now Meg lived alone with the damn cat, and they had both gotten stout and fussy with age the way everyone did eventually, rampant livery cars notwithstanding. Now Meg could do as she liked without fear of judgment. Meg could cut off all her hair (the hair Kate had claimed to envy because of its wave) into the universal crew cut of the distressed, as she did a few weeks after the accident. Meg could buy perfume-y, non-Kate-approved soap with a label like the wallpaper she would have in her entryway if she inhabited a rambling, Bloomsbury-ish house in the countryside—which of course she didn't, she never would, but she could have the soap. She could throw out the bottle if she got tired of the smell, hurling it right into the trash can even if it was still half full of perfectly good soap, and then buy another kind, whether it was made by a company that tested it on the eyeballs of baby monkeys or not. There was no one who would say a thing to her about it.

Meg slumped into the lumpy armchair she'd inherited, or more accurately, pillaged, from their grandmother's Upper West Side apartment. The grandmother had died several years after Kate, one of the many ways in which the universe revealed its shoddy organization. The curtains were open in Meg's living room, but she was too depleted to stand and draw them shut, and instead tortured herself by watching her neighbors across the way bustling in their bright kitchens, husbands handing wives glasses of wine, children climbing onto tables and being shooed off, people living life the way it appeared in well-designed catalogues.

Meg's apartment was a sublet, unofficially rent-stabilized because the owner was a kindly woman who had moved in with her wealthy partner (Meg and her landlady shared an aversion to using the word "boyfriend" to refer to adults over the age of fifty) but wanted to keep her own place just in case—because postmenopause love had no room for illusion—and the woman, a history professor who had bush-whacked through the wilds of the CUNY system all the way to the coveted, near-forgotten peak of tenure, had taken a shine to Meg, in the way that other single women often did. They had to look out for each other, after all. No one else remembered they existed.

And so the professor let Meg paint the bedroom walls a pale blue, and fixed the bathroom tiles when they cracked, but hadn't raised the rent once in ten years. She could have, of course. People would pay anything in New York, even in Meg's corner of what she called Prospect Heights but that the couple who had bought the two-bedroom downstairs—the white horsemen of the apocalypse, as Meg thought of them—called "North North Park Slope" ("No-No-Slo," she mocked them to James over brunch). Particularly since Meg's apartment, though small, had a deck, and Brooklynites were so crazy for outdoor space you'd think they'd forgotten the outdoors was just sitting there, waiting for them, outdoors. But the clanging concrete world outside wasn't quite the same, was it, as your own living room–sized deck fringed with leafy growing things. Meg's deck did, after all, mean a green place to sit first thing in the morning, undisturbed, reading, with her tea, in pajamas even, which made her practically the richest person in the city.

It was here, in her second-floor sanctuary, in a rather ordinary-looking eight-flat on a street lined with nearly identical buildings, in this unassuming pocket of the borough, that Kate's ghost had begun to visit Meg. Or at least, Meg was sure she felt something. A presence. A wispy, immaterial *someone.* Like now, as she leaned back in the grandmotherly chair, conscious of the way her hair grease—a friend had convinced her to give up shampoo, and Meg wasn't sure it was going at all well—melted into the embroidery of fruit on the doily her grandmother had always draped over the back of the dusty rose chair and that Meg left there, rather than preserving it as she likely should have, Meg closed her eyes and let Kate know she was ready.

It wasn't anything as material as a rush of cold air. It wasn't a sound or anything shifting unexpectedly or a window shutting or a rush of wind. It wasn't a vapor. It wasn't a shape. It wasn't the sound of Kate's voice warped by alternate dimensions. It wasn't a smell—though how welcome that would have been, a whiff of not just her unscent-ed-but-somehow-scented Whole Foods soap or that hint of yoga studio incense she'd absorbed but *her,* that Kate-like Kate-scent of Kate that, after a few years, had worn off her cardigan that Meg kept in a bureau drawer. It was only a feeling, a sense of comfort, a certain Kate-liness in the air.

James, when Meg tried to explain it over Eggs Benedict balanced on a bistro table, insisted this was not actually Kate's ghost but more like a memory, that what Meg was doing in these sessions was what normal people called praying, a chatty battle against oblivion. It was a good thing to do if it made her feel better, he said, as if condescending to a red-state believer, his voice plummy with an implied *Of course it's pointless and all in your head, but* do *go on if you like.* She forgave him. He was, after all—or to her anyway—still a boy. James had only just turned twenty when Kate died, and Meg sometimes thought that, as a result, he had better learned how to live his adult life without Kate in it, and that maybe even to him the two were tantamount—Kateless-ness, real life. Besides, James liked rules and regulations. James placed a premium on being conventional, so much so that he, at thirty, was married, showed a keen interest in moving up professionally, investing his money, purchasing property, and obtaining a child. And he was gay. Meanwhile Meg, a lady clinging to the cliff of her baby-bearing years, whose parents would have lost limbs to see her married, saw the entire enterprise as a farce. Then again, she was aware that it was a privilege to be able to pick and choose conventionality, to choose, in her case, against it.

The teakettle hooted and Meg leapt to tend to it. Virginia Wolf sat on the kitchen counter, glaring, whipping her tail around the cup. Meg fished the strands out with her spoon not because she was squeamish but because cat hair in tea seemed such an indicator of the unwell iteration of spinsterhood. She steeped the tea, squeezed, and set aside the tea bag for the impending second cup, and settled back into the chair with the intent of summoning her sister for a chat when the earthquake struck. No, because there weren't earthquakes here, but yes, because something was shaking the apartment, vibrating Meg's teeth with noise so loud she almost didn't register it as a noise. The angry ghosts of the city, rising up. Or wait, no, construction downstairs.

"You're kidding me," Meg said to the floor. "Really? Fucking *really*?" There was no sense in closing her eyes and trying to be Zen about it. The couple who had bought the co-op downstairs was the bane of her existence. The renovations never seemed to stop. If they weren't fixing up the room for the baby (due sometime in winter), they were rewiring the electricity or rezoning the floors or something, or, most recently, gutting the kitchen because, really, it was *horrifying* and *utterly unusable*—of course the kitchen was identical to Meg's, but she just stared when the new neighbor said it.

Meg had been rubbed the wrong way on the wrong day and, like Virginia Wolf the Cat, was prone to getting tetchy. She stormed downstairs and rapped on the door before she could lose her nerve. She needed to be mad, to stay mad, in order to be able to say, when the pretty pregnant lady opened the door, increasing the noise's volume tenfold, "*What* is that noise? What *is* that?"

The neighbor—her name was Marjorie, or something like it—smiled. "Oh, that? I'm so sorry, Meg, I meant to warn you." She pathologically used Meg's name in conversation, as if to underline Meg's own inability to remember hers. Margit, was it? Maybe Marguerite, or no, sure Meg would remember a name so fancy and yet so like her own. She'd always wanted a fancy name of her own—poor little Meg Anne Rhys. There had been a brief period in undergrad when she tried to go by Annika—which she realized belatedly she must have lifted from the worrywart neighbor-girl in *Pippi Longstocking,* unconsciously fuddy-duddy even when trying to escape herself. It wasn't her name though, and it showed.

The neighbor, M-name, rubbed her swelling belly as if to remind Meg why she had to be nice to her. Meg shifted her weight in the hallway. She hadn't put her shoes back on before running down the stairs and now regretted the dorm-room feel of her stocking feet. M-name continued, "It's the door. We're putting in a side door." She had to shout over the din of jackhammers or whatever they were. "They got a late start, and I guess there was just one thing they wanted to finish—I'm so sorry, they were supposed to be done by the time people were getting home from work!" M-name was a freelancer of some sort and professed an impossible ignorance of the working hours of the civilized world. "We—well, here, come on in, take a look!"

Meg waved her hands in front of her face. "No. I don't need to see. It's just—it's insanely loud upstairs," she said as bitingly as she could. There was no fury like the fury of an apartment-dweller constructed against. "It's very invasive, and—wait, *what* are you doing?" The apartment was a two-bedroom (she'd been invited to the previous residents' low-key New Year's Eve parties a couple times, had known the apartment when it was the sparse domain of IKEA-devoted roommates); there was access to the backyard shared with the other first floor apartment, but there was also a concrete slab alongside the building, near where the trashcans loitered in a stinking gang, and M-name gestured airily toward it now: "We're putting in a door to the side patio."

The jackhammering stopped, and Meg put a hand to her temple. "The 'side patio'? Really? You mean the trash area?"

M-name smiled apologetically. "When we closed on the place, the previous owners told us that was actually our space. So we're building a wall separating out the trash area and what will be our eensy little side patio. And the door will go out here. It'll be really cute. You'll have to come grill with us!"

Grilling, grilling. What was so great about grilling? All summer long, all anyone in New York wanted to talk about was grilling and the best routes to drive out of the city, in order to do more grilling. If M-name and mate wanted to grill so passionately, why hadn't they been real about who they were and gone to Westchester and left the damn trash yard alone? Meg was nothing like a vegetarian but had retained or maybe adopted some of Kate's abhorrence at the medieval sight of a raw hunk of meat laid out over fire and maintained a native New Yorker's disgust at transplants trying to have it all—rooftop gardens and backyard chickens and fire escape beehives. *Just accept the concrete,* she wanted to scream. *It's terrible and unnatural and it is what you have chosen because something in you is broken, otherwise you would live somewhere normal, so just accept it already!*

"I mean," added M-name, "if you're still here this summer."

Meg was already tired of talking to this lady, who had been smiling and nodding the entire time, like a gorilla trying to emulate a human. "No," Meg said, in a not-unfriendly way, "I don't think I will be down to grill because—wait, what? Why would I not be here this summer?"

M-name made her eyes anime-big. "Uh-oh, did I do an oopsie?" she said, with innocence that was, if not feigned, then rather unsettling.

"Sorry, what are you talking about?"

"Because your apartment's going up for sale, I mean. Oh, I think I did make a boo-boo. I'm sure the owner wanted to tell you herself. I'm on the co-op board, and it came up at last week's meeting. She's going to make a pretty profit off it, and I tell you what, she bought it for a heckuva lot less than what we paid for this place last year!"

Meg's face burned. Her landlord? Her real estate guardian angel, who had never raised her rent, who had talked about how women had to look out for each other, with whom Meg had had a goddamned *understanding*? She would not faint in front of this wretched breeder; she couldn't give her the satisfaction. She put a hand in the doorjamb to steady herself. M-name patted her hand and Meg twitched, fought the urge to slap her away, said, "I see."

"Ooh. Ooh, so you really didn't know. Oh shoot, oopsie-woopsie, bad on me. Well, she's going to talk to you in the next few days about showing the apartment to realtors and the hours for open houses and all that good stuff. Unless *you're* planning to make an offer! I know you've been there for ages! It is just you, right? Sometimes I can't tell how many sets of footsteps are swanning around up there."

"Just me. Yes," *you nosy bitch,* she didn't say. Meg's body was on fire, her heart melting down into her calves. There went her whole carefully planned life, her safe harbor in the storm, her sanctuary in the inhospitable world. She wanted to punish M-name for delivering the news. "Well, and the ghost. There's a rather noisy ghost up there, I hope it doesn't bother you guys too much. Gosh, I hope it doesn't come down here!"

M-name laughed, but her eyes flickered with the panic of realizing that your already-eccentric neighbor has come unhinged right there in your doorway. But maybe—even at her lowest, Meg was never completely without hope—just maybe a fear was lodging itself within M-name's vapid, happy heart. Maybe she would spend a few nights rendered sleepless by inchoate fear. Meg was nothing if not optimistic.

She turned on her fuzzy-socked heel. "They really need to stop drilling by five. It's too loud. You're being rude." She stalked down the hall, up the stairs. A door. A door! What gumption they had, expanding like a rapacious army of a family, gobbling up bits of common space with their gentrifiers' sense of manifest destiny. M-name could reliably be found down by the mailboxes, squawking about the new espresso bar down the block, by which she meant more white people in the neighborhood. M-name had probably led the charge to exile the subletters, to purify the building of the unsavory renters in their midst. *They look like the rest of us,* Meg could picture her saying at the board meeting, *but they are financially* insecure. *They come and go. It's not good for the building. Think of our property values! Think of the children!* And Meg's landlady had probably had no choice but to acquiesce. Meg was one of only two renters in the building. Her landlady would probably call tomorrow, all apologies, and explain what was happening to Meg in a way that would assuage her current feeling, which was that she had been gutted like a fish on a Chinatown sidewalk. As with all disasters, the specter of eviction seemed both utterly surprising and like she ought to have seen it coming all along.

Now Meg's peaceful night, her time with Kate, potentially her entire adult life: blown to smithereens. But no, she wouldn't get hysterical; she would pad back upstairs, she would lock her door and replace the bicycle barricade, she would scoop up the cat and breathe in its dusty bookstore smell and stroke its fawn-skin ears until it leapt away, and then she would take her now-tepid tea out onto the deck even though it was muggy and threatening rain, and the jackhammer sound would call out plangently, and sure, Kate could come to her even here, even outside, even tonight. Even though it was loud and difficult to concentrate. Because this was what had been welling up in Meg all day, what welled up every day, as she went about her life, riding her bicycle, helping library patrons, feeding the cat, scolding the neighbors, seeming normal, seeming like she had absorbed the decade-old footnote to her personal history (went to Pratt, majored in Library Sciences, contracted shingles, got her nose pierced, studied abroad in Rome, let the nose-piercing scab over and heal, got a dead sister, got a cat), and what by the end of every single boring ordinary run-of-the-mill day she was full to brimming with: "Kate," Meg whispered into her tea. "I think I will never get used to you being gone."

It was the same thing she always said, but it was like saying "I love you" to a live-in lover—you always meant it, you always had to say it, you always *wanted* to say it, even though you knew each time you said it, you wrung it out a little more, like a washcloth getting twisted into dry cloth jerky. Kate knew. Kate was sorry. Kate missed Meg too, and James, and Mom and Dad, and life.

There was no answer, no ghostly rattle from spectral Kate, but Meg knew. She knew that she knew.

# 3

**OF COURSE**, Meg's wasn't the only haunted house in the city that never rests. There was a house I once knew well, on Holland Avenue. If you could wrench off the front and peer in at the resulting dollhouse, you would see the stacked stories. On a sticky summer evening, for example, as new renters attempted to settle into the sepulchral apartment downstairs—a young couple, arranging themselves in their first shared home, arguing over whose desk should go where in the office off the kitchen, which suddenly seemed drafty, didn't it? Should they contact the landlord? Or? Tape the windows? Or? Why was it so *cold* in there, mid-summer? Why was the window always sliding shut, the door always slamming open? It was his fault, she insisted, and he countered no, it was her fault!—And—why did they both feel so *weird*? It couldn't be just the move, could it? The apartment gave them an ominous chill every now and then, for no apparent reason. Was it a mistake to move in together, was that it? Or the neighborhood, was it still too marginal? They were so close to the projects after all. Whatever the reason, they both felt angered, somehow, stirred up, not entirely themselves.

Meanwhile, on the second story, a woman squinted at a book. She had lived there long enough to settle into the creepiness, to ignore the cold spots, to cohabitate with what was not after all a malicious spirit. She was more troubled, in fact, by the book. Her friend had recommended it, Oprah had recommended it, but she just couldn't get into it somehow. Was it her or the book? She didn't like the idea that she was wrong about it, but she didn't like the idea that everyone else was wrong about it either. She put down the book and looked warily at the door to her son's room, slightly ajar to let in the crack of light that he swore foiled monsters. Timid monsters, apparently, afraid of something as slight as light. She was used to the shuffling sounds of new neighbors settling in. This was the fifth set in four years.

Her apartment had been just right for her son and herself—the two small bedrooms, the tidy kitchen clad in stock rental laminate fixtures, even the oddly bifurcated living room, which the landlord told her had probably once been adjoining bedrooms, back when the house was one family's country home. She liked the peeling ivy-patterned wallpaper in her bedroom, though her girlfriends told her it was nasty and that she needed to have the landlord repaint the room for her. He would get around to it on his own, probably, eventually. He was a funny kind of gentleman landlord, with his professorial elbow patches and natty suits, nothing like the overwrought Hasids she'd so often rented from. He never fixed anything himself but hired young men from the neighborhood in an overly politically correct way. She knew that he himself lived in hoity-toity Park Slope, with all the rich white people and their SUV-strollers, and that this was his only rental property, and that he tried to do a good job—when he stopped by, he brought treats for her four-year-old, and spoke to him respectfully, as if he were indeed a tiny man—but she also knew that there was nothing to be done about the ghosts in the house. What could he do, evict them?

She'd been in the downstairs apartment a few times, and she tried to picture it now as she padded to her kitchen to make a cup of decaf black tea, moving quietly as a shade so as not to wake up the boy, who was, despite being a city kid his whole life, a light sleeper.

The mother dumped sugar in her tea, watched the corporeal white lumps dissipate in the darkness. She listened to the new downstairs people thump a box, muffled voices flaring in anger, and looked again at her son's door. They had a lot of stuff, these people, heavy boxes of books, indecently large antique furniture. So they'd probably stick it out for the whole year, with a haul like that. But no longer. Despite all the house had to offer, in a city where people would pay thousands for a literal trash heap ("needs TLC"), despite its historical charm and reasonable rent and quiet location. Quiet was a commodity in Brooklyn, almost a place in itself, a city-state of brain-space. And it was quiet there. But some people (the mother shook her head to think of it) just couldn't abide a simple thing like a ghost.

# 4

**THE BROOKLYN COLLECTION** was one of the few remaining places in
the world—or at least in New York, which to Meg meant essentially
the same thing—where quiet was a priority, where shushing was still
*de rigueur.* This had been Meg's default joke, when asked what on earth
a person studied in Library Sciences school. "I'm majoring in hushing,"
she would say, "it's a lost art." And then sometimes, if she'd had a cocktail, she'd pull down her cat-eye glasses and wink. The "sexy librarian"
trope was something every Information Science scholar had to deal
with in one way or another, and it was best to decide your stance early
and stick to it, like with giving money to panhandlers on the subway.

Truly it *was* a lost art, the shushing, the hushing, she was reminded
when a caffeine yen lured her from her nun's cloister of the Brooklyn
Collection into the bowels of the library. The Central Library, home
to six thousand books and one ghost—Agatha Cunningham, age
six—was meant to itself approximate the shape of an open book—a
neat architectural trick few of its patrons acknowledged as they waited
grumpily for their turns on the public computers—with the atrium
serving as its spine. At one end/page of the atrium was the entryway to
the Children's Library; at the other end/page, the glorious Languages
and Literature sections; at the other axis lay the Information Com-
mons, which sounded so much more exalted than what it was, less a
Library of Alexandria–style chamber of wonders and more a mob of

internet portals, in truth, the part of the library that the Bookish Orthodox like Meg wished didn't need to exist at all. Like many librarians in the city system, despite being devoted to books, Meg had cut her teeth at an underfunded branch deep in a Bengali enclave of Brooklyn, teaching recent immigrants how to Google. She still associated search engines with the smell of curry.

The atrium ceiling soared to the heights of knowledge or at least the second floor, where strung along the balcony hallway like beads on an abacus were the small specific universes of the Brooklyn Collection, History/Biography, Science/Technology, and so on. The result of this secular Pantheon, an unfortunate side effect unforeseen to good old Githens and Keally as they designed the space, was a constant pullulating cacophony. In the deafening lobby, the circulation counter huddled along one wall, while in the opposite corner crouched the pandering—Meg felt, despite patronizing it daily—espresso-and-pie café, so that her coffee breaks were soundtracked with the screams from storytime—Youth Wing, standing-room only—ricocheting around like racquetballs: pinging, tinny, percussive. "Shh," said Meg to no one, "shh."

It was on such a day, Meg standing on line for coffee and already physically craving the quiet of the upstairs as much as she'd physically craved the coffee, when she saw a man cooing at a Don Rickles–faced toddler who did not feel like waiting its turn to check out a stack of Seuss. Meg knew the man, she did, and in a way that made her stomach deflate, only she wasn't sure why. She'd lived within New York City's radius for her whole life—formative years on the Upper West Side, college in Fort Greene, adulthood in Park Slope and then Prospect Heights, her escape from the nest imitating the limping, cloistered flight of a partridge—so he could have come from any chapter of her life. It happened frequently that someone lifted the book of Meg and shook the spine, sending pages flying every which way for her to put back in order.

After a minute of feeling ill at the sight of him—handsome, bland, Jewish-y, armored in a well-curated blend of preppiness and hipster-lite—Meg realized he was associated with Kate. Oh *yeah*. He was the ex. Or was it an ex- situation? They had of course never broken up.

It was some feminine-sounding name he had, a word full of vowelly air she hadn't understood until seeing it written down. She couldn't remember it now, only the breathy way Kate had said it.

"Meg!" he acted happy to see her, which was vaguely repulsive to her, and not just from him—as a rule, anyone who was that happy to see her turned her into a Groucho Marx routine. He had lifted the child now, and it squirmed around looking unpleasant, its nose leaking two honey-like ropes. Aryeh. That was his name. But she wouldn't say it.

"Hello," Meg said. She would be pleasant. Or she would be neutral. It wasn't his fault, none of it was his fault, except that he had the audacity to be standing there before her, breathing air, taking up space, existing all over the place. When someone you loved died, you never quite forgave everything else for being alive.

"I've been wondering if I'd run into you! I thought I remembered you worked here. Remy loves the storytime. We're here all the time. We've even learned to come early enough to get a ticket. I'm a stay-at-home dad now, it's pretty funny."

Was it? It didn't seem particularly out of character to Meg, but maybe he had different ideas about himself than what he telegraphed. People were so often mysteries only to themselves.

Aryeh seemed anxious, sweaty from the effort of seeing her or maybe holding the squirming child, whom Meg still couldn't get a handle on, age- or gender-wise, not that she was especially trying to. She didn't mean to be rude, but she did want her coffee, and so she stayed on the line until she'd ordered. "You sure you don't want the pumpkin spice latte?" the barista teased her, as he always did. "Pumpkin spice *es delicioso, por eso*! Come on, just this once? What kind of white lady are you, anyway?" Meg flashed him a smile, and to tell the truth she considered it every time—she had a weakness for the sickeningly sweet—but didn't know what they would joke about if she relented. They had a whole rapport that she counted on at this time of the day, and she was nothing if not devoted to her routines, so day after day, she pretended to be offended and demanded "real" coffee, claiming to put a premium on authenticity over novelty. And he wagged his finger and said, "*Mañana*! You gonna try it!"

When she turned away with her steaming paper cup, Aryeh and the child were still there. Meg closed her eyes to center herself. In moments of stress the lobby noise rubbed her raw. It had always struck Meg—particularly when she looked down from the second floor balcony and reflected that the library had begun its life as an ambitious Beaux-Arts palace before the Depression stalled it for a few decades, at which point the half-built ruin had been transformed into something else altogether—that the space wanted to be more elegant than it was. The same could have been said, she supposed, for the entire city. She wished she could have seen that original Beaux-Arts building brimming with people straight out of Edith Wharton, that the bodies shuffling about, near-nude on what was likely the last day of summer, were shaped into corsets and suits, that parasols were involved. Bustles. Hoop skirts. Top hats. Outside there would be horses and dust, sure, a deadly pollen of smallpox bobbing on the breeze, deeply problematic institutionalized racism, yes, a troubling lack of women's suffrage, definitely, but inside, there would be no sproingy dings of iPhones receiving text messages, no grown men in flip-flops.

Meg knelt so that she was at eye-level with the child, who had been released and now stood knock-kneed, as if poised to escape. "Hello, Remy," she said. She knew herself to have a rapport with children unique to nonparents; unlike most adults in their lives, she needed nothing from them.

Remy leaned close, pointed at her earrings. Meg tried to remember what earrings she was wearing. "Ah yes, those are called pearls," she told the child. "Oysters make them, in their guts, at the bottom of the sea." It was, like most things told to children in order to explain the world, mostly a lie. Meg's were polymer curds made God knew how, probably by exploited women somewhere dreadful, but she had calculated correctly, and the child's eyes grew wide, and he—Meg decided it was a he because she associated the name Remy with her seventh grade French textbook and a recurring gym-shorts-bedecked character on whom she'd had an aching crush—told her something unintelligible of his own experience of the ocean. Aryeh nodded adoringly.

Meg recalled the secular *shiva* they'd had at her parents' apartment, the way he, Aryeh, had come bearing a ruinous casserole, his eyes dry and his boots muddy, the way he'd sat miserably as Mrs. Fishman from 2E accosted him with her favorite memories of Kate, the way her mother had eaten the food to be polite, the way Meg had felt nothing but fury at this oaf compounding their family's tragedy with charred mushroom cream.

She stood up and smiled crisply. "Where does he get a name like Remy?" she asked. It wasn't meant to sound accusatory, only to remove from Aryeh's face the "I'm so sorry" smile. It had been almost ten years. People could stop being all "Oh, I'm so sorry" all the time. She couldn't, but they could. Meg blew on her coffee. The child was throwing picture books onto the floor now, trying to reclaim Meg's attention. Meg budgeted three more minutes for this encounter. She wanted the rest of her break for sitting outside in the sun, eyes closed, like a turtle.

"Oh, *she*—" said Aryeh, and Meg raised her eyebrows in recognition of her error—who could tell anymore! What had happened to gender anyway?—"Her mother is French, and she's named for her grandfather." Of course. Out of loyalty, Meg immediately hated the French wife, seeing her in a flash: a humorless cross between Jean Seberg and a mentally stable Emma Bovary, sitting in an office somewhere with a scarf tied chicly about her neck. Nothing next to Kate. A poor replacement, as everything was. And the little family probably lived in an improbably sunny apartment in Park Slope, and sent the child to French-language playgroup, and read Knausgaard in their couples' book group. Aryeh was still talking. "You look great, Meg, really. It's so great to see you. How are your parents, how are Nora and Martin? I feel terrible that we've fallen out of touch—"

"Oh, don't. We did that on purpose," Meg said, but he took it as a joke. She started backing away. She didn't think she'd be able to stand it if he said The Thing, oh please oh please, she thought, anything but The Thing, and then he said it, a little distracted, as he tracked Remy's weaving between the café tables of put-upon novelists scowling up from their laptops, "We've got to get together sometime."

Meg put a hand on his arm and said, with the equanimity she'd earned in her most recent half-decade or so of Not Really Giving a Fuck, "No. We really don't. But I'm here every weekday from nine to five, if you ever need me. Trust me, I know what it's like. I have my brother, I'm lucky that way. It's okay if you miss Kate and want to talk or something. It's fine."

The name slapped him almost audibly across the face. *Kate!* He was trying, poor thing, but he didn't know what to say. No one ever knew what to say, and it was nearly impossible for whatever they did say to be the right thing anyway, so she didn't actually mind the piscine way he opened and closed his mouth, and to make it easier on him, she smiled—a flashy smile, the one for men—and said, "So nice to see you. Your child is adorable. Enjoy the books." Then she went to the bathroom to reapply the red lipstick she habitually wore as a shield against the unironic form of spinsterhood, cleaned her cat-eye glasses on a fold of her skirt, and hurried back upstairs, feeling after all too weak for the bustle she was sure to encounter outside.

There was never a bustle in the Brooklyn Collection. There was hardly ever a buzz, merely a murmur. It was why Meg needed to be there, why she had fought for this job and would cling to it forever, whether she ever got a raise or promotion or not—after all, she had the kind of life in which it didn't much matter if she ever made much money. No one depended on her, she depended on no one, she made exactly enough to get by—or had anyway when she'd been guaranteed her atavistically low rent—and that was fine, that was good, that was how she wanted it. She didn't need savings; she didn't need travel or fancy things. She did need, for most hours of her day, profound quiet, or else things became disheveled in her neatly filed brain. So while she could never leave the city, she had at least found the very quietest part of it.

When she walked in, Head Librarian Helen was showing someone how to read the Sanborns, ancient fire insurance maps with onionskin palimpsests of precomputerized record keeping. Meg loved showing people the Sanborns. The know-it-all big sister in her experienced a clean high when telling people how to do things. "Here's the key," she'd tell amateur genealogists, "see, here's how you can tell which buildings were wood-frame." But she'd wasted time with the

modern-cultural-jumble of a family downstairs, and Helen had gotten the guy.

Meg took her coffee to her desk in the back room and placed it on
the cat-faced coaster beside the yellowed photograph of herself, James,
and Kate as knobby-kneed kids at the shore. It was such a clichéd image of summery childhood that it held no sting for her, no more so
than if it had been the picture that came in the frame or a still from
the flashback scene in a film.

Which was a lie, of course it was. In the aftermath of the Aryeh
encounter, she sipped her coffee and stared at the photo until the silence changed in tenor from inert to expectant. Someone had asked
something. Was asking.

"Honey? You all right?"

Meg stood too quickly, as if Helen had challenged her to a duel.
"Of course! What? Can I help the patron, is that what you asked?"

Helen frowned. "He wants the *internet*," she said, shrugging. She
always said the word "internet" dubiously, as if it were something that
hadn't proven its place in the universe, like string theory or Pluto.

The patron in question had all the earmarks of being Meg's favorite kind. She could tell by his demeanor he was pursuing a personal
project of some sort. They were the best researchers—guileless, easy to
please, hungry for guidance. And he was extremely good-looking, tall
and broad-shouldered, with startling, intelligent hazel eyes flashing
behind his glasses—which never hurt either. Well, sometimes it did
hurt actually, making it difficult to concentrate, making her lean in
too closely while pointing out keys or signatures, drawing her attention to her breath. (Did it stink? Was she panting? Would he mistake
her untreated low-grade asthma for lechery?)

He avoided her eyes (and he was *shy!*), but Meg felt that she knew
him completely just by the way he worried his large, clean hands together—he was a lifelong local, he was looking into a building his
family owned, convinced it was worth millions, since Brooklyn had
gotten gussied up all around without his parents noticing, busy as they
were with the business of actually living. Because the man was Black,
she guessed he lived in the pretty part of Bedford-Stuyvesant or the

mansion-y section of Lefferts Gardens. Of course, though Meg prided herself on knowing the texture of the borough, she frequently jumped to conclusions that were wrong and therefore borderline offensive, for example, pulling out the Sunset Park files for a Chinese woman only to be crisply corrected—it was a beach bungalow in the Rockaways that she needed to research, *actually*. Meg understood. She herself bristled at people's assumptions about her ("So can I talk to your husband?" plumbers and handymen always wanted to know). But in the city, you were constantly sizing people up in ways you'd never say out loud, especially if you were a woman who was often alone. Meg could evaluate a rumpled figure on the subway—dangerous or just wacky?—in an instant, as unemotional as a bird-watcher.

She glided—she'd had to learn how to move this way, the "creative movement" element of librarianship—over to the patron's side. "You needed help with the computer?" she asked in her hushiest voice. He startled, despite her gentle approach. He had nervous eyes, for which Meg was thankful; his shifting gaze made it easier for her to stare at him. But she wouldn't be weird, she would stay focused, she was at work, he needed her help. He had something he needed to get off his chest. He shrugged and said: "The lady thought I could find the lock number on some website . . . ?"

Lock number. Helen tended to rush incomprehensibly through the steps of building research, a task she found beneath her, being a genealogy gal herself. Patrons were left not understanding even what actual words had been said. "Block and lot number, maybe?" Meg supplied. He nodded uncertainly.

Meg gestured to their computer, an outdated box with a poorly calibrated screen. "I'm trying to find out some information about my dad's house," he said. He spoke cleanly and precisely, like a scientist or a mathematician, or, she tried not to think, someone on the IT-end of the autism spectrum. She nodded. She knew. "It's obviously an old house. My dad says it's been there since at least the thirties. He's had tenants for a long time, but their leases are all up soon, and the place needs some renovation before we can sell. We just wanted to know—well—a little bit about the history of the place. You know?"

"Sure, of course," said Meg, summoning the ACRIS database and watching the man out of the corner of her eye. She offered him the computer stool. He genteelly refused, standing at a distance behind her. "And what exactly do you want to know about it?"

He scratched his head, considering. She waited. Sometimes people just needed to talk. Meg took in his slightly rumpled shirt, his leather wristwatch, his buzzed-short hair, his exceptional eyebrows with stray strands snaking every which way. Maybe he was a high school teacher or a professor of some sort. English. Sociology. At LIU or Brooklyn College. Or one of the better charter high schools. Maybe he owned— she took in the tan animal fur clinging to his pant legs—a Cocker Spaniel or a tabby cat.

"How old it is? If there's ever been a fire? If additions were added?" Meg prompted, knowing these weren't right but giving him time to warm up. "Original owners?" She asked for the street address and typed rapidly, her coffee frothing volcanically in her gut, the hot-guy-adrenaline lighting up her synapses. "Here, you can see the basics. Block and lot number, zoning documents. Certificates of Occupancy. This is kind of neat." She clicked to bring up a crooked scan of the house's Bill of Sale from 1931 and zoomed in on the scrawled signature. She loved seeing the handwriting, that tangible reminder that behind these records there had been, all along, people, actual alive people, living their stories, never thinking that someday a real estate receipt would be all that remained of them, and yet because of that signature, were somehow still alive.

"Ye-ah. Perhaps. Yes. I think so. I've been compiling a list from the Criss-Cross directory of all the residents before he bought it in the seventies."

Meg smiled. "Ooh, very good. You know what you're doing, I see."

The man laughed. "Well, I do a lot of research for my work, so I'm used to archives and that kind of thing. The problem here is, well. I guess—I'm not exactly sure what I'm looking for. Stories, really. If anything . . . *unusual* ever happened here. In the house, I mean." He rubbed his forehead. "I don't know. The original owners would be interesting to know. Or . . ." He still hadn't met Meg's gaze. "It's a strange house," he said finally, as the records with the block and lot number materialized on the screen. "My dad—he's always had a hard time getting tenants to stay. I always wonder why, you know? It's a nice old house. Good bones, as they say. Everyone's supposed to love 'prewar charm' right? It's pre-*all* the wars."

Meg smiled. "Bed-Stuy, huh," she said, squinting at the Google Street View she'd opened in another browser window.

"My parents always called it that, but now people say it's Crown Heights. I don't know, when I think of Crown Heights, I think of all the Jews around Eastern Parkway." Meg nodded. It was one of those stretches of Brooklyn thickly populated with Hasidic Jews, distinctive in their wigs and *payot* and hats, the shop signs written in Hebrew and Yiddish. "But I guess even Crown Heights sounds better to folks than Bed-Stuy? Realtors," said the man, shrugging. Something between them relaxed; real estate angst, the lingua franca of New York. Realtors were always changing the name of a neighborhood to exaggerate a proximity or escape a troubled past, and it was funny unless you were apartment-hunting, in which case, it was confusing at best, infuriating at worst. Meg had grown up—her parents still lived—on a block now called "Prime Upper West Side" and dotted with million dollar properties that had been tenement rentals when she was in elementary school. To this day, she experienced a secret thrill when walking above Eighty-Sixth Street, which had been the absolute don't-go-there-or-you'll-immediately-become-a-junkie boundary of her youth. Now the only threat was that she'd spend too much on a kombucha.

"The most recent record I see is a purchase in 1970 by a Harmon Williams," said Meg.

The man nodded. "That's my dad. I'm Ellis," he said, holding out his hand for her to shake. She took it, registering electric shocks up and down her arm, her whole body warmed as if possessed or stricken with a fast-moving and deadly fever. "Meg Rhys," she said. "Nice to meet you." Malaria, maybe.

They moved back to the table, and Ellis told Meg about how, after inheriting quite a bit of 1970-dollars, his father had bought the house and lived there briefly in all its bohemian splendor with Ellis's mother, a politically active nurse. They'd been as committed to the troubled neighborhood as anyone, but once they had Ellis, they struggled with their consciences—sure, they wanted to help "bring the neighborhood up," but they also wanted their son to go to good schools, to imagine a future for himself defined by college and career and the great privilege of possibility. Harmon had taken a mentor's advice to divide up the house into apartments—cheaply and not that well, they could now admit—and rented them out for extra income while he and his family moved to an apartment in Park Slope.

He'd tried to be a good landlord, but it wasn't always easy. The house was spacious by Brooklyn standards, even had a fenced-in backyard one of the tenants' child liked to play in—true, it was surrounded by barbed wire and abutted a dead end, but still. It was something. People had concrete slabs for which they paid a premium. (Meg nodded meaningfully, trying to express just how well she knew what he meant, until she realized her neck was bobbling perhaps cartoonishly and tried to still it.) At least this outdoor space hosted some scrubby grass and a tenacious, if traumatized, cherry tree, Ellis explained. There was even a root cellar tenants could use for storage at no additional charge. But. The building was unignorably old and drafty, and the floors creaked, and the roof leaked, and the plumbing failed, and a huge public housing project loomed a few blocks away. "Then the riots in '91. How's a neighborhood supposed to move past that? My dad always says the city will never forgive Crown Heights for those riots." Ellis shook his head. "Anyway, now he's ready to fix it up and sell it. He's done, you know, ready to move on."

"I see," said Meg, chewing on the inside of her lip. Among the greatest benefits of librarian life (healthcare, a pension, the ability to waive late fees) were the masses of stories she got to collect. It was like being a hairdresser, only you didn't have to touch people. "Well. Let's start here. Now that we have the block and lot number, you'll want to check to make sure that the block and lot number hasn't changed, which we can do with these Sanborn maps we already have out. Did Helen explain how they work? They were meant to be simply fire insurance maps, but it so happens that because they recorded which houses were made of what, they also give us a way of imagining what these neighborhoods looked like." She surveyed the ones he had out and scurried off to select the right one for his address, birthing the huge bound volume with the steady hands of a rare documents midwife, and placing it on the table before him. They sat side by side at the large table, and she showed him the key, where to locate the block and lot number. Soon she was running her finger over the house in question.

"That's funny. It sits at a kind of a weird angle, doesn't it? Off the grid, a little bit? Well, if you want to find out when the house was actually built and its original owners, you'd look at the land conveyances, but our stacks and the online records don't go back that far—it's likely pre-1900s but has not been landmarked, do I have that right? So it wouldn't be in the digitized records, which is too bad. You could check out the city directories for the 1800s or visit the DOB." She was speaking too quickly now, channeling Helen—there was simply too much pleasure to be plumbed from the obedient progression of information—so she stopped and transcribed it for him. "Department of Buildings. Probably first you'll want to go to the Brooklyn Historical Society, and they should have the land conveyance, which will tell you the name of the first owner. And from there you can check the census listings to find who else was listed in the household. That will include family, servants, boarders, and so on." Meg paused. She tended to exhaust people quickly. She knew herself well enough by now to accept this.

"Right. Start at the beginning. That makes sense." Ellis Williams nodded. "It's an old house," he said again.

"Right." Meg pictured the Renaissance Revival brownstones for which Crown Heights was famous, with their crumbled, once-stately stonework and desiccated stained glass panels, the elegance still legible beneath the ruin, lining the avenues like architectural Norma Desmonds. Kate had briefly rented a room in an old Crown Heights mansion: a beautiful building on a terrifying block. "Funny that you're looking into all this history now, just as you're planning to sell it." Meg tried to make her voice sound casual, sifted through some papers as she spoke. "Did anything in particular spark your interest? Sometimes, when people begin renovations, they find artifacts that

make them wonder what their houses have seen, is why I ask." There
was a pause. Meg was about to move to fetch a city directory—which
she loved not as much as the fire maps, since they didn't seem as poetic, but which she still savored for their spidery scripts—when Ellis
clamped a hand on her arm and leaned forward. Her arm zipped with
electricity. They both looked around, but Helen and Gil had disappeared into the back archives.

Ellis moved his hand away as if embarrassed but kept his eyes fixed
on hers. "Is there a way"—he said in a husky near-whisper—"to see if
strange things have ever happened? To see if anyone has ever reported
. . . *strange things?*"

The hair on Meg's neck pricked up, like an improperly stroked cat.
"What kind of strange things do you mean, Mr. Williams?" Because
no one else was in the room, she leaned close to him, close enough
to see dark freckles faintly speckling his nose, and said, "You mean,
like, ghosts?"

He blinked. She'd said it aloud. She'd made it real.

There was a freighted silence, and then they both laughed nervously
and leaned back, as if they'd awkwardly kissed. "Now, I hear how that
sounds, Miss—sorry, what was your name again?"

"Rhys. Meg Rhys."

"That's a nice name. I like that name. Now Miss Rhys."

"Meg, please." Because if they were going to talk about this, they
were going to have to be friends, and because Meg had a name that
made people feel automatically friendly toward her, its cozy single syl-
lable and indistinct old-fashionedness like invitations to intimacy.

"Meg," he said. Her name sounded sweet in his voice. "I know it
sounds crazy. To be clear, I don't really believe in the idea myself. It's
the kind of thing my dad talks about, but, well. I'm a science guy myself.
Still. I mean, I've always wondered why the previous owner—this old
lady who had lived there since the thirties—was in such a hurry to un-
load the building. She sold it to my dad for a song, even by 1970s standards. And since then, well, like I said, strange things have happened
in this house. It's the first floor apartment. Upstairs, there's been the
same lady renting for a long time, and she seems fine. But downstairs.

Year after year, the tenants bolt. Sometimes before the lease is up. Who does that? Sometimes they leave half their stuff behind, never even ask about the security deposit—they just want out. A Haitian guy once told me, with a completely straight face, that we had some bad voodoo in that house." Now that he'd begun saying the things he'd never said, he seemed unable to stop. He leaned forward, went on urgently: "They complain, 'There's a cold spot in the middle of my bedroom.' We check the heat. Nothing. They say, 'There's a cat stuck in the walls, I hear it scratching and crying at night.' We check the walls. Nothing. They tell me their stuff moves around without them, their windows slam open and shut. My dad's replaced all the windows. No change. He's getting too old for this shit, you know? And the thing is." He looked down at his hands now, unable to meet her gaze. "I remember. I remember from spending time there as a kid. It just always had a weird feel to it. A weird, chilly something. Unsettling. Like we weren't welcome there. Like it wanted us out. My parents always told me I was imagining it, even though I knew they felt it too. But I wonder, you know?"

Meg nodded. "If there's a ghost."

"It's crazy, I know. But I've heard crazier, I guess. What if there was a murder or something, years ago, and some restless spirit's been squatting this whole time? My grandma always talked about spirits, and I swore she was just senile, but I gotta say, I'm beginning to wonder."

"It's really not unusual," Meg said. "We get haunted house questions a lot."

"My dad." Ellis sighed. "My dad is ready to be done with the place. He wants to renovate the house and sell it for a cool million. Just move on. He tells me some yuppie couple is going to snatch it up. The neighborhood is changing so fast, he thinks now is the time."

"He's probably not wrong. Brooklyn's infested with millionaires these days. They're like bedbugs; once they're there, it's so hard to get them out."

Ellis allowed a small smile. "Well, that'd be just fine with me. A million dollars would sure help my parents retire. I don't live nearby anymore, I'm just visiting right now, and I worry about them."

"Definitely, I hear you. So? What's your hesitation? Then the house would be someone else's problem."

"Well, exactly. It would be someone else's problem. How can we, in good faith, take someone's money for a house that might be—you know."

"Haunted."

"Sure."

"Now, Mr. Williams, that *is* unusual."

"What's that?"

"Ethics in real estate."

He smiled again and shrugged. "Maybe you're right."

"I usually am. But let's put that aside for a minute. Maybe we really can find out if something bad happened—or someone died or something—in your house, and you can do with that knowledge what you will." Her imagination had already sprinted off toward a gloriously vicious murder, blood seeping into a frilly Edwardian gown; a ghost woman floating down a curving staircase, hunting her wayward lover.

Meg moved toward the card catalogue with its typewritten hagiographies of city street names, but at that moment Helen appeared, reminding her that a group of middle school students would be arriving soon. Oh, the students! With their shifty postures and disdain for history, their poster boards and dioramas and accordingly minuscule sense of scale. Meg reluctantly excused herself to pull some noncirculating volumes for the undeserving tweens, and by the time she returned to the table, Ellis Williams was gone.

Oh well. She hoped he found his ghost, or whatever he was really looking for. So it went. She'd get a chapter of a person's story, they would confess something they'd never told anyone. Later she might see them on the street, and they would double-take but not wave, unable to place her. She was a living, breathing missed connection.

# 5

.

**LATER, AND CONSTANTLY,** she revisits it in her head, running through the day again and again. Maybe there is a code to crack, a way she can untangle it and make that whole hellacious summer go differently. The air of unease. The indecipherable whispers. The tension as palpable as the day's wet heat. Maybe if she'd noticed sooner—maybe if the whole world had—

But at the time she notices nothing. At the time she notices only that Jane has her doll, and that she wants her doll. She is nearly eleven years old, at the edge of being too old to play with dolls, and instead of taming the ferocity of her desire, this knowledge inflames her. She doesn't have much time! The time to play with the doll has nearly ended! And Jane has taken her, Jane has taken Lucretia. Lucretia isn't much, only an invertebrate dummy clad in gingham, her crudely painted face in a state of perpetual shock. But Lucretia is *hers*, not Jane's. Lucretia is, actually, the *only* thing that is hers. She pictures Lucretia cruelly snatched from the cot, maybe that morning while she was in the chapel, Lucretia roughly shoved beneath Jane's pallet, Lucretia's painted-on shock at having been so unjustly purloined and imprisoned, and her heart aches for the rag doll.

So she stomps through the creaking wooden halls. It is a sticky, sultry day, the heat stupefying in a way that multiplies her anger into rage without her permission. She yells *Jane! Jane! I will find you, you*

*naughty thing!* Imitating the voices of the Quakers who run the orphanage, prim, ashen ladies with silver hairdos and devotions to bon-
nets and Bible verses. She likes the power of her voice in the hall, the
echo that fills the space like an army reveille. *Jane! Do you want a
hiding?!*

It is Miss Murray who appears in the parlor doorway, her face set to
scolding. *Isn't this your outdoor air time?* Hands on hips. It's true, the
other girls are in the yard, playing with hoops. Even though it's hot,
way too hot that whole steamy summer, to do anything other than
stand listlessly and inhale the dust billowing up from the road, their
hoops dangling from their hands. That is meant to be playtime. She is
glad that at least it is Monday. She prefers the days they have lessons
to the days they have chapel. Sundays make her anxious and twitchy.
But today Dr. Smith dropped into her classroom for a science lesson.
She is going to be a doctor like Dr. Smith one day—she says this all the
time even when the other children laugh at her—and like Dr. Smith,
she is going to live in a big mansion built by white people and possibly
even have a white servant. Her own daughters will have one hundred
Lucretias. One thousand Lucretias. She herself will have a Lucretia as
big as a man.

When he comes to their classroom, she has to fight her desire to
climb into Dr. Smith's lap and stroke his muttonchops like she did
when she was smaller. Now it would mean something different, she is
almost old enough to understand that. But it burns in her, the desire
to be close to him. Like the other children there, she expends a lot of
energy believing that a family is out there waiting for her; that they
had to give her up when they fell on hard times, but that they will be
back soon to retrieve her. Sometimes she fantasizes that he, Dr. Smith,
is her father—that he will one day announce it and take her from the
asylum to live in his house with his wife and children. Other children.
She is still aglow.

Miss Murray is not aglow. Miss Murray's face looks like that of an
Irishman staggering home from the tavern—red anger splotched on
top of confusion.

*Yes but Jane is not out there and Jane has taken my—*

Miss Murray cannonballs her a silencing look. Miss Murray, who is usually so patient, so kind. What *is* all this? All the adults are on edge today, huddled in the parlor around a newspaper, speaking in hushed tones. So the girl turns around, slumps her shoulders, mopes down the hallway to the front door, sighing as dramatically as she can muster, like an actress in a melodrama, the theatre star Laura Keene transplanted to the Colored Orphan Asylum.

Outside, the other girls are giggling, twirling their hoops and sticks, their boots clacking against the flagstones. Their long, stiff skirts swish as they move. Usually the yard is noisy with the clomping of horses and carriages battling Fifth Avenue, a rocky, rutted path that leads toward the new park up north; usually they hear medicine men and fruit sellers peddling their wares and herds of pigs snuffling along, the usual Manhattan cacophony. It's a dusty part of town, far north of where most of the grown-up business is conducted, down in the sewage-and-cat-carcass-strewn streets of Tammany Hall's domain. She can remember when she first came to the orphanage (in a spotty way—she remembers the orphanage seeming new and strange but can't recall what life had been like before, or where, or with whom) that the land was even wilder back then, the stately plantation house seeming to rise from the dirt as if Miss Murray and the Miss Shotwells had grown it from a seed. Since those days, the sound of new construction has rarely ceased.

Today the street is eerily still, though no one seems to notice but her. She and Jane usually like leaning against the fence and peeking through the holes to catch a glimpse of the occasional pairs of fancy ladies promenading in hoop skirts and lacy parasols, making up stories about what they will do when they are fancy ladies themselves. But today something is different, as if her interior mope has transformed into weather. The sky presses down, gray as the woolen blankets on their cots. She notices, after a moment, that the air smells different than usual. She turns to an older girl. *Tillie, does it smell like burning to you?* Tillie shrugs, *Another slum fire down in Five Points, I wager.* She nods, though she is not satisfied with the answer.

As she stands out in the yard of the Colored Orphan Asylum,

heat baking up from the paving stones, the dull, diffuse sunlight pounding down on her head, the hair on her neck prickles. She can't shake the feeling: something is not right today. Not right at all. If she strains her ears, she can hear a—something. A distant, low roar. Like thunder, only constant. What on Earth could it be? It sounds Biblical in scale. She looks around at the other children in the yard, having forgotten all about Jane and Lucretia, studying faces to see how frightened she should be. Then Miss Shotwell, the younger one, steps out, and the girl takes one look at her face and knows the answer: very, very frightened.

*Children?* calls the Miss Shotwell, her voice terrible and strange. *Inside! Playtime is over! Right now! Quickly!*

A few of the girls groan. They congeal into their neat line and march up the front steps and into their home, as well-trained as any children in that chaotic muck of a city, armored by their boredom. Miss Shotwell hurries them in and shuts the door behind them, locking it, lowering a large wooden bolt they have never noticed before. The Miss Shotwells stand in the entryway, dressed in their gray dresses, the older in a darker gray, the younger, lighter, wringing their red hands. The girl studies the asylum matrons. *What has happened?* They exchange glances over the heads of the children but don't explain. *Just go to your beds. Just do hurry please. We must hide.*

*They won't come here,* the younger Miss Shotwell says, but she says it like a question.

Her sister doesn't look at her. *No, but we must take precautions.*

The girl blinks at them, rooted to the spot. *Who?* The older Miss Shotwell ignores this, places her cold hands on her shoulders, steers her toward the big girls' room, their cots lined up like stepping stones. *If anything happens,* Miss Shotwell whispers, *hide under your cot.*

Her mind races. If any *what* happens? What is the anything? What are the options of what the anythings might even be? The war? Has the war finally leaked into the city, oozed its way through the streets like the sewage in the slums? She pictures raggedy Confederate soldiers filling the chapel with the terrifying tenor of their rebel yells, brandishing bayonets at the matrons, at Dr. Smith. Her heart pounds as she follows the other children. In recent years she has heard about the war, of course, but has never actually seen it, never actually been a part of it, knows only faint details of its plot. The war stays on battlefields far away, the soldiers' blood seeping into hills and meadows she can hardly visualize. The only way she knows it's really happening, knows it in her bones, is that she's seen Union soldiers getting medals at presentations in the city (looking like the damaged characters from fairy stories, their limbs abbreviated or vanished, ancient faces on young bodies), but what the men have actually lived through remains invisible to her. The sound, meanwhile, grows louder, closer. What on earth could cause such a dull roar, if not an army? A stampede of Barnum's elephants? An erupting volcano?

In the girls' quarters she finds Jane, and all is forgiven, they cling to one another. The littler girls are already crying. Nobody even knows what they are frightened of yet, and the not-knowing is the scariest part, it crackles in her chest like tuberculosis, sealing her lungs with panic.

Now the good Dr. Smith appears, his voice booming over the din: *Children, try to stay calm. Listen to what I have to tell you. There is an angry mob in the city. They started the draft for conscription yesterday, and many Irish names were called, and there is a lot of anger. Surely the mob won't harm an orphanage, for the citizens of our city are God-fearing, Christian men, but to be safe, we are keeping you all inside until they pass. Don't be afraid, my children. God is with us.*

And then he is gone, off to talk to the boys, she imagines.

His words soothe her. Dr. Smith must be right. The Irish are as much a part of the city landscape as they themselves are, their good old boys running the police force and the fire department, their brogues familiar to her ear as the rest of the city music. The Irish have been forced to live in filthy slums of their own—the ramshackle village of Pigtown is not far from the Black town of Seneca Village, up north just a ways, where the new Central Park is being constructed (where many of the children suspect their families live, saving their pennies until they can afford to take their so-called orphans back home). Yes, they are poor, and angry, but even the maddest mob of

drunk Irishmen would not attack an *orphanage*. The children have
learned in their daily lessons (a part of their tidy, well-cared-for life
here at the asylum that they take for granted) about religion, and
about God, and about how people are at their heart good, and about
how God loves them all.

Later she tries to remember how long it is before the mob torches
the building. A few seconds? An hour? But all she can summon up is
what she first hears as an eerie twinkle of chimes and quickly translates
into broken glass. Jane, who after all is smaller than her, a year younger
but also physically tiny, a birdish little thing, cries out, sobs against her
chest. She strokes Jane's braids, the way she imagines a mother would.
*Shh, shh. There, there.*

The noise floods in from outside—racketing, angry, a stomachache
of sound. The rancid stench of a city on fire. Miss Shotwell again, with
her brow furrowed, her eyes flashing, fear on her like a funny hat. *Children, hurry, follow me, take one thing if you must but then leave everything else behind, hurry now.* The girl freezes when she hears they can
take something with them. She knows what that means, some interior,
primal part of her knows: it means they are never coming back. She
watches the children snatch their dolls, their cast iron trinkets, their
sad scraps of blankets from the homes they no longer remember.

They can hear the inhuman shouting of the mob now, and to her
deep shock, the sound is of the voices of women and children, cheering
as they throw bricks through the windows and doors of the orphanage. The voices scream the ugliest of words, singeing her ears. What?
No. Because this can't be happening. Like Dr. Smith had said, no one
would burn an orphanage. There is some mistake here. A mistake has
been made.

Her memory breaks it apart when reliving it. More than a flash at a
time is too much to bear:

The smothering heat of the day made hotter by the building in
flames . . . The dirty faces of jeering children in the mob, waving clubs
studded with nails . . . Florence, one of the smallest girls, grabbing a
Bible as they are rushed through the rooms . . . The constant, almost
cheerful trill of glass splintering in the air . . . The moment when a fire

company rolls up, and her immediate relief turns to ice as she realizes the firemen, like the police force, have joined the mob. That they are not there to help. That no one is coming to help.

The thought that turns her knees to aspic as they pass through the back door out into the inferno: Lucretia, her one doll, her best friend her whole lonely life, is somewhere inside. But there is no time to go back and find her. They are rushed out the door, all 233 of them, holding hands like paper dolls. Jane cries, but Jane always cries. Most of them don't. The desperation is too thick in the air, takes concentration to move through. Miss Murray and the Miss Shotwells hurry about them, all the matrons close-walking on either side of the lines, as if a woman's body could shield a child.

As the children march down Forty-Second Street, she looks over her shoulder in time to see the mob storm inside her lovely home, ransacking the fine chapel and the ladies' parlor. She can't even think about it. She never wants to see what that gleaming, stately building looks like afterwards. She never sees the asylum again. She follows the matrons into the volcano of the crowd.

By some miracle the mob lets them pass. One of the firefighters shouts, "They're children, for God's sakes! They haven't done anything! Let them go!" and the crowd of women and children separates, like the Red Sea, to let them escape, though this doesn't stop the mob from continuing to torch the asylum.

So they aren't stoned or torched, but the girl doesn't look up at any faces as they go. In fact she is no longer a girl. She turns to stone. They march through the columns of smoke, beneath the low sky. This looks familiar, and in a moment she realizes why—it is as if the illustrations of hell from the children's Bible back at the asylum has come to life. A devil skips by on cloven hooves, taunting them. Or maybe it's a mean-spirited child, but she won't look up to see. Probably she should cry big wrenching sobbing gasps like Jane who weeps as she clutches her hand, but she can't, because she is made of stone. It won't even matter if they burn her because she is made of stone. So that's good. Stone is safe. Through fire and brimstone, through inferno and evil, she goes. The sky is the color of mud. This must be it, the end of the world. Or certainly the end of the city. No place can survive a battle like this with its soul intact. The city she knows and loves, her home on earth, is over.

She tries not to look up, but a movement out of the corner of her eye makes her forget, and that's when she sees a man swaying limply from a tree. She is not sure what she is seeing until Miss Murray catches her and hisses, *Don't look at that, child, concentrate on walking forward,* and that's when she knows it is what she thinks. Throughout the city there are men hanging from trees and lampposts, their faces ghoulish masks with bugged-out eyes, like poor Lucretia's stunned expression. In this city, in this time, after Abolition, as the country fights to free the slaves, as colored people are doctors and businessmen and landowners and preachers and free. Still they are strung up, dead, in the middle of the day.

The girl knows then that everyone is lying. She might be a child, but even she can see: this mob isn't mad about the army's draft. This mob is mad about something she doesn't even understand. Something the mob doesn't even understand. Something for which there is no actual solution.

One fireman, one good fireman in that whole God-forsaken city, the one who speaks up and makes people let them pass, tries to put the fire out, tries to save the orphanage. He fails, of course. You can't fight a tide of evil that easily. But in all the chaos, he, or maybe another fireman, takes some of the children to hide in a fire station; another group is stashed in the police headquarters; a brave widow takes a couple dozen into her home; the girl and Jane and most of the rest are shuffled onto a ferry boat that sails to Blackwell's Island.

She forgets a lot of the details, especially after she is dead. But one thing she never loses is the view from that boat as it glides through the East River to the jagged sliver of an island where the denizens of the lunatic asylum, penitentiary, and smallpox hospital haunt the edge of city, near Manhattan but not of it. As they near the dark, spooky island that is meant to save them, she watches Manhattan—shrouded in smoke, muscular with flame—shrink, until it looks like a model of a city, a dollhouse town.

They feel safe on the island that first night when the dark, low, heavy skies finally break open and the rain begins. She and Jane stand by a window and hold hands and watch the rain extinguish the city. The riots are not over yet. The riots will never actually end. But the fires go out. Night falls, and rain falls, and plumes of smoke rise up from the city like wraiths.

# 6

**STEAM SNAKED UP** from Meg's tea. "I saw Aryeh at the library," she said. "Remember that guy? Kate's old boyfriend? He's married, he has a kid. Do you think that would be weird for Kate to know? It makes me mad. Is that weird? It's weird. Not that I think it should have been Kate marrying him, of course she could have done better. She would have done better. If she'd had a chance. Also, I think I'm getting kicked out of my apartment," she told the tea. "So, it's the end of the world, basically. The end of my life as I know it. Here comes my bag lady future, sooner than I thought. Good thing I've been stockpiling empty cat food cans. I can build a tin tower to live in, do homelessness right, like the Fisher King! Kinda have fun with it, you know?"

Her brother James sighed across the table. "Nice to know you're maintaining your sense of perspective," he said dryly. "And I'm fine, thanks for asking."

Meg looked up. "Sorry, Jamie." She adopted a falsely cheery tone, a newscaster smile. "Hello, person! How is being a person alive in the world treating you today?"

"Terrible! Miserable. Nightmarish. First of all—"

"I *know*." They both glared at the family who had annexed their preferred square foot of space in the vaguely French café. At the head of the table loomed a portly baby in a high chair, waving a spoon like a small, irrational queen. That was *their* spot of 10:00 a.m. light. It had been theirs for *years*. *They* had met here every Sunday and sat at that table back when the baby's parents were still Midwestern graduate students nursing indistinct big city dreams. *They* were supposed to be eating the first meal served that day, not the baby's poorly groomed, overly bespectacled father. The bistro table with the bench was the perfect corner for unfolding the Sunday Review, as the mother was now, shaking out a kink in the newsprint with an authoritative crack. The injustice rankled.

But that was silly, Meg knew that. In the grand scheme of things, she could let the table-stealers live. Someone else's brunch, even at *Meg and James's* table, didn't keep Meg and James from sitting at the *other* tiny table near the *other* window, from catching up on the week over too-large plates of food. Someone else's waffles did not take away her own. It was a lesson she seemed to have to perpetually teach herself, as if she woke each day scrubbed clean of any accrued wisdom, like a gigantic, ambulatory goldfish. What was that, that had flared in her sinuses when she'd seen the idyllic triad in their preferred brunch spot? It was hard to know. Privilege, she knew that was actually its name, but somehow saying it didn't exorcise her frustration.

This new other table was situated by the front door, and the picture window offered a view of Fifth Avenue. Meg watched a van with a huge eyeball painted on the side amble down the street. Only a few years earlier this block had been barren enough that James and Eugene were able to buy a two-bedroom co-op with noncrusty prewar moldings, 35 percent down. Now even this scrubby stretch of Park Slope crawled with brunchers, pairs of young women swinging string bags full of apples from the end-of-the-season farmers' market, couples armed with paper cups of coffee, strollers and strollers and strollers. This wasn't even the only place to meet James on Sunday mornings anymore, although they kept at it out of tradition. That was the kind of family they were, habitual about vacations (two weeks in the Berkshires every August), fetishistic about pets (generations of mentally ill beagles), loyal to holiday rituals, even those that had been chosen entirely by accident (Christmas Eve at La Caridad, the Cuban/Cantonese place on Broadway, first visited the year their mother firebombed the ham). Sometimes Meg wondered if these arbitrary traditions were the only scaffolding their family had anymore, given all that had not gone according to plan.

The more she looked out the window, the more confused she felt: why did children dress so strangely these days? So many capes and crowns! James followed her eyes and said, "Halloween, Meg. It's Halloween."

"Oh *yeah*." Meg shuddered. There was no day of the year she hated more than Halloween. No wonder she had blocked it out.

The waiter sidled by. Meg ordered the day's special, Nutella-stuffed French Toast with candied oranges. James made a horrified face, ordered the Eggs Benedict, "like a goddamned grown-up," he said.

Meg considered her little brother. He *was* a goddamned grown-up. He was married; he owned a co-op; he had *investments* for heaven's sake. He wore a watch, meticulously updated a leather-bound planner, read the newspaper in print even when on the subway, folding it into origami rectangles with the care of someone preserving an ancient art. After brunch, James was going to pick up Eugene so they could go see a new exhibit of botanical sketches at the Morgan Library. He would invite Meg to come, of course, but Meg would refuse, saying she already spent quite enough time in libraries, thank you very much, which was empirically true. More importantly for Meg, she needed the time alone. He knew she was this way and respected it, sometimes even claimed to envy it. James didn't know what to do with more than an hour alone. He and Eugene spent every instant of their free time together, filling their calendar with quiet, adult amusements: family-unfriendly museums, silent auctions, parties at art galleries.

James the Grown-up stared intently at something over Meg's shoulder. She turned to see and then leaned over the table and hissed, "Stop eye-kidnapping that baby."

"I wasn't!" But he had been rather aggressively eyeing the baby occupying his usual seat. "I do like her sweater," he conceded. It was a nubby garment the color of a squirrel, with triangular ears stitched to the hood. The neighborhood children all seemed to have signed some sort of whimsy contract requiring them to imitate woodland creatures whenever possible. Every time Meg walked through Prospect Park, she tripped over a child with a tail or cub-ears or whiskers of some sort.

She clucked her tongue. "You don't want a baby, you want a Pinterest page."

"Probably," said James, but he was smiling oddly, like someone caught admitting to a crush.

"So anyway," Meg said, after she had blown ripples across the surface of her steaming tea. "How's Eugene?"

"Fine," said James. Eugene was always fine. It was Eugene's mission in life to be *fine*. All troubles, large and small, beaded and rolled from him like water off a duck. In this way he was the opposite of Meg and James and their whole family, the anti-Rhys. "He's going for a jog before he makes his Sunday soup. You know how he is. His weekends are all about making other people's weekends look lazy and weak. Yesterday he volunteered at the food bank."

Meg rolled her eyes. "The Lance Armstrong of weekends."

"Without the use of performance-enhancing drugs, of course."

"Naturally. How's work?"

"Don't ask."

"Okay, I won't. In fact, I don't even know what you do. I'm sure it's something very respectable and that you do a good job at it."

James nodded. "That's pretty much it. So what's all this about your apartment?"

"Oh right! I'm getting kicked out. My annoying neighbor told me first, and then my landlady sent me an email. An email! She's selling. The co-op board is trying to root out all the wicked renters and subletters." Meg was suddenly near tears. The apartment had become part of her, an exoskeleton that allowed her mushy, defenseless body to survive. This was an unfamiliar pain—dull, sometimes ignorable, crawling through her belly like indigestion. She didn't want to cry, focused her eyes out the window instead, studying the community garden across the street that had until recently been an empty lot fertile with broken glass, rat nests, drug dealers. Scabrous roses rattled against the garden's fence, having survived the first frost and now looking for more ways to show their strength. Maybe growing in the rocky urban soil had given them superpowers, and maybe any moment they would reach out and bend the bars and scurry down the street, their roots agile as spider legs, leaving a trail of dirt in their wake. But James was waiting for an answer. He had said something, was waiting, she could tell by the way he was looking at her, by the taut quality of air between them. "Sorry, what?"

He sighed. "I'm saying," he said in a slightly louder voice, as if talking to a lost tourist, "I can help you. We will figure it out. Eugene has a client whose wife is this super awesome real estate agent, she actually specializes in affordable rentals because she's like, I don't know, idealistic or something. And anyway you know, if you need first and last months' rent for a place, or even somewhere to stay, you know Eugene and I can help."

Warmth settled in Meg's chest, surging with love for the boy she'd spent so many years torturing. "Thanks, Jamie. I'm sure it'll be fine. But that's nice."

James sipped his coffee. "And you know Mom and Dad would be overjoyed to have you move back in," he added, raising an eyebrow.

The warmth bottomed out. Meg scowled. "You're an asshole, you know that?" How humiliating would that be, the spinster daughter living at home, caring for her elderly parents, like an emotionally stunted Jane Eyre without even a hope of a Mr. Rochester, in a humid, rent-controlled 2.5 apartment? There, after all, was the fear, the ultimate fear of the woman alone: that she wouldn't be able to hack it. That the world would consider itself proven right, that she had needed a husband after all, for the financial stability if nothing else. There she was, like the desiccated postprime roses in the alley-garden, slamming her once-pretty head against a once-welcome fence. But this was all so silly. She was probably just hungry because, where on earth was her breakfast? The café had never been so crowded before. Here came all the people, flooding in, taking over everything that had once been hers. She hated everyone who walked in the door, accusing each one of being the well-to-do buyer about to snatch her apartment, her life, away from her, resenting the confidence that came with having enough money to not think about money.

"I was only kidding, you know," James said. "Don't be so negative, Megs. You haven't even looked for a new place yet, right? At least look before you get all depressed and hopeless." James. What did he know? James's life was cozy and well-considered. James was married (to a man, as their father conceded, granting the quizzical shrug with which he greeted all of life's mysteries—his wife's desire for Botox, the Disneyfication of Times Square, flavored coffee drinks); you didn't need to worry about James any more. This was the thought. It was old-fashioned, it was inaccurate, but still, when someone paired off, you thought, *Well, phew. Don't need to worry about that one anymore. That one won't die alone. That one is all set.*

When Meg thought of her brother in the abstract (when he wasn't sitting there in front of her, being the consummate adult), she pictured roller skating down the Central Park Ramble, and little James running behind, never being able to catch up. Sometimes her memory was considerate enough to elide Kate, skating along somewhere between them. And yet now he was the one skating ahead, confidently navigating the path without even seeming to think about navigating, and Meg was losing her way, and Kate was, well.

"This guy came into the library," Meg said suddenly, just to change the subject, "trying to research a haunted house." Their food finally arrived. She stabbed her French toast with a fork.

"Really?" James said. "He said that? He came in and said 'I'm here to look up a ghost'?" His role in their relationship was to be the skeptic, the brother-Scully to her sister-Mulder.

Meg chewed, the powdered sugar dusting her sweater like diorama snow. (She picked up speed, skated ahead, coasting over bumps in the path.) "No, silly. Of course not. But he had that shifty demeanor, like you just knew something was up. Okay, so he has this old house. Over a hundred years old, probably some turn-of-the-century rich Manhattanite's getaway. I mean, I'm guessing. In Crown Heights—you know that Bed-Stuy/Crown Heights area?—and of course, same old story, he sees a gold mine and wants to renovate and sell to some enterprising yuppies who will pay a million dollars and then open up an espresso bar in the neighborhood—I mean, I'm projecting, but still."

James perked up. "Yeah? What's it like over there? Really, are prices still low?"

"Yes, James. Prices are still low. It's the fucking ghetto. I mean, there are literally housing projects down the block. Boarded-up buildings left and right. You're not ready for it. It's not ready for you."

"I don't know. I read one of those *New York Magazine* stories about that neighborhood that makes you feel like a jerk for not already knowing about the thing they're writing about nobody knowing about—"

"About the wine bar? I know, I read that too. Different end of Crown Heights. The Jews are already being gentrified out, poor things. First Williamsburg, now this! They either have to keep creeping further into Brooklyn or just relent and convert to hipster. Maybe that's easier. They've already got the facial hair."

James sighed. "It's probably already over. Anything I find out about is already over. New York City was over before we were born. America's been over for decades."

Meg stared at him for a minute, chewing. "Oh? So where are we right now, pray tell? Mars?"

James waved his hand. "Go on."

"I was saying it's the other end of Crown Heights, you and Eugene are way too white, so you can stop with your real estate lust. Besides, what's your problem? You have a great apartment already."

"Eugene isn't white," James said, though it was a weak argument. Eugene, beautiful part-Black, part-Puerto Rican, part-Native American, mostly Connecticut Eugene, was white enough. Eugene wore oxfords. Eugene celebrated Hanukkah. Eugene lived with James, in Park Slope, where they made play dates for their dog. Who took Prozac. The dog, that is; Eugene self-medicated with green smoothies and hot yoga.

Over at their usual table, the smug trio was packing up to go, the table littered with crumbs of the Styrofoam-like substance the baby had been consuming. Meg watched James watch the baby toddle across the floor in three lurching, triumphant steps before teetering and being swept up by its mother and tucked into a papoose.

As they ate, Meg told him about Ellis Williams's descriptions of odd phenomena, talking with the urgent pushiness (she could hear it in her own voice, tried to tone it down without any luck) of those storefront psychics desperate to make you believe, or else convincing themselves that coincidence equaled truth, like how a person in turmoil (so, anyone) would read her horoscope and be struck speechless at the undeniable, obvious truth in the trite words ("you're in turmoil"), the message that might relate to any human anywhere. Yes, they were all in turmoil. Yes, life was hard, or anyway everyone's life seemed hard to them.

Kate had never met them for brunch in this café. Kate had not seen James graduate from NYU. Kate had never been to James's apartment. Kate had never met Eugene. All of this helped James, Meg guessed. James had barely gotten to the age at which family members reveal themselves to be actual people, hardly had the chance to start seeing Kate, really *seeing* her, when—poof—she was gone.

So maybe James didn't get lost the way Meg did, remembering, out of nowhere, a trip to the Met that they had somehow convinced their parents they were ready for—just the three kids, alone, and James only five years old. This made Kate nearly ten, fawn-leggy and lovely, a girl who could pass for a young lady but often chose to act more like a goony kid James's age, and Meg a sage fifteen. Meg felt her siblings were ready for some art history, she told their parents (who were ready for a Sunday to themselves). But Meg's real MO was to impose upon her impressionable brother and sister a sense of adventure. Meg waited until they were on the crosstown bus to show James the decayed paperback chapter book she had given Kate to study, which concerned the adventures of siblings who ran away to live in the museum. James looked troubled, but Meg ignored the worry emanating from him like a smell. For the first decade or so of his life, Meg and Kate considered James to be more of an experiment than a mate.

On the bus, instead of looking at James trying not to cry, Meg watched out the window and couldn't have really seen what she seemed to remember seeing, which was the characters from the book, standing on Central Park East, holding up and studying a large city map.

At the Met itself, everything was new. They'd been there a million times with their parents and on school trips, but it was as if Meg had never seen it at all before that trip with her siblings: Miles of gleaming ramps that seemed to have been placed there expressly for James to race up and down; bloody battle pictures Meg found to show him; the Temple of Dendur suddenly their own personal wishing pond. Up and up and up to the rooms that their parents pooh-poohed as "just decorative," and which the kids loved the most—arranged with fancy furniture, silent and eerie as an enormous dollhouse. They would sleep in that canopy bed, the girls plotted, they would dine on the resin food at the regal banquet table. They would never go home again.

James ruined it all by bursting into tears, at which point Meg had scooped him up—she liked to pretend in public to be his mother, dressing in high collars and long skirts and affecting a pair of wire-rim spectacles long before she needed a prescription—and comforted him. "There, there, little dear," she said soothingly, more like *Little Women*'s Marmee than like their actual mother. "We're only playing a game. Right, Katie? We're just being silly." James had nodded and snuffled, and then they'd gone to the café where Kate had consumed—Meg could remember this most clearly of all—a piece of chocolate cake, a chocolate pudding cup, and a glass of chocolate milk. When she thought of Kate this way, squishing pudding between her teeth thoughtfully as she paged through the chapter book for reference, she knew that she had never died. That no one ever did.

In a harried moment once, James had accused Meg of using Being In Mourning as her pastime, the way some people got really into CrossFit. She had responded maturely and calmly, by snapping that it wasn't her fault if he was in denial. Neither one of them was entirely wrong. But it wasn't like this haunted house business was all her. So many patrons at the library wanted to talk about haunted houses, people who had never met her before—they always gravitated toward her for those requests—and so Meg knew it was real, and not simply one of her many weird theories about the world. Of course, patrons at the library also thought that computers could capture their souls, but never mind all that.

"And? So? Did you go to his house and meet the ghost?" James said, not terribly nicely.

Meg sipped her tea archly. "No. Then I had to do something else. And he left."

"And that was it? That's the whole thing? Cool story, bro."

"Oh shush. Yes, that was it, and yes, I'll probably never see him again, and no, I'll never get to meet his ghost, but I just think it's interesting, that's all." She looked out the window for a minute. "Sometimes I think that's why I have this job. For the every once in a while when someone wants to find out if his house is haunted."

"Do people really believe in it, though? I mean, come on, Meg. They don't *really*, right? Outside of TLC original programming? Believe that there are ghosts? I mean, it's New York, buildings are old, they settle, they creak, neighbors make weird sounds, and the first thought is: *That couldn't just be the super practicing Zumba, it must be something supernatural?!* It's absurd."

"Yes, *act*ually, many people believe in hauntings. And it's not like in the movies, *act*ually, drawers sliding open and windows slamming and all that dramatic stuff, I'll have you know. It's usually more of a feeling people get. Don't you ever get that feeling, like when you're alone but you're not alone? And anyway, why is it so terribly hard to imagine that in a city where millions of people have died, there would be a kind of residue left behind? A something—maybe not like the green blobby guy from *Ghostbusters*, not a *figure* like that—but some bit of their essence left behind. I mean, really, don't you think it means *something* that so many different people from all over the world have, for so long, had this idea of ghosts, of spirits, of hauntings? This guy from the library, he was saying every year the tenants in the downstairs apartment move out in a hurry. They don't know each other, the rent is low, the place sounds nice . . . now why would this be?"

"Um, maybe it's a rundown apartment in the ghetto, like you just said? Maybe the landlord does a crappy job of vetting his renters? Maybe it's New York City and people move around a lot?"

Meg glared at him, drank the dregs of her tea. There was a silence. "Also, the guy was super hot," she added.

"Ah!" said James. "Well. Now I find your story interesting."

"I know," she sighed. "He really was. But now I'll probably never see him again so, you know."

"So you've just had the perfect relationship. All desire and possibility."

"Right. And some intense smoldering-gaze exchanges. If only we were Edwardian enough to be satisfied by that!"

"Right." James paused. "Slimer."

"What?"

"The green blobby guy from *Ghostbusters*. His name was Slimer."

"I know, James."

"Okay."

"I know that. I know who Slimer is."

"Wait, are you *crying?*" James leaned forward. Meg swiped her cheeks with flat hands. "Are you crying?" he said again, dumb with confusion. "About . . . Slimer?"

"Yes," Meg said. She found a handkerchief in her bag, dabbed beneath her glasses. "Yes, I just can't believe it about Slimer. He left us much too soon."

"Well, what is it?"

"You'll make fun of me."

"Probably, yes."

"It's Kate. Kate knows to visit me in my apartment. I mean, I've always felt her presence there. And if I move—who knows if she'll find me again, you know?"

To her relief, James didn't laugh, or even smirk. "I know what you mean," he said slowly. "I do. Remember when I was dating that guy who moved to Queens and then I never saw him again?"

"Oh yeah. Well, he was on the R line, right? That never would have worked out."

"Seriously. But, the point is, I'm sure Kate will find you anywhere."

She knew it pained him to say it, skeptical as he was, weary as he was of her spectral gossip. She smiled, patted his hand. "Thanks, Jamie."

James paid the check and Meg protested and James protested her protest, the elaborate kabuki of two people with imbalanced incomes at bill-time. He had money. She didn't. It was no use pretending.

They walked down the avenue together. James took her arm and said, "Don't worry about the apartment. Seriously. You have us to help." And then, after a deep breath, he added, "Speaking of help. You'd make a great aunt, you know that?"

Meg laughed. "Oh boy. Talking about burying the lede. And what ever do you mean by that, Jamie dear?"

James took in a long breath, letting the city sounds chatter between them, their conversation a ventriloquy of F train rumble and livery car honk and pigeon flutter. There was a rustle of wind, a downpour of yellow. Gingko.

Finally James said, "Well." They stopped to look at the Halloween display up in the barbershop window. The remaining Rhys offspring were the last nontourists in the world to actually stop and look in windows. It was an unofficially official part of their Sunday walks. Making eye contact with a plastic skeleton leaning rakishly against a vintage barbershop pole, James said, "We're going to have a baby." Meg turned to face him, blinking, and he corrected himself, "We want to have a baby. I mean. We're starting the process."

She put her hands on his arms. Even after all these years, she was always surprised to find herself a head shorter than her little brother, and yet she was, and the older they grew, the more their age difference seemed to diminish, in that unlikely algebra of siblings. "Jamie! We've been talking for an hour, and you didn't think to mention it? What on earth is wrong with you? That's wonderful!"

Her first thoughts were of course selfish. Their parents ached for grandkids with the fervor of the starved, and they had only just recently seemed to notice that their forty-year-old single daughter was not producing a litter of onesie-wearers in this lifetime. Nora and Martin had developed an unsettling habit that summer of taking their neighbor's six-year-old son out for ice cream, buying toys for him everywhere they went. The substitute grandchild's apartment must have been a traffic jam of die-cast cars from seaside towns up and down the East Coast. Really, James was giving Meg a great gift: a nag-free future.

They resumed their walk, headed down a side street toward the park. "Wow, James! That's really, really great," said Meg again. She tucked her arm comfortably in his and squeezed. "So! Tell me. Tell me what that means."

"Well, we've talked about it a lot, obviously, and we'd like to have some genetic say in the matter. I think we're going to try to find an egg donor and a surrogate—probably not from the same person because that's a whole other *thing*."

"Huh!" Meg was trying to have the correct response, without entirely knowing what that was. They stopped to admire a still-blooming bush of yellow roses in front of a brownstone. "Okay, so, whose sperm? Or—what should I say? Who will be the genetic father? Is that correct?"

He rolled his eyes. "We're thinking Eugene for this one. I want a baby that looks like him. And then the idea is: if it works, and we still have any money left, we'd have another in a couple years and use mine."

They continued to stroll. From somewhere—James's brain?—came the mewling wail of an infant.

"That's some advanced planning," Meg observed. "What's this baby's college application list looking like?" She said it lightly, she hoped.

"I know, I know. We're just trying to see the long road. You know? To make sure this is the right time, the right thing. Eugene is pretty sure he's going to be made partner soon. I'd hope to be home for a bit with the baby I guess, but who knows if my firm would go for it. I'm an architect, by the way, did you know that? We'll get a nanny I guess, I don't know. I just know we both want to, we want to be fathers, and if I'm going to have a kid, I don't want it to be all alone. You have to have a sibling, you know?"

Meg watched his face shift. They were always, in a way, secretly talking about Kate. Maybe that was all a ghost really was, after all.

"Okay. You guys are good planners, you really are. I know you'll figure it all out. You guys will be such great parents! This baby is already so lucky. He's going to have it all—love, gymnastics class, Momofuku. But it's not—I mean, *you* know—babies aren't symbolic, right? Once they are born, they are, you know, themselves. Greedy creatures chewing on the edges of your fancy coffee table. It's not going to make you feel—"

"I know, I know. Jeez, Meg."

"Okay. Okay." She took a deep breath. "Have you told Mom and Dad yet?"

"God no. I won't tell them until it's a sure thing."

"That's a good idea. In fact, maybe just wait until the kid's in preschool. You know how they are."

They crossed Prospect Park West, entered the park. Meg kicked through piles of dead leaves. Though she didn't want to jinx anything, she allowed herself to imagine a Eugenian little imp throwing itself into a pile of maple leaves. Most of the trees hadn't yet changed in the park; fall was still a caricature of itself; people wore sweaters too thick for the temperature and scarves they didn't need because they couldn't wait. There was the usual frenzy over pumpkin spice lattes at Starbucks. The park looked limp and peaked, as if the trees might forget about changing color altogether and suddenly find themselves standing there naked and snowy one morning. But Meg knew if they walked down to the Nethermead or the Long Meadow, there would be something to see. There would be at least one bright yellow tree to make them feel that time was passing as it was meant to, even though it was warmer than it should have been, even though all around them picnickers and dog walkers and child-minders were taking off their cardigans regretfully.

Meg hopped on a trampoline of mousy leaves. "Okay, and? What else? You're not going to leave your apartment," she commanded.

"No. Not yet. It would be fine for one kid. We'll put a door between our bedroom and the office, make the office into a little nursery. I don't really need an office at home anyway. I have a laptop. We can move the bookshelves to the living room. People do it all the time."

Meg nodded over-enthusiastically. "Absolutely," she said. She was forcing her excitement a little, but it seemed to be what was called for. "That room is perfect. Just put up a door. Right. There's that window in there, and it has such a sweet view of the courtyard. Perfect. How exciting. I'll babysit, of course. I won't even charge that much." She winked.

"Are you *winking* at me?"

"Am I? Did I? Sweet Jesus, how *cute* of me. Funny, someone winked at me recently, and I thought, what in the hell, who *winks*? But it must have planted in me a desire to wink. How was it, the wink? Did it look forced?"

James laughed. "No, it looked okay."

"Good. Thank you for telling me. I'll use that then. Maybe I'll become a person who winks. God, the future is really full of possibility, isn't it?"

"Remarkable."

"How auntly of me, really! Is there a word for that? Aunt-ish? Unfair, since uncles have 'avuncular.' 'Avauntular?' No? Well, that's institutional sexism for you."

They walked on, out of the park now and through the narrow side streets where it seemed trick-or-treating had begun, braving the clumped crowds of costumed children. Before dark, Meg was okay with Halloween, more or less. In the daytime, it was still a holiday of children—little girls flouncing in princess dresses, plastic crowns askew in hair taut with sugar; boys disguised fiercely as ninjas and knights and commandos and superheroes; older kids in menacing masks; babies roped into their parents' elaborate grown-up jokes, dressed as parts of movies they'd never see.

Still, she leaned against James as they passed the ghoulish decorations. Meg disliked the skeletons arranged to look like they were escaping from graves. She extra-disliked anything resembling a body. The more weight it had, the worse she felt about it; a hay-stuffed zombie slung over a banister was bad enough, but a mannequin swaying heavily from a tree could undo her. The fake gravestones were bad, but even worse when there was a whole yard of them, worse still if a child had made them, writing in a crooked child-scrawl the death dates of Dracula and Michael Myers and Rebecca DeWinter (well, it was Brooklyn after all). Meg envied the children, the careless way they screamed at skeletons on display and then raced past them with the bravery that the promise of a mini Snickers could instill, the way death was still a joke to them, so much so that Grim Reaper and Bloody Doctor and even Old Person were nothing more than costume ideas.

Worst of all, in the season of bedsheet ghouls and suggestive vampires, was the crime scene tape. The ghosts were one thing—the white, truncated cylinders that appeared on signs or shirts or cookies were so abstract that Meg made no connection between them and the ghosts she knew. But the crime scene tape was crime scene tape, and it would always be to her the scene of Kate's accident, the livery car stopped as if something could be thrown into reverse and taken back, the continent of blood on the pavement, the body bag. There was likely an anthropological reason for the uptick in crime scene tape as decoration this year, probably due to some quirk of Chinese factory production schedules, it had overtaken the dollar stores that a few years before had been largely stocked with Day-Glo purple cobwebs. Now it seemed every other door was criss-crossed with caution tape, and the yellow flicker of it, the way it shuddered in the wind or when a door slammed shut, made Meg sick to her stomach, made her angry with everyone around her, for whom a crime scene meant Hollywood, for whom ghosts were decorations, for whom thinking about death was optional, occasional.

She and her brother held each other's arms and faced the cutesy death all around together, walking up Seventh Avenue and then zig-zagging over to Fifth, back to the restaurant where Meg had locked her bike. Meg biked home, thinking about something James had told her before, about his nagging sense that you couldn't really live a life without having a family, not *really*; she had chided him for being old-fashioned, though she knew he wasn't alone in his feeling. But when Meg thought about reproducing (a foregone conclusion at this point, anyway, pretty much), she felt only fear gripping her kneecaps like cold hands. Look at the heartache their own parents had suffered. Why open oneself up to that? How could James stand the risk?

Meg stopped at a stoplight, putting a foot down to steady the bike as a bus rattled by. She was going to prove to everyone that her life—her singledom, childlessness, her low-powered career path, her anorexic bank account and quiet lack of accomplishments—meant something. Somehow she was going to make something happen, extract some meaning from the mundane progression of days, buck everyone's expectations of what made a life worthwhile. Somehow.

Meg looked up, and somehow there they were, the family from brunch, the squirrel-baby now snoozing in the carrier against the mother's chest, the bespectacled parents studying the map at the bus stop and having, she could tell by their body language, a muted argument about how to get somewhere. The father hissed at the mother. The mother pointed, mutely but furiously, as if they had to keep quiet or the baby would awaken and know they were unsure. As if they could mask the fact that they didn't always know how to map the way.

# 7

**IT IS NOT NEWS** to her that grown people behave erratically. She has lived with the knowledge that a mother gave her up, a mother who must have been a broken leg, a loose woman, a nightwalker. She has grown up surrounded by children whose mothers have given them up. It is a sad fact of the asylum that few of the orphans are actually orphans. The children she knows have shadowy pasts at workhouses or Bellevue or on the streets selling matches or worse. Adults are, for the most part, dangerous and untrustworthy. The exceptions being the ladies who run the asylum, Miss Murray and the Miss Shotwells, who are good and kind, the other matrons with their soothing voices. And Dr. Smith, of course. Dr. Smith, who speaks like a president, who insists that they be proper at all times, who is always telling the children that they must grow up to be something. That they must learn to read and write—it is *crucial* that they read and write—and learn a trade, like he has. It is important, he tells them, because right now the world is watching. The world is waiting for them to fail, to prove that they are inferior and can't handle freedom, and it is their job to live well for all the folks who never got the chance. This he tells them again and again. They can be something. They *must* be something.

She wants to be a doctor, like him. She selects this somewhat haphazardly and then molds herself to it. She will be a doctor. Because she likes the way pieces fit together, because she likes to mother people like

little Jane, and because she is in little-kid-love with Dr. Smith, and a
desire to be a doctor will please him.

He knows this, and maybe this is why she is singled out. A few days
after the asylum burns, Dr. Smith appears at her side to tell her about
the place where she is going next. He says her name, and the way he
says it makes her heart stop. Is she in trouble? No, she is special, and
she is smart, and because she is so serious about her studies, and because she wants to train to be a doctor, he thinks she will be the right
one for it, for this new home. *As soon as it is safe to travel*, the good
doctor says, *you will go. Word has gotten out about what happened to
the asylum, and people are trying to help us place all of you children. A
family I know has offered to adopt a girl. A very good family. Educated
people, God-fearing churchgoers, with four girls of their own already.* She
asks if they are nearby, thinking of Jane, who has always been her sister
up until now. Dr. Smith shakes his head. *No, they live in a small farming settlement across the river. And it's a special place. Wait till you get
there, you will see what I mean.* This he says with a twinkle in his eye,
the first inkling of anything like happiness she has detected in anyone
since this whole ordeal began. *It's called Weeksville.*

She stands by the shore watching the river, which resembles cooking
grease mixed with pig slop, lap queasily against the rocks. In the harbor, ship masts stab upwards like the picked-clean ribs of a Union boy's
carcass. She plans out her dramatic farewell. She will cast a hand to
her brow and sigh like her heart is breaking. She will shake her stiff
pigtails in sorrow. She will slump her shoulders and squint her eyes
and everything about her appearance will express to the matrons how
deeply unhappy she is to be separated from Jane, from everyone she
knows in this whole lonely universe, and maybe they will change their
minds. Maybe they will prostrate themselves at her feet and beg her
forgiveness. Or maybe the country family will agree to take Jane too.
Or maybe the city will pull itself together, reassembling its broken bits
the way an illusionist reconnects a sawed-apart lady. Perhaps she ought
to try her hand at rending her garments, something she has seen other

broken-down people doing in the days after the riots, so complete and animal is their grief.

But even as she is leaving for the unimaginable new future, she is an asylum kid through and through. As Dr. Smith has often told them, they are the best-behaved and most civilized children in all of New York—not just of all the colored children, he'd said, but of *all* the children—and this is important. It is important for life in the asylum, and it is important to prove to the world that it can be done. And besides, even now, even after all the brutality she's seen, she can't bear the thought of the glare the matrons would shoot her if she were to tug roughly at her starched white smock. Well, it used to be kept clean and bright anyway; once they are refugees on Blackwell's Island, the orphans take on a distinctly orphan-y appearance that she can tell troubles the tidy Miss Shotwells. The usually well-groomed children have gone smudged and sloppy, like urchins from the almshouse, or the illustrations of London street life from one of Mr. Dickens's stories they pore over when Dr. Smith can obtain a magazine for them.

In the end, Miss Murray calls her over to go, and all she can do is stare mutely at the faces she has seen every day for as long as she can remember. *Fare thee well*, they say dully, envious of her for leaving. Jane weeps. She wants to run and hold her, but some part of her that has been hammered down into a thin metallic veneer holds her steady. *All right then*, she says to Jane, to all of them. *Take care.*

Miss Murray clutches her carpetbag as they board the skiff that will carry them to Manhattan. It occurs to the girl, used to being mindful of adults and their moods, that Miss Murray is nervous. Miss Murray catches her watching and squeezes her arm with a smile that is meant to be reassuring. *Well then*, she says briskly. *Feels odd to be heading back this way, does it not? Never fear, my child, the violence has ended.* The girl looks at the black husk of the city and nods. She is ready for adults to stop lying to her.

A grizzled, ancient sailor steers their skiff. He smiles at her as they push off into the river, revealing a toothless grin like the Headless Horseman's jack-o-lantern. *Are ye setting out to calmer seas, then?* he says suddenly.

The girl looks away, studying the tarry detritus bobbing on the current. *Yes sir*, she murmurs.

The sailor opens his mouth, and an evil-sounding cackle bubbles from his throat. *I remember my first voyage out*, he tells her, not seeming to care if she wants to hear a story or not. She looks to Miss Murray for reassurance—is this normal? How is she to know how people act outside the asylum walls?—but Miss Murray is studying her handkerchief as if it were embroidered with fascinating runes. The sailor continues, *I was but fifteen, not much older than you are, and I conscripted myself to defend my country. War of 1812. Those were the good old days. We fought with valor back then! Not like these cowards today, doing whatever they can to avoid a fight. These damn immigrants burning down their own city, so-called, to prove they're more American than the—*

*Sir,* Miss Murray says. *If you please. She is but a child, remember.*

*Of course, forgive me, madams.* The sailor laughs with unnerving volume, a laugh that transforms into a throaty cough.

Maybe it is possible to sink down through the bottom of the boat, to disappear completely into the watery world beneath. Maybe a misty maiden will grip her by the throat, take her to a comfortable lair for sirens and kelpies, like the old charwoman at the asylum had told them about as they gathered round her coal bin, hungry for stories. A bump jolts her out of her reverie; here they are, back on Manhattan.

The sailor has taken them to the lower end of the island, by the seaport, where the girl will board the ferry that takes her across the sound to a wild stretch of farmland called Brooklyn. Her heart thrums in her throat, as noisy and vibrating as the steamships in the harbor. Miss Murray hurries her off the rickety skiff, orders the sailor to wait, then steers her through the maze of dockworkers, weaving between mountains of cargo and herds of leering men who smell sour and shout at Miss Murray: *We musta missed that one!* or *Got yourself a good-looking specimen there, how much you think she'll fetch?* The girl stays as close to Miss Murray as she can, clinging to her hand. Miss Murray holds herself differently here, under the threatening eyes of the men. Miss Murray is as out-of-place in that unsavory seaport as the girl herself, all but glowing in her prim Quaker dress, her lips pressed thin. The girl knows that they are near the heart of the Manhattan slave trade, that down the canyon of Wall Street is the place where people were once bought and sold here in their own city. She recalls Dr. Smith's stories with a shudder. It might have been her own family shackled there, mere yards from where she and Miss Murray now hurry along. A wild pig clonks headlong into the girl's leg, and she stifles a scream, pressing even closer to Miss Murray, her chest clanging with panic.

She can hardly catch her breath as they weave through the chaos. The air is hazy with smoke from factories and steamships and maybe still the riot fires, darkened with a tang of sewage and biological rot. The stench makes her realize what she's never been so viscerally conscious of before—that she is improbably lucky to have spent her childhood up at the asylum, where the air is sweet and fresh. Was. That the matrons who founded the asylum, who bought the gracious manor and fed and housed and educated poor children there, are angels on this wretched earth. That she is leaving them. That her whole childhood—with its clean aprons and hoop games and ragdolls and lessons and prayers, with its sturdy stone walls and their implicit promise that the problems of the outside world would not breach the keep—has ended. Tears spring to her eyes. But she isn't a girl anymore, remember? So it doesn't even matter. She has to remind herself of this frequently if she is going to get though this next whatever-it-is. She is made out of stone. She wipes at her eyes once, fiercely.

Her ears ring with the clatter of wagon wheels on cobblestone, the monstrous squeal of cable cars, the crude voices of peddlers and newsboys, a rhythmic marching she imagines is a regiment of soldiers but doesn't dare to turn her head toward. She is surprised not to see any Black faces in the crowd, not even among the beggars. Perhaps everyone ran the day of the riots and have not come back, seeking shelter in the woods, or the countryside where she is headed, or who knows, boarding ocean liners back to Africa. Perhaps there is no one like her left in that whole entire city. She has never felt so lonely in her whole lonely life.

When they reach the ferry landing, Miss Murray purchases her ticket and hands her the carpetbag. The girl stares dumbly at it. She herself does not own a thing. (She can't let herself think about Lucretia, surely a pile of ash by now.) She can't imagine what might be in the bag. But she is happy to have something to hold onto, as if the weight of the bag will keep her fastened to the boat. Miss Murray sits her down on a bench near the window, holds her shoulders as she looks her in the eyes. *Do not talk to anyone,* she said. *Do not let anyone accost you. You are safe while you are on this boat. As soon as the boat stops, ask the ferryman to walk you to the dock. Do not go without him. He is a friend of Dr. Smith's and knows to help you. A man will be waiting for you at the dock. His name is Mr. Jenkins. He is a good man. He will take you to your new home. Do not go with anyone else besides Mr. Jenkins. Do you understand, my child?*

She nods, blinking back tears. Her face has forgotten that it is stone. *Oh, Miss Murray,* she whispers and reaches out, and Miss Murray gives her a quick hug, pats her shoulder, and says, not exactly looking into her eyes, *Bless you, child*, before disappearing into the crowd, slipping through the people trying to board.

The ferry heaves across the sound, and once again Manhattan shrinks. They lumber past a sprawling, turreted building that at first she thinks might be a castle, surrounded by strings of pearls, wait, no, people lined up on gangplanks, white cloths over the heads of the women. Servants entering the castle. Or no, maybe it's a kind of asylum, or a hospital, and the people from the boats are waiting to get in. *Castle Clinton,* says a girl to her, tapping on the window. She starts. Do not talk to anyone, Miss Murray had warned. She nods mutely. The girl is a few years older than she, with a vague Irish brogue to her speech, but skin a color like she's never seen—light brown, like a sapling's bark, neither black like her nor white like Miss Murray. This brown girl nods knowingly, *Me paw came trough after the Great Hunger,* she explains, though this explains nothing. *Came to America, where he heared the streets'd be paved with gold,* she says, with a giggle that borders on hysterical. A harsh adult voice rings out through the crowd then, and the girl rolls her eyes and zips away from the window, toward her invisible mother.

When the boat docks, the people begin to file off, and just as Miss Murray had said, the ferryman appears. Without a word, he takes her small hand into his large, dark clubbed fingers, and leads her down the gangplank. She marvels at the texture of his skin, rough and criss-crossed with scars the likes of which she has never seen. She is so distracted by the wooden block that is his hand that she doesn't, at first, take in her surroundings. It is only after the ferryman has located Mr. Jenkins and handed her off that she looks around. The Fulton Ferry landing is much like the dock in Manhattan, but the air seems clearer, and it's quieter. Seagulls circle the bay. Horses whinny conversational-ly from their posts, hitched to omnibuses driven by natty men who lift their top hats and wave to her as she stares. A murder of crows darkens the skies overhead, cawing as they flock toward the East.

Mr. Jenkins greets her cordially and escorts her to the railroad sta-tion nearby, where they board the Brooklyn and Jamaica Railroad, a monster of a steam engine that looks familiar for some reason. An in-stant later she realizes why, that a boy back at the asylum had treasured a cast iron keepsake of this very train. She had never known the toy was a copy of a real train. She wonders now if the boy had suspected. What the other children would say if they knew that she was on a fine, gleaming train, chugging through the countryside.

For the first time, the day takes on the tenor of an adventure. From the relative calm and quiet of the train car, she watches fields and farms tumble greenly past the windows, regaining some sense of her-self as the train picks up speed. She remembers, with a little smile, the dramatic farewell she had planned only a few hours earlier, when she'd been a different, younger, sillier girl.

Mr. Jenkins, who has hardly said a word to her, looks up from his newspaper—*Frederick Douglass's Paper,* she reads—and sees her smil-ing. *Are you glad to be coming to live with us, then?*

The girl blinks at him. *With you?* She had assumed that he—a Black man with skin as dark as any African she'd ever met, and the wiry body of the servants she'd seen when the asylum hosted fund-raising picnics for wealthy donors—was a hired hand sent to fetch her. Her heart bottoms out, a dented skiff run aground. She is to be living with the servants, then. In the servants' quarters of some plantation house, no doubt, not slavery but close enough, and the fate of most girls like her. Here she'd thought she was so different. She'd thought she would continue school, grow up to be a doctor, have a fine house like Dr. Smith. Why would Dr. Smith play such a dastardly trick? After all of the horrors of the past few days, now is when, her hands still folded primly in the lap of her singed asylum uniform, she bursts into tears.

They are heaving, racking sobs, tears like Jane cries, tears like she hasn't cried since—well, ever. Tears that vaguely recall, deep in her humors, some nascent preasylum babyhood she has erased her own memories of. She bends over her lap and weeps, the train's rattle vibrating her cries into an unsettling keen. She cries for herself, and for the asylum, and for the soldiers in the war, and for her damned mother and father, wherever they are. She cries until she can't breathe, and then she sits up and digs out her handkerchief and has paused to take in a shuddering breath when she realizes that the man, Mr. Jenkins, is laughing.

She stops crying, stunned. *Are you—laughing at me?*

He shakes his head, trying to suppress the chuckles behind a smile. *My dear girl. Forgive me. I don't mean to laugh. I know you've been through a lot.* He is attempting seriousness, now. He pats her hand in a fatherly way. *It's not so bad out in the countryside. I daresay you will even enjoy it. Our life is simple, it is true. My own daughters—I have four of them, and I know you will get on fine with them—do complain that it is dull compared with the big city excitement they read about in novels, but I promise you we have fun. In a few weeks, we'll have one of the biggest picnics of the year at Suydam Pond! Fiddlers and dancing and footraces and a feast of clams and oysters, and swings for the children. And wait until you see our school, our principal is practically world-famous. And—*

*You mean—*Her face burns. She snuffles, dabbing at her eyes with the handkerchief. *You are—? It is your home that I—?* She isn't even sure what she wants to ask, so she blurts out, *I'm not to be a servant?* Now his laughter reassures rather than riles her. *No, no, no, child. You're not anyone's servant.* He produces from somewhere his own handkerchief, since hers has been thoroughly defiled with her phlegm. She studies the cloth for a moment before applying it to her wet cheeks. It is clean and soft, and someone has beautifully embroidered the initials JJ along with a compass rose in a corner. She runs her fingers over the compass as he explains, *In addition to the farming we do at the house, I'm a lighterman at the docks. When I was a younger man, I worked on a merchant ship and sailed the seas.*

Only now does she understand, and she remembers how Dr. Smith had told her she was going to a special place, and then she laughs a watery laugh, feeling foolish and relieved in equal measure. *So you are the farmer. You are the man of the house. And you have agreed to adopt an orphan, er, me.*

He nods, sticks out his hand for her to shake. *Forgive my manners, I don't know what came over me there at the station. Allow me to formally introduce myself. Jacob Jenkins,* he says, *of Weeksville, New York. Very pleased to make your acquaintance, Madam.* She tilts her head as daintily as she can, like she imagines Mary Todd Lincoln might when meeting Queen Victoria for tea. *The pleasure is all mine,* she says primly, and then blushes when he takes her hand and kisses it, as she has always dreamed that someone might.

# 8

**ELLIS WILLIAMS** was back.

Meg looked up from the front desk, and there he was, opening the heavy glass double doors to the Brooklyn Collection by pushing the handle, not pressing his palms flat on the glass and leaving greasy graffiti like many men did, the sort of men who spread their legs on the subway as if they were bower birds staking their claim with elaborate nests of pant leg, duffel bag, Sudoku pages—how men loved to take up space—no, he gripped the stainless steel handles, paused to let the vacuum seal whoosh, then pushed the rest of the way, and so she guessed that he was a standing-up-for-women kind of subway rider, and having made this clever observation, she believed she knew all there was to know about him. Even though it had been days, she knew him with hypnopompic clarity, remembered his entire name immediately, endured a palpitation of joy. There was Ellis. He was different than other men, somehow. And he was back, he was hers, for this moment anyway, wasn't he?

For there he was, in a heavier-weight blazer now and a hand-knitted scarf (who had made him that scarf?)—the weather had turned brisk, with that abruptness autumn sometimes adopts, like a conversation icing over in the wake of a faux pas. As a rule, Meg developed a passion for anyone who came asking about haunted houses, but this was different. There was the jolt of recognition, the moment of hope—like falling in love for a minute with someone at a party simply because he has made eye contact with you and then looked quickly away. But more, even more than love. Because, in the end, one didn't actually want to be in love, not anymore. Love hadn't been able to explain anything since the days of Isabel Archer. No, Meg didn't want love. What she wanted was to understand something about the world, something about her own existence. Love couldn't help you there. Only death could.

So Meg looked at Ellis and Ellis looked at her and the air between them burned like a firecracker fuse and then they both looked away before impact, the way one really didn't do with a library patron. When one was a prim and proper librarian, one smiled crisply and said, if anything, "You're back! How may I help you today?"

He rubbed adorably at his head, his gaze darting along the shelves. She took the opportunity to study him: He was tall, but not overly so, muscular in a way that had not particularly appealed to her until recently, which she was sure meant it was one of those hormonal things wherein your aging body began to panic about procreating and sent urgent messages to your not-yet-aged-out loins to hurry up and mate with a hearty specimen of manhood—in fact, she was certain she'd read something like that in the Tuesday *Science Times*. There was something forbidding about him, not quite open, and he was too broad-shouldered and unsmiling to seem friendly—but then there were those kittenish hazel eyes and unrealistically curly eyelashes, and the strong jawline and cleft chin of every man she'd ever loved, and his cardigan sweater, and thick tortoiseshell glasses that leant him a vaguely bookish mien . . . Meg assembled her face into her tightest Dorothea Brooke smile and pushed her spectacles up her nose.

Ellis smiled at being recognized. "Hey. Meg, right? You were so helpful last week."

"I'm very glad. How goes the research?"

"Okay. I'm kind of rushing a bit because I head back to Chicago soon."

Meg's heart did not sink because why should she care? She became very busy shuffling papers. "Oh? So you're just here visiting?"

"That's right."

"I assume there's been some sort of pizza-comparison field test?" (*Please stop being so stupid*, Meg told her brain.)

Ellis smiled, just slightly. "Not exactly. It's—it's complicated."

Meg nodded. "It *is*. Deep dish, pan, thin crust."

He paused, as if deciding whether to take the bait. Then: "Right. To fold or not to fold."

"That *is* the question."

"So—" and he told her how he had gone to the Brooklyn Historical Society, had spent an afternoon in that platonic ideal of a library, all hush and gleam, the spiral staircases Jack-and-the-Beanstalking up into stacks. He had flipped through ancient city directories and land conveyances, had become acquainted with the waxing and waning of the plot itself. He had gone to the Department of Buildings, he had sifted through the digitized records. He had compiled a list of occupants and sellers and buyers back to the early twentieth century. He had tracked down the original deed for the land—1839!—but had not yet found a name for who actually built the house upon it, or who the very first dwellers might have been. He had come this far, worked this hard, only to have to say to Meg, almost apologetically, "I have to head back home soon, though, back to Chicago, and I'm not sure how much I'll be able to do from there"—she nodded with celerity, knowing well her role as Good Listener—"but I think what I'm actually looking for is, well, to know who may have died in the building."

Meg nodded. She knew. After all, Meg had not only been cohabiting with her sister's spirit for the past decade or so, and she had also, professionally speaking, shepherded dozens of would-be ghost hunters through the Brooklyn Collection's hallowed halls. There was the first—oh, one always remembered the first—a middle-aged woman of occult appearance, seeking to cleanse her Windsor Terrace yoga studio of a spirit given to slamming windows shut during Shavasana. Meg had helped her wade through the Sanborns and local newspaper archives, and they'd discovered that indeed, a fire had ravaged the building in the 1970s; an article embalmed in microfiche revealed the blaze had snuffed out a neighborhood old-timer, who apparently maintained his dread of hippies from beyond the grave. There was the Brooklyn Heights family with a thumping basement; as it turned out, the stately brownstone had once been a stop on the Underground Railroad. Meg's particular favorite was the South Slope home where the taps turned on by themselves, doors opened and closed, food disappeared, eerie chattering was heard in the night, and where, after weeks of researching likely haunters interred in Green-Wood Cemetery across the street, the residents discovered a family of raccoons living in the roof. There was an explanation for everything. It just wasn't always the one you expected.

The thing was, as much as Meg understood his dilemma, there *wasn't* exactly a concrete way she could help. Unless the death had been notable in some headline-making way, searching addresses by deaths was simply not a function of the library records. She explained to Ellis that if you knew a person's name and wanted to find where that specific person's death had occurred, you could find death records here, or you could check census records there, but doing it the other way around was more complicated. It was weird to think about these things. If Kate had haunted the street corner where she died, how would anyone ever track it back to her, to the girl she had been when alive? How, for that matter, did Kate know how to track Meg down, where to visit her now? Was there some sort of dead person GPS system?

There was no one else in the Brooklyn Collection, so Meg swooped from behind the desk and pulled some volumes, mostly as props, and then transected the room, leading Ellis to a table where they could sit across from each other. He placed his hands on the table's scarred surface. She presented to him a noncirculating anthology of famous New York City ghost stories and a guide to genealogy—neither would help him, but she pushed them forward anyway, so that he would have something to do with his hands, a movement of mercy. "That's great that you found the deed. You can start to track down everyone who lived in the house. Or at least everyone who was officially on the books—that early there would likely have been undocumented family members or household help living in the house. Those people slip through the cracks, you know. And that area used to be this posh bedroom community for rich Manhattanites—that's why there are all those fancy brownstones. Like the Hamptons for the robber baron set." Meg was getting excited despite herself, picturing a spectral Victorian suffragette descending a staircase.

"I don't know," Ellis said slowly, "I think the house is older than that. It's not a brownstone, you know, it's an old wood-frame. The land they bought in 1839, and the house must have been built soon after. It took some doing. The records—I thought it would be easier to figure it all out."

Meg nodded. "Oh right. I remember—we looked at the Sanborns to get the original block and lot numbers—right, of *course,* it was wood, not a brownstone, duh, sorry—and then you had to run around tracking down the land conveyances—it gets tricky when you go pre-1900s. Did your family know the house was so old?"

"We had an idea. It's a funny, slanting, shambling old thing. I think I told you this last time, maybe, but it is almost like a farmhouse. I've always wondered if it might predate Brooklyn altogether."

"Sure. Of *course,*" said Meg, forgetting to be self-conscious. "It's even earlier than the twentieth-century Manhattan bourgeois. 1839—that's before Brooklyn was Brooklyn. There wasn't a bridge, I'm not sure whether the IRT trains went that far yet. Wait, maybe that was before there was even a train in Brooklyn at all. It surely *was* an old farmhouse." She knit her brow, concentrating. "Right! This was all field and farm back then, and Manhattan was a ferry ride away and was all Five Points and cholera and the draft riots and war. The Civil War! I mean, can you imagine? It might have been part of Crow Hill, this settlement that was famous for the huge amounts of crows that flew overhead, attracted by the carcasses of pigs from the slaughterhouses. You know, pigs used to run freely all throughout New York City."

"History buff, huh?"

"Yeah, a bit," Meg said, trying to will her face not to flush. She gestured around the room. "I mean, you know. City history is kind of my whole thing." Which was a perfectly, utterly moronic thing to say, so that was good, at least, that this humiliation was out of the way. She was the prim librarian, the talking history book. Of course she was.

Meg stood up suddenly and swept into the back appointment-and-pencils-only section where they stored the rare books, rejoining Ellis a moment later with a well-worn copy of Eugene L. Armbruster's *The Eastern District of Brooklyn.* "This is a classic. It's the first place to start, really, if you want to brush up on your Brooklyn history. He can be a touch racist,"—she flushed, inevitably—was it possible for her to sound stupider? What would she say next, something about the brilliance of Robert E. Lee?—"but he's not terrible considering the tenor of the times. Keep in mind that even though slavery had been officially abolished, New York City had the most slaves of any northern city, was crawling with blackbirders trying to capture runaway slaves, and the economy of the city was dependent on maintaining this whole myth of Black inferiority—I mean—you know." Deep breath. Yes. Yes, it was possible. It wasn't like any of it had been her idea—slavery, Jim Crow, Vanilla Ice. But still. Who wanted this message from her?

She talked faster and faster because suddenly she couldn't stop: "This book is kind of a chatty history of the beginnings of Brooklyn. So you might find it informative. That pre-Civil War era is not really my time period of expertise, but you know, I've learned a lot from working here. And yes, I like history. I mean, don't you? Doesn't everybody, whether they know it or not? It can explain so much about what's happening today, and I know Americans are famous for our indifference to our own history, but whether or not we remember all the dates and names and battles, that history is all around us. Like in your neighborhood! Crown Heights has such a legacy of racial tensions—and how could it not, going from farm land to mansion row, then falling into disrepair and becoming a slum, becoming infamous for the riot in the '90s—you know that's still what auto-fills when you Google 'Crown Heights'?—'Crown Heights *Riot*'?—and how can that not work its way into contemporary conversations about gentrification, this business of adding the white hipsters to this kind of already uneasy mix of Hasidic Jews and African Americans? The history is alive all around you, even if you're not conscious of the details." She took a deep breath, practically panting. Then—because why not?—she added the teacherly sound bite she often included in this presentation, "Surely your house has a story to tell."

"So I've noticed," said Ellis dryly. But at least there was a friendly-ish crinkle around his eyes. It was almost unconscionable of her, as they spoke of war and injustice and the dead, to note this shift, so familiar from her years of dating, this movement where he opened up ever so slightly, where he turned to you, noticing you, where something in his eyes changed, almost imperceptible—*almost*. Silly to pretend, though, that you couldn't feel it when someone's body started sending your body secret messages through the air, to act as if you weren't receiving the hormonal telegrams. Even when it was impossible—when there was nowhere for it all to go. Hello hello hello STOP.

The glass doors opened. It was only Helen, who nodded briefly at Meg as she walked straight to the back office; Helen's greatest passion in life was catching Gil, the new guy, poring over his fantasy baseball scores on the computer when he was supposed to be scouring lists of upcoming publications for relevance to the collection. Still, her presence brought Meg back to herself. She ran her hand over the books—how she loved the supple leather binding of the Armbruster, how she thrilled to the crinkle of brittle plastic shrouding the ghost story collection. "Anyway, knowing the history of your home and the lot is interesting, but I'm not sure that helps you, except that it might prove informative to learn a bit more about the era in which your house was built. To be perfectly honest, it's going to be really hard to find out if someone died there. Especially if it was early in the house's history. In those days, record keeping was not what it is now, and families were big, and there were probably lots of people living there at any given time—"

"And slaves. Right? Or escaped slaves. Who wouldn't have been recorded? I was trying to tell my dad that, but he was like, 'Do your best, son, just try to track down who lived here.' Like I'm one of his students doing a research paper. I don't even know why he's assigned me this insane task. It's like he just needs a way to keep me busy while I'm here, or something."

Ellis spread his hands across the table, and in that moment, Meg noticed his wedding ring. And why should that make her insides de-flate? And why should she even notice? It was not what she wanted, and if it was what other people wanted, if certain men with certain curly eyelashes wanted to be married to certain other women in Chicago, well, good for them. Marriage, that mouse trap of the soul. She tried to un-notice, standing up again, as if acting busy would protect her, and strode to the flat files, sifting through maps. Though a map was not what they needed. For some things there were no maps.

"Well, you know," she said, trying to refocus, "now that I think of it, there was a rather prominent settlement of free African American landowners near your part of Crown Heights. It was called Weeksville."

"Oh, sure," said Ellis. "Of course. I remember my dad telling me about that. They found it again in the '60s or something?"

"Right." Meg searched for the details in her crowded filing cabinet of a brain. "Some guy from Pratt flew over the neighborhood in a prop plane and identified the pregrid diagonal of Hunterfly Road. And this woman in the neighborhood championed saving the houses when they wanted to knock it all down to expand the parkway. School kids helped with the archeological dig."

Ellis was silent.

"What?" Meg said.

"Remember when we were looking at that map, and you pointed out that the house's lot is a little wonky, like tilted off the grid kinda?"

"Yes," said Meg slowly.

"I wonder—I mean, it's an old frame farmhouse—"

"Like the Weeksville houses."

"Right. Like the houses they preserved."

He wasn't really that closed-off, she realized, watching his curiosity light up his face—the crisp, overly polite reserve didn't even fit him quite right, hung on his shoulders like an oversized coat. He seemed, rather, to be very, very sad about something. His eyes were dullish, but something alert in his posture suggested they weren't always.

Meg said, to say something, "They kept quite good records, actually, in Weeksville. The contemporary iteration of the *Brooklyn Daily Eagle* wrote these horrible screeds about the community, as if it were this den of chaos and iniquity, but then in the 1960s those amateur archeologists rediscovered the settlement and found all sorts of evidence that it was solidly middle-class, that there were all these educated, literate people—churches and a school and an old person's convalescent home and all these gentlemen farmers whose wives were literate enough to write letters and keep diaries and—well, all sorts of things. Here," because, awfully, a doddering old couple had wandered in and stood at the empty reference desk blinking expectantly—"let me quickly grab you the file." It was a manila folder stuffed with clippings and Xeroxes, plucked from the filing cabinet with its folders of neighborhoods, the filing cabinet that for Meg *was* the shape of the city, so that when a friend suggested brunch in Ditmas Park, Meg thought not of the subway stop she would need but of the Ditmas Park History file in the cabinet, as if brunch might be found neatly filed there.

Meg handed the folder to Ellis and distractedly helped the old couple find the Coney Island paraphernalia they were the millionth people to think they were the first to think of. Then Helen had a question in back, and Gil needed help privately in the Map Room—a proposition that only sounded suggestive, in fact meant he was too incompetent to run the Xerox machine—and by the time she was returning to her post, Ellis was leaving, turning to say, "Thank you again, you've been so helpful." And a final smoldering look up and down, worthy of a Mr. Rochester, a Mr. Darcy, or perhaps only misinterpreted by Meg's overactive imagination, no more than the hormonal fallout of menopause's quickening.

So that story was over. So he was gone. Again. Gone, likely, back to Chicago, where the pizza had too much cheese, and his life had too much of a wife, a woman who waited for him, knitting another scarf for another winter. The Weeksville file was reassembled with conspicuous neatness, like a bed remade after a tussle. Ellis wouldn't find what he was looking for because he was looking for a ghost, and one never found a ghost unless the ghost wanted to be found. It would be fine. His parents would renovate, they would sell the house, the ghost would become an upwardly mobile yuppie family's problem. Or maybe Ellis would take the house. Maybe Ellis would move back, with this property in a gentrifying neighborhood as a nest egg, and maybe their paths would cross again. As unlikely as that seemed, stranger things had happened in New York City. Maybe they would run into each other at brunch one day, Ellis pulling out a chair for a beautiful wife with Michelle Obama forearms, Meg on a first date with a chelonian retiree who had misled her with a profile picture taken during the Bush administration. The first one.

Meg took a deep breath, straightened her skirt, smoothed her form-fitting top out of her middle-age-middle-waist-rolls, and ducked her head into the back office to tell Helen she was taking her lunch break. Helen nodded without looking up. Helen didn't look up even as she said, "We really have to stop encouraging patrons with silly projects, don't you agree? There have been some complaints. The library director is displeased. We are a resource for serious researchers, not a psychic hotline, wouldn't you say?"

Meg was speechless. A resource for serious researchers? Most of the visitors to the library were using their public computers to play Minecraft. She hardly thought her vague interest in the occult was causing the death of public intellectual discourse. But she just nodded, too tired to speak. Helen made no indication that the conversation was over, or that in fact it had ever even begun, so she slipped away.

Maybe Meg was the ghost. Maybe no one could actually see her at all.

The atrium downstairs swelled with the afterbirth of yet another infernal singalong, and Meg's solar plexus pulsed with dread at the thought of running into Kate's boyfriend and his androgynous child once again; without looking at any of the people around her or thinking very clearly, she scurried through the crowd and through the revolving doors outside. At least it was her lunch break.

In Meg's life, lunch had never really rebounded from the Kate days. Kate had been the best at lunch, in a way that made one realize that one had never before realized it was possible to not be the best at lunch. There was one summer in particular that had been truly the reign of lunch—Meg was nineteen, in college at Pratt but still living at home on the Upper West Side because despite what seemed like an unbearable cross-East River commute and the indignity of bunking with a high school freshman, subway tokens were a good deal cheaper than student housing or, even more ridiculous, a Brooklyn apartment (even back then) for someone already paying private college tuition. So that would have made Kate, what, fourteen. Kate had always been precocious, the inevitable birthright of a Manhattan-born younger sister, but this was the year she truly came into her own as a brainy, fearless heroine-of-a-chapter-book type. She seemed poised to skip altogether any era of awkwardness, inhabiting instead a quirky, unselfconscious, Eloise-meets-Pippi-Longstocking persona. This involved craze after craze—the winter had brought science experiments that, predictably enough, nearly blew up their rent-controlled kitchen, inducing in their mother such nervous fits they considered investing in (or trying to make) smelling salts, spring had involved a brief but passionate flirtation with bassoon, and summer was the age of picnics.

Kate eschewed the city kid requirement of overnight summer camp in the woods in favor of her library card, croquet set, and picnic blanket. ("Just as well," their father had breathed with relief, looking up from a pile of bills wrought by Pratt, orthodontia, and the private middle school they'd found for sensitive little James when fifth grade bullying had reached a frightening pitch.) Meg took a summer course in the mornings and then commuted back to Manhattan, where Kate would be waiting with her covered wicker basket and floppy hat—a getup that would have seemed like an affectation on anyone else—so that the two of them could walk to Central Park (no Jameses allowed) and picnic by Strawberry Fields. Kate often claimed to be following the ghost of John Lennon—his shooting was one of Meg's earliest memories, or at least watching her preschool teacher cry about it was—from the Dakota across the park. Then again, Kate had a habit of chatting with all of the many ghosts who frequented the park.

A few years earlier they wouldn't have been permitted to venture alone to that dark forest of buskers and homeless and flashers, oh my—for the longest time Meg associated Central Park with the fleshy, flaccid penis of a man who had ruined a friend's eighth birthday party with his lurid self-exposure—but the city was changing, the park was changing—fewer panhandlers, more picnics—and they were getting older, and now, in the brightest part of the day, they were allowed. Even then Meg would find herself staring into the sun-baked expanses of the park, watching emo boys play guitar, picturing with a shudder how dark the Ramble would be at night, trying to unremember the gruesome details of the Central Park jogger story—raped, beaten, left for dead, found naked and shattered—that had haunted her dreams only a few years earlier.

But Kate seemed oblivious to all of it, optimism her fatal flaw. Kate was a great innovator of the sandwich, a foodie before anyone used the word, and so in between pumping Meg for details on the sex life she had recently begun (the smarmy teaching assistant, who'd seemed like an easy mark, and then the only seemingly shy, as it turned out, boy from Victorian Literature), she would pass her a chicken salad and grape jelly on baguette, or a hard-boiled egg and liverwurst on a pumpernickel bagel from H&H. She'd befriended the morning manager at Zabar's, and as a result the Rhys family was rich in pickles and spreads. This was before the vegetarianism, before Kate had gotten so very serious about so very many things. This was the summer of lemonade-and-seltzer concoctions in thermoses clinking with ice, books spread around like Alice's drowsy pre-Wonderland afternoon, because, after all, Kate's excuse for this summery laying-about was the hefty recommended rising Freshman reading list provided by the LaGuardia High School English department.

In reality Meg probably remembered only two or three moments of that whole picnicky summer, which now made her feel—as she pored over the familiar lunch menu, as if she might try something new, when of course she wouldn't—robbed. Bereft. There ought to be an official brain chemistry exception when people died young, Meg felt; their family members ought to be allowed to remember more than the average person, their minds ought to shuffle about, expelling all unnecessary television jingles and passwords and childhood friends' telephone numbers and all the other things you didn't actually need to remember, making megabytes for more memories of the dead. There ought to be a way to capture, to catalogue, to contain the intangibles of a person—their smells, the weight of their hugs, the way they changed a room for better or worse when they entered, their sheer energetic force, the themness of them.

Meg also remembered how Kate had thrown *Pride and Prejudice*—or was it *Sense and Sensibility*?—to the ground in a fit of disgust, flopping down on the checkered blanket and saying, "Are they serious? This is what this book is? It's a *soap opera,* for Chrissakes!"—the "Chrissakes" nicked from *Catcher in the Rye,* which Meg had taken the liberty of adding to the required reading list.

And that was it, really, what Meg could actually distinctly remember of that entire summer of her sister's life. That, and a handful of vague impressions. The brindled grass, a gingham sundress soft as a fawn's pelt. It would always seem impossible that there was none of Kate's life left ahead, left to the side, left in the back of a cupboard, left somewhere, still to be lived. Kate's life struck her sister as not *lost* but rather misplaced somehow. It couldn't be so permanent, something that had happened so quickly, could it? There must still be time to undo the impact of the car, to lift Kate from the sculpture of bent bike. How could she still miss Kate, after all these years?

But she did, with a kind of fury. She missed her as she headed to lunch, she missed her as she hurried down the grand staircase, flanked not with the regal stone lions of Manhattan's central branch—Patience and Fortitude, if *only*—but, because this was Brooklyn, with fountains for children to splash in. The library's front entrance was illuminated with golden bas-relief figures from literature: canonical creatures like Moby Dick, Walt Whitman, and Meg from *Little Women.* Yes, it had always seemed like a sign of something, though she wasn't exactly sure of what. Meg still rankled at having been named for the domestic one. Couldn't she have been a Jo? And for that matter, shouldn't the one on the library be the bookish Jo? She had once thought these things, anyway; now she was so used to the figures she barely looked at them—too seen to see, like the face of a family member, the shining shapes hardly figured in Meg's consciousness anymore, and whenever she walked by

she constructed them vaguely from memory rather than actually seeing them.

Meg inhaled the fumy air. While the library was across the street
from the boreal landscape of Prospect Park, the main entrance abutted
a traffic circle that made even livery car drivers gasp, muttering the
curse words of dying languages. In the center of the traffic circle rose
the Grand Army Arch, Brooklyn's horsey answer to the Arc d'Tri-
omphe, a monumental bit of scenery—dedicated "To The Defenders
of the Union," or as James joked, "the fender-benders of the union"—
that was almost every day lost on Meg, as she kept her eyes forward
rather than up, trained on the walk signal, sweeping her periphery
for suicidal bicyclists hurtling through stop lights. She hugged herself
against the chill and crossed the street—pausing for a strangely familiar van with an eerie eyeball painted on its side, which couldn't really
have tracked her as the vehicle passed—to the Prospect Heights side,
where a back alley housed the only decent place to eat lunch on those
days when even a coffee from the library café couldn't elevate her Tup-
perware of leftovers to suitable meal material. It would be more than
she wanted to spend on lunch but okay; she would go to the charming
lunch place and buy a nine-dollar turkey sandwich and it would be
quiet or there would be interesting music and she would look over her
draft of this month's Rhys's Pieces column for the library newsletter
(because of course her veto of the cutesy name had again been vetoed).
What did Ellis eat for lunch? she wondered. What did Ellis remember
about being a kid, in his version of New York? What would Ellis say if
she told him she talked every day to her dead sister?

Meg rubbed her forehead and stared at her longhand notes for her
newsletter column, scrawled on looseleaf notebook paper—her handwriting was elegant and loopy, a result of her anachronistic Palmer fix-
ation, the hand of another era altogether—*We mustn't think of digital
archiving as a force against print media, but rather as a way to protect our
priceless photographs, letters, maps, and other records, so that they may
be useful to our patrons while huddling safely, like birds waiting out a
storm, in the temperature-controlled archives. We are not witnessing the*

*death of print, or if we are, perhaps it is some comfort to know we are also
witnessing its extremely articulate afterlife.*

Meg knew she'd have to fix this—her logic was muddled, her language florid. As far as she knew, her only reader was a bag lady she'd once seen poring over the newsletter at the library café. Or perhaps that had been *her,* Meg herself, come back from the less-fortunate, post-eviction future to check in on the past.

She reluctantly took up her pencil, drew stakes through the hearts of her words.

What Meg needed was a new topic, a new muse. Writing about digitization seemed unbearably boring, much too small. And anyway, all she could actually think about was Ellis. His story. His house. His ghost. His . . . Ellis-ness. But she couldn't. Could she? She didn't know enough, not yet anyway. All she knew was that she wanted to know more, that it somehow seemed crucial to get to the bottom of it, and that she probably never would.

# 9

**WHEN THEY GET OFF THE TRAIN**, they step from the great hubbub of steam and noise and confusingly bright sunlight, straight into a cloud of excitable, giggling girls, Mr. Jenkins's daughters, all older than her and ready to coo over her cuteness. She relaxes back into childhood, a place she had thought was gone forever. One sister grabs her carpet-bag, one swishes the skirt of her dress and clucks her tongue at how dirty it is. They clearly have no concept of the hell that she has been through. They live in another world altogether out here, where sooty clothes are briskly washed on washing day because the fabric of life has not been so destroyed that sanitation has been completely forgotten. They have not had the order of their days exploded by war, not watched their home burn, not seen the edifice of freedom reveal its unsteady foundations. They are girls with neatly plaited hair and wide smiles, girls with a mother who darns their clothing when it tears, and their biggest concern is, as the eldest says, *Hurry now, we must get home for supper. Mother has made her famous roast duck!* The youngest moans in anticipatory pleasure, *Like Christmas Day!* And they smile at her—at her!—because her arrival has turned the day into a holiday. She begins to doubt any of her past—yesterday, her entire life—ever happened at all, so unlikely does it suddenly seem.

She cranes her head to see Jacob Jenkins trailing behind, stopping to greet this railroad employee or that neighbor strolling by. It takes a while to register, but when it does, it blooms in her head like the lilacs the Miss Shotwells used to grow in the asylum yard, bushy and showy and bright: every single face she sees is black. She stops in her tracks, looks all around. Here is an entire town of Black people, walking around in fine clothing, holding newspapers under their arms or parasols above their heads, as free as anything.

As they walk down bustling Troy Avenue, which feels almost like a block in the city—*There's the church! And there's our school! You'll go to that school with us, and we'll have ever so much fun!*—the girls pelt her with questions about the orphanage and the riot, which they consider a terribly exciting, if abstract, tale, but she soon loses their attention to a squabble over a hair ribbon. It's for the best. She's not ready to tell the story, which she hasn't yet formed into a story at all, which is still separate images and objects jangling around in the incomprehensible cabinet of wonders in her head. She's not sure she'll ever be ready to tell the story, to tell the truth. And for now, she wants to look around as they walk, to soak in her new surroundings, so quiet and boreal, as if they were a million miles away from Manhattan. People stare as they pass, not because of the color of her skin, but because she is so filthy. She probably smells like the riot. She boils with impatience for a bath and clean clothes. She is about to have clothes, she realizes, quickening her step, besides the stiff orphanage uniform. The dresses of the girls flit before her, the different patterns—all different!—fluttering as their legs move.

They climb hilly dirt roads surrounded by sand and scrub grass, fringed with Brobdingnagian trees. One of the sisters, a scholarly looking sort with wire-rim glasses perched on her nose, who holds a notebook in which she says she keeps scientific specimens, explains that these are oak, spruce, and pine trees. *I am going to be a scientist*, she adds gravely.

The girl nods. *I am going to be a doctor*, she answers. They regard each other respectfully as they scramble up a steep hill. At the top of the hill, the eldest girl stops, holds out a hand like a queen presenting her domain. Mr. Jenkins smiles indulgently. *Here, child, is Weeksville!* says the daughter. *Isn't it beautiful?*

It is. It is the most beautiful place she has ever seen. To the west, as the Jenkins girls point out in a confused chatter, each shouting over the next, are the roods and spires of Brooklyn, City of Churches, which she briefly spied when the ferry landed, where she and Mr. Jenkins had boarded the railroad what seems like a lifetime ago. To the east are the hills of Jamaica Bay. To the north rise the hills of New England across Long Island Sound. The scientific sister points out Suydam Pond in the hollow below the hill where they stand, where they fish and swim in the summer, they tell her, and ice skate all winter long. And arrayed all around are parks and forests and outcroppings of rustic wooden houses. They will cut through the Hunterfly Woods, they announce, and then they will be home at the Jenkins Farm. Home. She turns the word over in her head, like a marble in her hand. Home.

They make it sound like a quick little romp, but for a tired city girl, the walk through the woods to the house feels endless. She thinks of that morning, when she and Miss Murray embarked on the skiff. Was that today? Was that *her*? She is in a wild place now, trekking through a gully that shapes the wind into a gale, whipping her hair and skirt. Chickens race underfoot. Hickory nuts rain down from tree branches that bend over their path. The littlest girl disappears into the brush, reappearing a moment later with a sloppy handful of blackberries that she shares with them all.

The wooded path funnels out into a larger dirt road, rutted with deep carriage tracks, which the girls gingerly navigate. On either side of the road are frame houses with heavy timber gables, so different from the way buildings look back in the city. Each house has a small yard, most with kitchen gardens flourishing beside the gentle humps of middens, and in between the houses are thickets of woods, swells of hills, disks of ponds orangely reflecting the mellowing evening light. Now that it is starting to get dark, she notices there are no streetlamps, and she adds this to her tally of the oddities of country life (no sidewalks, no pavements, wildness everywhere), walks close to Mr. Jenkins as the sunlight dims. He pats her shoulder. *There is nothing to fear here*, he says. *The blackbirders don't come this far, and everyone looks out for each other*, nodding at a man who walks by, as if to prove it. She hadn't really been worried about blackbirders—hadn't even thought to fear being captured into slavery, after all, she's only a child, who would want a child?—but somehow his words soothe anyway.

Then they are at the house. *Here it is!* cry the sisters, tumbling up the stairs and into the front door. *Welcome,* says Mr. Jenkins. He invites her inside.

She has never been in a house like this before, or if she has, she doesn't remember it. Maybe once she was a baby in a home like this, with a mother and a father and the chattering sounds of family. It's possible. All she has ever really known is the asylum: enormous, divided into wings, cut through with long echoing halls.

The rooms in this house are small and warm and cluttered with artifacts of family life, bits of lace and vases of flowers and tintypes and Bibles, the floor scattered with jacks that Mr. Jenkins shakes his head at, newspapers and broadsheets folded on the end tables, fine wooden chairs and a velvet sofa crowding around the hearth. A delicious smell from the kitchen overpowers her—meaty and rich and abundant, nothing like the stews and porridges the asylum cook favored. Mrs. Jenkins steps out of the kitchen, wiping her hands on her apron, a smile illuminating her face.

*You're here! How did you find the voyage? What is your name? Tell me, my dear, what is your name.*

When the mother says her name, it is as if she were an infant being named for the first time, called into the world, given her place in it. When the mother says her name, she says, *Welcome home,* and she knows that for the first time in her life, she does, in fact, have a home.

She is overpowered by an exhaustion which drops onto her like a cloak as soon as she has eaten her lavish meal (the oily meat to which she is unused settles on top of her gut), a boisterous affair during which the girls pelt her with questions, and the mother attempts to get in some words about Weeksville and what life is like in a town of free Black people. The information ricochets around her head: The Jenkins are not the only family harboring refugees from the riots; in fact the town leaders and preachers have encouraged everyone to offer safe harbor to the persecuted. The town is already used to protecting runaways, is dotted with stops on the Underground Railroad (she is so tired that everything sounds like a dream, and she pictures a miniature version of the train she rode earlier in the day, chugging along through mole tunnels in the dirt)—surely she knows, Mr. Jenkins interjects, about the Fugitive Slave Act and how it has made white men think they can snatch up any Black person they see and sell them into slavery? She nods, sleepily, as it sounds like something Dr. Smith told them about once. But those things had seemed so far away from within the walls of the asylum. Can it be they are a part of everyday life in this strange town?

Mr. Jenkins is explaining how they help fugitives stay safe, how they help them to start their own lives as free men, when Mrs. Jenkins gently interrupts. *I think our little girl is tired, Jacob. She has had a long couple of days.* He nods, chuckling at himself, *Quite so, quite so,* and the girls jump up and swarm the table, clearing the dishes, beginning to wash them, as the mother boils water for the hot bath that the girl who has escaped the mob so desperately needs.

After a long, drowsy soak, she is given a clean, worn but carefully patched nightgown and shown her room. Her room. For the girls' bedroom upstairs is already so crowded that she is given a room of her own, a little chamber off the side of the kitchen, used mostly for storage, but now also for her. They show her the pallet they have placed on the part of the floor warmed by the kitchen fire on the other side of the wall. They show her the rag doll that the youngest daughter has decided to pass on to her. She hugs the rag doll to her chest, thinking of Lucretia, her eyes shining. The mother says, *So this room can be yours now. The keeping room is yours.*

## 10

**NORA RHYS**, matriarch of the prematurely edited Rhys clan, had worked her way up the Tenement Museum corporate ladder with the hunger of a pieceworker on her way to factory shift manager, all the way from genteel docent to her current star turn as a costumed interpreter. She'd called Meg one day, brimming with excitement, to tell her that, like a senior citizen Lana Turner, she'd been discovered at the soda fountain (well, the gift shop) by one of the curators. The former Granny Moore, matriarch of the 1860s family who had scraped out their meager living in the Lower East Side tenement, AKA the Irish Outsiders Tour, had gotten a bit part on Broadway, leaving the museum in a lurch. Could Meg believe that! (Meg could believe it, actually; she supposed that even in New York City, tap-dancing septuagenarians were in short supply.)

So now, four days a week, Nora traded her yoga gear for a calico housedress and had her chic silver bob professionally mussed in order to soliloquize about the potato famine. If only they'd been able to buy that building, Nora mused to her children, had it only gone co-op in 1869, what millionaires the Moore heirs would be.

A lingering teenagerishness had prevented Meg and James from going on one of their mother's tours for some months. "Come on," Meg had urged James over eggs and coffee at their usual table, "Don't you want to hear Mom's 'Irish accent'? I'm dying to hear her talk potatoes." She adopted a Vaudevillian version of their mother's Upper-West drawl, "'Oy vey, the potatoes are gone! But, between us, good riddance, you know? Who needs all the starch? Here, try some hard-tack beef, high protein, locally sourced, no nitrites, that stuff gives you cancer you know.'"

They'd shared a laugh, deemed the whole scenario ridiculous. But there it was, James occupied with his hypothetical family, booked with surrogate meetings (the nonexistent baby already irritatingly time-consuming), and here Meg was, alone on the Lower East Side of Manhattan, on a perfectly good Saturday off of work that really should have been devoted to apartment searching, or packing the sad evidence of her life into boxes reconstituted from her neighbor's recycling bins, or at most ideally of all, curling up with Virginia Wolf and Virginia Woolf—she'd just checked out the recently discovered new Woolf novel, which she read a few chapters of on the train and reluctantly dog-eared when her stop butted in.

The day felt gray. There seemed to be no temperature to it, no character at all besides grayish, coldish, fallish. Refugee leaves whipped across the wide Second Avenue crosswalk, hurling themselves between groggy hipsters headed brunchwards, erstwhile art stars en route to clock in at American Apparel, bright-eyed tourists checking their maps for Katz's Deli.

Meg pulled her cloak tighter around herself, shivered on the street corner, waiting for the light to change. A pigeon landed beside her, stared at her boot for a minute, then shook its head disapprovingly and took off uptown. Meg tried to clear her head, walking down the street her mother walked down every day. What must it all look like to Nora? The museum was perilously close to where Kate's accident had been. That fucking city! New York City was so small, really—when one took to the streets—that one was always traveling in biographical circles; of course the museum was close, everything was. A few years back, when Hurricane Sandy had decimated swathes of the city's coasts, Meg had found herself understanding why people hung around, rebuilding in the same old floodplains. Logic might tell you to leave, but you couldn't outrun your own life.

After Kate's death Nora had thrown herself into her curating work—besides, James was in college at that point, and she needed something to occupy her mind—and then, upon losing her job and declaring herself retired, had become a fulltime volunteer, toiling for free at every institution that would have her, before falling in particular love with the Tenement Museum. Meg wondered how aware Nora herself was of the connection: first she loses her (favorite) daughter, then she devotes herself to a place that tells the stories of the dead, recreating the tales of hard-luck New Yorkers, people for whom life was spirit-crushingly hard, people from whom the city took everything. Maybe Meg would work up the nerve to ask about it sometime, but they would all need drinks first, possibly also to wait another decade or so.

The intern selling tickets had been primed for her visit and directed Meg up the rickety stairs to the Moore's nineteenth-century walk-up Junior 4. There, huddled over a farm table spread with plastic food, stood a slight grandmotherly figure in a headscarf and apron, hunched over something. Piecework? No, Nora looked up from her phone. "Meggie! You made it!"

Meg laughed, hugged her mother, despite her sense that the ground beneath her feet quivered, that reality was unlatching itself from its usual place and shimmering around, rearranging itself the way furniture moved in a room. There was her mother, lumpy in nineteenth-century drab, like something out of Dickens; they stood chatting at a kitchen table, but one set with rough-hewn earthenware, not the Fish's Eddy plates of the Rhyses' Upper West Side Here-and-Now. It was as if she'd entered her childhood bedroom only to find everything shifted six inches to the right. A memorized world slightly, but irrevocably, altered.

Nora showed her daughter through the railroad apartment, kitted out with period furniture and museum replicas of appealing heft, pleasant reality-approximaters. Here was a loom, here was a coffee pot. All the artifacts of a life. There were the mats on which all seven family members had managed to sleep, in the one true bedroom. "I can just hear the realtor pitching it to the Moores," Meg joked out of defensive impulse, shivering in the dim passageway. "Cozy, intimate, perfect for

families. Sun-drenched." Universal real estate code, as she was painfully aware these days, for subterranean, crepuscular.

Her mother played along. "Perfect for moles, more like it. Can you
imagine? And they'd traveled across the ocean, left their country and
everything they knew, for this. For the chance to work in a factory and
live in a closet of an apartment in a city that still didn't have municipal
sanitation. Well, I guess it was better than famine and death. Everyone's just looking for a place to call their own, in the end."

"'I moved to America and all I got was this typhus,'" Meg muttered,
fingering a quilt draped over a chair. "You know, Mom, you look great
in calico."

Nora/Granny Moore laughed and twirled. "Quite a getup, isn't it?
You know, Granny Moore was only in her sixties when she died. Look
at the source photo." She handed Meg a print she kept in her apron
pocket for the tours.

Meg studied the puckered face. "She looks about ninety."

"Right? All those carbs. And no sunscreen."

"And a life of hard labor."

"Isn't this so great? Are you going to stay for the performance? I
mean, tour?"

"Of course, Mom." Meg sat gingerly on one of the caned chairs,
which groaned beneath her; she spread her hands on the table, trying
to feel the room. She hefted a cast-resin onion in her hand, took a pretend bite. "No wonder there was so much hunger! This is terrible!"

Her mother laughed obligingly, straightened her headscarf. What
work had her mother done to inhabit her character, and why did Meg
only wonder now? She knew her mother took her role very seriously,
intimidated by taking on the role a serious actor usually played. Meg
wondered for the first time if they had been researching the same
things, taking themselves back to the same era at the same time. Her
mother's pretend new life shared temporal space with the Williamses'
haunted house, didn't it? Meg could just see Granny Moore and Ellis's
farmer ghost, passing each other on a dusty Five Points avenue.

"Funny to think," said Nora, as if reading Meg's mind, "that my own
Grandma Milly might have walked by Granny Moore on the street."

"Oh?"

"Sure, my grandmother and her older brother came over sometime in the 1860s and then ended up on the Lower East Side for a few years before they left the city." Meg had heard her mother's version of this family history before, and in her current real estate-obsessed state of mind, it struck her as either particularly funny or particularly crazy-making. The Jewish refugees from the unspecified, now-forgotten area of probably-Germany, arriving in the chaos of the city, processed through Castle Clinton in what was now Battery Park, before Ellis Island had even taken on its famous role—it was the New York City version of having had relatives come over on the Mayflower. Meg was a legit New Yorker—her relatives had been exploited for cheap labor in the garment industry since Day One! Of course, those ur-Rosenfelds had dropped their Yiddish, cleaned up their names, assimilated as much as possible, migrated out of the city as soon as they possibly could; when Nora's mother had still been alive, she would remark on how, for generations, they had strived to get out of little apartments in crowded areas of the city, and here were kids like Meg and James, plunking down huge amounts of money to live in places with so-called "lively foot traffic." Of course, it was nicer to be around a lot of people in an era of public sanitation and indoor plumbing, Meg assumed, when "vibrant street life" indicated coffee shops and cute stores rather than peddlers and, like, streetwalkers. Still, funny (maybe) to think that if those hapless immigrant teenagers had been able to invest in real estate, their first homes in Manhattan would now be worth millions, that the hovels where they had first huddled were now highly in demand. To think of all the energy directed toward excluding and scapegoating Jews and the Irish and other unloved immigrants, how it had resolved into something else, like a cloud of pollution lodged in the sky, able to reposition itself but not to dissipate altogether.

"Do you ever wonder about the things she made?" Meg said suddenly, having never thought of it herself until that very moment. "Like, when they were working in a garment factory—what were they making?" She was struck by a visceral desire to touch the fabric her great-grandmother had stitched, to slip on a dress her teenaged relative had hemmed.

Nora/Granny Moore blinked back at her. "Well, no actually. The thought never occurred to me." She paused. "My mother had the rag doll her mother had brought over on the boat, or what was left of it. The story was she had pulled the stuffing out and snuck it in her pocket, even though their parents had told them to bring only the essentials. She was too old to be playing with dolls, of course, starting a new life in a new country, which would daunt most adults. So it's kind of heart-breaking to think of her wanting that little bit of girlhood with her."

Meg smiled, squinted, trying to imagine it. "Do you remember her? What was she like?"

Nora laughed. "Of course I remember her! She was mean, mean, mean. A tiny and tough and terrifying lady. She would watch me when I was little and rap my knuckles with a ruler if I misbehaved. Every move she made reminded you that life used to be much, much rougher."

Why had Meg never thought to research her own great-grand-mother, that whole downtrodden wing of the family treehouse? Other people's histories had always interested her, but her own—who knew? It felt so *known*, so woven into the fabric of everyone's understanding of New York City, a story too often told. Her mother's family had come with early waves of Jewish immigrants; her father's family had come with later waves of Welsh immigrants. Every white person in America was some kind of unexceptional European mutt, weren't they? So what?

But that didn't make Milly any more real to Meg, a century-and-a-half on. She pictured Milly sitting in Granny Moore's stiff-backed wooden chair in the corner of the room, a smudged child in a ragged woolen coat, her emptied doll's hand poking out from a pocket. Milly's arms were crossed, her face stern. *We left our home forever, we became adults at fourteen, we came here to America, where we were told life would be better for us, for* you, *and this is what you do with it? You work at a job, you look at a computer, you bitch about your brunch? This is the great American promise? This is what we sacrificed for? So you could internet-date and buy nine-dollar avocado toasts?*

Meg sucked in a breath, preparing to defend herself. Milly just closed her eyes, shook her head, disappeared. Meg looked at her mother for commiseration, but Nora was busy Instagramming a selfie.

There was a hum in the air, a familiar buzz. Probably just the lights and the fans—one wouldn't expect tourists to live an hour the way these people had their whole lives; they would have demanded their twenty-five dollars back in an instant. Did the ghosts of the house feel privileged or mined? Meg pictured them huddled near the ceiling, critiquing the various performances. "I was *never* that *fat!*" the fourteen-year-old Greek star of the Meet Victoria Confino Tour would whisper to the sweatshop workers who had died before she moved in, glaring at the NYU theatre student stretching her best dress.

The rest of Meg's mother's other family assembled. The roles of Mr. and Mrs. Moore were played by a couple of out-of-work character actors. (Nora confided in a whispered aside that Mrs. Moore was a bit of a diva, but they kept her on board because, having had a line as Brothel Madame 1 in a PBS cowboy series, she was uniquely qualified in the time period.) "So, you're Mother's other daughter! Hello, sister!" When Mrs. Moore laughed, she showed teeth blackened with Poor-Dental-Hygiene makeup.

Meg stood at the back of the tour group, behind a mother-daughter trip from Texas—next they were headed, a mother in a sparkly I Heart NYC T-shirt revealed, to the Hard Rock Café—and watched Nora perform a passable Granny Moore. It was hard to believe, in their "Kiss Me, I'm Irish" city, that once the Irish had been despised immigrants, that when they flooded the Lower East Side in the late nineteenth century, seeking asylum from their famine-ravaged country, they had faced mistrust and discrimination—they were Catholic, after all, and poor, living with multiple generations crammed into tiny tenements without basic amenities. (The Texas mothers loved this, gasping and widening their mascara-crusted eyes. "Here?" one exclaimed, gesturing around the tiny rooms. "Ma house has five thousand square feet for five people and we're cramped as hail!" The other mothers tittered in commiseration.)

Jobs had been scarce, the Moores explained, "No Irish Need Apply" signs barring immigrants from even low-paying positions, so many had found employment instead with the privately run police and firefighting forces, laying the groundwork for contemporary New York's blue collar demographics. Meg got a kick out of watching the visitors nod and murmur—there was something wonderful about the moment when you learned a bit of information about the past that seemed to make the present fall into place, when it all jostled into place, an ace move on a mental Rubik's cube, the backstory that explained what you never even realized was a mystery—and there was something wonderful about watching people have that moment themselves. She could tell Nora liked it too, getting more and more animated as the audience responded.

After the horrors of life before sanitation and Wi-Fi had been fully revealed, the tour group filed down the stairs. The mothers kept their hands on their preteen daughters' shoulders, as if they could keep them from spinning off into the terrifying ether of their womanly futures.

Nora plopped down at the table, pulling a Luna Bar out of her apron pocket. "So?"

Meg accepted the food-like chunk her mother offered. "That was great. You're really great at this! Who knew? Has Dad seen?" She tugged her shawl closer around her shoulders, feeling tired and frozen.

"Yes, though you know, he thinks I'm crazy to do this. He still thinks I should come do the bookkeeping at the firm, like I did when we were first married." Nora shook her head, then reached up to tighten her kerchief. "He never seemed to notice how bored I was working for him!"

Meg chewed the bar and looked around the replica apartment. The poor Irish family, scraping by in a chaotic city that hated them, had been both more and less free than the farmers out in Weeksville. Part of Nora's Granny Moore spiel had included the information, novel to some and to others, too obvious to bear mention, that in Civil War–era New York, Irish immigrants had been almost as reviled as Blacks, that the Draft Riots had turned the tide further against Irish. What a terrifying time to be alive—even more so than the present, Meg thought, with its super-bugs and psychos with machine guns and Snapchat—

everyday life must have been so hard and dull and filthy. It was a terrible thing, if you only had one life to live in this world, to have been born before vaccinations and running water and affordable reading material. Meg felt a pang of—what was it?—love. Love for her stupid, small, sad little life. Pounding, pulsing gratitude for every quiet day at the library, every bicycle ride through the park, every evening she met a man at a bar or stayed home with a book, every one of the innumerable pleasures that made her life what it was, whether Great-Grandma Milly would have seen it as a waste or not.

But what was the connection? Her mind was too thick; she'd stayed up too late reading, sleepless with anxiety ever since she'd been given her apartment marching orders, and she couldn't quite think. Her mother and the Moores in their Manhattan tenement. Her own great-grandmother and her trip across the sea. Ellis and his haunted farmhouse. What *was* it that she was almost understanding?

The intern peeked in her head: the next tour group ran into delays on their East River cruise ship and cancelled, so Nora had a break. She shrugged off her kerchief. "Come on, Megelah, I'll give you the walking tour for free. Consider it like a Friends and Family Groupon."

Meg linked arms with her mother, and they strolled out into the busy avenue.

"What you were saying," Meg said, casting about for conversation, wanting desperately to avoid talking about her own real estate woes, and having been forbidden from mentioning James and Eugene's latest developments, "about working for Dad. Did you like doing that when you were first married? What had you thought you would do?"

Nora blinked. This was clearly not the conversation she'd meant to have, and before answering, she pointed out to Meg where the good horse-hitching posts on Orchard Street had been, where the streetcar would have stopped. "Convenient for Whole Foods," she said, with the worn inflections of an over-told joke. "What did you just ask me? Oh, working for Dad. Well, you know. We met in college of course. I was at Sarah Lawrence." Meg nodded as if her mother hadn't bragged about this treasured accomplishment every day of her entire life. "I was a very good student, you know. I graduated with honors in art history.

Look at that sign—luxury condos. This was all slums of course." For a second, Meg thought Nora meant that when she was in college, it was all slums, and maybe she did. The city's history was nothing if not checkered. "Did you know there was a big problem with dead cats piling up on the streets? Can you imagine? In the 1860s, I mean, not the 1960s."

Meg had the unsettling sense that she was seeing all the layers of the city transposed over one another, like scrims in a play going haywire. The narrow, dusty streets were fringed with furry corpses; instead of pansy-filled tree pits, sidewalks contained waystations of gelled filth. People like paper dolls, dressed now in superimposed top hats and hoopskirts. Out of the corner of her eye, the truck passing by became an omnibus pulled by horses.

You had to train yourself to block out so much to live in the city, just to walk down a street intact. Even as a born-and-bred city kid, Meg had learned this every summer when they returned from their summer stays at the Berkshires. In the city, it was frowned upon but also actually treacherous to stand on a sidewalk and look long enough to see what was there. Life almost never allowed it.

They turned a corner and Nora continued, "I guess I didn't have much of a plan outside of Dad. I mean, it was the '60s, you know, and all my college friends were feminists and hippies, and it wasn't very much in vogue to say you were going to school to pass the time until getting married. You don't believe me, but it was very progressive there, and there was a lot of, well, conscious raising." Meg knew she was meant to ask for clarification here but couldn't quite bear to. The trolley rattled past, wait, no, the train rumbled beneath their feet. The sky darkened. Maybe it would rain. Maybe it would snow. Maybe there would be an earthquake, a hurricane, a flood, a plague. "I probably had a vague idea of going into curating. I had always loved museums. But I didn't know anyone who did that; I couldn't figure out what steps you took to actually get to one of those jobs. And really, and this was not popular to say during the summer of love, probably even less so now, but—I mostly wanted to have a family. I just did. I just always knew that I did. So Dad and I got married, I worked for his firm for a few years and we hung out and had some great dinner parties and that kind of thing, and then you were born, and I was so, so happy."

"That's sweet, Mom. It really is. You were a great mom. I mean, you are a great mom. But it's funny." Meg tried to think of how to say it. Of how Kate would have said it, Kate who, even as a troublemaking teenager, had somehow had more sympathy for their parents. "You know, now that more and more of my friends are moms, I realize, when I talk to them, how conflicted they are. Of course they love their kids, but they're surprised by how hard it all is, and they feel they've lost part of themselves. You never had any inkling of that?" She was worried, she could almost admit to herself, about James and Eugene, about what they barely seemed to realize they were getting themselves into. No one *needed* to have kids anymore, did they? Well, someone needed to, in a perpetrating-the-human-race kind of way, but not *them*. They could have pets and summer homes and time to read! Was there anything else you needed? Really, really needed?

Nora squinted into the sky. "Look, up there is where one of the first water towers in the city went. Can you imagine what a change that was? There wasn't a public sewage system until 1865!"

They crossed the street again, entering a community garden through the open iron gate. Nora sat on a bench fringed with dormant honeysuckle, patted beside her to indicate Meg should sit too. Meg guessed they were done with the heart-to-heart, and when her mother took a breath, Meg expected a talk on the history of the Green Thumb Community Garden System. Instead Nora said, "I don't know if you can believe me, but it was really all I ever wanted. Martin, and you kids. I had friends who wanted careers, friends who wanted big houses in the suburbs, friends who wanted to drop out and join communes in Tibet. I know, trust me, I get it. But my family was where I found my meaning." She hugged Meg in an uncharacteristic burst of physical affection that Meg guessed was more Granny Moore that Nora Rhys. This was not the kind of conversation they usually had—they weren't exactly a "heart-to-heart" kind of family. Meg leaned in to her mother's sharp, birdish bones, feeling, as she always did beside her mother, ridiculously large and excessively soft.

She wanted to say to her mother, *Don't worry about me. I have meaning. There is meaning elsewhere.* She wanted to brandish a perfectly apt quotation from a memorized poem. She wanted most of all to exude the kind of confidence that would stop her mother from questioning whether she was okay, whether her childless life could ever be meaningful. In the aftermath of Kate, Meg's job was, if nothing else, to be okay, to need no concern. But she couldn't think of what to say in time, and the moment passed.

They stood up and started back toward Orchard Street. Meg knew this much: her mother seemed livelier, as if lit from within, since she had been working at the museum. She could keep on saying that it was only to keep busy, but Meg knew, and Nora knew, that there was more to it than that. There were so many different ways to live in the world—this was what Nora said all day to groups of visitors, every time she showed them the photo of ancient sixty-year-old Granny Moore, every time she delivered her heartfelt speech about that rough passage across the imagined Atlantic. There were so many different worlds in the world.

Meg hugged her mother goodbye at the museum's front door. Nora tied her kerchief back on. "Okay, Megelah. Dad wants you to come to dinner soon. You could even bring someone, if you . . ."

Meg squinted down the street. There it shimmered—the horse hoof clomp on cobblestone, the dust swirling in the air, the reek of kerosene and compost, the far-off rumble of an angry mob. On the corner, a small girl selling flowers? No, of course not, a child with an oversized lollipop, waiting for her mother to finish chatting to another mother. "No, Mom, I'm not seeing anyone right now. You know that."

Nora smiled and patted her cheeks. "Okay, okay! I guess I do. You have a great day, my girl. Thanks for coming. Be careful out there."

On her way into the city, Meg had been mourning her free day at home, plotting her expeditious return to the apartment as soon as she could muster in order to read. Now that she was here, she felt the need to walk, walk, walk, to walk and look, the way you only really could, or she only could, in the city. She always needed a minute after her mother, some time without talking. She was glad now that James hadn't come, though she remembered to text him: "How's the surrogate?" (He and Eugene had spent the morning with a woman they hoped might carry their baby, so it was hard to say which Rhys had had the weirder day.) A few moments later, her phone buzzed. "Hm. Crazy. Powered by Jesus. ☹"

Meg slipped the phone back into her lumpy satchel and walked. She felt a great physical itch to move her body across the island, to outwalk the voice in her head nagging her that today was the day to get serious about looking for apartments, diving deep into the rental listings, which struck her after a few cursory scrolls as being even more depressing and devoid of hope than OkCupid. Without considering her itinerary, she headed south on Orchard out of instinct, trying to see clearly the various histories of her path—recognizing a café where she'd once met Kate, an apartment building she was pretty sure she'd had a one-night stand in sometime during graduate school. Soon she was mindlessly weaving in and out of the crowds as one did, wearing the pungent prerain air like an extra cloak, breathing in the fragrant hot nut vending carts and sewer fumes. Meg always waited for the walk signal at crosswalks, everyone in her family did, eyeing traffic with earned suspicion. She took a right on Canal Street, enjoying the seedy clamor of Chinatown, stepping over bowls of sickly turtles for sale, walking past bins of unidentifiable fruits and boxes of silvery dried fish. Perpetually unable to walk by words without reading them, Meg looked for a story in the cheap T-shirts hung like flags above the Rolex and Louis Vuitton bootleggers' shops. "New York Fuckin' City," read one shirt, and "If you see da police, WARN A BROTHER" (arranged in a cheap imitation of the Warner Brothers logo), and "It's not a bald patch, it's a solar panel for a sex machine." Meg could imagine many things—for example, the early Chinese immigrants who had once lined the streets with their carts and cases, wearing the conical hats and skinny mustaches that would later become racist caricatures—but she could not for the life of her imagine seeing one of the silly T-shirts and wanting to purchase one, to wear it on her body, to present it as one's sartorial emissary in the world. *This is who I am, this is my experience of the world: Scarface ordering a pizza.* Then again, there were so very many ways to live in the world. Who could say?

Meg passed beneath the roar of the Manhattan Bridge. Once she hit Baxter Street, she finally understood what she was doing. She headed south ]on Baxter past Columbus Park, where Asian senior citizens played eerie flutes, and the trees were strung with bamboo birdcages, tiny canaries singing plaintively into the din. She was near the ghost of Five Points now, the notorious slum of nineteenth-century New York where Irish and free Blacks vied for scant space; in the Civil War era, it had been a warren of alleys fringing a polluted quagmire of a pond from which cholera radiated like the music of an overenthusiastic car radio.

Meg took out her phone for a moment to consult a glowing Google Map of the area, confirming when she was at the place, the very eye of what had been the Five Points storm. She stood there on the pavement expecting to feel something. She even dared to close her eyes.

She was immediately jostled by a pair of gangly teenagers bouncing a basketball between them, their limbs impossibly elongated beneath jerseys. "Move it, lady," one of them spat out as they pushed past. Well, that was probably historically accurate too, the free-floating venom.

Maybe she should keep walking. Yes, she would walk all the way down to the bottom of the island, she should go to Ground Zero, where the new World Trade Tower cast its long shining shadow, where the reflecting pools cut into the ground, where the rubble had once smoldered, where the ghosts of terrorist attacks mingled with the ghosts of the West African slaves buried deep beneath lower Manhattan. She would walk on to Battery Park, where Milly and her brother had shuffled through the lines at Castle Clinton, a rehabbed structure where you could now buy tickets to visit the Statue of Liberty. She would get a hot dog from a vendor and stare at the sea. She would jump into the diseased water and swim out to where it was clear, maybe all the way back to Europe. Or she would take a boat to the Statue of Liberty and climb all the steps with all the Japanese tourists and, at the top, she would look at the city from Liberty's crown and then jump out and float down like confetti. But first she needed to sit down for a minute.

Meg looked for a place to rest—there was a corny-looking red sauce Italian place, flanked by storefronts demarcated with Chinese characters, but she wasn't hungry. She made her way back across the street to Columbus Park. She couldn't have possibly felt more white and spinster-y, more Brooklyn-y, than she did sitting there on a bench beneath a row of birdcages, though she was apparently invisible to everyone who walked by.

What a miserable thing to have as a pet, Meg thought, watching the parakeets shiver in the wind. Tiny winged dinosaurs behind bars. How *sad*.

Birdcages always made her think of Kate, who had once acquired one of the famous Brooklyn parrots who noisily colonized the neighborhoods near the baroque Green-Wood Cemetery. She had found it injured in the park while visiting friends, had scooped it into her picnic basket and taken it to the vet. (The family was used to her animal-saving ways, having watched her nurse baby mice to health and splint the wings of three separate injured pigeons.) "Parrots? In Brooklyn? Are you crazy?" their father had said, but Nora knew the context: "Yes, of course, remember? They escaped from a boat, I heard about it ages ago. They're tropical birds, meant to be pets, but a colony of them went outer-borough and feral." "Like the hipsters!" Martin had replied, guffawing at his own joke.

So for a few months Meg and Kate had roomed with the incredibly noisy, ill-tempered Monk Parakeet, a fluorescent green thing given to swinging endlessly on the swing Kate installed in its cage, prone to screaming accusatorily at them whenever they entered or exited the room. The parrot soon died, presumably of pure pique, but Kate kept the cage, ushering in a brief obsession with vintage cages of all sorts, in that way certain girls are drawn to uncanny dressmaker's forms and haberdasher's molds. After Kate's death, James had talked Meg out of getting a tattoo of a bird flying out of a cage. She knew he was right—it was a little on-the-nose, symbolically—but she also knew she still might get it one day.

A guttural cry jerked her head up, scanning for a victim. Nothing had changed in the park, but there again was that shimmer, that dislocating sense that things were shifting about. Meg studied the people around her. No one seemed to register anything out of the ordinary. An elderly woman pushed a shopping cart of unidentifiable melons; two men muttered at one another over a game of chess; a couple of small children kicked a ball into the bushes as their mothers scolded them. There wasn't an earthquake. There wasn't a bomb blast. What was it, then, that made Meg grip the bench beneath her? A sudden vision of a woman in rags, running with a torch. What was that? A young man, covered in soot, looking back over his shoulder? What was *that*? A swell of sound, like a speaker cutting out and in again: voices, bugles, horse whinnies, fire crackles—then quiet again. Meg shook her head. She had to get home. She had to lie down, close her eyes. She was losing it. Yes, she'd been chatting with Kate for years, but this was different. This felt out-of-control, like it was enveloping her, closing in without her permission.

She decided not to walk anymore after all, but to get home as soon as possible. While she still had a home! Meg hurried back toward the train, got stuck behind a crowd of French tourists at a stoplight. She was close enough to touch them, almost did. There were times in the city when one longed to reach out, to rub a shoulder, just because everyone was so close, because you were all humans, because you could. But it would have broken the entire city if everyone did that. It only worked, this crazy way they lived, because people respected the imagined spaces between them, because you *didn't* reach over to the restaurant table an inch away from yours and sip their water, because you *didn't* make eye contact with the neighbor whose living room you could see every inch of as he sat on his couch and you sat on yours. So Meg couldn't rub someone's shoulder, platonically and without subtext. It wasn't done. She wouldn't be the one to do it. But she would compensate in a way invisible to everyone but her: be overly chatty with the newsstand man from whom she bought the Sunday *Times*, engaging in the mundane time-travelling available only at Manhattan newsstands on Saturday afternoons. She would tip too lavishly in the deli counter cup when she stopped for a coffee to warm her hands. Because being so close to so many people could, after all, be so very lonely.

# 11

BECAUSE THE HOUSE is a noisy, joyful, ruckusing place when she is alive and even when she is dead. Because she has started getting used to the house, has begun to feel as though someday she might fit in here in this new town, in this new life. Because she has only lived there for a year and she is not ready to quit it. Gas lamp. Woodstove. Kitchen hearth. The scuffling family sounds. Molasses. Johnnycake. Chicken shriek. The pipe smoke of Mr. Jenkins. The warm rough hands of Mrs. Jenkins. The upstairs bedroom filled to bursting with the four sisters and sometimes a couple of cousins.

Most of the time she doesn't mind that her pallet in the keeping room is so close to the fire. No one comments on this. A fire brought her here, a fire that almost killed her. Still, there is not the thought that sleeping near the hearth will inspire in her any feeling other than warmth. It is true, the warmth is a comfort. But that whole year she has trouble sleeping. She worries that the Jenkinses will be disturbed by her shouts, but she can't seem to help it: Every night she wakes at least once, crying out, hears the glass breaking, feels the flame, smells the burning wood, sees the halls crawling with people who shouldn't be there, sees Dr. Smith's face resolve into a fossil of worry, hears Jane crying, crying, crying as they move in a line through the mob. Every night she rolls over beneath the quilt and sighs and goes back to sleep.

After all, it's not so bad here. For one thing, she has, for the first time in her life, a door.

And the pantry along the wall of the keeping room, stocked with tins. She's never seen food like this and loses herself staring, as if it were a museum exhibit of marble statuary or something else equally exotic. This amuses the sisters, the four sisters with buttons down their backs as if fastening their spines closed, but she can't help it. She has never seen anything like it! Food in a silver can, like a tool or a jewel, solid and shining and smelling (she sniffs) like nothing. Like nothing at all. And yet the idea is food hides inside. Inside the can dressed up in a label with a picture of a tomato or a fish, like a practical joke. Who would be so silly as to buy such food? Anything at all could be inside. There is no peeking until it's opened, and there's no reclosing after that. It could be anything at all—she imagines a tiny family of demons, a bloated rat, a fistful of cloud.

The tins come from boats in the dock where Mr. Jenkins works. They have the small farm, the large garden, but by day he is a lighterman. The fathers here are longshoremen and lightermen and stevedores, words like songs. They leave early in the morning, on wagons, because, out here in the country, there are no streetcars. She knows she is in no position to be a snob, a waif like her without even her own people, but oh how she misses the city. She tells the sisters things that make their jaws drop. *Oh sure*, she says, *we got to take walks to the new Central Park they are constructing, where white ladies in bustles and parasols promenade around like queens.* As if just the telling of it meant she had broken off a chunk of their grandness that she could keep in her pocket. *Oh sure, we rode the streetcar and had a fine Christmas meal in a fancy hall*, even though it had been only once and she hardly remembers it. The girls ooh and ahh, country girls who have never seen Manhattan. There are beehives behind the house, and a kitchen garden they try to teach her to tend, and a broken-down cow. But no streetcars. No bridge to the city, though there are impossible-sounding plans to build one over the river. And so the men leave early to get to the dock to work there, and sometimes they come back with exotic objects that have traveled on boats from Europe. Tins of food. A violin. A printed calendar with a smiling apple-cheeked mermaid on it, a white-person calendar for marking white-person time and white-person holidays. A four-poster bed for the master bedroom, off the kitchen, off the keeping room, by the hearth, where it is warm. For her, a charity society has made a quilt. The ladies at the church are forever quilting, quilting, quilting. The quilt is a thing that is hers now. Her pallet and quilt in the warm spot, like a housecat. Her pallet and quilt and door. Her door. Her place.

The sisters swarm, wanting to know the horrors of the asylum. They hold out a map of their father's, and she sees just how far they are from where the asylum used to stand. The truth is it was wonderful there. Her life there was her real life, remains her real life. She tries to describe summer nights on the front steps with Jane, watching the ladies and gentlemen passing by in swoopy skirts and long tall hats teetering into the sky, the horses as beautiful as beasts from stories. Or playing hoops out in the yard with the other girls. They want to know, wide-eyed, about her mother, her father. She can tell them nothing. She hears one say to the other, hiding behind the clothesline, that her mother was a nightwalker. It's possible. She doesn't know. They ask where she got her name. She doesn't know. Maybe her mama cared for her as a baby and gave her a name and then died. Maybe, that is, she only left because she had to. Maybe Dr. Smith himself named her for a long-lost love. She likes this idea best.

Just as Mr. Jenkins had promised, a few weeks after she arrives, there is a big picnic at Suydam Pond. The excitement in the town is palpable, and early on the morning of the party, she and the Jenkins girls go to help Mrs. Jenkins and the women in her church group, the regal-sounding Abyssinian Benevolent Daughters of Esther, get everything ready. Some strong young men from the church set up a dance floor in the middle of the woods, and it looks exactly like something from a fairy tale, like a fairy tale she read in Jane's book, now ash, like something out of it itself. A small band rehearses jaunty tunes in the clearing, the flute, harp, and violins trilling into the sweet August air. For the children, swings are tied from sturdy branches. The youngest

Jenkins sister leaps happily onto one and starts pumping her legs. The motion of something swinging from a tree turns her stomach, though, and she leaves the thicket. Maybe someone needs help with the refreshments.

She means to assist Mr. Jenkins and the pastor with the heavy carts of clams and oysters they are hitching near the kegs of lager, but the men don't notice her and continue a heated argument. The pastor is shaking his head at the lager. *I don't like it,* he is saying. *Look at everything we've done to be taken seriously. We are God-fearing, we educate our children, we help the infirm and elderly and destitute. What will the Europeans think if we are drunkenly carousing? If Mr. Cornelius's speech turns from a rally into a rowdy demonstration?*

*Drunkenly carousing? A rowdy demonstration?!* She is surprised to hear Mr. Jenkins flare up at the pastor, having only heard him speak in gentle, fatherly tones, and she ducks behind the keg, suddenly hungry for the whole conversation. *Do you not recall what occurred mere weeks ago in Manhattan? Was July 13 so long ago? And who was it who burned the city down? Who was it who drank and caroused and rioted and looted? Who lynched innocent men and torched an orphanage?*

The pastor shakes his head sorrowfully. *I know it. I know it. But don't you see, Jacob? Don't you see, we have to be better than them? We have to remind the ruling classes of themselves, not of the other unfortunates. We cannot be as bad as the immigrants. We must be as good as the wealthy.*

Mr. Jenkins sounds impatient. *It's only a picnic. Mr. Cornelius will give his speech on abolition and everyone will cheer. Some of the men will drink. Old Eliezer will be too much in his cups, and someone will drag him home to Bannon's Barracks. But it will not get out of hand. It will not reflect poorly on anyone.* Then, more calmly, *Besides, do you really think Rachel would arrange an event that would cause any trouble? We will raise some money for the church ladies, that's all. Trust me.*

Someone calls to the men then, and the girl scampers away before her eavesdropping can be discovered. The whole conversation delights her. So dramatic! So grave! She falls a little bit in love with this new side of Mr. Jenkins: the rebel. She skips around the grounds, stopping now to make daisy chains with the sisters to decorate the refreshment table, then taking off again and stopping at the edge of the field to watch the baseball team, The Weeksville Unknowns, warming up for the exhibition game they will play later that afternoon. Everything exciting is happening all at once, and the day is bright and burnished as Miss Shotwell's fancy serving platter, and she is nearly drunk with the smell of sun-baked grass and the sweet sounds of the music. She spins and spins and collapses into the meadow. Everything before was a dream, she decides, and only this part of her life is real.

Sure enough, it is a good-natured garden party, and sure enough, only old Eliezer (a house-breaker, allegedly, from the unsavory fringe of town, though watching him stagger to music she can't imagine him breaking anything other than the tin stein he waves around) drinks too much. Mrs. Jenkins and the other Daughters of Esther circulate a jar for donations, raising money to provide burial insurance for women and children, which strikes the girl as a dark reason for festivities, but an important cause nonetheless. Meanwhile she sips her thirteenth glass of lemonade.

When the famous Mr. Cornelius takes the podium, she realizes he is a blind man, about nine hundred years old, who speaks stirringly about abolition. She sits on the grass to listen. Jack, an older boy she knows slightly, who helps out with the Jenkins' beehives sometimes, materializes at her side. He leans in to whisper to her, and the whole side of her body prickles. *A bore, isn't it?* he hisses. She nods, not daring to look at him. *He wants us to all enlist, to join that doomed war. Nice, right? He's too old to, but by all means the rest of us should go lose our limbs.* She can smell his sweat. She steals a look at him, then pretends to concentrate on the speech again.

*I don't know*, she whispers back. *Maybe he's right that it will help us to be taken more seriously by the Europeans?* Repeating what she'd heard the pastor say earlier, hoping it makes her sound smart and grown-up. She self-consciously adjusts her calico dress, the daisy chain one of the sisters threaded in her hair.

Jack laughs. *I think I'd rather hop on a boat back to Africa, wouldn't you?*

*I, sir, have never been to Africa,* she tells him crisply. *Though I wouldn't mind going back to Manhattan someday.*

He laughs again, and she sits very straight now, wondering if anyone sees them. She fantasizes that one of the Jenkins girls is watching, inflamed by envy that she, the poor orphan, is the recipient of handsome Jack's conversational charms.

*Come,* Jack says, and they shuffle away from the speech, through the field, into the forest where the dance floor is. He invites her to dance, but she has never danced and invents a grave foot injury, so instead they watch the other dancers and giggle together at the way old Eliezer hurls himself around.

After the picnic, watching out the window of the keeping room becomes one of her main pastimes. Whenever Mrs. Jenkins needs eggs or honey, she is the first to volunteer and dashes outside, always hoping for a glimpse of Jack. Sometimes he is working in the garden and sends her a friendly wave, and that is enough to fuel her for days. She is growing up, after all, she tells herself. Soon she is going to be a woman. She might as well be in love with someone.

Despite all the fun of the picnic and all their lighthearted family meals and outings, despite the nights when music and dancing take over the first floor of the house, the uncle who owns a camera documenting it all before drinking moonshine and snoring until dawn on the parlor sofa, the Jenkinses are serious people. They seem to forget she can hear them from her room off the kitchen when they host evening meetings in the parlor. Or maybe they don't care that she can hear. Maybe they want her to hear. She fantasizes that one night she will hear Jacob Jenkins say, *You know who would make a fine apprentice for the doctor?* Or *I love my girls, but let me show you the finest student at all of Colored School No. 2!* And her shyness will fall away like a snake's skin, and she will make a grand entrance into the parlor, where the important people of the town will clap and cheer.

Disappointingly, she doesn't seem to be a much-discussed topic, other than in the abstract: the Orphanage Problem. Women from Mrs. Jenkins's church group come over to quilt with the mother and older sisters and look at her sympathetically. What is to be done with her and everyone like her, now that the mobs have revealed the fault lines of the city? What is to be done with the whole burnt frame of New York? The city is ruined, they say. The city is over. The once-mighty city smolders, like the ribcage of a burnt-up hen.

There is a volcano under the city. That's what everyone says. Who knew there was so much anger and hatred, so hotly just below the surface?

It is unceasingly strange, after so many years in the world of children, to hear these adult voices at night as she lies awake on her pallet. She listens in anyway, makes notes in the diary that the scientific sister gave her. During one of the meetings she listens to from her pallet, the men discuss taking up arms. *Let us not forget the Riots so quickly,* a man with a low voice says. *We must take arms. Every home in Weeksville should have a loaded rifle by the door, in case the mob decides to visit us.* The girl shivers, hugs her rag doll close. Another man shouts, *We must do more than that! Like Mr. Morel says, we should emigrate to the West Indies and leave this shattered country behind.* Another interrupts, *No, no, Liberia. Personally, I plan to join the African Colonization Society and start a fine new life back where I belong.* The next voice she recognizes as Mr. Jenkins, and she sits up, strains closer to the door in order to hear. Mr. Jenkins says, with commanding calm, *Where we belong? Where we belong is here, our home. The white man's ancestors once lived elsewhere too, or does no one remember that? I have no more relationship with Africa than President Lincoln does with England, or wherever his squeaky people are from.* The men chuckle. *No,* says Mr. Jenkins, *this is my country, no matter what Jeff Davis and his curs may say, and what is more, I will fight for my country.*

What follows is a boisterous debate about whether or not they ought to join the war. She remembers what Jack had said about it, and as if hearing her thoughts, the man with the low voice rumbles in protest: *Enlist? For what?!* They argue deep into the night: Leave their homes and families and freedom, for ten dollars a month, not even offered the bounty the white soldiers get? And with the prospect of a dog's death at the hand of bloodthirsty rebels if they are captured?

No, no, this is not a country they can fight for yet, some of them say. The others argue about emancipation, saying that freedom for all is the best cause there is. That the sight of these sable warriors in uniform shows people they are strong and brave and can fight, worthy of citizenship. Their voices thrum throughout the first floor, militant and harsh, as if the village were already preparing for war. Which war, she can't be sure.

After a while she pulls her quilt over her ears, tired of the jagged edges to their voices. Even when Mrs. Jenkins pipes in, she sounds cacophonous and shrill, entirely unlike her daytime self. The girl wiggles down under her quilt and, as her eyes adjust to the dark, consults with her rag doll. *Are you glad I've come to live here with you?* she asks the doll. The doll answers seriously, in the affirmative. *I'm ever so glad you were here waiting for me. You really understand me, don't you?* The doll says yes. *How is it that I have not yet given you a name?* she asks the doll, *Forgive me, won't you? You need a name. I think I will call you Jane.* The doll is happy then, and they cuddle all night in the warmth of the keeping room.

She is pleased to be going to school with the big girls, puffs up like a rooster as they walk together through the town. She is behind them in her studies but swallows her pride, remembers what a gift it is to be getting to go to Colored School No. 2, with its handsome and charismatic principal, known across the country as a speaker and activist. The principal is Black, the teachers are all Black, and many of the children are Black, but there are white kids there too, that's how good the school is. The Germans and other immigrants who settle nearby want to use their school too. The teachers are unperturbed by the fact that many of the adults in Weeksville can't read. As Mr. Morel, their principal, intones at school meetings, *Reading will buy you a future. Being literate makes anything possible.* Everyone in town smiles at her as she walks from the house on Holland Avenue all the way down to Troy Avenue with the Jenkins girls, clutching their schoolbooks and slates like shields.

At night, after finishing her chores, she sits in the keeping room and writes in the diary. *O, who will ever care about my meagr words, she writes, & what I think? The business of the world is grave inded in this time. And don't laugh, diary, for it's a fact—I sometimes think I can grow up and help. There are so meny things I wish to do, viz., finish school, find a way to repay the kind Jenkinses, become a doctor, make my way back to the orphans. I pray for the power to help them. Also I wold very much like to some day have a corset and pierced ears.*

As she writes herself into existence, she begins to believe more and more in each possibility. It is as if by committing the words to paper the events are born and fly off into the future, where they wait for her.

# 12

**FOR YEARS** Meg had been able to keep loving her city, excusing its many inconveniences—she forgave New York for the slush-spray of uber-angry Uber drivers, the calf-strain of walkups, the withered produce for which she paid a premium—she ignored the pollution that caked in her nostrils, the labyrinthine processes one endured each morning just to obtain coffee, croissant, newspaper—didn't even mind too much about the bag ladies yodeling into dumpsters as if they were karaoke rooms—in part because she had always been in the city, the city had always been in her, so that she experienced the carapace of architecture as so much a part of her body she wasn't sure her systems would continue to work elsewhere, feared in fact that in the bright clear light of a place like Long Island or LA, she would find herself unable to stand upright, pale and unmuscled as a limb left too long in a cast—and in part because of her apartment. She had been, these ten years, a person blessed in the way of real estate. It had become part of her identity, one of the things about her—*Meg? Right, the one with the silver streak in her hair, the one who's read every book, who rides her bicycle all over town, who has a dead sister and an alive cat, and who has that amazing unbelievable apartment—yes,* that *Meg.* She was accustomed, when bringing a man home from a bar or library lecture, to hearing impressed wolf-whistles at her balcony. When she was feeling showy, there was deep pleasure to be had just by telling someone what she paid in rent. "But the wood floors! The moldings! The claw foot tub! The huge windows and built-in bookshelves!" girlfriends would say. Meg would affect a modest smile. "I know," she would say, shrugging, "it's crazy." It was like having a hidden talent, or a trophy casually displayed on a bathroom shelf ("Oh that? That's my Emmy, NBD."). People regarded her differently because she was that rare bird: a self-supporting Brooklynite with a beautiful home, a renter who had finagled her way into her own shining spot of that cruelly expensive city, a single woman who had outwitted the system.

Until now.

Her landlady had given her (delivered, apologetically, with a bouquet of out-of-season hyacinths) the official notice. She had until the end of the calendar year. "Kicked out at Christmas," Meg grumbled to James, as they trudged to an open house on Bergen Street.

"Don't be dramatic," he said. "She's giving you over two months. That's nice of her. You have plenty of time."

"But it's the principle of the thing." He couldn't disagree, or anyway he didn't dare. "It's my apartment. It's my *home*. And I'll never be able to afford anything nearly as good. This city hates the single." They arrived at the only slightly decrepit brownstone and scaled the steep stairs to the third floor. "This is hardly Prospect Heights, by the way," Meg said to no one in particular, lifting a hunk of peeling hallway carpet with her toe. "If I'd wanted to look in Crown Heights, I would have said Crown Heights. I don't see why everyone has to be so fucking sly. Like I'm not going to notice, once I'm here?"

James sighed a long-suffering sigh. He had been the one who insisted finding a new place would be "no bigs;" he had offered to come with. But it had been a while for both of them. They'd forgotten how demoralizing the process could be and now faced the stock of run-down 1BRs with the dismay of a recent divorcee at a singles mixer: So *this* was what was available? Meg stepped into the musty-smelling living room. The entire apartment was visible from where she stood—kitchenette at one end, foyer and bathroom door at the other. A real estate agent with the mien of a substitute teacher's substitute teacher greeted them uncertainly. Meg held up a hand, silencing the pleasantries. "Where's the bedroom."

"Ah, yes, right here, is this perfect cozy—"

"That's a foyer."

James squinted. "It's perfect for, like, a telephone table."

Meg turned around.

The agent started, "Oh but it's such a great deal, let me show you—"

Meg and James started down the stairs. "I'm a grown woman," Meg called back, "and when I say I need a one-bedroom apartment in Prospect Heights, I *don't* mean I'd like to see a *studio* in *Crown Heights.*"

Some murmurs from the agent wafted down the stairs—"sun-drenched," they could hear, and "great for entertaining!"—silenced by the building's front door, which Meg slammed shut.

"I thought you loved Crown Heights. I thought you were all about Crown Heights. I thought the best ghosts of the city lived here."

"Shut up. Please."

"Okay," said James after several blocks of silence. "Let's not get hysterical."

"Hysterical, Jamie? *Hysterical*? Oh, what, am I making this up, how awful every apartment we've seen is? Is that my problem? The musty studio stacked high with porn videos and reeking of mushroom? The astro-turfed living room with the window facing the goat slaughterhouse? Am I suffering from *hysteria*? Is it my wandering womb causing me womanly madness, is that my problem? Where's my phrenologist, where's the bloodletter?! Someone send me to a sanitarium, please!" Meg shook her hands in the air.

"All right. Bad choice of words. Just, slow down, will you?"

Meg took a deep breath, adjusted her pace.

"Anyway, I thought you liked history."

"I hardly think 'decrepit and moldering' is the same as 'historical charm.'"

"Suit yourself. But that apartment's carpet was legit from another era."

"You're hilarious. See how hard I'm laughing? Let's stop here and get a tea or something. I need a break." They were straddling the neighborhoods' border now and ducked into a schmancy Prospect Heights café with exposed brick walls and enormous plate glass windows, stood on the line in a fat beam of sunlight. James studied the rows of colorful macarons on display like jewels in a museum. But Meg couldn't relax, shifted around, glared at the attractive pale people camped out at every café table, their slender silver laptops humming in chorus, their casual wealth and general wellbeing surrounding them like auras. "Look at all these people. All these people with their espressos and their flat whites, taking a break from their perfect little Prospect Heights homes, with their fancy haircuts and hipster handbags and their summers in the Hamptons."

James snorted, still eying the sweets. "You don't know any of that."

"Sure I do. Look at that guy—over there in the corner. He's writing poems. Longhand. In a Moleskine. He has a wife and kids—how can he afford to be a poet, in this neighborhood? Daddy was a banker, I guarantee it."

James craned his neck, whispered, "How do you know he can afford it? Maybe he's a longshoreman during the week. Maybe he's stealing fifteen minutes away from his basement hovel to write, and the rest of the time he's working his fingers to the bone. Wallace Stevens was an insurance executive you know." He paused. "You told me that. I don't even know who Wallace Stevens is. Anyway, how do you know he has a wife and kids?"

They inched up in the line. The woman ahead of them was coming to terms with her desire to buy every single cupcake. Meg sighed loudly. "Look—wedding ring. And look at his back."

There was indeed a smattering of something sparkly clinging to the poet's black turtleneck. "Stickers!" James whispered. "Oh man, is that my future? Walking around all day without realizing there are shiny stars all over my back?"

"Yes." They were at the front of the line now, but Meg's vitriol had neutralized any hunger they might have had. James ordered an iced herbal tea to justify the detour, and the Rhyses launched back out onto the street, roiling with tides of brunching families and women brandishing boutique shopping bags. The next appointment was a few blocks away, comfortably in Meg's price range but ominously described as "good for shares," which usually meant no living room, or a kitchenette fit only for Millennial roommates living on strict diets of Seamless. Despite her limited budget, Meg had ruled out renting a room in someone else's place. Her solitude was crucial.

"Why do you even want to stay in this neighborhood," James said, sipping the flowery tea, "if you hate everyone here so much?"

Meg glared at him. A tow-headed toddler ran past her, nearly knocking her over, chased by a gaunt blonde calling, "Chip! No, Chippy!" and to Meg, "Watch *out*!" James gestured after them, as if presenting the evidence.

In truth she didn't quite know. She was comfortable there. It was familiar. She never shopped at its tiny boutiques selling too-cute dresses and overly jocular mugs, couldn't afford them but also just didn't like them, usually preferred dim sum in gritty Chinatown dives to a fussy prix fixe at a fusion café with three tables. She liked the local used bookstore but only sort of. She appreciated the bike lanes and the proximity to the park and her job, yes, but if she was going to be honest with herself, it was probably more a matter of habit than anything else. She found herself with no idea of what she was going to do, and usually if there was one thing Meg Rhys knew, it was what she was going to do.

The next address turned out to be a stolid apartment building straight out of Cold War Stalingrad; Meg couldn't even work up the energy to go inside. James left her in charge of his plastic cup of melting ice and went up without her. Within moments he reappeared, shaking his head.

"What? What?"

James just shook his head some more. Then he lifted a finger in the air, like a sailor checking for a breeze. Finally he said, "Something is going to come up, Meg. I know it is. It definitely is. But just—not this. Not today." They slumped together down on the wide concrete step in front of the building. Meg took off her glasses and rubbed her eyes. So far that day they'd seen a spacious two-bedroom that looked exactly as if someone had been murdered in it five minutes before they'd arrived; a "garden apartment" that turned out to be a concrete basement with windows like the swollen-shut eyes of a seasonal allergy sufferer; a fifth-floor walkup distinguished by a complete lack of kitchen appliances ("They plan to install some?" the agent had said uncertainly); a floor-through with windows facing brick walls and a closet too shallow for a single hanger; showers in kitchens, house-shares without doors, and more cramped studios than they could shake a stick at. And each of the dystopian places had been just slightly above Meg's price range.

"How can it be," Meg said, "that in this whole big city, there is no living space to fit me?"

"It's not," James said. "You can't give up. You'll find it."

She wanted to believe him. She had to believe him. Her life in New York could not be over, could not end in this unceremonious, cruel way. They sat there for a long time, until a delivery truck with a creepy eye painted on the side parked in front of them, and they had to move on in order to get some air.

They didn't find anything, of course. Meg went to work in despair.

"So." He leaned over her desk, having materialized out of nowhere. Ellis Williams. Apparently this was a thing now? It was. It was a thing. Meg tried not to look too pleased.

"How may I help you, sir?" she intoned, doing her best reference-desk crone.

Ellis raised an eyebrow, and she laughed at her own nerdiness, and he smiled at her guffaw, or at least she guessed that's what it was. She studied him. A glittery spray of rain formed a map of tearstains on the shoulders of his camel coat. Today he offered no slip of paper, came armed with no manila folder. She wondered what his father's latest directive had been, and what else were they looking for, and for how long they could wait, held hostage by a petulant ghost, before life—and the inevitable renovations it always required—had to move on. Ellis looked once, quickly, around the room. Meg did too, not wanting Helen hearing what they were inevitably about to discuss. The Brooklyn Collection was empty. For some reason rainy days kept people away from what Meg knew was the best place to be on a rainy day, the drops sluicing onto the Collection's windows, rat-a-tat-tatting with exquisite noisiness. She was hyperaware of the rain sounds just then, of the heat and heft of her body, of having worn the wrong socks and being forced to feel them sliding down her ankles, again and again, slouchy reminders of the human body's many structural flaws.

Ellis said, "I just have to tell you the latest developments." Meg couldn't pin down his tone. Ironic? Sarcastic? What was the difference between the two again? He smiled crookedly, his eyes as sad as ever.

"Oh? Did you find some new records?"

"You aren't going to believe this, Ms. Rhys, but something happened to me in the world, *not* inside a book."

Now she knew she was being teased. She leaned back and folded her arms across her chest. "Is that so! I've never *heard* of such a thing! But it reminds me of something I read about once, actually—"

"Do you have a minute?"

Meg set aside the Prospect Heights clippings she'd been filing—okay, so maybe she had been mournfully sifting through the stories of the neighborhood she was sure she'd be forced to leave when her lease was up; the annoying thing was she recognized these stages of guilt, knew she was lingering between denial and guilt, and hated that her mind was so predictable—and gestured toward one of the large tables, where they could both sit. "Step into my office," she said. They sat across from each other. No danger of touching.

Ellis worried his hands together.

"I just had the weirdest fucking morning of my life, excuse my French, and I have to tell someone about it. You're the only person in this whole city who won't just tell me I'm crazy." He smiled slightly, though his eyes were cold.

"Or if I do, I'll also have a good reference for a shrink," Meg said.

Ellis's eyes warmed then, crinkles fanning beside them. "Exactly."

"Okay. So. Shoot."

He took a deep breath and launched into his story.

That morning, Ellis had stepped blinking out of the subway station. The longer he stood there trying to remember the shortest way to walk, the more painfully aware he was of how he had become an outsider in his own city. He tried to walk purposefully but almost immediately made a wrong turn. Despite having visited the neighborhood frequently as a kid, he'd never quite become fluent in it. His father had come up in a neighborhood a lot like this one, but way up in the northern reaches of the pre-arson wave Bronx, and had always loved to tell him about how it was a rough place where you were always aware of which crew ran which street, whose side you needed to be on; an island society where the native patois was a complicated combination of looks and nods and handshakes; a childhood in which Harmon had never met a white person until college.

So anyway Ellis was feeling out-of-place as he walked down the desolate block populated by boarded-up shops, old men smoking cigarillos on crumbling stoops, and storefront churches in need of fresh paint, realizing how far he had to go. In fact, it was painfully clear to him that he had taken the wrong subway altogether, like a goddamn tourist.

He wasn't a tourist. He also wasn't a handyman. And yet he had been tasked by his father to fix, of all things, a broken door. So Ellis kept walking in what he supposed was the direction of his father's house.

His father's Crown Heights house had always creeped him out, and maybe because of that, he hadn't been there in years. Since moving to Chicago, trips home to Brooklyn had been brief and crowded with Williams obligations, the centerpiece of every visit a walking tour of the neighborhood where he'd grown up, going, "This used to be a squat. Now it's million-dollar co-ops!" Or "This is a frozen yogurt place now? That's hilarious. This used to be where you could buy girly magazines behind the counter." Everything seemed to be a frozen yogurt place now. He couldn't figure out why anyone would even want to live in Brooklyn anymore unless they really, really loved frozen yogurt. (Meg laughed at this—she knew that feeling so well.)

Now his father wanted to renovate and sell the broken-down Crown Heights house. If they played their cards right, they could probably get some gay couple to buy the house for a million bucks. That was how things happened for these down-and-out neighborhoods, wasn't it? That was how even humble college professors made their fortunes in the city: decades of patience. Lying in wait like a real estate panther.

But the first step was the front door. Literally. The front door's hinge had broken, and now Ellis had been dispatched to fix it because despite being some of the smartest people he'd ever known, Ellis's parents still thought the "engineer" part of his title qualified him to moonlight as a carpenter. So there was Ellis, being put to work as an Extreme Renovator: Haunted House Edition.

The house on Holland Avenue was pretty much like he'd remembered it. Like when he ran into high school friends on the F train, he recognized the bone structure, the mannerisms, pieced together what vibrant young thing had faded into the iteration standing before him. His father's house had always struck him as what was left over. Left over from *what*, Ellis couldn't say.

It was a house you would keep on walking past if you had any city sense at all. The whitewashed three-story wood-frame (smushed in between a ratty apartment block on one side and a forbidding garage on the other, set at a weird angle on the lot, down at a dead end where the street was truncated by the roaring river that was Atlantic Avenue) sounded great on paper. It even managed to look charming in his father's perennial Craigslist rental notice. But in real life it exuded the unsteadiness of a subway creep, the building equivalent of the guy with too many plastic bags. It was nothing you could put into words, only a sort of ice encasing your spine, a shudder, an internal groan. This was no spooky mansion on the hill, no eerie country estate left vacant and Halloween-y, waiting for an unsuspecting sleuth to creep around the shrouded furniture. It was only a house dwarfed by its utilitarian, pseudo-industrial surroundings. Only a house that was a little *off*.

The tiny lawn was tidy as ever, mowed into Harmon's signature stripes. Ellis looked down as he walked (avoiding the house's eerie stare) up the walkway made of poured concrete combed neatly as freshly plaited hair. The windows were ordinary, not lidded by boards like a movie haunted house; the roof, reaching up into a witch's hat of a peak, recently and responsibly re-tarred. The house was old but the foundation was firm. The locks were sturdy but not so clustered along entries as to betray excessive fear of burglary.

As Ellis recalled it, the first floor apartment was nice enough, with a sunny living room facing what was a relatively quiet street, a kitchen of civilized size, a bedroom that—it was true—lacked a closet of very convincing dimensions, but with that extra room off the kitchen, in the back of the house, overlooking the slightly feral backyard, a dining room or an office or a nursery or a spacious mudroom, undesignated space being one of the most significant of Brooklyn miracles. When he still lived in town, Ellis had often been the one to show the apartment to potential renters, and at the sight of this room (a plain chamber with a four-paned window and its own back entrance, with its screen door that reminded former suburbanites subconsciously of home, this simple space of possibilities, this potential art studio or collection display or guest room or library or yoga studio or bicycle storage), he would see the potential renters' eyes light up, their lives opening up in front of them. They would marvel at the low rent and he would nod. "It's near a great middle school," Ellis would recite, as his father had instructed him, "and a big playground with basketball courts! Quiet, residential area! Nice neighbors!"

And so year after year, renters ignored the tingles in their scalps, the shivers in their stomachs, because after all, most people, most twenty-first century Americans, most New Yorkers, were skilled at ignoring their instincts. You had to ignore most things in order to go on living without going insane. They rented the place, and they stayed as long as they could stand, and then, boom, they were gone.

So the house had always been a problem. It was the inexplicable creepiness of the place, even as tidy as they kept it, that instilled a kind of fury in the neighbors. It was the unsettled feeling that descended as soon as you stepped near the house itself, particularly the first floor, particularly the room in the back. The keeping room.

Ellis had Googled "replacing a door hinge" and studied some wobbly YouTube videos, so he had his wooden shims ready to prop up the sagging door, his cheap brass hinges because the kooky handyman online preferred them to the fancier ones. He crouched by the door, opened his bag, stirred around for the wrench and work gloves.

Then all in the same instant, he stood up again and the door shot open, flinging forward with such force he was knocked backwards, clutching his nose, stunned on the ground and waiting for blood to start pouring from his face. It didn't, but he still needed some time to recover himself. The door flapped innocently. "What the fuck," said Ellis, his butt on the ground, his hands on his face. "Hey, man, watch it! I'm working on the door here, be careful!"

But no one came out of the door. The pain thudded through Ellis's head, a visceral reminder of the few times he'd been punched in the face: horsing around with the Bronx cousins; a college-era brawl in a bar. "Hello?"

There was no one.

He pushed himself up and, shaking off the stars that swarmed his vision, peered into the front hall. But no one was there. There was a pocket of ice in the air—he remembered now the weird thermodynamics of the house, how it was given to stagnant air and sudden cold drafts. The small, carpeted entryway needed fresh paint and better lighting, but besides that looked relatively normal. The door to the first floor apartment stood directly to Ellis's right, closed and (he discovered when, despite himself, he gave it a little shove) locked. He heard no sound on the creaking stairs, no footsteps overhead. "Hello? Anyone home? It's Ellis Williams, Harmon's son," he added, "uh, the landlord, you know," realizing belatedly that his entry (a big man busting in through the door, clumsy and cursing) might be disconcerting to any lingering tenants, had they not already moved out as they were supposed to.

Ellis muttered to himself as he stepped into the hallway. "Damn worn out hinges. Rusty springs. That spooky fucking draft . . ." He entered the house, leaving his tool bag loitering on the stoop and the door hanging open. The carpet in the hallway was clean but threadbare, a hypnotic hexagonal pattern he remembered studying as a child. Seeing the pattern and breathing the hallway's smell reminded Ellis how, as a kid, he had raced up and down the stairs of that old Holland house as fast as he could, to avoid the ghost that chased him around. He had a distinct sense memory of how it felt to have it—her—nipping at his heels as he ran. His mother would always shush him, maintaining it was simply a creaky old house and would he please stop making a racket for the renters. He remembered liking the ghost he invented to play with, finding her not scary but fun.

As if reading his thoughts, the front door slammed shut behind him. He jumped, yelled, "Shit!" Ellis reached again for the doorknob, only the door wouldn't open. Ellis had slammed his open palm against the door, ignoring the pain twinkling across his fingertips. He rattled the doorknob pointlessly. "Come on," he muttered to the door. Then he heard the door lock, the deadbolt sliding shut with ominous finality.

"Hello? Is someone there?" he yelled into the crack between the door and the wall. Then he remembered about the peephole and pressed his eye to it.

Of course, there was no one there.

He rattled the knob some more before slapping the door and turning away, disgusted. Stomped upstairs to pound on that apartment door. No answer. Stomped downstairs to pound on that apartment door again, as if the tenants might have materialized in the past minute. Nothing. The only other door went down to the basement, and everyone knew you weren't supposed to go down to the basement. But after rattling the front door some more, trying futilely to shimmy it open with his AmEx and then sharing more of his feelings with the slab of wood, Ellis couldn't see another option.

He walked through the creaky front hall to the basement door, opened it, and, foolishly, whispered "Hello?" down the stairs, before shaking his head and commanding himself: "You are a grown-ass man, man. Go down the damn stairs." Ducking on the steep steps so he didn't concuss himself on top of everything else, Ellis felt his breath catching in his chest. He couldn't find the switch and thus shuffled along in the dim light afforded by the casement windows. The basement air was clammy, necrotic. There was again, always, that eerie feeling of being watched, that sense that someone nearby was not just watching but in fact raging, sulking, plotting. Impossibly, he sensed he was walking into an ambush.

Ellis remembered that beyond the storage crates, beyond the ancient bicycles piled like skeletons in catacombs, beyond the monstrous furnace with its menacing green eye, there was another set of rickety, termite-nibbled steps leading up to the cellar door. He tried to move quickly toward the door, shuddering with the distinct feeling his heels were being nipped at by that old grouchy ghost. That fucking house. Had his mind all mixed-up and spooky too.

The presence he had always felt in that house, the whatever-it-was, swarmed toward him. He heard the basement door slam shut overhead, grunted with fear despite himself. A bluish fog of icy air enveloped him. Ellis stumbled away, heart racing, blood crashing noisily against his skull. He found the back stairs, flung himself up them, fumbled with the lock, and slammed his shoulder so hard against the cellar doors that when he heard a splintering, he imagined for a confused instant it must be his own bones cracking. But it was the door, which flew open, birthing Ellis up and out of the aperture like a baby born in a taxi, breathless, grunting, in an inhuman rush.

As he lay there panting, a delivery truck puttered down the street, its side painted with a triangle encasing an enormous eyeball, an eye that seemed to track him as the truck drove slowly on, made a clumsy U-turn at the dead end, and passed him by again.

Ellis blinked at Meg, looking exhausted, exhausted by the experience itself, exhausted by the telling.

She blinked back at him. "So, your house tried to eat you!" she translated.

He looked pained for a moment, then laughed. "I guess so. I guess it did."

"Jesus."

"I know."

Meg shuffled some papers, bit the end of her pencil. "Okay, this is none of my business, and you don't have to answer—but why *did* you come here? I mean why aren't you back in Chicago? Did you come here for the house? Or, I mean, did you know you would get so involved? With the house?"

Ellis nodded, like he was agreeing with her. "Well, yeah. Stuff got kinda messed up at home—I'm officially on a leave of absence from my job. I guess I wasn't—well. My wife. Rachel."

Meg was conscious of holding very still, like a cat trying to hide.

"She—passed away. Ah. Six months ago."

"Oh, God."

"Cancer. It all happened really fast. It was—it's been—well you know. A really strange time."

"I see. Oh, God, I'm so sorry, Ellis."

Tears sprung to her eyes, tears she quickly pressed away with brisk fingertips. And she had been envious of this unknown woman, this supposedly lucky lady. When she really dug deep, examined herself unvarnished, what an asshole Meg was! Meg considered all Ellis had told her, everything he harbored, all the turmoil she knew filled his days, and how disturbing she knew it was to have such supernatural experiences mucking up the normal life you were trying to have. She knew he probably wished his ghost was Rachel, wished that he had a gentle wifely presence alongside him at all times, rather than battling this malevolent force in his father's home. His wife's death had simply made him more receptive to messages from the beyond, which was a mindfuck of spiritual proportions. How disobedient life could be, refusing to fit in the story shape you'd imagined for it.

Meg leaned forward. "Ellis," she said.

"Yes, Meg?" he said.

"That really, really sucks."

"Well, yeah. It does. It really, really sucks."

There was a pause.

"Ellis."

"Yes, Meg?"

"I think I'd like to go to your house."

## 13

*ONCE YOU ARE DEAD*, it's difficult to have a new thought. You mostly are what you were. It's why you get fixated on places and people. It's why you get stuck haunting. How can you move on, when you aren't alive to change?

Sometimes, as she gusts around the house, she can still see it the way her living eyes recorded it. There are instruments in the parlor. Crinolines in the closets. Furniture from abroad. Oil lanterns smoking in sconces. Food in tins. The calendar on the wall. Ice delivered in a huge block once a week and domesticated in the black iron box in the kitchen. There are Bibles, newspapers, broadsides with the news of war.

Sometimes she thinks she hears Jane. The person Jane, not the doll. Over her Christmas in Weeksville, it is arranged for Jane to come see her. It turns out that Jane has stayed with the matrons and the other children, that after some time on Blackwell Island, they'd gone to a new orphan asylum built up in a pastoral land called Harlem where colored people headed after the fiery riot. Bringing the orphans to Weeksville requires arrangements of exceeding difficulty and unlikeliness, but someone, probably Dr. Smith, makes it happen, and all the remaining asylum children are brought to the world-famous, okay maybe city-famous, Suydam Pond for an ice skating excursion. She sees Miss Murray and the older Miss Shotwell and the younger Miss Shotwell for the first time since that terrible day when she left, and she can't help but leap toward them, as if she were meeting her own mother.

Maybe her new family can see how empty she feels here, surrounded by all their love, and helps make the reunion happen. Jane is practically her sister coming up. Being together for this moment is the happiest she will ever feel. She is crushed by nostalgia for the asylum. She wants to go back with Jane and sleep in a row of metal beds with all the girls again, even though she knows it is crazy to say this, probably sinful to think it, even though now that she thinks about it, she was one of the oldest girls there and was likely about to be sent elsewhere anyway, to work in someone's home, perhaps. By sending her here to Weeksville, Dr. Smith has bought her some childhood. She is so grateful she can hardly look his way when the orphans arrive. The new sisters as usual make speech unnecessary, invade the space between them, fawn over Jane's curls which are, after all, extraordinary.

On the day the orphans come, Mr. Morel hosts a Christmas celebration at the AME Church. A huge spruce tree out front is hung with candles and books and shining packages for the children. Every child gets to choose one, and watching the orphans pick their baubles, the girl is so proud it's as if she'd made it all happen herself. She herself selects a children's primer on phrenology, which she clutches to her heart. Mr. Morel gives talk on scientific process, poking a finger in molasses to teach about adhesion, encouraging each child to try. Even the unscientifically inclined are eager to poke their fingers into the jar of sweet, sticky stuff. Then he announces that he is going to crown the queen of the school, and a hush falls over the crowd. Since it's her first Christmas there, the girl has no idea what this means, can only parse the other students' excitement to know it's something big. Mr. Morel holds a beautiful white wreath and a crown of woven mistletoe and lace ribbon. The sight of them takes her breath away. Then he looks right at her, where she is standing up front, clutching Jane's hand and that of the scientific sister, and calls her name.

*Me?* She says, unable to believe it.

Mr. Morel smiles. *You.*

She joins him in the front of the crowd, in front of the tree, and he places the crown on her head, hands her a gift, a tiny leather-bound Bible of her own, and everyone cheers. Later Jane laughs at her—*I never ever saw you smile so big!* She beams. She waves. She is a star on the stage, an opera diva, a celebrity speaker addressing Congress. She is a famous doctor delivering a lecture on biology. She's a respected abolitionist promoting a book she has written on suffrage. Most of all, she is wearing a *crown*. She grins and grins, feeling the heft of the crown on the plaits Mrs. Jenkins gave her that morning, feeling the sun of Mr. Morel's approval on her skin. Little old her: queen of the school.

Then they all gather round for cider and brown betty, before filing to the edge of Suydam Pond to lace up their skates. As the Jenkins girls had told her the instant she arrived in town, ice skating is a mania among the local children and adults. The orphans have of course never been, and, keeping on her crown, she imperiously shows them what to do. They watch her with awe as she glides out onto the ice. She is wobblier than the Jenkins sisters but steadier than she has any right to be. As she skates across the pond, avoiding the dips and bumps she knows by heart from their winter of afterschool recreation, flakes of snow begin to gently sift down. God is making a cake, she thinks hysterically, and I am a part of it.

Jane is overjoyed by the skating pond. When she thinks of Jane now, it is like this: twirling clumsily but beautifully on skates, laughing more loudly than she ever has before, slipping, sliding, laughing, huge snowflakes on her eyelashes, dusting her curls. Why doesn't she ever see Jane now? There are so many spirits in the city. It is hard to know how it works. As time passes she is more feeling than thought anyway. More impulse than intelligence.

When she remembers Jane on the ice that day, she remembers that she, too, has a name. She hears Jane screaming at her as they careen across the ice. She hears Jane calling her name, and she knows that the people who are trying to destroy her house have names too, and people who love them, and reasons they need to stay alive.

But when demolition begins, when they come to strip the walls, when they take her door from its hinges, something black boils over in her. She is scared the way a fox is scared in the woods. All she has is the fear; she is transformed into fear. She is only feeling and the only feeling is scared. The fear becomes an atmosphere. This is the most dangerous thing.

It's like when they are building the big parkway and tearing down everything all around the house, and the safe feeling of the house is infected with the noise and the fear of the people living in it, because they are trying to tear down everything. It is only scared people turning mad and then turning useful that saves the zigzag of Hunterfly Road from being pulverized.

She doesn't believe in haunting—of course not, one of Dr. Smith's well-behaved asylum girls through and through, the promising student, the queen of Mr. Morel's school—but she needs the people to know she is upset. She needs to throw a book, to slam a door. She needs to gather up her everything to use it to hurt them. The fear thunders up, and she hears horse clamor and breathes street dust, she is cold and shivering from her fever and she is hot from the fire, marching away from the Colored Orphan Asylum.

There is Jane, attempting a figure eight on the ice, stumbling, laughing, looping again. Calling her name. But she turns away. All she has is this house. This place. This is no time for a name.

After she dies, the family, shocked by the failure of their good deed, hurt that their largesse would be answered with tragedy, doesn't talk much about her. Her name is unspoken for so long that she forgets. That is the danger. Even she knows this, or maybe only she knows this: That is when you find yourself capable of cruelty, of haunting. When you've completely and forever forgotten your name.

# 14

**"SO WHAT."** A bird call echoed from deep within the classroom forest, and Meg willed her face not to flush—she would not fall prey to that blend of apathy and daring that was a locus of power only in grade school, as the eighth graders before her couldn't yet know. Going into middle schools to teach research workshops like these was the most loathed of the librarians' compulsory tasks, but it was required by the same state arts board grant that had provided funding for a year's worth of acquisitions, so Helen had told Meg and Gil, in her Helen sort of way, to suck it up. Still, the very idea that someone whose entire job training had, until this point, encompassed the ordering, shelving, archiving, and recommending of dusty folios, might be qualified to lead a group of rowdy school children in a forty-two-minute workshop about non-Google researching—a practice that struck the children as being as absurd as say, entering a wardrobe as a means of traveling to another world—was in a way rather cruel. These were children who couldn't read maps, children who lived according to the oral histories of their GPS devices, who saw the city as a series of lists rather than in any particular shape. These were children for whom "history" was something to erase on the search engine before leaving a public computer, for whom "character" indicated the limits of a tweet, for whom "stories" were images translated by filters. Books seemed relentlessly unresponsive to them, ludicrously unsearchable. It wasn't like there weren't any brains in the bunch. It was more that they expected too much too quickly, and while Meg didn't think they were entirely unjustified in their thirst for excess, she did wish there were some way to reach into their heads and massage their cortexes or whatever it would take to get them to slow down enough to absorb the printed word. But that gift, the teaching talent of a Socrates or at least the *Dead Poets Society* guy, was one Meg lacked.

Gil was even worse than Meg, if that were possible, because he thought of himself as being about the same age as the students, and more than the wise librarian with useful information about using the NYPL Digital Map Warper, wished to present himself as a buddy, the cool substitute teacher who said, "Call me Mr. G," winked at the girls, and sat backwards on the chair. Meg thought it best to keep her hostility toward him as masked as possible. Besides, he was her only ally against the "So whats."

The classroom was a forbidding place, with meager natural light and insufficient heat. Leaks dribbled down the exterior wall in lurid orange rivulets. The halls of these public schools deep in the reaches of Brooklyn were all cinder block and flickering fluorescence and broken linoleum, metal detectors at the entrances manned by unsmiling security guards, the kids anarchic with a noisy bravado that made Meg feel faint, so on these days, she wore boots with heels as high as she could muster and stacked her arms with a Wonder Woman's worth of bronze bangles she'd found in Kate's dresser. She'd never seen Kate wear them, but they must have been hers and somehow this helped, both that they had been Kate's and that Kate had not frequently worn them. The mornings before classroom visits were solemn ones in the Brooklyn Collection, with Meg checking her file folder again and again, downing coffee like it would save her. She was probably only imagining the smirk on Helen's face when she waved goodbye. There would be one of the great advantages of life as Head Librarian (but now Helen was saying she felt so terrifically well, that she was sure her work kept her going, and thank goodness that retirement was still a long ways off)—not having to do classroom visits.

Meg loved the city with her whole heart. It was the people she wasn't crazy about.

The feeling was mutual. The eighth graders of PS One-Oh-Something in this pre-pregentrifying swath of Bedford-Stuyvesant cared exactly zero straws for Meg, her prim high collar and severe bun and painterly lipstick and stacks of worksheets, her dour insistence on correct pronunciation. Who was this white lady here, trying to tell them their business, their history, their life stories? When she offered free Brooklyn Collection bookmarks, they scoffed. What use did these children have for a bookmark? Meg could tell, burning in their half-lidded glares, that they would never believe it if she told them she, too, had once been a disaffected youth. That she had felt the same contempt they now felt for everything. That she, too, had thought adults couldn't possibly *get* it. That she was a creature of lust and compassion and fits and foibles, just like them. That she, too, had wanted so much, without knowing exactly what, that she, too, had expected her life to turn out to be extraordinary without any real effort on her part. And that it didn't matter that they didn't care because she would be there, lecturing on building histories and research methods, for exactly five minutes more, at which point she would go back to her life as a grown-up, while they had to trudge on to the cafeteria and high school and the SATs and the rest of puberty. Meg shivered thinking about it.

Still, when the second "Yeah, so *what*?" was lobbed at her, Meg froze, working to not look frightened. Gil took the bullet. "So *what*," he said, leaping off his backwards chair like a spry inspirational substitute teacher, "is that kids like you have made some major discoveries in the history of this city. Did you know that?"

The energy crackled, shifted. The kids' eyes opened slightly wider. Meg stepped back, watching him. The classroom teacher looked up from her desk where she was taking advantage of the library-sent babysitters to grade a stack of papers. Gil and Meg were the only two white people in the room, a phenomenon Meg kept trying to unnotice because it didn't matter, because she was ashamed at herself for even noticing, because she expected herself to be more post-race than that, but which nonetheless made her self-conscious, as if everything she did or said represented more than just Meg herself. She thought, for an instant, of Ellis, of what it would be like to connect her life with the life of a Black man, if it would feel different from a love affair with someone who looked like her, different from dating the Korean-by-way-of-Queens guy she'd been briefly obsessed with, if it was imperialist to even have the thought. What if they had a child, she and Ellis? What would she tell a child, who the world would see as Black, about how to behave, how to speak, how to protect himself? How would she know how to deal with her hair?

Meg shook her head. There was no love, there was no affair with Ellis, and there were certainly no future children. Her frequent Ellis-flashes actually had little to do with the de facto segregation of urban public high schools and everything to do with the heat she felt every time she pictured him—Ellis, Ellis himself—and then, by weird transference, did an extra bit of research as if confused penance, so that, in effect, she had begun lusting for a haunted house.

Gil gesticulated with his pale hands—he had skin so pale his fingers were translucent, pink as prawns—as if communicating in semaphore. "Listen to this, homies"—Meg cringed, but the kids didn't seem to register the word choice as offensive—"Miss Rhys here has been helping one of our library patrons do some research on a really cool, super old house that's not too far from here." Meg stared. Who knew he'd been paying attention? It figured. There were no secrets in the Brooklyn Collection. Miss Rhys. Jesus. "It might even be a part of Weeksville. Tell me you all know about Weeksville, right? No? You *guys*. Dudes, seriously. It was *dope*. It was right around here, a settlement of free African Americans in the mid nineteenth-century. Does that ring a bell? 1850s, 1860s? What was happening at that time? Come on, fam, Civil War, hello? Anyone? Okay, so dig it, this was *before* the Civil War. There were slaves in *Manhattan*, and they had this whole free utopia here in Brooklyn, when it was all farmland, where Black dudes were not only free but owned their own land." Meg watched the students. For some reason her heart was thudding. They betrayed nothing—but they were still, they were listening. Gil! "And then it got forgotten, and then guess who found it again? Some Pratt professor had a theory about where to find it but needed to see from above. So homeboy flew over Brooklyn in a tiny prop plane—pre-9/11, you could do crazy stuff like that I guess—and spotted something weird from the air: Three old houses all crooked, not on the city grid at all. Guess why?" Silence, but with a different texture than before; they weren't bored anymore, they were expectant. "Because they predated the current city grid! They were on what used to be this crazy old farm trail called Hunter-fly Road. And guess who, in the, what, Meg, I mean, Miss Rhys, the 1960s?—uncovered the whole thing? School kids. Students, like you, in your very own neighborhood—they did the first archeological dig."

Well, shit. He had them completely transfixed. Meg knew she should be happy, that, after all, the point was to teach the community about the magnificent treasures of the library and the rich tapestry of their city's history, and that now she could step back and maybe work the slide projector and let him finish up and, soon enough, go to lunch. But there was something that irked her about having done a bad job, having had to be saved by Gil, having not thought to tell the students about the inspiring child archeologists of Weeksville herself. It was her story, and he had stolen it!

The grump followed Meg out of the classroom, growled as she pretended to listen to Gil enthuse about kids high-fiving him on their way out. She stared out the window as Gil drove the library van down Eastern Parkway with the blithe speed of someone to whom nothing bad had ever happened.

The neighborhood they found themselves driving through had two or three selves, none of which Meg was intimately acquainted with. There was Black Crown Heights: Islanders who ran Caribbean food restaurants and sold Jamaican textiles from gritty storefronts, women legendary for their weave, voodoo shops that kept the good stuff (the real stuff) in back for people who knew how to ask, the famous West Indian Day parade—an annual pageant of music and dance and color that made every other parade in the world look positively stygian. Meg had gone to the parade a couple times but never lasted more than a few moments before the sensory load overwhelmed her, and she had to disappear into the first quiet place she could find, usually someone else's church or library branch.

South of the Parkway were the Chabad-Lubavitchers, the ultra-orthodox Jews in their suits and black hats: improbable amounts of children bouncing alongside their improbably young mothers, old men with voluminous beards whispering to their prayer books on the subway, yeshiva boys walking in groups on Saturdays, tzitzit tassels swishing at their sides, speaking a language Meg couldn't quite pin down—Hebrew? Yiddish? Sometimes it sounded like French or Portuguese, or maybe they were polyglots and she really was identifying all those different tongues. Meg harbored a certain appreciation for the Lubavitch devotion to the written word and to costuming—the women dressed in long skirts and dark shades, like Meg herself, except that the younger women had a more carefully curated fashion sense than she did, always looking as put-together as 1950s housewives. Plus they often dressed their kids in matching outfits, which appealed to Meg for a reason she couldn't put her finger on. She knew, somehow— from her mother?—that it was a religious sect focused on the spiritual, though from the outside, seeing the dingy storefront synagogues and covered-up women, she couldn't quite parse it, distracted by bile every time she saw a woman shepherding what she deemed an oppressive number of young.

She felt no chime of sympathy, despite having been raised Jewish-ish—lighting candles and singing prayers in what was probably terrible Hebrew at Hanukkah, devoting a sizable chunk of her adolescence to weeping over *The Diary of Anne Frank* and myopically wishing something dramatic might happen to her someday that would make her childhood journals publishably poignant. But Meg's relationship with her mother's stifled religion was incoherent at best. She liked Woody Allen movies and often imagined she had a cold; she was *that* kind of Jewish. Meg assumed these otherworldly people didn't see her as having any claim to Judaism at all, and in prophylactic defensiveness, she mentally categorized them as something completely different from the Jews she knew, like her childhood neighbor Mrs. Fishman, who said "Oy" a lot and, every Passover, waterboarded a carp in her bathtub before sacrificing it for gefilte fish. So whenever she passed groups of Hasids, she felt more like a befuddled tourist—her messy hair called into relief by the Barbie-like wigs of the young mothers, her lack of comprehension rendering the kosher restaurants and various yeshivas and head-covering shops (not to mention why the women wore wigs in the first place) mysterious—than as if she were among the like-minded.

In the past few years the Northern-most edge of the neighborhood had been addended with hipsters hungry for rentals near Washington and Franklin Avenues, colorful with tattoos and curious hair, locking their fixed-gear bikes to lampposts outside the wine bars and cafés that, to the old guard, had seemed to spring up like mushrooms, growing overnight, potentially poisonous.

The idea of the city was that all these things happened in harmony and it was beautiful. But everyone who actually lived in the city knew it wasn't so simple.

When discussing neighborhoods, one necessarily spoke in code: "Crown Heights is up-and-coming," one white mother at the Brooklyn Children's Museum (plopped oddly in the middle of the neighborhood) might say to another, meaning that artists were moving in, like canaries who would gauge whether the minority populations would quietly decamp as rents increased, à la the Latinos in Bushwick, or staunchly hold their ground, having bought homes in cash and staked their claims more permanently, à la the Chinese in Sunset Park. "I see," the other white mother would respond, "but how are the schools?" Meg had been recently text-harangued by a friend with school-age kids for having made this dismissive observation over birthday drinks for another friend, that people were always saying "But how are the schools?" as a way to not sound racist when talking about neighborhoods; the mother had been silent, but later messaged Meg: *It doesn't make me racist to want Annabelle to go to a good school where they have, like, books in the library. You know?* Meg had apologized with an invisibly insincere emoji. *Of course.* No one was racist, no one craved homogeneity, it wasn't *that*. But.

Meg—thoughtful, analytical, often-self-critical Meg—considered herself complicit in none of this. James had teased her about this recently at an open house, as she grumbled about the willowy, fedora-clad couple who had immediately rented the only decent apartment they'd seen all day. "Hipsters," she'd muttered. "Gentrifiers."

James had laughed at her. "What makes them hipsters and not you?" As if it weren't obvious! Meg was a lifelong New Yorker! Her life wasn't financed by some mysterious benefactor in a way that allowed her to work as an artisanal honey farmer or boutique owner or some other nonjob job, and yes she was white, but she wasn't as white as *those* people, and she liked gritty New York, not just frozen yogurt New York, and anyway she would never wear a fedora. She liked living near books and coffee, was that so terrible? But before she could say any of that, Mr. Hipster had said from beneath his brushy mustache, "We're really still recovering from Burning Man," and Meg had only had to gesture to indicate, "See?"

"So," James had said as they reluctantly left the sunny apartment, leaving Mr. and Ms. Hipster-Hipster to fill out their rental agreement and plunk down their first and last month's rent, "If you hate hipsters so much, why do you have to live in your hipster white person neighborhood? How are you not part of the force of gentrification, *madam?*"

"Oh please, seriously? You and I both know I'm not rich enough to drive up anyone's property values. No one's getting forced out of their family home because a poor old spinster lady is renting a $1,500/month one bedroom."

"So it's because you're not helping the neighborhood to improve."

"Oh! What? See! Oh gotcha there." She'd wagged her finger at him. "You. And why are rich people necessarily considered an improvement? *Sir?* Aren't the poor and crazy people why we love this city?"

James raised an eyebrow. "I suppose so. Then again, I'm sure no one enjoys being poor and/or crazy in order to provide you with some interesting people-watching, but, okay, I take your point."

It gnawed at her, of course it did. What *was* her place in the city? Meg did feel, really, like she had an unalienable right to be able to pick and choose where she lived, or that she *should*, anyway. The fact that her finances were complicating this had made her indignant. And maybe this was exactly her privilege speaking. After all, the instant

Meg had been made to feel that forces beyond her control were shaping her life, she became enraged. It all seemed so *unfair*. And inevitably, just as she was starting to get really heated about it, a patron at the library would ask about the Lenape Indians as if in some secret Jungian rebuke. As if to say: *You know who else has been kicked out of their home? You know who else has watched other people take what they think should be theirs? EVERYONE.*

She thought about the kids in the class they'd just visited, that school that was, as far as she could see, all-Black, that clearly lacked the book-stuffed shelves and computers and art supplies and class pets of the largely white schools they visited in other sections of Brooklyn. If she had children, would she, in complete honesty, want them to be the only white children in a school? What would that mean? How had this happened to their country, that everyone knew that saying a school was all-this or all-that was coded language for a good school or a bad school, a school with resources or without?

Then there was Ellis, who had mentioned in one of their increasingly discursive conversations, that his parents had made a point of raising him not in the Crown Heights house but in a neighborhood where there would be kids of all sorts, but especially kids whose parents believed in good grades, who expected college and graduate school, who shared, in other words, Meg's sense that the world owed them a certain kind of life.

There was something else to it too, though. Meg often felt uncomfortable, out-of-joint, and had thus sought out a life that made her feel okay—the library, her friends, her hours of solitude. You tried to find like-minded people and then found yourself in a life so guarded by those other like-minded people that you couldn't see over their heads, couldn't remember what they were guarding against.

Meanwhile, the library van chugged along the parkway. "You know, we're right by the house," Meg said suddenly to Gil, actually thinking only *Ellis*. "The house I've been researching, the one you were telling the students about." *Ellis*. She invented a way, in a flash, to make it about work: "Want to stop by? He told me he'd be there working on it and to stop by whenever. You could tell me what you think. You've been to the Weeksville Historical Society, right?" Of course he had—he'd gone with Kathryn, the cute children's librarian, to one of the hipster-y Weeksville garden parties that summer, had worn seersucker and done the Charleston and engaged Kathryn in some boozy necking, as Kathryn had whispered to Meg at the next very awkward staff meeting. But it occurred to Meg that Gil really could be of use now (even as she could almost hear James scoffing. *So you asked a coworker to check if it seemed haunted? Was that your version of due diligence?*), with this project that she was having so much trouble seeing clearly. "You have fresh eyes. Maybe you could come take a look, tell me if this house seems like it could have been from Weeksville. Everything Ellis has found suggests it's the same era, and it's really only a few blocks away from the other Weeksville houses. We haven't found any true proof yet, but it's credible enough to—you know, the next step is trying to obtain a grant from the city to investigate if it could become landmarked, become part of the museum maybe, and that could be really great for this family—"

After reading and thinking about it so much, Meg's need to see the house itself was suddenly palpable, tangling with the need to see Ellis; two flavors of lust incongruously braided together. (She texted Ellis—was he there? Were visitors okay?) She wanted to find out if they'd found anything as the contractors scraped away the first layers of the interior, and she wanted Ellis to have all the answers for her, and she wanted to have all the answers for him; she wanted to be consumed by him; she wanted him to sweep her into his arms like Rhett Butler or the hot one from *The Hunger Games*, unable to control himself anymore; she wanted to die in a fire that was Ellis; she wanted to stop thinking about him, to go back to her normal self, to regain her normal brain with its excellent powers of concentration and imagination that made reading difficult books the ultimate pleasure; or wait, no, she only wanted to see the house for herself, of course, it was as simple as that; research purposes only. (His response materialized: Yes. She was welcome.)

Gil was nodding. "You don't have to convince me to play hooky, just tell me where to turn. What do we tell Helen?"

Meg peered at the cross streets and bit her lip. "Um, here I think? Wait no! Here! Here! Right. Sorry. Helen? Tell her we checked into a motel for an hour. Oh watch the road, I'm kidding. We inspired the shit out of the students, and they used their study hall period to learn more, I don't know. It won't take long. Maybe she won't notice. Turn right."

"Okie dokie. You better not be flirting with me, Miss Rhys."

"Oh please. Another right. I prefer Ms., by the way. I'm forty years old, I'm nobody's 'miss.'"

"Because that would be highly unprofesh." Gil moved his hand, and for a second she was afraid he was going to brush her knee, squeeze her thigh, but he only adjusted the rearview mirror, and she felt immediately ridiculous for having had the thought. "And it would seriously bum out this house guy."

Meg's face went tingly. "House guy? Okay, wait, I think this is it! No, keep going. Oh, here it is." She pointed, and they parked halfway in front of a driveway, leaving the blinkers on to hedge their bets, and Ellis was standing out in front, talking to the contractor.

"Yes, the house guy, you know, that guy right there." He tapped on the windshield glass. "The scholarly hunk from the wrong-side-of-the-parkway, who has done more quote- unquote research on this house than anyone ever in the history of the Brooklyn Collection, all while shooting you smoldering looks every time you turn your back because he's secretly in love with you. *That* one."

Meg searched for something in her bag, hiding her smile. "What do you know about the history of the Brooklyn Collection? You were hired about a minute ago. And in case you haven't heard, there's no such thing as love." If he had a response to this, she didn't hear it.

They stepped out of the van in unison, moving with shared purpose, like a third-rate Sherlock and Watson, a pair of junior Miss Marples. Inside the grim school, Meg had not noticed the screaming blueness of the sky, the determined cheer of the sun. It was, in reality, a fine, bright day. The run-down block looked almost beautiful; everything did on a day like that. Including Ellis, facing away from her, as usual.

The haunted house was not at all how Meg pictured it when she was sifting through crumbling journals tattooed with spidery script, squinting at daguerreotypes of unsmiling women in frilled collars. This was no urban Manderley. It was—the house itself, finally, inevitably—rather small, crammed between a forbidding industrial something and a six-flat brownstone with smoke damage like eye shadow ringing the closed-up windows. Meg had seen images of the house but had forgotten to age it in her mind. Somehow she always pictured it still existing in the past, a tidy farm wood frame with green shutters, surrounded by pasture. It must be part of Weeksville after all, if she pictured it like this, so specifically, more like a memory than a possibility. Maybe Kate could see it. Maybe that happened if you were a ghost, maybe you lived in a palimpsest of the city, each era mingling together, the streets parades of period-dress shades. Where had such an image come from otherwise? Because Meg could clearly see a kitchen garden out front, right there where they stood on the sidewalk that bisected the truncated front yard, and beehives and wandering ducks and a listless cow out back where the fields stretched for acres before the next farmhouse. Why now should she hear the clop of horse-drawn carriage, smell the dust rising off the road and the animals, and beyond, something baking in the kitchen? Were these phantoms merely a result of her excellent grasp of history, the spawn of an overactive imagination meeting too many books? Or was it something else?

Maybe Kate was here with her. Maybe that was the sudden peace she felt now. Or maybe it was the broad smile spreading across Ellis's face as he turned and saw her and stepped across the yard to where she and Gil loitered like timid trick-or-treaters. "What brings you here?" Ellis said to her, but in a way that felt like the warmest greeting imaginable.

Meg gathered herself up and resisted the urge to leap into his arms, though he held them close enough to touch her woolen pea coat in greeting. There was no such thing as love. "We were doing a research workshop at a middle school not too far from here, and I realized we were nearby," (oh so casual, as if she hadn't been thinking of him and his proximity the whole time) "and I figured maybe Gil here could give us his impression of the house, as he's coming fresh to it and all." The "us" hung in the air, as if she'd kissed him.

"Oh. Yes." Ellis turned to Gil, a bit stiffly. "Yeah, of course, man! Want to come take a look? It's empty right now, all the tenants have gone, and we've cleaned and stripped the walls. The downstairs kitchen is demolished, so you'll have to be careful but, well, come in, come in." This was being downright friendly, for him. Who knew why she was perpetually drawn to these withdrawn types, these Mr. Darcy-men with their wounded standoffishness? Heaven knew there were easier ways. Surely there existed men who allowed themselves to open, men who could open her. Relationships with them, those friendly, happy-go-lucky types, were probably such joys, brimming with double dates, cheery vacation rentals including boisterous groups of friends, uncomplicated nights spent cuddled up watching things like *Love Actually* without mocking dissections. And yet unmoody men disgusted her for irrational reasons, for no reason, even though she knew, having gone down this road before, that moody men eventually exhausted her with their moodiness too.

She suffered a thrill from the slight smile Ellis allowed her. She followed him into his house. Gil trailed behind, arming the van's alarm with a squawk that was vaguely embarrassing, like a mother clutching her handbag as she walked by a group of slatternly teenagers.

The house felt wrong, Meg could tell as soon as she stepped in. She recognized the buzzing unaloneness. It's what all those novels meant, why everyone was always so freaked out in Shirley Jackson books, Meg realized—this otherworldly feeling, this *thing* you couldn't put your finger on, this uncanny dread that fisted your stomach and wouldn't let go. She swallowed hard. Ellis offered an arm. "Careful. The floor's a mess." She was so startled that she slipped her arm in his, let him draw her closer, the side of her body twinkling almost audibly. He pulled her close, said in a low voice, close enough that she could feel his breath on her ear, "You feel it too. I can tell by your face."

She turned nervously and saw Gil pretending to study a scrap of wallpaper still scabbed on the wall, unsuccessfully hiding a smirk. He didn't seem to sense the malevolent ice in the house, the angry cold that shuddered through Meg. Meg looked up at Ellis wonderingly. "What *is* that?" she whispered.

He shook his head, but she could tell there was some small relief now that they were talking about it, together. Just because a thing didn't make sense didn't mean you had to ignore it. They picked their way into the rubble pile of the kitchen, where the icy anger churned in the air. As if she'd been shoved, Meg leaned into Ellis, feeling faint. The whole room reverberated in a soundless scream, thick with an expectant air of panic, like being in a crowded place where something unspeakable has just happened—it wasn't a sound or a sight, but a deep, palpable unease. Ellis looked for Gil, who had stayed respectfully in the front parlor, peering into the fireplace, and then back at Meg. "It's gotten so much worse since they did the kitchen yesterday," he said quietly but urgently. "We thought that would make it better. The—the—"

"Ghost," supplied Meg.

He shrugged, showing his palms, the sight of which evoked a confused tenderness in Meg. She couldn't trust her emotions right now, awash as she was in so damn many of them. Was this what it felt like to be pregnant? Her mother-friends described the swell of hormones, the high-and-low rush of every-feeling-all-the-time, like PMS but always. Maybe Meg was pregnant with something after all. She tried to breathe, worked to stay calm, to quell the inner voice saying *I am going to fucking freak the fuck out.*

Ellis spoke in a hush, "The worst of it was always in this part of the house. Remember I told you how this first floor apartment was always losing tenants? Some would say it was haunted, a few were downright hysterical, but even the quiet ones always moved out. We thought the demolition would help somehow. Like something was trapped in the walls, I don't know, I know that doesn't make sense, but shit, does any of it? And it's so bad, Meg. The contractor said he can't get his men to work. The other day, one of the guys tripped on a tool he swore he didn't leave on the stairs and damn near killed himself falling down.

He said yesterday paint cans were *literally* flying. Dad was here last night and says he heard a child crying in the room off the kitchen. My father! He's a reasonable, logical guy, trust me."

Meg moved around the room, arms slightly spread, hair pricking all down her neck and forearms. "It's so weird," she whispered.

Ellis nodded. "Weird is the word for it, definitely." He met her eyes and snorted. "I can't believe I'm having this conversation."

She'd heard that sentence before, and on this exact topic, somewhat endlessly in the past ten years. In the aftermath of Kate, she was prone to having unbelievable conversations. She didn't mean to become the Ghost Lady, one never meant to; she'd meant to become the serious, brainy lady who believed only in literature, whose intellect would arm her. She had never been especially drawn to the occult; she'd never huddled under her blankets reading ghost stories as a child; when her erstwhile best friend Madlena had dragged her to a *retablos* shop on the Lower East Side for shrine materials, Meg had been spooked by the eerie flicker of the tall Latino-style yahrzeit candles. She scoffed when white people celebrated Day of the Dead. She never joined her morbid artist friends on their pilgrimages to Green-Wood Cemetery to do headstone rubbings and pose for boozy Instagrams. She hated ghost movies (with the exception of *The Ghost and Mrs. Muir*, a classic about a woman cowriting a book with a ghost—what was not to love there, really?). In graduate school she'd written a lengthy paper debunking Victorian Spiritualists—this, before Kate's death—presenting one of the most persuasive arguments against the so-called ghost conjurers the professor had ever read (or so he scribbled in the margins). And yet.

And yet there had been Walter, a lovely man, with whom Meg had unofficially cohabitated for nearly two years, a brilliant yet nonthreatening physicist with a fascinating reddish beard, whom her parents and nosy bystanders had hoped might be The One, who had one day asked her, curiously, meaning well, the poor man, over breakfast, "Don't you think it's about time you started getting over Kate?"

Meg had stabbed her egg in its over-easy heart. She could still remember the gruesome way it had bled over her plate, the yolky feel of well-meaning-Walter's dumb stare. It wasn't that he was a bad person, or a bad mate even. He had made her that very meal of eggs and coffee! He cleaned up after himself. He asked her questions about her day and at gift-giving times, offered rare copies of her favorite books. He was reverent in bed, worshipful with his too-narrow hands, ridiculous on such a big man but somehow charming. He was forthcoming with affection, with his willingness to be loved, and she had worked hard to appreciate that. And yet, she knew in that egg-stabbing moment, he would never understand. They would never live on the same planet. She'd said, "Of course not. Why would I ever want to get over her? She's my sister."

Walter had leaned over, put his dainty hand on hers, awfully. "She *was* your sister. It's been years since she—since the accident."

Meg had stood up abruptly. It had been five years then. No time at all. There had been no reason her sister should die. There were people like Walter who were allowed to think that death was for the finished, who only knew funerals as underpopulated crowds of bent white heads and bewildered great-grandchildren. Meg was no longer one of his people. Theirs was a culture clash too profound to move past.

Now, here, in a haunted house, Ellis understood why Meg shivered and wrapped her arms around herself; had Meg said, which she wouldn't, "She's here, she's always with me," Ellis would have known she meant Kate, her dead sister, and he would have nodded and maybe he would have said, "So is she," meaning Rachel, his dead wife, and Meg would have nodded. Walter had suggested she try Paxil. They hadn't spoken in years. He was married to another physicist and they'd had twin boys, Meg had heard somewhere. That seemed about right. That seemed, like other people's futures always did, inevitable.

Now Meg could be the one to look into Ellis's eyes and say, "It's okay. It's an okay conversation to have. Something weird is happening in your house. It's not like you're the first or only one to say it. It would be weirder to pretend nothing was happening at all."

Cue Gil, of course, having heard only her last sentence. He arched his eyebrows. She knew she would never hear the end of his teasing; taken out of context, it *had* sounded like something out of the thumbed-through romance novels that warmed library kiosks for an instant at a time before getting checked out to another hungry patron. But she didn't want to explain about the ghost, sensing that Ellis would be even more embarrassed to be thought occult than to be thought in love. She had to let Gil think they were discussing the "nothing that was happening" between the two of them, that she and Ellis were about to fall into a camera-ready, face-smushing, hair-breathing smooch. The whole situation was impossible. Meg flushed and, to avoid Gil, walked past Ellis into the small room off the kitchen. Ellis's arm darted out. "Wait. Wait, Meg, it's even worse in there."

Gil smiled blankly. "Wha-at are we talking about here? The construction?"

Meg stepped through the doorway. There was a nonsensical moment when she wanted to escape her discomfort—they weren't in love! There was no secret affair! What a preposterous thought! Or was it!— enough to prefer that whirlpool of cold and turmoil, as if a restless, angered soul were ping-ponging around in a fury. The wallpaper had been flayed off the wood plank walls, the fixtures stripped, the floorboards partially exhumed, but mostly it was a cavern of raw pain. Meg nearly stumbled backward, whispered without forethought, "What is it you want?"

"What? Meg? You talking to me?" Gil was saying. "We should probably head back to work, you know, if you're all done here . . ." But Ellis was the only one she could see. He knelt before her—she had somehow dropped to her knees—and took her chilled hands in his. Past him she was sure she saw a flicker—it was only an instant—of a foggy figure in a dress darting across the room.

Meg stifled a scream, stutter-stepped backwards, standing up and stepping back and tripping over a loose plank all at the same time. Ellis helped her up, pushed her back into the kitchen, where she turned and closed her eyes and shuddered. They managed their way into the parlor. Gil was pacing nervously near the door, talking to Ellis now, having abandoned hope of getting an answer out of Meg, who was trying to compose herself by leaning on the mantel and doing some yoga breathing, which she sucked at—yoga, calming, breathing, all of it.

"Whoa, Meg, you okay there?" Gil said uncomfortably, and without waiting for an answer, rattled on to Ellis, "Things are always a mess at this stage of a renovation, I'm sure. You guys fixing this place up to sell or what? It'll be really nice, I can tell already." Even Gil, so fearless in the classroom, so blasé so much of the time, sounded shaken as he tried to make casual conversation. So much of the struggle of it all was trying to act normal, not wanting to seem crazy. Or maybe Gil was only reacting to her own weirdness; maybe to him she seemed to have observed some messy construction and contracted a case of the vapors. It had been a mistake to take him here, of course, to think he could protect her somehow. To think anyone could be protected at all.

Ellis spoke, looking the whole time at Meg. "I don't know. Our idea was always to fix it up and sell it, but it's going, uh, weird. Things have gotten really weird." They made their way out of the house—how had people survived on that floor for even one year at a time?—Meg had to go out onto the street in order to breathe.

Gil kept talking, clueless, apparently sensing nothing at all out of the ordinary. "I guess if you found out it was part of Weeksville, it could become part of the historical society? Maybe there would be some funds to restore it? But the thing is—and this is me as a regular dude talking, not as a research librarian, you dig—why even try to landmark it, when you'd probably make a lot more money selling it to some rich Europeans, or like, Chinese investors, right? Just call this Up-and-Coming Park Slope Far North East, right?" Gil's attempt at a joke froze, shattered to the ground. Meg could only stare at him, distracted by the faintest echo of piano music. She cocked her head. "What's that sound? Ellis?"

His eyes were wide. He nodded very slightly. Meg felt an odd pressure at her back, like tiny hands pushing her. Out. They had to get away from that house. She wanted to smile at Ellis but it wasn't working. She couldn't say anything in front of Gil. The whole thing was too preposterous. "We have to go," she managed.

Ellis's eyes bore into hers.

Gil clapped his hands together. "Right! Well! Back to the old grindstone! Good to see you, man," and he shook Ellis's hand awkwardly. On their way out the door, Meg looked back at Ellis. He was watching her so intently she felt naked. She had the thought then, as she had before, that he could do something terrible to her—it was clearer now, like a smell on a freezing cold night, the thought in her head crystallized by being shaken and scared—he could do something terrible. He could gut her. She didn't know what or how, but she also didn't care. There was permission in the thought. It was a good thing love didn't exist, wasn't it?

Back in the van, a predictable conversation unfolded: Gil laughed and noted how weird she'd been acting at the house; Meg apologized, stammered something about how she hadn't had any breakfast and was suffering from low blood sugar. He sounded unconvinced but offered to stop at the grimy-looking Dunkin' Donuts they were driving by, and she laughed at the thought of presenting Helen with a paper crate of sprinkle-covered munchkins, so they decided to go for it. She was grateful to Gil for not pressing her too much, for not taking the opportunity to tease her about Ellis, for making her laugh. She was almost, as a result, able to get through the rest of the day without making too many weird guttural utterances.

She wrapped herself in her routines as if in a blanket. Closed up the Brooklyn Collection. Checked out her books on hold. Rode her bike home, pumping her legs angrily, cursing at every reckless driver. Lugged the bike into her apartment, closed the door, parked the bike against it, started her tea. Petted the cat. (Fuck. Had she been making sure to look for pet-friendly apartments when scouring the real estate sites? She had to admit, somehow she had kind of forgotten about the cat.) Took her tea and sat in her chair and closed her eyes. Waited. For something. A message, a visit, a feeling of peace. After about thirty seconds of that, she'd pop up and grab her laptop and start looking up more about Weeksville, more about the era of Ellis Williams's house. As if she might find something, anything at all, that would crack the story. She listened to Civil War–era music. She squeezed her eyes shut and tried to imagine life then, what it was like, what a person might think about, how a person might die, why they might decide to haunt a house.

Of course, Meg had always been prone to obsessing. Maybe this was why she and Kate had understood one another so well. They would share a run of chapter books, passing them up and down between bunks, reading each of the series in a row, Kate always one book behind Meg, taking turns pitching to a higher reading level ("What is 'ejaculating'?" Kate wanted to know while struggling through *Anne of Green Gables* at age eight, causing Meg to explode into laughter, and then when calm, to provide the unsatisfactory answer "speaking with great emphasis") or a lower one (Meg could read two *Sweet Valley Twins* for every one Kate got through, but tried to pace herself out of charity). There was a month or two of tropical fish mania (then the years of waiting for the fish to die so they could stop spending their Sunday nights cleaning the stupid tank); a good six months of detective work fueled by *Harriet the Spy*, a pair of composition notebooks, and some mysterious sounds that echoed down from the upstairs neighbors' bedroom at night. They were a team, Meg and Kate, Kate and Meg. James they loved(ish), but as an afterthought, a little brother sidecar to their bicycle built for two.

In later years Meg's tendency to fixate on things began to seem less precocious and more plain old obsessive. There was the frantic, *By Grand Central Station I Sat Down and Wept*–style love for the Swedish exchange student who lived in 6C for junior year and who promptly disappeared into the preinternet ether upon his return to Scandinavia. She was sure she would die of it. Then just as passionately and overwhelmingly came the decision to become a librarian, which prompted visits to every single branch of each of the three library systems in the city (New York City, Queens, and Brooklyn), as well as research facilities in every major university in the Tri-State area.

When Kate died, no one was surprised that it—her death, the Katelessness of the world—became Meg's new hobby; she was the one who convinced their family lawyer to press charges on the livery car driver; she was the one who dug up his previous DUI; she was the one who—it must be admitted—waited for his wife outside of the doughnut shop where she, the wife, worked, who cornered her one dark night. Meg was the one who insisted they keep Kate's ashes. There were so many things that happened when someone young died unexpectedly, so many odds and ends to deal with all at once. Had Kate wanted to be buried in the cemetery in Queens where their grandparents had purchased plots when they retired? Did she want to be embalmed—that seemed unlikely, given her ecological bent—or cremated? Who could say? Each option seemed equally ghastly. The only thing they wanted was to not dispose of Kate at all.

And that was only in the first few weeks. After that, there were her things to remove from her rental apartment, her student loans to deal with, the endless detritus of a life interrupted. Picking up Kate's dirty clothes off her floor was a particular torture that Meg insisted on inflicting upon herself, deconstructing the mounds of clothes Kate had dropped here and there, shaking out the dresses that looked as if Kate might have simply vanished while wearing them, sniffing them all as she went. A postcard came to their parents' apartment the day after the funeral (it had been packed with sobbing young people, most of whom Meg had never seen before), reminding Kate that she was due for a dental visit. Meg was the one to call the dentist office and tell them to stop sending the damn cards, angry that they hadn't somehow known, that they didn't somehow check to see if people had been killed in a terrible accident every time they sent out reminder postcards with clipart of huge smiling teeth clutching scepter-sized toothbrushes. Meg stormed the bank, armed with the proper paperwork and appropriate amount of Kleenex to get the remaining money out of Kate's bank account. Meg convinced their parents to send the money to Greenpeace because Kate had sometimes volunteered for them. Meg (having guessed her password on the third try) went through Kate's email and MySpace accounts. Meg assigned herself the job of giving away Kate's clothes and books and then kept most of them. Meg, more than any of them, adopted the identity of Kate's mourner.

They were all heartbroken, of course they were. But for some reason, Meg sunk into it more; or maybe the very fact that she got so sunken down in her grief freed the rest of them, or required them, to adopt stiff upper lips, to say things like "Nothing like getting back into the swing of things," (from their father, when he went back to work the next week, not knowing what else to do with himself) or "God never gives you more than you can handle," (the worst kind of pablum, and from their mother of all people). It was, after all, kind of a luxury to be able to wallow so melodramatically. She had the time. She had the freedom. She had the strength, in an odd way—she could go to her deepest well of grief and still be able to come back up, which she must have known on some level even while wallowing in the thick of it—and which made it safe to descend. Her only responsibilities were to rage and cry and disbelieve and miss and sleep until her body ached and then to start the process again, to rage and cry and disbelieve and miss. It was inhuman, unbearable, unbelievable, how much she *missed*, how even when she considered the best possible outcome, allowed herself to believe that one day she would begin to feel less assaulted, she knew that the missing would never end. There was no way it *could* end. And maybe part of what she was mourning was not just her sister but herself, the self she had once been, the self un-waterlogged by misery.

It was only after months of this tonic immobility that she stopped wearing black like a Victorian widow, that she started seeing people again in any context other than work, going places besides the compulsory, stepping back into the flow of life in the city, feeling that it was permitted to smile or laugh or lose herself for a few hours in a fictional world. Books, more than ever, became her salvation. In those first, raw years, the remaining Rhyses found themselves gathering often but rarely talking about anything deeper than the weather: Her mother snuck to *shul* to pray; her father numbed himself with hours of television, gallons of wine, and an unwholesome attention to James' NYU career; James, meanwhile, paid almost no attention to said NYU career at all, descending instead into an oneiric underworld of clubs and party drugs; Meg read.

Oddly, she craved books about love, probably because she understood that she would never feel it again, because it suddenly seemed as foreign and far-fetched as another planet. She spent weekends immobile in bed, rereading *Madame Bovary* and *Anna Karenina*, until that wasn't enough, as if her senses were permanently dulled. She craved books about lust, the more depraved the better: *Lolita* gave way to *The*

*Sexual Life of Catherine M.*, novels with names like *Endless Love, Enduring Love, Days of Abandonment*. It wasn't that the death and the sex felt connected in a specific way, not yet; only that she needed to shock her brain into something else as elemental as grief, something as difficult to talk about and as dangerous. And since she wasn't yet ready for fucking, she read about it.

In the intervening years, other obsessions had sprung up—for a while it was, actually, fucking, a desperate hunger for one-night stands, though she eventually moved on to long-distance biking, which felt just as satisfying—but nothing ever eclipsed Kate. When Meg had first started to sense Kate in her home—it began with hearing her voice, feeling a cool hand pressing her arm the way Kate did when she really wanted to make a point—she had thrown herself into ghost research (coming to the conclusion that everyone who believed in ghosts was a kook, not that this made *her* believe any less).

A few men had worn the mantle of her obsession for brief periods. Walter, whom she'd been with the longest, had made her feel the least obsessive of all, which had probably been part of the appeal of the whole even-keeled affair. The worst obsession had been, naturally, a married man, but in the end even Meg hadn't had the constitution for that; as a reader of fiction, she had too much empathy for every character involved to be able to forget about the wife for long.

Then Ellis Williams had alighted. Now Meg spirited home noncirculating volumes of local history and ancient journals, pored over Weeksville census reports, read nineteenth century *Brooklyn Daily Eagle* articles on her laptop until her retinas burned. She squirreled away every clue or potentially interesting story she found (Smallpox outbreak! A burnt-down orphanage!), imagining that she and Ellis would meet to revel in each small victory over coffees in the library café, and things would feel buzzy in that thrilling way, like when one *New Yorker* article she read happened to dovetail in poetic and unlikely ways with something her mother had just emailed her, and suddenly the whole world had felt connected and magical, and it would be more so this time because it was shared with Ellis, because it would cause Ellis to smile, to lean forward, to burn his gaze into her eyes in thanks.

How happy she would be to present some small offering to Ellis, some chance of dispelling some iota of his pain.

And yet. James' question was valid: then what? Would the voodoo ladies on Franklin Avenue be able to use some Yoruba magic that would, like a realtor burning a vanilla candle, make the house salable again?

So Meg sat with her laptop in her grandmother's old chair—her thinking chair, her talking-to-Kate chair—closed all the windows on the computer and reopened the browser, the Google bar suggestively blank. She typed in "How to Talk to a Ghost." The first entry was a blog called, naturally, *How to Talk to a Ghost*, curated by a lady in upstate New York whose profile picture skewed heavily purple. The posts were long and unfortunately fonted in lavender Comic Sans on black, so to avoid feeling as though she were having a seizure, Meg selected all the text and pasted it into a text file. Once she had, though, she lost herself in the blog. Post after post detailed a story of a famous haunting or someone who had come to the blogger with a story of a ghost. There was no inkling of either skepticism or boosterism; the author made no claims of being a seer or a ghost-hunter, called herself merely a scribe. Here was a Midwestern farmhouse beset by flying objects, the result of a murdered farmhand seeking retribution. There was a Scandinavian chalet, given to moaning through the outmoded talking tubes once used to summon the servants—a child getting lost during hide-and-seek and gruesomely dying at the foot of the stairs. Now a city subway tunnel troubled by ten times the usual volume of collisions—crushed transit workers could really hold grudges—and then a Parisian apartment, left locked for decades, only to be opened when new neighbors noticed a strange chill and persistent smell of almonds—for courtesans murdered by their husbands did not like to be ignored.

Meg had read her share of haunted house stories, of course, but the ghosts never turned out to be very effective at staying ghosts. *The Turn of the Screw*, *The Little Friend*, *The Fall of the House of Usher*— the hauntings rang true, but then disappointingly, the novelists were too urbane for such magic, and the "ghosts" always turned out to be manifestations of characters' psychological distress. There was never a conclusion, never a ghost brought to rest. It irked Meg to think that her reality was less sophisticated than the books she liked—her, literary Meg, living a life in *genre*! And yet, her ghosts were so persistent, and her belief that she was not insane so firm, that the online trove of earnest ghost tales struck her as immensely helpful.

When dealing with a ghost who is causing mischief, instructed the violet blogger in her matter-of-fact FAQ, it is best to set aside judgment and think clearly. 1) What does the ghost want? 2) How can you give the ghost enough of what he or she wants to quiet his or her restless spirit down? In most cases (Meg read) the ghost just wants to be left alone in its home, like an elderly person resisting removal to a nursing facility. Is there a way to allow, the upstate spiritualist urged her readers to consider, the ghost some space? To cede some bit of turf? "Otherwise you shall find yourself battling forever more, like the Israelis and the Palestinians, or Islanders and the Sea," concluded the FAQs. Meg's eyes ached from staring at the screen for so long in her dark apartment. It was nearly midnight. She couldn't tell whether the pronouncement she had read was profound or completely unhinged.

She sighed, closed her computer, and took the cat into her arms. "Okay, Wolfy," Meg murmured. There she was. The unsettling Williams house visit still churned in her gut like an emotional appendicitis. Meg paced around her tiny living room, stroking Virginia Wolf's fur, flashing for the millionth time to the image of Kate holding that same cat, scrawny and greasy as it was then.

"Let's think. Wolfy? Think with me. Kate, are you here? You guys, help me, okay?" A raucous peal of laughter unfurled up from somewhere and Meg froze—*Kate?!*—only to realize it was the people downstairs. There was apartment living for you—just when you were feeling so alone you were asking your cat and ghost for help, there was a reminder that you were never alone at all, which somehow made your home feel emptier than ever. Meg shook her head, continued in her regular conversational volume, pacing around noisily, because—Fuck 'em. "Lots of people have died in that house, probably. So why does this one hang around, haunting the keeping room? What does it want from us? What can we give it?"

Her answer came in the form of a thumping so loud Meg gasped. She stopped walking, dropped the cat, who glared at her before stalking to the olive-colored velvet loveseat. There it was again—THUMP. THUMP. THUMP. Meg gasped again, but now she was murmuring: "Those *ass*holes." Admittedly, she had been pacing around and it was late. But they had been vibrating the entire building with their fucking construction for weeks, adding their stupid door, getting ready for their stupid baby, filling the air with their stupid life debris. Meg took a deep breath, then headed for the door and stomped downstairs.

M-name—Marlene? Mabel?—opened the door. She was smiling, wearing pajamas, wooden spoon in her hand. The smell of baking cookies swarmed like a virus. "Hi, Meg!" the neighbor chirped.

Meg was taken aback by the friendliness. She blinked at M-name. Maybe it was Melissa. Melinda. Something perky and fun. Mandy? "Okay, why are you thumping on the ceiling? I mean, I know it's late, but I'm not exactly having a party up there. If you guys have a problem, you can come up and talk to me like adults, you know."

The husband appeared behind M-name. "Hiya Meg," he said. "Can we give you some cookies? Someone's nesting!" He held a hand parallel to his wife's head and then pointed at it with the exaggerated motions of a corny comedian.

M-name smiled indulgently and then reached out to Meg, who flinched. "Oh honey, we didn't thump on the ceiling. You mean like with a broom?" She mimed the action with the spatula in her hands, apparently unaware that it looked exactly as if she were giving the utensil a rigorous hand job. "We wouldn't, you know us! We would never!"

Meg *didn't* know them actually, other than that they were the kind of people who said things like "You know us!" She let it slide. "Oh. You didn't?" They looked at each other and shook their heads. The husband disappeared into the kitchen. Meg flushed. "God, sorry. I— it sounded so much like someone was banging on my floor. I guess it could have been from upstairs? God, that's so weird. I'm—sorry, I must have seemed really rude." The husband rematerialized holding a paper plate of warm cookies. "Oh no. No, no. I couldn't."

"You have to!" said the husband.

"Otherwise we'll bang on the ceiling all night!" chimed in the wife, and they both chuckled. Meg mumbled a thank you and another apology and another thank you and backed down the hall. She was properly mortified by the time she was back upstairs and slumped down onto her floor, ignoring the cat who came over to sniff the cookies. She was that lady. She was the crazy old maid in the attic, staging her own personal *Wide Sargasso Sea* right there in Prospect Heights. She was—

*Thump. Thump. Thump.* A thunderous, muffled thumping, not, she realized now, from the floor, but from—where? Meg pressed her ear to the interior wall, the exterior wall, stuck her head out the balcony door. The thumping was there, everywhere, and getting louder, and coming from nowhere in particular. She curled up in her chair and, trembling, hid like a child.

If there had been a way for Meg to blast her own door, to take up another square foot of space in the world, she would have. But Meg knew there was no opening one door without shutting another. For there they were, alive, stupidly, showily, all of them alive—Kate's boyfriend, Kate's sister, their brother, their parents, the downstairs neighbors and their unborn baby who would someday shriek in the echo-y alley, a one-hundred-year-old woman in the Bronx who consumed only tea, an eighty-five-year-old grandfather in Bensonhurst who never took his cholesterol medication, teenaged junkies who daily attempted murder on their own cellular structures, Ellis Williams—all of them, eating and sleeping and riding the subway, racking up library fines, wearing sandals, surrounded by ghosts they worked hard to ignore. For now, alive.

# 15

FIRST IT IS FEELING TIRED. She is so tired. She can't remember ever being so tired. Then a fever. She lies on her pallet. They try to move her to a bed. She doesn't want a bed; she wants her pallet and her quilt in the keeping room that is hers. She wants to stay in there with the door closed, the warmth from the hearth whispering through it. Her body aches. Her head aches. She hears murmurs—*pox*—and the word is leaden inside of her, a swallowed pill of dread. Not the hot fear of fire but worse, like she's done something wrong, been careless in her breathing.

Smallpox has been gusting through town, but no one thinks to ask if she has been inoculated like the other sisters, like most of the native children have. Something has gone wrong, and now she has the disease that filthy people get, the disease of the poor. She is disgusted with herself as she writhes in pain. In two weeks she's covered in blisters, transformed from the pretty girl she hadn't noticed she was into a monster, a tree trunk, a warning. *President Lincoln had smallpox and lived:* somehow this information sticks with her, and she holds it like a locket. She isn't even afraid of dying. She is afraid she will infect the other children, and the family will never forgive her. She is afraid she will go blind. She doesn't go blind. She does die, though. If she'd gone blind, would she be blind as a ghost? This is a thought that is often with her. So there, she is thankful for some things. She can see.

She can see her rope pallet and quilt being burned. The room is left open for a week even though it is winter. Though the Jenkins are a modern, scientific type, a witch healer is brought in to purify the space. *What can it hurt?* reasons Mrs. Jenkins, who is understandably shaken.

Death is a disappointment. She's been told there is a place called Heaven. She's been told about a wonderful land, all fluffy and bright, humming with angels. Part of her has been expecting to meet a mother and father on a big shiny cloud. Harps and wings. Milk and honey. God, maybe, looking all rosy and welcoming, like Santa Claus. All the angels from the Bible skipping around, maybe playing with a hoop or ice skating. Grandparents and aunts and uncles and cousins, brothers and sisters. A whole big family. They would explain to her what went wrong, the awful reason they couldn't keep her. How they tried. How they've been waiting for her. There would be warmth and light and peace.

But there is no one on any other side waiting for her. Of course. She has never had any people. Why should she have people now. There is no one to welcome her over. Maybe this is why she never ends up leaving. Or maybe there was never anywhere else to go.

At the Orphan Asylum everyone believes in ghosts. They have to. They believe in everything. God and angels and the devil. Someone obtains a page from a new magazine. They huddle over a painting of a fat, pink-faced white man in a red hat. They study it. Then they believe in Santa Claus too. They believe in everything there is to believe. Because why not. Girls see the ghosts of their mothers every thunderstorm. What else have they got to do?

The orphans' ghosts are see-through people, shimmery selves in bedclothes. They float around. They moan. They have wisdom to share, like the meaningful spirits in Mr. Dickens's Christmas story. They speak in the mournful creaks of settling houses. In their world, everything is quiet and everything makes a lot of sound. There are no machines whirring and radios yelling and phonographs playing, like there are later. When she is a child, there are none of these things. There are noisy wooden floors and the sizzle of oil lamps. There are horses clomping. They yank rattly carriages. The air is noisy with locusts and dust. The night is quiet with locusts and ghosts.

The air in her house is now never still, and she is the air and it buzzes. If she still had feelings, she would long for the stillness. If she were still a child, she would pad around the house on child-ghost feet. But it's not like that.

Instead she stays in the keeping room. She is surprised, at first, that they let her, that no one sees or feels her. But they don't seem to, and she gets used to this. She has always been shy. The ability to observe completely undetected suits her.

She has lived in the house for only a year. But it is a child-year. An eternal year. She plans to stay forever. When she dies, she is eleven about to never turn twelve, and she knows what all children know, that time works differently at different times. That this year is more than a year. That this year is her life. That more than one thing can be happening at once. So she stays in the year forever. As if the year were a new village in which to live. She becomes fluent in the language of its novelty, a world she exists inside of as a deep sea diver stays alive in a bathysphere, dangled in the deep but not *of* it.

She inhabits this year of her life, this time when everything seems possible. This is the year she is sent to school and then comes home to furtively teach lessons in the yard, bossing around pinecones with what turns out to be natural authority. In this same way she inhabits the house. She holds her doll. She holds her book. She clings to it, reads it again and again, studies it harder than she's ever looked at anything in her life. Dr. Smith always said it was important that they read and write, that they learn a trade. In this way she will be able to build a life for herself; this is what she is told again and again. The book's ghost lives here too, a quiet friend. The doll's ghost.

There is no leaving the house. The keeping room is her place. She watches the sisters grow older. She watches the buttoned-up dresses get passed down to the smaller girls. She watches the salons continue in the parlor. Works up her nerve to join in and sing, too late, too late. Colored men do end up joining the war, including, to her surprise,

Jack the farmhand. The mass migration back to Africa never really takes hold. The Civil War ends, of course, and Emancipation stands, more or less. It is difficult to know if the country's wound has healed completely, or if it ever can. Homes have long memories, as she is in a unique position to know. History doesn't go anywhere. She feels this intimately, viscerally, that time is not a continuum but a substance, a quality of air. But maybe this is difficult for the living people to see.

The eldest girl gets married, moves out. There is a plague among the honeybees. The two middle sisters have a falling-out. One emigrates to Manhattan, is scarcely heard from again. The city creeps closer. The farms shrink back, like ice melting on the surface of the skating pond. How they love skating on the pond that winter, that one winter when she and the ice and the countryside all exist at once. That winter all any of the girls can talk about is skating, skating. The newspapers announce with mock gravity that the town "*has contracted ice skating fever.*"

She watches new crazes grip the town. She watches the bridge stretch across the East River like a greedy hand reaching for the jagged rock candy of Long Island. She watches the skating pond get filled in, disappear beneath asphalt. The eldest daughter moves back in, takes over the house.

This is her room. This is her door. Her pallet goes here, in the spot warmed by the kitchen hearth. Her quilt goes here. She goes here. She stays here. Even as the kitchen sounds and smells change. Even as there is more buzzing and clanging, more machinery, more lights and for longer, until it seems that it is never dark at all, light-bulbs hissing like cicadas trapped in terrariums, even as electricity winds through the walls like sparking kudzu. The icebox disappears. Shelves attach to the walls like barnacles. People coming and going, stomping, thumping, wearing less and less, clad in fabrics that seem unlike fabric at all and more like—what? Like reptiles, maybe, or some other smooth and unwelcoming creature.

The eldest daughter dies and the house is sold. The land conveyance updated with spidery script on a rectangle of paper. The rosebud wallpaper is torn off, walls denuded. The eldest daughter sulks in the upstairs bedroom briefly before dissolving, welcomed to the other side, probably, by her waiting relatives. Exactly what she herself does not have. The city grid chops the land into squares. Winding, lawless Hunterfly Road grows faint, nudged aside by the new parkway. Huge block buildings erupt across the street like a giant's lair. Other houses she knows as a child, where the family's friends live, where the kind nurse who tends to her lives, come crashing down or empty out and have their windows and doors boarded up, bandaged, silenced, like children going blind from smallpox. The church alone stays, almost a miracle.

City noise swells. At first she thinks she is imagining it, conjuring it out of decades of homesickness for Manhattan. But no, the city has followed her across the river and through the wilderness and all the way to this farmhouse, like a stray cat that can never really be left behind. Once a window in the house breaks—riots, a mob, not coming for her this time but still an angry mob, still a roiling, volcanic riot, the worst of people revealed—she has that familiar feeling, that knowledge that the city is over, the city is finished, the city is burning to the ground. Human civilization has failed. It is time to think of something else. The way she screams is that her whole being vibrates and rackets around the room like an electrical storm.

For the most part she just is. She is the room. The room is her.

In New York the neighborhood is always changing. Sometimes someone will die and immediately disappear, maybe welcomed into a secret afterlife club she is not invited into. But there are plenty of disgruntled souls who stick around, who brush past each other like strangers on a ferry platform, hurried and busy and inwardly focused. It's Brooklyn; there's a lot of them. Measles ghosts moaning and rashy, Spanish Influenza ghosts listlessly bobbing on the breeze. There are Plague ghosts haunted by their own decimated selves. Cholera ghosts wheezing in the wind. Consumption ghosts, barely wisps of anything. There are Yankee soldiers and Dutch farmers and Natives faint as onionskin paper. There are young men still angry at being lynched. There are women stunned at having died in childbirth. There are 1970s activists so noisy it's almost as if they still have bodies. There are children and old people and babies, and if you paid attention to all of them, you'd lose your mind.

After all, being a ghost is uncomfortable. You are every version of yourself at once. The baby version swarmed by inarticulate urges. The dying version dizzy with fear. You are your emotions and you are your own wordless ways of experiencing things. So it is no wonder that ghosts are known to act out. But only the really deranged among them actively wish to haunt. This is how she feels about it, even now attached to her good behavior that Dr. Smith so praised. She is quiet and polite. Mostly she keeps to the keeping room, where it is warm, where it is quiet, where it is hers.

But she has a flair for drama, as she always has. She has always wanted to be noticed.

Time swells around her. The room's name is changed, tonelessly, from the keeping room to the mudroom, or the office, or worst of all, "the spare." Machines buzz. Vinyl wallpaper plasters over the ivy pattern, over the secret note one of the sisters wrote to another sister in a closet. Paint adheres to decades of penciled growth charts. At some point, the crumbling fireplace starts to belch smoke into the house, collapses into itself like a bad snow fort. Someone replaces the chimney, unearthing the outgrown shoes the family had bricked in to ward off evil spirits who might wish to burn the house down, and, like fools, discarding them. Eventually the hearth is scraped out and filled in, even stupider.

The house is sliced and patched and torn open and stuck back together, as if undergoing sloppy surgery at the hands of a traveling medicine man, a con artist with a saw. The man comes who tries to make it three houses. The staircase is blocked off by heavy doors. She can feel the house choking, its airways clogged by carpet and mailboxes, its throat pierced by lock chains. The attic is given a slipshod bathroom. A rickety kitchen is plugged into the second floor, in what was the largest bedroom. At night, she can hear the hot plate sizzling up there. She spends several decades preparing herself for an electrical fire.

She is about a teaspoon-full interested in the living. They seem overly fleshy, shameless about being alive in a way that is slightly disgusting, shedding skin and nail clippings and hair like self-satisfied confetti. *Whee, we're alive, hurrah for us!* She doesn't bother them much. It would never occur to her to try to scare anyone. She watches them, that's all. She likes children, especially the very young ones, who don't fear her. They sense her and they don't fight it, as if they were still close enough to what came before to remember the other side. There is one little boy who adopts her as a playmate. They race up and down the stairs, play chase in the backyard. He never tries to tell her she doesn't exist. People often do this, without realizing it is quite a rude thing to say to a ghost. Sometimes she thinks he is the best friend she's ever had. But then she suffers that inevitable tragedy: he grows up, gives her the cold shoulder, moves away.

People use the ground floor as their whole home, couples and sometimes a small family. They sleep in the mother and father's bedroom. They complain about how small the closet is because they all seem to have the wardrobes of kings. Where the upright piano always stood in the parlor is now usually a hulking piece of furniture with a flickering moving-picture box where the people watch stories about ghosts and laugh or shiver.

While still alive, she doesn't tread across the floor long enough to wear it down, but the mother she lives with does. The floorboards in the kitchen retain that mother's habitual path, sing it with a creak. It is not the grease of her skin that smooths the window jamb where the sisters lean, watching the boys in the fields. Still she leaves a mark.

She doesn't mean to make the keeping room cold, but she does mean to keep it quiet, to rustle just a bit when the jangle gets to her. She makes her mark on the bones of the building. Everyone who ever lives in a house does. It would be silly to deny it.

Contractors know. It's hardest to hide from them. They tromp through soon after the last couple leaves the apartment. They measure and take notes and rub their whiskers. Hiding from a contractor is like hiding from a priest or a doctor. There's no point. They read her markings like an expert animal tracker. They are not impressed or scared or sentimental. But they do know.

*Oh*, says the foreman, slamming open the door—*her* door—stomping across the threshold, staring right through her until she fears she'll dissolve. It is not a fear of being discovered so much as it is shame. (If he can see her, does he see her smooth or pox-scarred?) This paw-fisted pale giant says, *I see your problem right here.*

*You do?* says the other man, sounding surprised.

He does?

He nods. He is staring into her eyes. She knows he isn't going to say what he knows, but only, *Foundation trouble. See it all the time in these old houses. Need to shore it up is all. This room here was a later addition, and they did it themselves most likely, and it's sagging, so the whole first floor is unsettled.*

Unsettled. He can't say the real problem because then the man will think he's crazy and won't hire him. But he has to know the real problem to be able to fix it, and the man who also knows, though he also won't say it, has to know that he knows. This is how people work. The foreman knows how to fix the house so it won't sag and also so people won't be afraid. He means to dig up her buried treasure, to tear down her door, to flatten her room. He means to make her leave. He means to kill her again.

But he better not. He better stay *out*!

She slams every door shut.

# 16

**THE DOOR OPENED**, Meg looked up, felt her whole body brighten. They had been texting rather intensely since exchanging numbers, and via text had gotten chummy, their friendship, or whatever this was, fast-forwarded by the tiny glowing words. The text had strayed from official historical research territory into general friendliness, but Meg wasn't sure how that might translate into real life.

"Hello, Mr. Williams. Nice to see you again." She tried to keep her voice measured. When you'd been Meg Rhys for as long as she had, you knew how to express your interest in a tamped-down way, cordial but not cloying, never *too* open, *too* vulnerable, but friendly, cautiously probing for the degree of returned friendliness—all of this coiled into a "hello," like a snake in a prank can.

"Meg," he said without his usual ironic reserve, coming close. Her heart flip-flopped. "I'm so sorry. About the other day. The house. It's—it's fucking weird, right? I'm sorry if you were—scared."

Meg had been—was still—terrified. But she was also Meg. So she smiled with her lips closed and made a near-laugh sound in her throat and said, "Scared? Me? Of course not. I'm used to a little haunting now and then. All part of a day's work."

His eyes crinkled around the edges, and he patted her hand—quickly—once.

She was thankful: that it was a chilly day, so that the Brooklyn

Collection's clanking heat would strike him as cozy rather than oppressive; that she had worn this particular sweater, which she knew set
off the color of her eyes and hugged her curves; that she had just applied crimson lipstick *and* consumed a breath mint; that she had, that
morning, enjoyed a jocular exchange with Kate, imbuing the balance
of the day with unparalleled lightness.

Ellis looked not at her eyes but down at the desk between them
like a teenager. He held out to her something that resembled a joint,
or no, a rolled piece of paper; she took it, their hands brushed, she
moved it quickly to her face and unrolled it and opened her eyes wide.
"This is fantastic!"

He explained: he had trekked back to the Department of Buildings to talk, this time, to the right guy in the right office, and a
Crypt-keeper-looking dude had finally dug up this certificate of occupancy (what she held was a mimeograph, as if even the historical
records existed only within layers of the past), which meant that
they finally had the name of the man who had purchased the land
on Holland Avenue and first built a house on it—a three-story wood
frame, what do you know—which meant they now had more or less
the name of everyone who had ever owned the house.

"I don't know, maybe now you can help us find out if this dude was
murdered or something? Or anything about him? His family stayed in
the house for a long time, apparently. Or maybe it was someone else, of
course. I don't know, maybe this doesn't help anything at all."

Meg clapped her hands, as if to shock him out of his torpor. "Yes!
Don't you see? This is wonderful!" Her voice was saturated with a false
optimism, but she couldn't seem to tone it down today—she felt a nagging responsibility to make things okay for him. It was part of her job,
sure, to assist the patron with his research, but if Meg was being honest
with herself (which occasionally she was), she recognized something in
Ellis, a subterranean sadness that spoke to her own. The physical Ellis
before her (an appealing enough physical form, to be sure) was only
the plot and beneath roiled subtext, waiting for a reader. Meg pushed
her glasses up her nose. "If we have his name," she said, watching Ellis
smile, as if despite himself, at her dorky enthusiasm, "we can look him

up in the census reports and find out what he did for a living, and his family's names. And if anything crazy happened to him, it's probably mentioned in the *Brooklyn Eagle* archive or something like that. This is great news, is what I'm saying. This has gone from a real-estate re-lated mystery to an excavation of a life story, and I have to admit, I'm partial to people." Her eyes flicked to his, his eyes warmed then flicked away. Had they officially converted from conversation to flirtation yet? Meg blinked, tried to focus. She brushed her fingers over the name. "Jacob Jenkins," she said. "Pleased to make your acquaintance."

She moved away from the podium and beckoned for Ellis to fol-low. "Sounds Dutch, doesn't it?" she said over her shoulder. "Makes sense, there were a lot of Dutch farmers around at that time. Holland Avenue. I get it." Meg perched on the stool in front of the computer, the exact spot where they'd first met. Ellis stood behind her. The pair of undergraduates who had been whispering over Whitman left the room (leaving the rare *Leaves of Grass* edition spread-eagled on the table, the way they probably left their "going-out" clothes wadded in their boozy wake), and Meg and Ellis were alone.

Meg expended much too much energy managing her posture on the rickety stool—balancing in a way that flattered her figure, not that she *cared* how she *looked* of course but rather out of a desire to main-tain her core strength, and at the same time, not wanting to appear *too* uptight—and thinking about where Ellis stood in relation to her burning body. He had positioned himself close behind her, but not too close. Anyway, she tapped quickly on the keyboard and made a *voila* flourish with her hands when it appeared on the screen—the census listing for Jacob Jenkins. "Oh my God, look!" she cried. Old man Jen-kins, it turned out, had been a full-time farmer who purchased the land from James Weeks, the former dockworker who had founded Weeksville. "Weeksville, we were right! And look—not Dutch."

Ellis squinted. "A Negro," he read, a small smile playing at the edg-es of his mouth. "A free Black landowner. Look at that."

"Now *that* is a story." Meg tapped at the screen with the little scroll of paper. "And look at his handwriting," she said, running a finger over the Spencerian script on the land conveyance. "He was a gentleman."

Ellis leaned in closer to see better and Meg's heart stopped. He smelled like soap and coffee. She was close enough to see the stubble on his cheek, which she studied, as if she might identify a pattern, a code, a message hidden in the hairs. But this wouldn't do. Meg didn't believe in love. She believed in research. She stood up, offered him the stool, invented an invisible, urgent task elsewhere.

He stayed. She returned after helping a flock of grad students and settling herself somewhat, showed him where he could find more records on good old Jacob Jenkins. Now and then she jumped up to extract from a filing cabinet an obese folder of clippings on this neighborhood or that event. Here was an editorial on rural Brooklyn's response to the harebrained idea of building a bridge between Brooklyn and Manhattan. Here was a series of letters written by New York City abolitionists, including Weeksville residents and a "JJ" that might well have been their man Jenkins? But might not have? At one point Ellis said, "This stuff seemed really boring when I was going through it with my dad," and Meg pursed her lips to curtail the grin. "It's all a bit better when you have some context," she allowed. It was only a fraction of what she meant, what she could never quite articulate about her work, about these moments—they were, in fact, otherworldly for her, transcendent. It was the closest she got to religion; it was the way she understood the world, or rather the only times that the world seemed to make sense to her—when she was putting together pieces, stitching a narrative from disparate sources.

"Look at this," Meg murmured, scrolling through another set of online archives. "Here's an article about how after this orphanage was burned down in the Draft Riots, a handful of orphans were adopted by residents of Weeksville. Not totally relevant, maybe, but kind of interesting."

"Huh," said Ellis. Then he laughed. "Shit, I'm getting goosebumps! Why? What are you doing to me?"

"Oh, that's a totally normal effect of the librarian-gypsy curse I just put on you, not to worry," Meg said.

Ellis nodded. "I see. That's cool. My grandma knows some pretty mean voodoo, so I should be all right."

"Good. We understand each other then." She scrolled some more. "You know about the Draft Riots, of course."

"Right. Don't forget my father is Professor Williams, of the casual dinner table historical oration. Horrible mob violence because people didn't want to get drafted for the Civil War, right? And a lot of the city was burned. Like in that terrible movie. Man, that movie was bad."

"*Gangs of New York*? I wouldn't call it 'historically accurate,' no. Or, 'good.' Right. The specifics were that African Americans were not eligible for the draft. And you could buy your way out of the draft for $300, which made it essentially a draft for only the poor and working class, which meant mostly the Irish."

Ellis nodded. "Oh yes. One year when I complained about the St. Patrick's Day parade, I got a rousing speech about the 'dirty Irish' and all the discrimination they once faced." He smiled ruefully and shook his head. "Having a history professor for a father can be—tiring."

Meg smiled. "I'd like to meet him." Then she cleared her throat, all business again. "So they—mostly the Irish, but soon enough the whole city—rioted for three days, and there were lynchings, and all this terrible violence, and as if that weren't enough to make you lose your faith in humanity, the mob burned down the Colored Orphan Asylum. Orphans!"

Ellis sat back, studied her face. "And people say Black folks love to riot," he said. She flushed again. He nudged her shoulder. "I'm messing with you, Meg. Relax." She could already tell it would take a long time to learn how to talk to him. "So some of the orphans ended up in Weeksville, huh?"

"That's what this says. Some of them were stowed on Roosevelt Island, which was, like, this long skinny strip of land where they had a maximum-security prison, a lunatic asylum, and a smallpox quarantine hospital. So that was probably a fun place for the orphans."

"Sounds like where I went to overnight camp."

Meg laughed. When was the last time she'd met someone *funny*?— even though every joke he made caused her some degree of distress, like she was never quite sure if she should laugh or not. She bustled over to the flat files and pulled out a map from the 1860s, spread it on the table, and leaned over it, tracing a finger along the Midtown area where the orphanage had once stood—now a stretch of shining office towers and upscale retail, near the alternate universe of the New York Public Library (was there a Manhattan Meg who worked there, buried in *their* local history archives?). She slid her finger across to the river, rested on an oval of land labeled Blackwell's Island. "I went through this big Nelly Bly phase in graduate school and wrote a paper on her research methods—one of the things she did was have herself committed to the Lunatic Asylum on Roosevelt Island, called Blackwell's Island then, and then she wrote this blistering exposé on their inhumane methods."

"Wait, hold up. I'm still at, 'big Nelly Bly phase.'"

"Um, *yeah*, doesn't everyone have one of those in college? You know, things get pretty crazy at Library Sciences school."

He snorted. "Hey, believe me, I know—I went to graduate school for biomedical engineering. So shit got pretty crazy there too, you know. I, like, learned how to make curry…how to make dumplings…"

Meg looked at him. "Biomedical engineering, huh?"

"We all have our dark sides."

She laughed. He *was* joking, right? He said everything with such a straight face, he was so quick, his words so precise, as if created by a 3D printer. *She* was used to being the one whose sarcasm disarmed people. "Right. So anyway. Nelly Bly. That's when I first learned about this island. Anyway, nice place to bring terrified orphans, right? Though I suppose that was the only place where they could be safe at the time."

Ellis considered this. "But not these ones, who ended up in Weeksville?"

Meg went back to the online archive, scrolled some more. "The people in Weeksville were used to sheltering other free Blacks from kidnappers and slave-traders, and I think there were even some Underground Railroad connections. So I bet their leaders encouraged families to take in the displaced orphans. They all felt responsible for each other." She paused. "Looks like one of the orphans was, for a time, living with Jacob Jenkins and his wife, Rachel."

Ellis recoiled, as if burned.

"What's wrong?"

He shook his head. "That name. Rachel. That's—that was my wife's name."

"Oh, Jesus. I'm so sorry, Ellis."

He stared at his hands. "It was the spring. This past spring." He paused. "There was this cherry blossom tree on the Medical Campus, right outside her window, and it bloomed the day she died, and her sister and mom were crying, like *There she is, that's Rachel*, and I lost it. I was like, *my wife is not a fucking flower.*" He shook his head. "Sorry, I don't know why I told you that. It just—It was really fast, really brutal. She found out she was sick, and less than a year later, she was gone. I—I don't usually tell people about it. I mean, I haven't much."

Meg leaned forward, over the map, and squeezed his hand, feeling ashamed at the way she'd been thinking about him, sizing him up like just another piece of dating meat. She said, "Shit." Then she said, "My sister. When she was twenty-five. Hit by a livery car and killed on impact. I know it's not the same thing, and I know it's stupid that people always want to tell you their own death stories, like it matters, or helps anything. I'm just saying that to let you know I understand, a little."

If only she could transmit to him everything she'd learned in the past ten years, point him toward some source that would help him to understand that new parts would grow around the mourning parts, but that the mourning parts would stay festering there in the center; she wished there were some citation that would save him the trouble of scraping through it all himself. There were those things you just had to learn yourself, like how it is possible to cry until you throw up (who knew?), like how the grief comes and goes and sometimes blindsides you when you least expect it, how you eventually go longer in between the bad moments and then feel guilty, how when you start to feel like a person capable of joy again, you fear that you are losing something. How no one will ever say the right thing. As if your bad memory and urge to spare yourself pain are doing what death couldn't—erasing your person forever.

But she knew he had to do all that himself. She didn't envy him having it all ahead. All she could do was to tell him, in a low, anesthe-tized voice, "We live in a different world, people like you and me."

He stared at her, like he'd been hungry for months and she had offered him a meal. "Does it get easier?"

Meg said, "No."

Ellis leaned back and regarded Meg for a moment and said, "Thank you. Thank you for saying that. I'm getting real sick of people telling me I'll feel happy soon, or there's some secret meaning in it all. I don't even know if I want to feel better. Does that sound crazy?"

"No," Meg said again. "I know exactly how you feel."

She was going to say more, or maybe he was, but just then a ghostly figure appeared at Meg's elbow, and they both started in terror. The child stood blinking at them, swaying slightly. Meg had to stop herself from reaching out to see if it was real, or if her hand would (as she assumed) go right through it. The child shimmered under the harsh overhead lights, then resolved. Meg laughed.

"Remy!"

She stood and took the child's hand. A real child! Of course it was! Meg said, almost apologetically, to Ellis, "I know this kid! I mean, I know her father. I mean, I know who he is. Hold on, don't go any-where," and then to Remy she cooed, the way you would speak to a puppy or a plant, "Aren't you a silly girl? What are you doing up here? Did you run away from storytime?" She had almost reached the glass doors when she saw Aryeh run down the hallway, turn, see them through the glass, and sigh with stagey relief. He pushed the doors open and fell to the child's feet, grabbing her pudgy hands.

"Remy! Don't you ever run off like that! Daddy was scared!"

Meg and Ellis shared a look. Meg had the weird feeling that they had lived through a lot together in the past few hours—the history of the city, the history of their own lives—but that seeing Aryeh broke the spell, reminded her of herself, reminded her that Ellis was a person there to do research, that she was only the librarian, that their stories didn't actually intersect.

Aryeh squeezed the grimy child to his chest. "I'm sorry, Meg. She doesn't like the singing part of storytime. They started 'Twinkle Twin-kle' and she just took off."

"I don't blame her," Ellis said under his breath, raising his eyebrows.

Aryeh knelt and scolded the kid some more in his semiotically cir-cuitous way: "Remy, was that a good choice? I don't think that that was a good choice, do you? Daddy didn't like that, okay? You can't run away from Daddy, okay?" Meg thought she heard Ellis clucking his tongue, like an old woman on the city bus, and for a moment she dis-approved of his disapproval; even as she frowned at Aryeh's frictionless manner with his daughter, she was aware that parenting was probably a whole lot easier in the absence of children. She wondered how James and Eugene would parent their future baby. Would they be ridiculous? Was there a way to not be ridiculous?

She tried to meet Ellis's eye, but he was deep in thought, far away somewhere within himself, remembering something he hadn't thought about in a long time.

"Well, my brain is full," Ellis said, gathering his things, stacking the papers and books that would stay at the library. The light slanting in the windows at the far end of the Brooklyn Collection, which faced a leafy edge of Prospect Park, had gone golden around noon and then disappeared as it did every afternoon, leaving the shelves swathed in a premature dusk. They had failed to find anything too promisingly macabre about "Jake," as Ellis had started calling him. Stories had the right to unfurl themselves slowly—of course they did—but that didn't stop people from getting impatient.

"I never took my lunch break," Meg said impulsively, feeling stupid immediately afterwards. "I mean. I could now. They have good pie in the café downstairs. If you're not busy. You could. I mean, I could."

To her surprise, Ellis smiled, agreed. "Sure. We could toast good old Jake and the rest of the Jenkins family."

They took the stairs down, the people on the escalator floating past them like spirits ascending to heaven, or at least History/Biographies.

Meg had the apple. Ellis had a buttery, caramel-y cream something with a glaze like a vitreous humor. Of course they didn't know each other well enough to try bites of each other's pies, but for a second, Meg hoped that someday they would (strictly in order to maximize her pie-flavor-trying, she told herself). Meg sipped her coffee. "Should we try to be normal for a minute?" she asked him.

He looked up, startled. "What?"

She rubbed at her temples, tried not to run her fingers too many times through her hair, which was a nervous tic of hers she knew was probably unsanitary. "We've spent an awful lot of time together talking about, you know, death, disaster, more death. I wonder, like— what do you do back in Chicago?"

A vein twitched in his jaw. He paused, as if considering what to say. "Um, I work in biomedical engineering."

"Oh, right! Cool!" Meg poked her fork in the air at him. "Actually. I have no idea what that means!"

Ellis laughed. "Maybe I shouldn't tell you, then! You might change your mind." He forked some custard to the side of his plate, left it jiggling viscously there. "Right now—or, I'm, er, on leave right now, you know—but before that, I worked at a medical device company overseeing synthetics. I didn't love it, but you know how it is. Life. You get comfortable. You want to spend your weekends relaxing with your— relaxing. I had an easy job that ended when I clocked out at night, you know? I'm pretty into prosthetics. My postdoc work was about designing artificial eyes, but it was hard to get funding to pursue it, and I just kinda got comfortable in my job and, you know. Got lazy. I think I'd like to focus more on that, on research," he said, as if deciding as he said it: "The bionic eyeball." He watched her face, waiting for her response.

Meg slammed her fork down and leaned forward. "You. Are. Kidding. Me."

Ellis shook his head. "Afraid not, ma'am. I know, I know, my parents were hoping that premed degree would mean I became a surgeon. It's still hard to explain to them what I do. Ask my dad." And he adopted a stentorian lecture hall voice, "'I just *know* my boy could have been a doctor, he really could have *made* something of himself.'"

"That's not what I mean at all. I think it's amazing! Bionic eyes. How *poetic*!"

Ellis laughed again. "Not really. Not the actual work of it. I'm essentially a medical-class factory hand."

"I am *sure* that's not true, Ellis. I *know* it isn't true."

His name felt sweet in her mouth.

Now that he'd relaxed somewhat, Meg realized she'd had him all wrong. He wasn't distant and forbidding, he wasn't just another moody guy; he was shy, and he was in pain, but also, he was easy to talk to. Every time he made her laugh, she forgot, for a moment, about everything else.

He told her things she knew he wouldn't tell her if they weren't strangers, or even if they were on an actual date. How he had first met his wife, how he had first seen her walking through the door of the sandwich shop at the University of Chicago student union building, how she had the sweetest face he'd ever seen, how—probably because he'd been eating a meatball sub at the time—he would forever associate Rachel with something nourishing, in some kind of weird Pavlovian love response. How when they lived in their first apartment together, a fourth-floor walkup in a student housing slum, which she had made bright and cheery by hanging Caribbean-print tapestries from her aunties in Trinidad, they had cemented their relationship by cooking for one another. How Rachel had tried, for their first meal in the apartment, to cook callaloo, how even though she'd grown up in Illinois, she remembered the bright green stew from influential summer visits to her mother's hometown on the Island, how it had all gone wrong, how the apartment smelled like scorched taro for days. How that night they had eaten a deep-dish pizza instead and watched a Bulls game and then suddenly, out of nowhere, Rachel had said, *I want our babies to have some Island culture, you know, to hear steel pan and taste real callaloo like I did growing up,* and how they had never talked about babies or even marriage, but how he loved that she would say something so forward, so crazy, so uncool.

How they'd married, and when Rachel turned thirty, the biologist in her announced that, scientifically speaking, it was the Right Time for Babies, and when she didn't get pregnant right away, they shrugged and took some nice vacations, she drank a special herbal tea, she meditated and did yoga and read some Oprah-endorsed book on positive thinking. When she went to her doctor for a referral to a fertility specialist, she found out instead that she had advanced-stage aggressive breast cancer, which (she knew immediately, from an article she'd read in one of the medical journals she pored over in the bathtub the way other women devour romance novels) was, for reasons no one yet understood, common in young Black women, and very, very lethal. How she never did perfect the callaloo.

These kinds of confidences demanded an exchange, but it almost didn't seem fair—Meg was so used to talking about Kate, so articulate about her loss, so accustomed to the idea of it, that it wasn't an even trade; she didn't have as much at stake. Still, she shared her story as a kind of offering: the shock of the phone call, the immolation of the aftermath.

She had never been married? He wanted to know.

"Kate?"

"No, you."

"Of course not! I'd have to give up my spinster librarian card." A pause. "Have I mentioned I live with a cat?"

"Only one?"

"Just the one. I do talk to her a lot though."

"Does she answer back?"

"Sometimes."

It was one of the best conversations she had ever had (and Meg was a talker). They stayed much longer than her lunch break should have been—she was greeted on her return with a deadly glare from Head Librarian Helen. But it was worth it. They had covered advances in biomed engineering and library sciences, mourning rituals in American and Caribbean cultures, whaling, modern art, cats, basketball, New York City mayors, the Chicago mafia, pickle relish, the afterlife, pie, mothers: everything. Maybe it was just Ellis's interest—he seemed so *interested* in every little thought she had. He seemed to find *her* interesting, which made her wonder how foreign her buttoned-up bookishness seemed to him. Was she a living manifestation of a stereotype to him, a sort he'd only ever seen in cheeseball movies? Maybe it didn't matter. He was never only waiting for his turn to talk. He drank her in; he laughed at her jokes; he met her eyes. When she described Kate's funeral, he didn't look away. He nodded. He heard. Here was someone who would understand how fucking sad she was, how relentlessly lonely, and she knew it in him, too—she could help him, even, maybe, as the wound mercifully started to scab. They lived a lifetime in an hour at a wobbling café table in the library lobby—they courted, fucked, married, fought, made up, grew old, died—without touching one other once.

Then Meg looked at her wristwatch and sighed. "Well, back to the grindstone. Thanks for the pie, Mr. Williams." She stood up.

Ellis stood too. "Yeah, no problem. I mean, thank you. I mean! You're welcome. Thanks for your help. Come by the house anytime you want. I mean. If you want to. Or, I'll be back, I'm sure. Or, you know."

She smiled and shook his hand a bit stiffly, like a caricature of business exchange. "I'll have my people contact your people."

He watched her go. Suddenly there was an inkling of light. No one could ever fix it. But at least they understood each other.

# 17

**AS HER HOUSE** is pulled limb from limb, she musters herself together. The past hundred and fifty years have been a process of dispersal. She has settled in to the keeping room, has left parts of herself scattered around, like a kid careless with blocks on a rug. The room was the vessel. Now the door has been torn off. Now the contractor says things loudly, so he knows she can hear. *Better to take this whole room off. A back porch. A nice three-season porch. Is what you want here. This room, it's unsound.*

This room is unsound. But this room is her body.

Still the construction workers come and break off pieces of her house. They strip the walls naked, tearing off paper while the walls cringe and whimper. They chip away at the patched-up hearth. They wrench her door from its hinges, and her whole self winces. They violate the room that is now her body.

So now she needs a body. She needs to materialize.

It is not easy to remember your body after 150 years. It is like trying to remember a smell. She remembers certain feelings but not how they felt. It occurs to her to start from the outside. To remember her clothes. The sack-like dress and apron from the asylum. Or no, the new dress she is given when she gets to Weeksville. The first dress she can remember that is her own. That isn't identical to a hundred other girls'. Mrs. Jenkins could have given her a hand-me-down from the sisters, but no, she has made it just for her; she sews it on a machine that whirs throughout the house, a huge industrious cricket. She has never felt a fabric like this, gauzy as she imagines a wedding veil might be. Voile, Mrs. Jenkins calls it. She finds herself whispering the word to herself like an incantation. Voile. Voile. Voile. It is a word that sounds exactly like what it is. Like magic in a conjurer's show—voila! A dress as delicate as the handkerchief of a lady-in-waiting. As sunny as the curtains in a grand house's parlor. A whisper of a dress, so impossibly thin and delicate, she hides from chores to examine the tiny rows of strawberries printed on the fabric, positioning herself in a beam of mote-filled sunlight. She has never had a dress with pictures on it. Admires herself in the puffed short sleeves, the gathered bodice, the gathered skirt. Collects pebbles in the field just to have something to place in the pocket. The dress changes her. It changes her to have a pocket, to have fairy strawberries blooming across her heart. To have a summer dress. As in, different from a winter dress.

If she gathers up all of herself to remember the dress, it begins to be possible. A flicker of how a hand fits into a pocket. How stays pressed to her belly, an uncomforting hug. Remembering eyelet drawers reminds her of her legs, how they would get tired from walking, the tingle when they'd fall asleep. The bonnet she wore whenever she went out in the fields, it creates her head, her hair, which was coarse and unruly, nothing like Jane's enviable curls.

She'd so looked forward to a corset. To a hoopskirt. To a woman's body to fill them. To wear clinking bracelets, golden, one on each wrist. She'd wanted, as they said at the church, to pray and do good works and seek heavenly rewards and all of it. But also, and more achingly, she'd wanted to someday have tiny golden hoops in her pierced ears.

When she goes further back, recalls the Orphan Asylum, it gets worse. The fire, the shouting, the Black fear of the draft riots, of that whole nightmare time, burns in her. She loses the part of her that thinks it is wrong to haunt. The part of her that thinks at all. She is all roiling flame, all fox-fear, her soul boiled down to a captured shriek, a tortured child. Which is, after all, what she is, all she ever was. Remembering the dress's puff sleeve calls up her arm, and when she screws herself up into the memory of the feel of the arm, she can work on moving the memory of the arm. When she pulls together every scrap that she can, all the bits of self she has scattered around the room, she can almost move something. She can rattle a window. She can turn the air icy. She can knock over a glass, pull out a drawer. She can puff herself up into a foggy specter and swoop across the room, and she thinks maybe they can see her for a second, or some of them can. She is so very happy to hear the clank, see the crash, to see the man whirl around, to sense his own fox-fear. She wants them to feel not just haunted but hunted. To know how it is to be an orphan in a fire. To be made a stranger in your own country, your own city, your own home. Your own body. To be forced out.

She grows stronger, fills the dress in her mind. She slams doors, rejoicing in the shudder. She shoves people's backs, recoiling at the fleshy heat. The more the people feel afraid, the more she knows it is working, the more powerful she becomes. In this way, she feeds herself. In this way, she grows.

Harm becomes her cloak, her atmosphere, her country. She screams into the faces of the people. She stares into their unseeing eyes. She relishes the way they quake. At little old her! At the girl who wasn't brave enough to sing out loud in a living room! Now she scatters tacks across the floor. She grows stronger until she can move cans of paint to send grown men tumbling down the stairs. She can, every once in a while, find it in herself to break a glass, hide the jagged bits. The room was hers. If they can take it, she can make it a torture chamber.

# 18

**THERE WAS NO PUTTING IT OFF.** Nora and Martin Rhys tolerated being ignored by their children for a maximum of a day, and this particular summons for dinner had been issued nearly a week earlier. There was something they wanted to tell everyone, Nora told Meg over the phone. A chill slalomed down Meg's spine. This could mean one of two things: someone was dying, or real estate was changing hands. Potentially, both. Meg and James pow-wowed via Gchat in the afternoon while they were supposed to be working, concluded that the Rhyses were, once again, being tempted by their landlords to take a buyout on the rent-stabilized apartment for which they wrote a heart-stoppingly small check each month.

It was the Rhys family fortune, that quirk of the New York rental market, a treasure chest in the shape of what wasn't there. What her parents had on their side was neither sound investments nor savvy business acumen but merely the relentless march of time; they had had the tenacity or stupidity to have let their kids play unsupervised on dirty streets where they had to dodge drunken Vietnam vets; they had had the energy to clear away syringes and broken glass so that the neighborhood association could plant in the tree pits. Her parents had made good on their lefty Liberal politics and reared their young in the grit of the city, had celebrated budget date nights (Mrs. Fishman supervising the kids' television watching and then heading home to 2E once they seemed convincingly asleep) at Big Nick's Pizzeria or Williams Bar-B-Q or Gray's Papaya—they deserved their current glut of chichi restaurants and upscale retail and potential buy-out windfall.

And all her parents wanted in this moment was a family dinner, a good old Friday night pseudo-Sabbath, a habit Nora Rhys—née Rosenfeld—had slipped by her staunchly atheist, steadfastly antireligion, and strenuously antibrisket husband so long ago that he now considered it as their own family tradition, involving challah bread for no other reason than that Friday was the day on which Fairway sold it, and a pair of candles purely for ambiance. Scraps of the Jewish traditions her grandparents had shed with alacrity, in their hunger to fit in, Nora slipped back into their lives when no one was looking.

So after an afternoon of work spent distracted by a febrile desire for Ellis Williams to swoop back by, Meg closed up the Brooklyn Collection and stopped at the Hold shelf downstairs for her weekend haul. A slim volume of recently discovered poems by Sappho; a Lydia Davis novella about a haunted house; an inspirational writing manual by Harper Lee. Small talk with the circ clerk seemed an unbearable workout, a spin-class of the mind. She was so tired, and when Meg was tired, even just looking people in the eye felt hard, hard, hard. And yet, here she was, stowing her reading material into her satchel, leaving her bike securely locked to the Bookmobile gas pump, because her brother would not like her to bring it on the train and would not allow her to ride home, denying her an escape route—and yet, it was understandable—of course it was—given Kate, that no one liked her to ride across the bridge at night, or anywhere at night, or anywhere, ever.

She headed to meet James and Eugene beneath the Soldiers' and Sailors' Memorial Arch, the Parisian-looking Civil War tribute bumpy with statuary: there were everyone's old pals Lincoln and Grant, there were the muscular representatives of the Army and Navy, and piloting the bronze quadriga on top of the arch, a winged lady Meg had always assumed was a bellicose goddess until her architect brother explained it was Columbia, AKA the triumphant America represented as the Ur Manic Pixie Dream Girl. Somehow this had become their usual meeting place, ringed by deadly traffic, convenient only to the sexy Neptune fountain beneath the arch.

Meg sucked in a gasp when she saw them there, such beautiful boys—though Eugene was closer to her age than James's, they both seemed so young to her, probably because they were so happy, sated by their childlike belief in love. Well, she was feeling sentimental today. Before they saw her, James said something to Eugene, and Eugene rubbed his shoulder in such a tender way that Meg thought for a moment that her heart would flatten out, like a whoopee cushion under an unsuspecting auntie.

They talked about nothing for forty-five minutes straight on the 2/3 journey to the ancestral home. The boys had just gotten a SodaStream seltzer machine. Eugene confided in Meg, "It's seriously life-changing. And we haven't even *tried* any flavor syrups yet."

Meg stared at him. "You're the whitest person I know, Eugene. Honestly."

He laughed too loudly, because Eugene was one of those people who gave you too much credit, who laughed so generously at your jokes that you felt guilty for how undeserving the joke had been. The race issue was a real one—she remembered, with a pang, how he'd accused her of being afraid of Black men when she'd said someone looked sketchy on the subway—but it made it better to joke about it, to inch up to the edge of what was okay to say. It made it seem like you weren't afraid then, and Meg was suddenly desperate to prove that she wasn't. So when he said, "I'm sure that's not true, Miss Welsh-Scots-Irish-Cornwall-Dover-Queen-Mother-Rhys," she answered, "Beg pardon?" in the snootiest, most-like-their-Welsh-grandma-she-could-muster voice. "I'm hardly white. In fact—" and she lowered her voice as if divulging something unspeakable—"*I'm a bit Jewish.*"

"That's right," James said. "Of the ancient clan of UWS crypto-Jews-by-association, who, according to sacred religious tradition, bedeck their Christmas trees strictly in blue and white."

"Precisely," said Meg. She felt too weary for the jokey banter, but it was their shared language, and she had the sense the dinner ahead would be arduous enough without James having to worry about her being crabby. Which reminded her: "Speaking of nothing related to this at all, are you going to tell Mom and Dad tonight? About the baby?"

James and Eugene shared a married-person look of panic so palpable it had a gravitational pull. "No, no, no," said James. "We wanted to wait—you know how they are, they get so carried away with everything—and we wanted to wait until we have a surrogate."

"Pregnant," Eugene said. "Until we have a surrogate pregnant."

"Until Eugene gets a girl knocked up," Meg translated. "Okay. It's up to you of course. But I'd think they'd be excited. They could use some good news like that, you know?"

James shot her a dirty look. "Really, Meg? I thought you'd be on my side about this. No one understands how crazy they are like you do. Don't pretend they wouldn't be unbearable."

Of course he was right. But Meg was tired and crabby. She wanted to be home with a book and the cat and Kate's ghost. She didn't feel like watching young people with nifty ankle boots and bright smiles and well-planned hair clamber aboard the train in the city, noisy with excitement about the happy hours ahead. So it wasn't fair, but she did what one could only do with a sibling or a spouse—what one would never do with a friend or lover—she raised an eyebrow, stared out the window, and said, bitchily, "Whatever you want, Jamie."

Just then, the train stopped abruptly, going dark. An elderly woman behind a Chinese newspaper squeaked in panic. A third of the people on the crowded-but-not-packed train whipped their heads around, looking for fire or flood or terrorists; a third grumbled and swore under their breath about delays; another third didn't so much as flinch, absorbed in their magazines or phones.

It happened; trains stopped; things happened. But Meg couldn't ignore an uncomfortable prickle this time, an eerie off-ness. The train air went clammy. The lights flickered on again and then off again. The silent crowd awaited the train conductor's garbled announcement. They were all ready for the explanation—*Tell us there is a garbage train ahead, or a signal problem, make it clear, make it something simple and understandable and easily solved.* Instead, only silence, only the uncomfortably still train. Meg made her eyes wide.

"What?" said James "What?"

Meg just shook her head, the corners of her mouth turning up slightly, her palms parallel with the train's low ceiling. "It's weird, right? It's just really weird."

James leaned close to her, raising one eyebrow, mocking now. "What, the train? Does everything have to be weird, Meg? What, like, a ghost stopped the train? Like the ghosts of the city are fucking with us because you're uncovering their spooooooky secrets?"

The woman with the Chinese newspaper stood up abruptly and shuffled to the far side of the car, as if their conversation smelled.

"Well, I don't know if I'd go that far," Meg said.

But in that moment, the train seemed to close in around them. How long could they stay in the tunnel, really? Meg envisioned them squeezing out the doors, inching along the ledge against the tunnel wall, picking their way over rats and Mole People and Ninja Turtles and a hundred years of garbage. She looked out of the black window now, blinded by the tunnel, reflecting herself back. The lights in the train flicked from dim to dark (more muffled squeaks from the panicky lady), and for an awful instant, Meg thought she could see into the tunnel. Instead of the usual struts and work lights and graffiti, she saw faces. Hundreds and hundreds of faces. They stood very still, looking pale but bored, as if waiting for the train doors to open. Ordinary-looking people and old-timey-looking people and ancient-looking people of all ages and colors, standing in the tunnel, staring through the window. At her. Any second now, the familiar *ding-dong* would sound, the doors would open, and they would all come rushing onto the train, jostling for space. She couldn't breathe.

Then the lights flicked back on, and the speakers rattled with the conductor's garbled voice (Meg jumped, James and Eugene eyed her) making everything normal, alchemized back into metal and plastic and human flesh all over again: "Sorryforthedelay, train'llbemovingshortly," and everyone grumbled and sighed like normal, and the this-isn't-real-this-is-like-a-movie-or-maybe-like-a-nightmare feeling faded somewhat, and the engines started up, and off the train rumbled up-town.

Eventually they arrived at the Seventy-Second Street stop and emerged out of the tunnel into the sparkling world, the windows of apartment towers nacreous in the evening light. They walked up Broadway. It was one of the first crisp evenings of the fall, the waning sun burnishing the trees growing from pits that had been receptacles for trash and hypodermic needles when Meg and James were small. The avenue, having long outgrown its dingy adolescence, bristled with people heading out to dinner at the fancy eateries that had replaced the delis and greasy spoons and empty storefronts of their youth. Eugene fell back to let by a flock of tourists, thunderous with wheeled luggage, and Meg and James walked side by side, and it was good to be with her little brother in a moment when Manhattan felt lively, the excitement of the newly minted weekend crackling all around, and her bad mood softened when they turned west on Seventy-Fifth and could see that, in the distance, beyond West End Avenue, the leaves were beginning to change in Riverside Park.

By the time they reached their parents' building, Meg felt recovered somewhat, although she retained the unfamiliar itch of an un-answered question in the hyperanswerable world. It seemed like she should be able to do an advanced search on NYU's Bobcat site and have it solved and over with, the preoccupation she knew was at the root of her slump—not James's happy marriage or future baby and her own lack of either, of course not—but rather: *What does Ellis Williams think? About haunted houses. About his haunted house. About ghosts. About me.* Having a crush—that's what this was, surely; she'd been around the block enough to identify this ache in her chest and to know it wasn't love, which didn't actually exist anyway—was a bit like being haunted. When you have a crush, like when you have a ghost, you are never really alone. The specter of Ellis chased Meg through her day. *What if I ran into him right now? What if he is thinking of me right now?*

But when you were a big girl, when you knew there was no point in such an infatuation, you were able to pull your socks up and ignore it. You focused on the here-and-now. You walked up the steps to your childhood home and didn't at all picture Ellis watching you, smoldering with desire.

Despite everything, there was always a degree of comfort in coming home. In the nearly two decades since Meg had lived within its hallowed halls and wainscoted walls, the Rhys apartment had not changed nearly so much as the neighborhood around it. Meg remembered being allowed to play outside in the grimy streets with only a neighbor-kids-pack's worth of supervision, with the simple directive never never NEVER to go above Eighty-Sixth Street. (Meg allowed herself to imagine that while she had been playing Red Rover on West End Avenue, Ellis had been shouting, "Let Meg come over!" somewhere across the East River, living his parallel life in pregentrification Brooklyn—before she erased the silly picture from her mind.)

Back then there were junkies in Riverside Park—the drug kind, not the "addicted to jogging" kind—and you were brainwashed from birth to identify and avoid them. In her early teens, Meg realized the mystifying place on Seventy-Fourth called Plato's Retreat had nothing to do with philosophy at all but was instead, disappointingly, a tawdry sex club. There were boarded-up storefronts on Amsterdam Avenue. The rickety IRT trains that ran to their neighborhood were rusty red, to combat the graffiti that coated most of the subway lines—she remembered her shock, late in teen-hood, at learning that, beneath the scrawled tags, most of the city's train cars were actually silver. But as time passed, Meg was less and less sure that any of this was actually remembered from life. What if television and movies had erased her actual '70s and '80s New York, like Giuliani sand-blasting away a scrim of graffiti?

Meg pressed their parents' number, and they waited to be buzzed in. The building's super, creating a firework-like-spray as he "fixed" a socket in the lobby, greeted a trim white woman pushing a double stroller before high-fiving Meg and James and Eugene, for he remembered them, always, and asked about their jobs, and winked at Meg and said horrible things like "Still living the swinging single life, I see!"

with such a kindly old manner that she almost forgave him, but only because she'd known him since she was a girl.

Meg wanted to make peace, even though the rift she'd felt between them had probably been imagined, so in the elevator, she hugged James and said, "Hold him back! Don't let him press all the buttons!"—as he had on every elevator ride between 1986 and 1988, rendering each trip to fifth floor an epic journey. Eugene laughed obligingly—filling what had always been Kate's role—and James gamely pretended to struggle toward the buttons.

Then they were home, in the echo-y hallway of Floor Five, and James leaned on the buzzer so that it bleated out its unbearable rasp like a goat keening in distress, and Nora opened the door and hugged all three of them at once and exclaimed, "My babies! You made it!" She kissed Eugene extra-hard on the cheek, like always, and said, "Uch, you're so handsome it's disgusting."

In the kitchen their father was wrestling with a wine cork. James took over the task, and soon Meg was setting the table and Eugene was being shown photographs—on Nora's smartphone—of their recent bird-watching trip to Antarctica. You had to hand it to them, Nora and Martin were exceptional at being semi-retired.

A wheel of baked brie was installed on the coffee table, which caused Meg and James to share a worried look—they were in this for the long haul, if appetizers were involved. But they said nothing, sat dutifully on the sagging couch and took their glasses of wine. James made a teetering sandwich of Melba toast and brie, even though Meg could tell the caloric accumulation of each bite was making him wince. "So what's up, guys?" she asked, when her parents had perched in their habitual armchairs. A jazz CD whined a vespine drone. She could smell an apple crisp baking. Dread stirred in her belly.

"'What's up'?" said Martin, looking around comically, as if searching for whom they might be speaking to. "Whatever do you mean, dear daughter? Why should something be 'up' in order for our family to come together? And hello, how are you?"

Nora waved her hand at him, then stroked her silver bob back into place. "I may have mentioned there was a little bit of news." Meg wondered for an instant how she knew—*Ellis?*—and then remembered no, there was no news, Ellis was not news, he was just a person she had met. And thought about. Now and then.

"Oh-ho! Well, aren't I always the last to know," said Martin. He was obviously feeling jolly. It made him so happy to have the whole family, such that it was, together that it was pathetic really—Meg had to look away from his beaming face. It was like watching a priest enjoying an ice cream cone in the park, a joy you weren't meant to witness. "Well if there's news, I can't wait to hear it."

"It's not a big deal or anything. I don't want to give the wrong impression." Nora leaned forward, excitement precipitating from her grin. "But . . . Mrs. Fishman is moving to a home."

There was a long silence, during which Eugene stifled a chuckle, and James could not, quite. "Mrs. Fishman? Old Mrs. Fishman, who's lived in 2E since Peter Stuyvesant was a schoolboy? She's still alive?"

Nora pursed her lips and looked to Meg for help. "Yes, old Mrs. Fishman. She's one of the last renters in the building—"

"Besides the old paupers you see before you, of course." They laughed about it, but Meg knew it irked her father—how the building, in which they had once been the most well-to-do of all the renters, had gone co-op all around them; how the new tenants (who paid "market rates") got access to the recent additions like the exercise center, while the old stalwarts (who had made the neighborhood what it was, who had once the racial minority and who had liked it that way) got access mostly to dirty looks in the laundry room. But today Martin just tucked his thumbs into his invisible suspenders and did a little Charlie Chaplin-esque Little Tramp wiggle.

Meg stared at her father, who raised his glass. "You're awfully Vaudevillean today, Dad. So you guys, what gives? You're that happy to get rid of her?"

"Good riddance!" James said, leaning back and putting his feet up on the coffee table's ziggurat of *National Geographics*. He turned to Eugene. "As I recall, she gave out raisins at Halloween."

"Bit-o-Honeys," Meg corrected him. "Almost as bad. You're thinking of Sanchez. 2B. The monster with the raisins."

It was dangerous territory, the past. One was always treading an inch away from Kate. Because it had been Kate who had called kindly Mrs. Sanchez a monster after her raisin offering. Meg could still picture tiny Kate indignant in her Minnie Mouse costume and slipper socks (the great joy of apartment building trick-or-treating), skidding down the hall with her mouse tail waggling behind, emptying the erstwhile fruit down the elevator shaft.

Nora, a creature of perpetual motion, waved her hands around again. "So Mrs. Fishman, you know, has no family. *Very* sad." She nodded knowingly toward Meg at the "no family" part. There was a subtext of warning whenever her mother spoke of Family, when she tsked her tongue at women (never men, of course not) who had committed that great crime against nature that was getting old without procreating. Nora rhapsodized about her own days as a young mother, apparently having expunged from memory any sleepless nights or fussy infants— though Meg had been old enough when James was born to remember his early iteration as a screaming colicky baby, to recall precisely how the whole family had gone insane from lack of sleep for years on end. Nora had wiped clean any traces of toddler tantrums on the 2 or marital strain or floundering of self, all of which Meg's friends-who-had-become-mothers loved to confess on their rare nights out. Even then, even after they complained about the price of preschools and how they missed pooping alone (what did that even mean? Meg wondered), they would get dreamy, the mothers would, describing for Meg a cute thing the baby had done, or a precocious quip of the preschooler.

From the outside, to Meg, parenthood seemed a constant process of vowing, of confirming one's unchangeable choice, of recommitting to the task, the way she imagined nuns must operate, only in this case, "it" was the work of loving motherhood, the work of not mourning the life one spent one's twenties feverishly building, the work of remembering the truth of oneself, of existence. But parenthood was supposed to be a shortcut to meaning. If you were a parent, you weren't supposed to need to search for the meaning of life anymore. There it was; it was the baby. Or maybe you were only too busy to wonder about such things anymore, subsumed as your mind was by smaller-scale quandaries:

what kind of childbirth; what kind of diaper; what kind of elementary school; soccer or no; chocolate milk or no; God or no. What was the truth of oneself, of existence? But more urgently, who would fundraise for the PTA?

Nora could claim that meaning was without, that family was all, that Meg simply didn't know it because of course she'd never experienced the love one had for one's children—oh, it was heartbreaking when Nora said things like that because, while she never said Kate's name, it whispered all around—but Meg knew better. Meg knew if she only could read enough books and study enough history and think it all through clearly enough, she would find meaning, *the* meaning. The *real* one. "But," her mother had said over a tea tray of petit-fours and steaming pots of chamomile, when they met for Meg's fortieth birthday at one of those embarrassingly dear teashops meant for grandmothers and beribboned granddaughters, "you'll never know that feeling of a hand slipping into yours and a tiny voice calling, 'Mama!'" As if having a child were a neat hobby to pick up, a catalogue of sweet moments, and not an entirely different life altogether. "That's true," Meg had replied, efforting the rage out of her voice, "and I will also never know what it's like to perform scientific experiments in zero gravity, or hunt a buffalo across the plains on horseback, or do long division in my head. I only have the one life, you know." And this came out sounding more freighted than she meant, which was maybe okay, maybe it was okay to remind her mother, just subtly and only occasionally, that she wasn't capable of living Kate's life for her. Kate would have been a beaming bride, a glowing mother, the woman at whom everyone sighed and said they didn't know how she did it all so gracefully. That would have been fine. That would have been great. But Meg wasn't Kate. Not even now that there was no Kate to be Kate.

Still—not that she would have ever admitted it to her mother—Meg longed to be the maiden aunt. She hoped James and Eugene would find parenthood to be meaningful, and while they were at it, she hoped they would have a girl. She and the girl would spend afternoons together browsing at Books of Wonder, and Meg would buy her her first *Wizard of Oz* chapter book, and they would start reading it together over buttered scones at Alice's Teacup, up by her parents' place. Meg had no desire to be a mother, Nora was mistaken about that; it was three hours at a time with a child that Meg wanted. That would be enough. That had been enough for old Mrs. Fishman in 2E, who had entertained the neighbor children with leaf-shaped cookies and tepid cranberry cocktail, had listened to their stories with the absolutely rapt attention their parents could never offer, and then had sent them back down the hall to their own apartments in time for her to go claim her senior discount seats at the symphony.

"Mrs. Fishman was a teenager when she secretly married her high school sweetheart a month before he shipped off with the navy, and she never remarried after he died in the war," Nora said now to Eugene, as the family endured the purgatory of living room appetizers.

"'The war' being World War II," James added.

"That's, ah, a long mourning period," said Eugene.

"So anyway, Mrs. Fishman has been in the building longer than anyone except us."

"She moved in when the building was *new*," said Martin, always proud to inject a bit of New York trivia he imagined his history-buff wife and daughter might not know.

"That would be 1942," James translated for Eugene, who whistled.

Meg frowned. "I can't do math. So that makes her—what?"

Nora took over now, leaning forward. "Ninety-two. So she tells me she doesn't want to take the buy-out from the co-op board. She tells me—I was down there last weekend, you know I always take her breakfast on Saturdays"—this with a sly glance to see if Martin's attention was piqued, which it wasn't; Meg alone knew her mother's dirty secret, that for years, right in their very own building, right under her father's unsuspecting nose, every Shabbos she and old Mrs. Fishman had read Talmud and *davvened* together—"and so she tells me, out of the blue, she says, 'Nora, I know I can't take care of myself anymore.' And as you know, she doesn't have *any* children. No family. No one to help her in her old age. Very sad." A pause for emphasis. Meg studied a crack in the ceiling, which upon inspection seemed to trace Broadway's entire tilting trajectory along the island. "Sooo, her

girlhood friend Bessie lives in a home across town and wants Mrs.
Fishman to move in too. They do everything for them, and there's a
Bingo night, and a library with large-print Sudoku, and Mrs. Fishman's pension will pay for it. But she wants to keep the apartment in
her name. She only needs someone to move in and sublet." Another
pause, this one theatrical, accompanied by jazz hands. "Do you know
what this means? Do you have any idea what she pays in rent?" Nora
didn't wait for an answer, whipped up in a froth of real estate lust.
"One hundred fifty dollars. One hundred fifty dollars a month, for
this same apartment as ours! Two and a half bedrooms!"

James interjected, for Eugene's benefit, "That means two bedrooms
plus a closet to stow your extra child in," but the self-deprecating joke
fell flat, the fate of any quip that reminded them of their original family size.

"What happens when she dies?" Eugene asked. "I mean, sorry. But
she probably only has another, what, twenty-five, thirty years left in
her?" Nora giggled, always charmed by her son-in-law. "Who inherits
the apartment?"

"Oh," said Nora, "well, us, of course. We're in her will. She told me
in the '90s. We've always been close, you know." Meg and James exchanged a wide-eyed look. What other secrets did their parents have
to reveal tonight?

"Admit it, Mom," James said, "you and Mrs. Fishman have been secret lovers for years."

Martin laughed uproariously at this, but Nora only rolled her eyes
and turned to Meg. "My point is," said Nora, "We told her you would
take it, Meg! Think of how much money you would save! And since
you're getting kicked out of your old place, the timing is grand, don't
you think? Think of how much room there would be to grow!"

Meg flushed, James choked on a half-laugh, and Eugene, sweet
Eugene, even Eugene couldn't take it and got up abruptly to refill his
glass. "Nora, I'm going to check on your apple crisp if you don't mind.
It smells just exactly right!" he called from the galley kitchen, as far
away from the living room as one could get without running into a
bedroom to hide under a mattress.

"Thanks, my love!" she trilled.

"Me?" Meg finally recovered enough to say. "I don't need room to grow!" It was a strange thing that happened when Meg was with her mother. They had been able to have an exchange that felt so intimate, so un-fraught, so *real*, when Meg visited Nora at the museum, when Nora was in historical dress, when they were removed from the here-and-now. She remembered that as a child, too, she had been able to confide in her mother only when they were looking at something together—facing a painting at an art museum, or walking down a busy street. Here in their present-day lives, in the Rhyses's actual apartment, it seemed impossible that Meg might get her mother, or any of them, to understand what she was even saying. "I mean, yes, I need an apartment, but Man*hattan*? *Here*? Surely you remember the library where I will probably work forever, all the way in Brooklyn, an hour away on a good day? And where I live in a universe of Brooklyn history, I mean, my *life*, my life's *work*, is in Brooklyn, not Manhattan, *and* I mean, maybe no one's noticed, but I don't have a family. And Mom, I never will. I don't even have a boyfriend. What do I need more space for? A troll doll collection? Mom, if anyone needs 'room to grow' it's James!"

Nora's head swiveled. "James? Why?"

James's face drained of color. "I don't want the apartment, Meg. Mom, no one wants the apartment. I've been there, I remember. It smells like old lady and gefilte fish. There are rugs over the carpet, which is probably installed over more carpet. Sublet it and sell it when she dies or something, I don't know."

Nora was getting flustered now. "Why is everyone in this family such a grouch all the time? You know that Oprah doctor guy says being positive actually makes you live longer?"

It was a perfectly ridiculous thing to say, and of course Nora already knew this the moment she closed her mouth. Had having a positive attitude helped Kate to live longer? But Meg wasn't so insensitive that she would say it, only insensitive enough to snap, "James and Eugene are the ones who need more space. They're married, in case no one's noticed," (it was an unfair jab, when their parents really did try to be sensitive to "all of it," as Martin called his son's sexual orientation) "and *they're* the ones who are going to have a baby, not me."

Another ear-drum-smashing silence. The jazz CD had stopped, Meg noticed first. Then she looked at James, triumphant for a split second until she saw his face. "Oh. Oops. Oh, Jamie. I'm sorry. I mean. I mean, maybe they might have a baby? Someday? Right guys?" Eugene was nowhere to be seen, as if he'd actually managed to disappear into the apple crisp, snorkeling under the surface of bubbling butter in order to avoid the awkwardness.

"You're having a what?" Nora looked genuinely befuddled, as if Meg had announced a stork was delivering a bundle to the roof of James's co-op. "But—how?"

Martin drained his wine glass and set it down a decibel too firmly on the end table. "That's not really the question, is it, my blushing bride? The question is, How soon? When can we babysit? Congratulations, son!" He stood up, ready for a hug. James looked wanly from him to Meg and back to his father again. There was nothing to do but stand and take the hug. Meg buried her face in her hands.

"What?" Nora said again, as if in a daze.

No one was sure whose job it was then to finish explaining, and mercifully, Eugene swooped in, announcing that dinner was ready as if he'd cooked the whole thing himself—and he probably had, happily for all involved, added a few discreet sprinkles of the seasonings Nora tended to skimp on, like salt, so that everyone, including Nora, would exclaim with wonder at how exceptionally delicious the matzoh ball soup was, how flavorful the beef. Eugene, Meg could tell, had already forgiven her. James probably never would.

But like all families everywhere, they survived. They sat down to dinner. Eugene took over, explaining with grace and good humor how they planned to stir up a baby, what the first meetings with the doctor had been like, how they had been waiting for the right time to tell Nora and Martin, who would make the best grandparents of all times, and how, by the way, Nora had really outdone herself with the gravy tonight. By the end of dinner, Nora was urging them to consult with Dr. Moon, a fertility guru who had overseen the birth of her cousin's daughter's best friend's twins, and they were now in Gifted and Talented kindergarten, and James and Meg had a good laugh over this specious claim—"I'm not saying Dr. Moon ONLY makes Gifted and Talented children," Nora protested, which only made James and Meg hoot louder—"Artisanal babies!" Meg managed—and the deal-of-the-century rent-controlled apartment was momentarily forgotten.

Afterward everyone gathered with bowls of apple crisp in the living room. Meg escaped to her old bedroom. With the scrupulous unsentimentality of apartment dwellers, her parents had stripped the room of its girlish detritus the moment their children had left. The room held no suburban-style fane to her youth, no shelves of porcelain dolls and eyeless teddies, no photo strips of her high school buddies cinematically stuck to a vanity, no Depeche Mode posters peeling from roseate wallpaper. Most of the room had become an office, with a laminate desk and ergonomic chair that looked stolen from a middle-management cubicle.

The bunk beds remained, taking up a good third of the room, waiting for imaginary grandchildren to visit. Meg wondered if the six-year-old neighbor her parents were so fixated on had ever climbed into the lower bunk—Kate's—ever rested his playground-grubby shoes on the white marcelled quilt Kate had chosen over all the fluffy pink silliness in the world, had ever snuggled the stuffed bunny she'd left behind. It was a sad-looking thing, afflicted with the alopecia of the extravagantly loved. The cottontail had been named Nubby; for years Meg had tried to correct what she assumed was little Kate's mispronunciation of "bunny." She wouldn't touch it. But she would move deeper into the room, striated with streetlights so familiar they were like the sound of her own breathing. From the living room she heard a peal of her mother's laughter, the rumbling undertow of Eugene's voice.

Then, without thinking very carefully about it, Meg did something that she hadn't done in a long time. She opened the closet door.

It was the apartment version of a creepy house's basement: the place you really shouldn't go, the door you just don't open. Meg gagged at the sharp tang of mothballs. There was a neat row of photo albums languishing on the shelf. Nora had kept all of Kate's report cards and diaries and letters—chatty missives to pen pals who had been passionately beloved for a few months, then forgotten. Those were stacked neatly in shoeboxes, tied with incongruously festive ribbons. But Meg was here for the dresses.

Throughout the years Nora had saved their most precious dresses (as ranked by Nora, anyway). The baby dresses huddled on the left-hand side of the closet, like the cramped beginning of an overworked sentence. Then came the super-sweet Peter Pan collared numbers she'd stuffed them into on kindergarten picture days, the matching Laura Ashley florals for a neighbor's wedding. The black-white-and-red plaid jumpers they'd worn to cousins' Bar Mitzvahs. The strange, flowing, asymmetrical dream catcher of a dress Kate had worn when she went to prom with her gay friend, to prove some sort of point. The witchy black dress Meg had chosen for her own nonprom prom, when she and her friends had snuck into a dance club in the Meatpacking District instead. It was like a greatest hits album of girlhood, a sheaf of fabric from each year of their young lives, a timeline that ended abruptly in adulthood as they moved out and, well.

All the way on the right, punctuating the row, shrouded in a metallic bag like a specimen out of 1960s sci-fi, was (Meg unzipped it slightly to take a peek, to finger the silk) Nora's wedding dress, with its long cream-colored sleeves and poofy shoulders. Meg could parse the subtext here. It was waiting, *just in case* anyone ever felt like getting married, *just in case* anyone ever wanted to wear it themselves. The wedding dress hung stuck in time, cryogenically paused; it had fit Kate, who had slipped it on one day out of curiosity, but it was way too small for Meg. Kate and Nora were slim, angular, but Meg had always been buxom and solid-boned and soft all over, as if she'd emerged from another gene pool entirely. The wedding gown might have fit her at eleven, possibly, but it certainly didn't now. And besides.

Meg zipped up the bag and ran her hands over the other dresses. She took out Kate's prom dress and sniffed it (mothball-y) and hugged it close. But this felt stupid. It didn't do whatever she wanted it to do.

The dress had once held Kate's body, but this was only something she was thinking, not something she was feeling.

Then she picked up her own prom dress. She still liked the pearl buttons running down its back, like the hand-carved pegs on Laura Ingalls Wilder's good calico. The black bodice was lacy but stretchy. Meg glanced at the closed door and began to undress.

It still fit. Sort of. Differently. It was skin-tight now, more like Spanx than it meant to be. But it worked, it did what Meg had wanted the other dress to do.

Meg lay down on the bottom bunk squeezed into her ridiculous goth gown, the fishtail swishing around her chunky wool socks. She closed her eyes. There it was, the muscle memory of being a girl. Of being young and just filling out her own body. There only seemed to be repellent language with which to describe it—blossoming, blooming, budding, as if a girl were more flower than human. That wasn't how she remembered it happening. Flowers budded slowly, delicately, unfurling translucent petals. Girlhood was fierce and sweaty and muscly and messy. There was aching and stretching and blood, lots of blood. It had often been violent—what went on in her brain, what happened to her body, later, what boys did to her (and these were the gentlest of Morrissey-loving young men! They weren't brutalizing her, it was just that there was a certain amount of invading of personal space that was really unavoidable). Until she was about nineteen, all of her emotions, positive or negative, had felt like onslaughts. And the worst of it was that no one took you seriously because you were a girl, because they thought you were being hysterical, which you were, but that didn't mean you weren't also to be taken seriously. Meg had enjoyed being herself only once she had discovered the specific power that she, Meg herself, could wield. It wasn't beauty, or charisma, or sexiness, or carelessness, or any of the other things a teenage girl was supposed to have or want, but rather what she could do with her brain, in the classroom, when she had fully processed the text they were discussing, when she understood the subtleties no one else did. There was a certain kind of power in being smarter than everyone else in the room. Books were her Rosetta Stone for understanding the rest of school, maybe even the rest of the world. Now she knew who she was, now she didn't worry about filling out her own space.

It was a terrible thing that some girls only ever got to be girls. Meg thought of all the research she'd been doing, of that earlier era in which so many children died before being adults. Those girls who never got to grow into their actual bodies. Was it a problem of costuming? Was there some cosmic closet in which their grown-up dresses had simply been lost, so that there was nothing for their selves to wear, no way for their selves to grow bigger, no space for them to fill? Were there Weeksville-era girls stuck ghosting around because their future corsets had gone lost?

Meg sat up woozily, nearly bonking her head on the bedframe. She had fallen asleep. Or she had drunk too much wine with dinner. Her family still made muffled music in the living room. She looked down and laughed—here she was, mummified in a decades-old Betsey Johnson wrapper. How would she ever get out of that thing?

But she did (the answer turned out to be: carefully), and she dressed in her regular clothes and smoothed her hair. She wasn't quite ready to rejoin her family. She would go back soon, help her father load the dishwasher—she would start dropping hints that she was tired a full thirty minutes before she wanted to leave, to return to the home she had carefully constructed for herself out of bits and bobs over the years. She would offer to walk her brother's idiotic pet when she was back in Brooklyn so they stay out and catch a movie at the Walter Reade, and she would pray they would refuse her offer.

For now she stood close to a framed map her parents had hung above the desk and peered at it—a weathered old thing (or maybe fake-weathered) depicting the lawless land of Five Points–era Manhattan, that her mother had probably picked up from the discount bin at the museum gift shop. Meg lost herself for a moment tracing the ancient roads, marveling as always at the wide-open green space her parents' neighborhood had once been, at the prepark wilds of what was not yet Central Park. If she closed her eyes, she could almost hear the clomp of horse hoof, smell the dust of the dirt roads, feel the press of unwashed people teeming in the lower part of the city. It was a transporting enough moment that when the door of the room slammed shut, she stifled a scream and whirled around, half-expecting to be accosted by tubercular ragpicker.

Of course she was alone. Alone in her childhood bedroom. Alone but *not*. The room didn't feel right, suddenly, did not feel like a normal room. She could not quite discern why. It wasn't cold, it wasn't whispering, there were no suspicious shadows or fogs, but Meg knew that she was unalone in that room. She felt crazed, bristly all over, her ears swelling with seashell sounds that must have only been the blood in her skull but were deafening, the hair on her neck and arms pricking up like a cat's. Could this be Kate? It didn't feel like their usual conversation.

Meg closed her eyes, shook her head, took a deep breath, opened her eyes again and forced herself to look around the room, to acknowledge how utterly ordinary it was. She left quickly, pulling the door open a little too hard so that it slammed again, this time against the interior wall.

"Honey?" called Nora. "What's all the slamming? Are you okay?"

Meg moved down the hallway, fighting a surge of panic. "That was so weird, the door just slammed shut on its own. Are you sure that wasn't any of you?"

James shook his head. "Of course not. Must have been a draft."

"In an apartment with closed windows. And no cross breeze, as we all remember from those summers before we got air conditioning." Meg stood for a moment, too unsettled to sit, and then busied herself with clearing plates.

"So?" said James, sounding tired. "What are you saying? It was a ghost? It was Kate's ghost who slammed the door? Kate's mad we didn't save her any apple crisp? What are you getting at, Meg? What do you want us to say?"

"James!" said Nora.

"She's the one who's always talking about ghosts!"

"You sound exactly six years old," Meg said from the dining room. "*'She started it!'*"

But it was payback time for the botched baby announcement, and

James said, "Meg's been helping people at the library research haunted houses. That's what she does at 'work.' People actually believe this stuff!"

As usual, Eugene, who must have been exhausted by this point, and indeed stood up as if preparing to depart, saved them all. "My boss totally believes in haunted houses. She's trying to get us to go on this haunted New York tour thing as, like, a team-building event?" Soon they were onto a topic much more comfortably in Nora's purview—walking tours of the city—and Meg hid in the kitchen, methodically loading the dishwasher. When Eugene and James announced they had to get home to take out their dog (Meg had changed her mind, she would not take on their responsibility for them), they said their good-byes. On her way out her mother kissed her and said, "Well, remember what I said about the apartment, honey. Mrs. Fishman isn't leaving for a couple of months. There's plenty of time."

Being out in the crisp evening helped Meg to unclench. Once they stepped onto the leafy street and felt the delicious coolness on their skin, they agreed to walk through Riverside Park on the way to the train, and now they slowed their pace to a stroll. They had all been inside all day—work, the train, the apartment—and shared a sense of feeling starved for air.

"What is it about that apartment that makes me so insane?" Meg said after a minute.

"It's the apartment's fault now, is it?" James said.

"Ha. Ha. Ha."

"Well, it *is* a bit stuffy in there," Eugene conceded.

Meg shook her hair out, adjusted to hold her bag on her other shoulder, retied her scarf, the bright knitted scarf she loved that suddenly seemed intentionally "funky" when she left Brooklyn. It didn't seem possible to feel comfortable in her body just then. "Seriously," she said, buttoning up her coat against the chill gusting from the river, "I would lose my mind if I moved back into that building. I mean, really? Slinking back to the Upper West after all these years? I don't fit in here at all, not anymore anyway. I always feel like the ladies here are looking at me like they think I'm homeless or something, because I don't dress in Prada."

"That's just their faces, Meg. Plastic surgery is a terrible thing," said James.

"You know, it's not like you'd be moving in with your parents," said Eugene.

"It *is* though, kind of," said Meg, hearing the deflated sadness in her own voice. "They would be in my business every second. You know how hard I've worked to create an independent life? To be on my own? To pay my way, to do things how I want? When I'm in my apartment, in my neighborhood in Brooklyn, I feel normal. I feel like me. When I'm in that building, I feel transported back to childhood, like I'm an awkward teenager again. Like Kate should be there with me. Like things are missing, things are broken."

Eugene nodded sympathetically. "I get it," he said, "but maybe that's just because whenever you're there, you actually are visiting them—your own apartment would of course be your own apartment."

"Yeah, and Meg, I mean, listen to yourself. That's a pretty small comfort zone you've created for yourself. You can't leave your neighborhood and still be yourself, still enjoy your life? Really? Of all the problems people have in the world."

"James, you're not being helpful. I mean, I know! I'm not saying it's the end of the world. I'm just saying it sucks. I want to choose how to live my life, and I'm too poor to. And I'm not even poor. It just—sucks. Why can't a single woman with a decent income support herself? What is this world, anyway?"

"But maybe living in that building wouldn't even be so bad, is what I'm saying. Think about it—you'd be so near Mom and Dad for when . . ." James trailed off.

"For what? For when they get old and sick, and my duty as the spinster daughter is to devote my life to caring for them? What fucking year is this anyway?" Meg knew she was being terrible. She knew not wanting to nurse your elderly parents, dreading the task of shepherding them toward death, was not the kind of thing normal people admitted to. She took a deep breath, tried to lighten the mood. "Eugene, you've never seen Fishman's apartment. It's basically papier-mâchéd in layers of old lady sadness."

Eugene chuckled politely, and they continued in silence.

Riverside Park was serene in the early evening. They stood at the top of the steep stairs, staring out at the river, where the lights of New Jersey looked like coins scattered across velvet. The river's earthy petrichor always surprised Meg. How was it that this vein of water still managed to belong to nature? The banks were paved, the waterway clogged with boats. Overhead, sightseeing helicopters buzzed bellicosely. Impulsively she ran down the stairs, drawn to the river. James and Eugene trailed behind.

She headed north on the footpath, past the scrubby soccer field beneath the lacy fretwork of the Henry Hudson Parkway, where they'd cheered on Kate's team during her short-lived soccer craze. Meg vividly recalled one of the team dads—a firefighter, if she was remembering correctly—sniffing at James, "You don't play no sports? Whattsamatta witchu?" and thinking for the first time, *Wait, other people notice that Jamie isn't like most boys, too?*

A handful of sunset fisherman lingered at the shore. Couples called to their dogs in the dog run or strolled arm-in-arm along the water. A chilly wind rattled the dead leaves in the trees.

"Maybe we can come up with some great reason to tell your parents why you don't want the apartment," Eugene said after a minute.

Meg nodded, smiling slightly. "Oh, yeah, that's a good idea. Like, we heard Fishman's got bedbugs." She could hardly manage the words without shuddering. Bedbugs, the living plague of New York City.

"We heard she's got her husband's corpse locked in the second bedroom," James said. They laughed. This was far less disgusting than bedbugs.

"Word is," said Meg, "an office tower is going up next door and is going to block all the windows."

"New regulations," said James, "make it illegal for there to be too many weirdos on one block, and this one is full up. And definitely too many gays, which is why we are out of the running, despite our wonderful BABY NEWS that we weren't going to share yet, thank you very much."

Meg shrugged. "How many times can I say I'm sorry. I'm *sorry*."

"Mm-hm," said James.

The boys stopped to look out over the river. To give them a moment, Meg took out her phone and pretended to check it, brazen with the expensive hunk of electronics in a way she never would have been in the park of ten years ago, when she'd always walked with her five dollars of mugging money tucked in her pocket, the rest of her cash wadded in her sock.

She knew James was still angry with her, but she also knew that he would forgive her eventually, like he always did. They'd been through so much together, more than most siblings, probably. She remembered staring down the gully of West End Avenue with him, waiting for the light to cross so they could come to this very park, after dragging him away from a party in the K-hole of his early twenties, when his fuguestate life had involved way too many party drugs, when he'd been slipping toward a scary slope. James had seemed to float just outside of his body for a few years. Who could blame him? He was young, he was beautiful, and a potent mix of grief and ketamine exempted him from fully inhabiting his grown-up life—focusing on architecture school, being decent to people, even just paying his bills.

They had sat on a bench looking over the river, icy in February, and she'd said, as gently as she could manage, *Kate's life is over, but yours is not. You had goddamn well better enjoy the fuck out of it.* Of course, that was what he'd thought he was doing, there in the pulse and flicker of the Meatpacking District discos. He'd been sure it at least *looked* like he was having a lot of fun. So it wasn't surprising that Meg's confrontation had shocked him, angered him. Who was she to lecture him, he'd shouted—James, who never shouted. It had taken them months to heal the rift. But of course it had healed, James had healed, they had put one foot in front of the other and kept moving.

James and Eugene resumed their stroll, and Meg followed, temporarily blindsided by gratitude to Eugene for his kindness to her fuckedup little brother. Clubs and drugs and one-night stands—that life had seemed exciting to James at the time, but had it been real? Real life was the pavement beneath their feet, the railing to their left, the bicyclists whizzing by to their right, the sky streaked with dark clouds like hemoglobin above. Real life was the park, which had looked so satisfyingly menacing in *The Warriors*, so convincingly dreamlike in *You've Got Mail*, its Hollywood selves absorbing her childhood memories of it.

There was the minimalist playground where they'd played as kids, seeming hilarious now, a grim row of 1970s metal equipment looking about as welcoming as robotic spiders: seesaws, swings, slides, the end. They pointed it out to Eugene for the millionth time, and for the millionth time, he pretended to be impressed. Then James said suddenly, "I still have PTSD from that playground. Kate gave me so much shit for being afraid of the jungle gym."

Meg blinked at him. "What?"

"Yeah, don't you remember that?

"Remember *what*?"

"I was always afraid to climb, and she gave me so much shit about it. Then one time I mustered up my nerve and got to the top, and then I was, like, stranded—just paralyzed with fear. I couldn't figure out how to get down. I must have been about five or six. And Kate was yelling, 'James Rhys, you are a sissy!'"

"She was not. I don't remember that!"

"Maybe you weren't there. You would have been like fifteen then, maybe you were, I don't know, off reading Proust somewhere. But it definitely happened. And all the other kids started chanting, 'SIS-SY! SIS-SY!'"

"They did *not*." Meg couldn't even exactly pinpoint why this story was upsetting her so much, but her heart raced, she felt blood boil up to her face, and she started walking faster, past the playground. "James, shut up, will you?"

"Aw, now that's not nice. Did you hear that? Big sisters are so cruel," James said to Eugene, a strange smile crimping his lips. "It's true though, it's one of my core childhood memories. Ask my therapist. Part of it was I knew there was something about that word, 'sissy,' that it meant more than just, like, being a wuss, and I knew it was something bad, very bad, but I couldn't quite figure out *what* it was, you know? And Richie Evans was there, remember that kid? And I'd always had a crush on him though I didn't even know what that meant then, I just knew I could never stop looking at him, and that made him uncomfortable, made him act meaner rather than nicer. And, anyway, so he's down there too, yelling, 'SIS-SY! SIS-SY!' And *then* he starts hefting a rock in his hand and saying to Kate, 'I know how to help him down!' I mean, I had nightmares about it for weeks. Oh and then, you know what, you definitely were there, Meg, because I think—this part is fuzzier, but I *think*—you pulled me down and told me not to be a silly goose and care so much if people teased me."

Meg shook her head. "I don't know, James."

"Aw, poor kid! I would have helped you down, sweetie. I would have made them stop." Eugene slung his arm around James's shoulders and James burrowed into him. What a baby he still was, really, sometimes, Meg couldn't help but think.

Meg said, "I can't imagine Kate doing that, even on her worst day ever. I mean, really."

"Really?" James wasn't looking at her now, was watching a group of teenagers wrestling like lanky puppies on the grass. "You know, that's always seemed to me to be the weirdest part of it, is this revisionist history that has taken hold. Like, I loved Kate, I miss her every day, just like you guys, but really, Kate was never a bully? Kate wasn't kinda crazy? Oh no, now we remember and say, Kate was so *spirited*. Like, remember when Kate ran away from home, and everyone was in a complete terrified panic the whole day?"

"She didn't really run away," Meg said. "I mean, she was just in 2E."

"Right, but no one knew that, and she left that dramatic note, and Mom was freaking the fuck out."

"She was a character," said Meg.

"Right. What a character! What spunk! She bullied littler kids on the playground, she ran away from home, she nearly dropped out of high school, she was constantly turning friends into enemies, shedding people like skin—oh, she was just such a free spirit, is that it?"

Meg stopped now, encased in the ice of James's voice. "Are you serious? What are you even doing right now?"

Even Eugene was unsettled. "Okay, we're all tired. Let's head to the subway and go home, you guys."

"No, I want to hear this. Do tell, James! What else bothered you about our dead sister?"

James shook his head. "It's just kind of fucked up how you memorialize her as this perfect person, like as if she wasn't kind of OCD and manic, like she wasn't kind of hard to be around sometimes. Like, she wasn't a saint, you know? She wasn't always nice."

"Who is?" exploded Meg. Yelling now. They were those people yelling at each other in the park. You were always walking by some drama in the city, but Meg hated to actually be the drama, the *flâneur*'s entertainment. "I'm sorry, you can't be sad when someone dies unless they were a perfect person? Is that how it works, James?"

James didn't answer. Then he said, quietly, "I can't remember the last conversation I had with her. That's always bothered me. I can't remember the last time we spoke. But I think it was an argument in a stranger's living room. Did you ever know that? She'd shown up at this house party in Alphabet City, we didn't expect to see each other, but instead of being happy to see me, she freaked out and started yelling about how I better not be doing coke in the bathroom."

"And were you?" Meg said.

"Of course! But that's not the point. I just told her she needed to mind her own business and that if she ever told Mom and Dad, I would never speak to her again." They were all quiet then. The park was dark now. Meg had the weird feeling that she only existed when she was in the corona of one of the wrought iron lampposts, and that, between spotlights, she became immaterial. James said, "Of course I never apologized. Never got the chance. I figured there was time. I mean, usually you—you just assume there's time." Eugene murmured something soothing, but Meg found herself unable to respond.

Meg would have preferred to keep walking, tracing the park as far up the spine of Manhattan as it would go, moving until her legs thrummed with blood, passing in and out of light. But she felt the pressure of James and Eugene, how much they would need a train ride together to cool off, to talk about normal things, to not part ways in an angry huff. So they headed out past the Soldiers' and Sailors' Monument, the phallic cousin of the other Civil War monument near Meg's library. Why did the city need two different monuments for the same war, anyway?

The monument's white columns glowed eerily. The bronze door at the base stood locked shut, as she had always seen it; the colonnade emblazoned with heady praise of Civil War soldiers. Meg and James had seen Shakespeare performed on the back steps; as kids they had watched *The Odd Couple* replayed on television, pleased to spot the monument and other bits of their neighborhood in the movie's backgrounds. She tried to look at the structure now for a moment, to see it as if it were brand new, as if she hadn't seen it a thousand times, to see what it would look like if she moved back to the old neighborhood and saw it every day. After all, as Nora had said, there was still time to take the apartment. There was plenty of time.

But that wasn't really true, was it? There never had been plenty of time; there never would be. Meg had been profligate with her time, and now, as she walked hurriedly down the subway steps, she wished there were a way to make more of it. But it wasn't more future she wanted, or even more present. What Meg Rhys wanted was more past.

# 19

**THE HOUSE** on Holland Avenue knew its own story. It might have told its people if only it knew how. A house has no secrets from itself.

The house on Holland Avenue was not happy. The door, which it had worked so hard to loosen, now stuck onto tight new hinges and wedged shut against its will. The people left, and the house didn't like that. Houses like to have people. Houses like movement and light and noise.

Any house in the city gets accustomed to change, to being plastered and painted and prodded. Anyone who has lived in an old house has noticed a certain slant. A warp. An angle. A thickness here, a worn spot here. People don't think much about *how* the house got bent out of shape. They believe only that it is wrong for a floor to tilt one direction. It is irritating that skewed moldings prevent precise picture-hanging. Because a house holds the shape of everyone who lived there before, like a garment stepped out of. The dogs that birthed puppies beneath the front porch lent their afterbirth to the foundation, teaching the house to nurture. Raucous salons bequeathed the parlor a certain give, like the well-conditioned limbs of an athlete. The kitchen floorboards wore the weight of dozens of women, their cooking patterns impressed in the wood. A child in 1910 developed a nervous habit of knocking on an upstairs doorframe, and the woman who lived there next wondered why the door never wanted to stay closed. The stories of the past were sealed into the walls, inscribed on crumpled newspapers balled in the insulation—a riot caused by the price of flour, an epidemic of smallpox, a craze for roller skating—like a layer of fat beneath the house's skin.

Hundreds of people had lived in the house over the course of its life. Decades of Williamses' renters, some leaving before they could even make an imprint on the house's bones. The Williamses themselves, briefly, as optimistic newlyweds. The woman from whom the Williamses had bought the house. Her aunt, who had been born on the living room floor and lived in those rooms her entire ninety years. Her sisters; for a time, a wayward niece. That family when young, a clattering mass of girls and cousins and visitors, always warm with cooking, vibrating with singing. Dogs and cats and babies and old folks and rats and spiders and generations of everything, Black people and white people and Asian people and Latino people and everyone in between. Country people and city people. Smart people and stupid people. Slobs and neatniks. Fixer-uppers and runner-downers.

This time felt different. The house sensed, with something like animal instinct, that it was about to be eviscerated.

Here came the stripping, the layers of paint and wallpaper shorn from its walls the unceremonious way you'd buzz a sheep. Appliances plucked from the kitchens, leaving gaping holes. The first floor apartment stood empty, half-stripped, exposed as a woman in the aftermath of an assault. The house didn't like that. The house especially didn't like too much movement in the small room off the kitchen, the keeping room, where beneath the floor was buried a secret.

# 20

**THEY WALKED** across the meadow, enveloped in a silence distinct from the clangor of the avenue, while a black V of geese passed overhead, drawing a graph of migration across the paper of the sky. A checkerboard of heritage crops and native grasses rustled in the breeze, the plants pallid at the end of their lives. From within one of the farmhouses came sounds indicating life. Behind the houses, white cloths shivered on a clothesline, like burial shrouds hung out to dry. They stood there for what seemed like a long time. Surely someone would come greet them, welcome them in, tell them where they should be.

Outside, beyond the gates, a loud voice made her jump. The ideas she had about this place had come from without, and suddenly the boundaries between herself and her surroundings seemed to waver, to dissolve: In that dislocated moment, she wondered if people could actually see through her and what, if so, they saw there.

Then he placed a hand on her elbow, and Meg felt herself relax. Ellis allowed her a tiny smile, steering her toward the house at the end of the line, which she now realized was the visitor center. Her elbow jangled from the ended intimacy. It was funny, really, that they were doing this—Meg realized belatedly that this was essentially their first date, this shared trip to Weeksville, scavenging for clues. They were only a few blocks away from the Williamses' haunted house, and across the street loomed the Kingsborough Houses, a massive housing

project resembling a cross between an insane asylum and a penitentiary, but within the gates of the Weeksville Heritage Center, a quiet
farm sprung up before them. The rural calm was so complete that Meg
couldn't get her bearings. "Are they open? Are we supposed to be here?"
she wondered aloud to the empty field. Ellis shrugged, walked toward
the row of houses to their right, lined up perpendicular to the block of
Bergen Street where Meg had locked her bike after a harrowing ride.

That morning, her landlady's realtor had knocked on her door with
some potential buyers. There had been a miscommunication, and Meg
had never been warned. She was in her pajamas still, wrapped in an
unbecoming woolen shawl/blanket, drinking coffee on her terrace,
when the bell bleated through the air. Meg had felt exactly as if she
were naked, standing there trying not to visibly tremble as a gleam-
ingly blonde, obviously rich couple—you could tell they were rich just
from the fabrics of their clothes, their coats which were not just new
and clean but *fine*, ten years younger than her at least, which made it
somehow even worse, peered at her messy apartment. Strangers in nice
shoes, the soles subway-filthy, tromping across her rugs, looking at her
bedroom, her rumpled sheet still smelling of sleep, of her sleep. The
realtor faux-apologized for the intrusion but "since we're already here
. . ." Meg watched in horror as they moved around her space, touched
her things, reached down to pet her cat—Kate's cat. It was worse than
watching the hipsters rent the apartment she'd liked, a thousand
times worse.

The young woman frowned at the kitchen. "Oh gosh, it's like a dollhouse kitchen! Can you even cook anything in here?"

The man pointed to the terrace. "You could totally stick a barbecue
out there, though, right?"

"Totally!" The realtor seemed to position herself in front of Meg,
as if hiding a moldy spot on the wall. "I know this place is a bit small,
but that terrace is like a whole extra room. And this neighborhood is
just great—really up-and-coming. Lots of young couples and families."
Meg notwithstanding, obviously.

The moment they left, she had bolted the door behind them and
taken a long, searingly hot shower, as if she could wash their gazes off

her skin. It was *her* apartment, *her* life. Why should they get to move in and take it over? Why wasn't she good enough for her home, her neighborhood? She knew it was irrational, but it felt like some sort of conspiracy—her neighborhood wanted couples, wanted kids, wanted people to pay property taxes and join the PTA and start food cart festivals, not her. "Kate," Meg said, staring out her window, "what do I do?"

So after assembling her public self, Meg had spent the morning biking around beneath the last bright leaves of autumn. She shook off the unpleasant scene in the apartment, started thinking, as if accidentally, about Ellis. Ellis, Ellis, Ellis.

She had to move her body, to pump her legs until sweat sprang beneath her breasts, to ride until her crotch was sore. Nothing that she wanted to happen was going to happen, she was going to have to accept that. She was not going to be able to stay in her apartment, she was not going to find some amazing new place, she was not going to jump into bed with Ellis and confirm her suspicion that he understood her the way no one else ever would—that especially would just never, ever happen.

For one thing, he wasn't simply another hot guy given to Vronsky-esque smoldering. He was a library patron, which was one level of inappropriate, and one that didn't trouble her too terribly; but he was also a recent widower, an extra level of wrong that *did* trouble her, that troubled her very much. She knew what it was to be mourning. She knew what that first raw, exposed-nerve year was like. Meg knew that she ought to stay far, far away. Love was for stupid people, like the couple who had invaded her apartment that morning, who needed partners and the trappings of bourgeois life to validate themselves. She didn't need it. She didn't need any of that.

Riding her bike made Meg keenly aware of the city's elevation, the ache in her calf muscles a barometer of the former glacial moraine's remains, and traveling down streets with generous bus lanes but nonexistent bike lanes reminded her of the culture clash abutting neighborhoods could suffer. At the beginning of her ride in Prospect Heights, she had competed for bike lane right-of-way with spandex-clad cheetahs and parents balancing almond-milk lattes while they piloted their children in Dutch-designed bike wagons. As she entered Crown Heights, the lanes narrowed, the other bikes disappeared, and she found herself dodging aggressive Access-a-Ride van drivers and even more aggressive jaywalkers, who shouted at her as she rode past. Soon every face on the street was Black, and Meg, only a mile or so from where she lived, felt as out-of-place as James Baldwin in his tiny Swiss village. Why did it make her nervous to be so conspicuous? Why did she feel like everyone was staring at her, and if they were, so what? What did she think was going to happen, she admonished herself, and why should she even notice the askance looks? Why did she worry that people didn't like her being there, that strangers were mad at her for existing? Or was she imagining it all, and did no one even notice her at all?

By the time she met Ellis, she was feeling slightly deranged. But she had offered to come with in order to help him, she had to remind herself; she was there in a professional capacity. It was imperative that she knock this guileless tourist shit *off*. She pulled her hair from her sweating neck and took a deep breath.

The email exchange had gone like this:

Ellis: "I really appreciate your help on this. I can't help thinking there's something I'm missing here, something right under my nose."

Meg: "I understand completely. It's because you don't know exactly what you're looking for, so it's hard to know when you've found it. Or even gotten close. You're a scientist; you want answers in black and white. I mean, I'm guessing."

Ellis: "Yeah, and, well, it's complicated. Here's something though. Since Jenkins bought the land from Weeks, it must have been part of Weeksville. Should I just go to the Weeksville museum place, you know, the houses that are still there, and ask them what they think? My father keeps not-so-subtly suggesting that I do, but he teaches during the hours when they give tours. Have you been there? What do you think?"

Meg (switching, without comment, from her work email address to her Gmail): "I think that's a wonderful idea. I've been really wanting to go there myself. I'm off tomorrow. You know, in case you wanted some company." (Her heart beat faster as she typed the words, suddenly shy despite her decades of online dating, her continuing-education-master's degree in The Fine Art of First Dates; luckily she'd become an expert in the art of wording things ambiguously. Just in case their coffee date at the library had not been haunting his every thought as much as it had hers.)

Ellis: "There is a tour at three. I will be there."

And in that carefully worded do-si-do of emails, they had arranged this very super professional research mission.

Now they walked together, the Christmassy scent of Ellis's paper cup of tea unfurling in the air like a beckoning cartoon fog. "What is that?" Meg asked.

He smiled sheepishly. "Apple Spice Tea. I—Rachel got me hooked on it. I was so cold walking over here from the train I stopped in a bo-dega for this. Here, want a sip?"

Meg hesitated. She did, but it seemed too greedy, like stealing a kiss before he'd meant to offer it. "Let me smell it," she said, and she leaned over his cup and inhaled deeply, almost touching his hands but not quite. "That is wonderful. I haven't had tea like that since I found out coffee existed."

There were a million things she wanted to say to him. She wanted to ask about the house, about how he was doing, about when he was going back home to Chicago—she needed facts and figures, information she could chart. But she also needed to not seem needy and weird and not make this research trip into more than it was, which was an information-gathering mission on behalf of people researching a proj-ect, obviously. (She had decided to write a Rhys's Pieces series about different historical destinations in the city, which was an interesting idea for the newsletter and not at all an excuse.) She was still feeling jumpy and unsettled from her fight with James, or whatever that had been in Riverside Park—not a fight exactly, but a what? A confession? A challenge? An outpouring of—of what? But this was too many feel-ings all at once. In order to get through the day, Meg decided, she would have to change genders right then and there, a modern-day

Orlando. She became a man, nodded carelessly. "Okay," she therefore said, "so, let's do this."

They walked into the visitor's center together, Meg's whole side sparking whenever Ellis moved near. A very young, very cute woman sat at the desk nearest to the door. Behind her was a U of unpopulated desks, as if the rapture or a sudden staff meeting had whisked away her coworkers. The girl looked quickly from Ellis to Meg and back again, as if trying to take their relationship's temperature and make a swift diagnosis. Ellis smiled as she stood and moved toward them, her long skinny dreadlocks swaying, brass bangles clanking on her wrist. Meg felt something harden inside herself, watching Ellis watch the girl.

Meg crossed her arms over her sweater and studied the bookshelf beside her as Ellis and the girl chatted comfortably about the heritage center, about the neighborhood, about Caribbean food, about the old best place to get Doubles, the new best place to get Doubles. They had been standing there talking for several minutes before Meg realized the solitude of the office wasn't temporary—the computers were off, the chairs lacked sweaters or coats, the workspaces were clear—the girl was all alone there. The girl said something about budgets and cuts and offered to start the tour, since they were the only ones there for it. Meg nodded, stepping out into the yard again, chastising herself for feeling so ruffled. So Ellis was being polite to a pretty young thing who loved history, who was being polite back because it was her job. Why should Meg get so tetchy and feline about it?

Ellis held the door open for the girl, and the girl ducked under his arm and giggled and thanked him and then locked the door behind them. "This building houses the offices," she explained, battling with the key ring, "because it's actually a replica—the original burned down, so this isn't landmarked or anything." The tour guide continued in a sing-song, batting her eyelashes at Ellis but having clearly embarked on the memorized portion of her speech, "The new building you see on the far side of the field is going to house our permanent collections of photography and artifacts, as well as feature exciting, new exhibits. It is currently open only to special groups, but we hope to expand our hours . . ."

Meg squinted across the meadow at the modern block of the museum. She could almost see the long-ago farms busy with horse-drawn plows; the scrubby grass pocked by sandy patches; in the distance, oak, spruce, and pine spinneys; the large park, perhaps noisy with a picnic full of schoolchildren dressed in white tunics; further off, the deep green fringe of the Hunterfly Woods. She knew the area had been hilly, with a deep gorge that created stormy wind tunnels. Somewhere nearby had been Suydam Pond, where people got their water for washing, had picnics and parties in the summer, and skated when it froze in the winter. The wild topography of the land had been silenced by gridded streets, tamed with pavement. The Heritage Center was lovely, otherworldly, but it also was empty and smacked of municipal neglect; the dirty, trash-strewn streets nearby were chaotic with lawless traffic and unorthodox parking patterns, lined with crumbling houses and charmless storefronts. She would be mad too, she thought, if she had died and this had happened to the beautiful place she'd loved. Maybe the floating sense of fear she'd felt on the way here hadn't originated within her after all. How was a place to forget completely when it had been ravaged by riots, when it had been scorched and thrashed by the worst of humanity, again and again? How were people to forget? Maybe it was just that the whole damn city had PTSD. Maybe it was permanently embedded in the soil, like nuclear fallout, dormant but never entirely forgotten.

Ellis and the tour guide had started off without her. She followed them into the first building, a tiny structure with two mirrored houses connected like Siamese Twins. The tour guide recited, "This double-house has been carefully restored with furniture and artifacts from the mid-nineteenth century. Weeksville was an agrarian village at that time, founded by a stevedore named James Weeks in the 1830s, populated by free, land-owning African Americans—*before* the Emancipation Proclamation!" She ended every sentence on the same flat, slightly extended note, the universal cadence of tour guides. Meg was about to interrupt her—they didn't need the history lesson, actually—but then remembered how empty the visitor center had been. It was probably fun for the girl to actually get to practice her spiel.

Meg watched Ellis, who was studying the neat arrangements of artifacts on an end table—a Bible, a doily, a pair of spectacles. He pressed on a door gently but it didn't open, and he brought his hand down again before the tour guide noticed. Meg wanted to grab that hand and kiss it. What? No. She shook her head, turned her focus to the tour guide. "Residents enjoyed a number of professions, which included working on the docks, farming, and even being doctors and lawyers. There were schools, asylums, hospitals, and churches, one of which still stands just down the street, the Berean Missionary Baptist Church." Meg noted that Ellis had produced a spiral notebook from somewhere and was taking notes, nodding, like an A+ student. She smiled, walked slowly across the creaking wooden floors, listening to the lonesome music they made. The tour guide continued, her hands clasped: "The first African American woman physician in New York, Susan McKinney-Steward, was born here in Weeksville! And did you know, that when 1863 Draft Riots broke out in the Lower East Side of Manhattan, Weeksville served as a refuge for escaping African Americans!"

She beckoned them out of the house and into the next one. They exchanged a knowing smile, and Meg was healed. The next house was a 1900s two-story wood frame where an extended family had lived, and the next was a 1930s-era house dedicated to artifacts from the Great Depression. Ellis said nothing to Meg during the whole visit, except to mutter as they left the middle house, "This one looks a *lot* like my house." She nodded, some part of her pleased that the tour guide wouldn't know what he meant by this. But then she saw how close it really was, how similar the floor plan.

"What's this room here?" Meg asked the tour guide, pointing to a little room off the kitchen, just like the one at Ellis's house.

"Oh, I am so glad you asked—it's so interesting. There used to often be little rooms like this off the kitchen, and sometimes they were used to store food and other kitchen necessities, but also children or sometimes guests would sleep here because the kitchen fires kept it warm. They called it a 'keeping room.' Doesn't that sound so cozy?"

Meg nodded, wandered through the rooms as the tour guide continued her lilting speech. Ellis was so patient to listen to the whole thing, the simplified version of the world they'd been living and breathing in their research. Whatever that was, Meg didn't have it. She tiptoed up the creaking stairs, thick with centuries of paint, and found herself in a warren of bedrooms upstairs. The tour guide had said an eight-person family had lived in this home. Meg moved through the close rooms, trying to picture it, pausing to gaze out the window at the pastoral backyard. And she'd thought sharing a room with Kate was tough. How had eight people even physically wedged themselves into these tiny rooms? It would have been just a sea of beds, or else smaller beds than they were used to, or else—and she realized this was probably it—two or three kids to each small bed.

It was impossible to imagine a whole childhood like that, before the invention of privacy. Her adolescence had been defined by territorial battles with Kate. As she ran a finger along a doorjamb, she thought of the time she'd come home to find her vintage John Lennon & Yoko Ono poster replaced with a map of Tibet. "I'm going to run away from home," Kate had explained coolly, from where she reclined on Meg's bunk, "and go there."

"To *Tibet*?" Meg had spat, tired from a bad day of high school and a particularly jangling bus ride home. "That's the stupidest thing I've ever heard."

Kate, still new to her transcendental meditation kick, was ready for a fight. "How can that be? Unless you can't actually hear yourself talk."

The poster had been shredded, and the girls fought, really fought, slapping and pulling hair, until their mother had run in to separate them. "What is the matter with you two?!" Nora had cried.

And awfully Meg had said, still panting, "I want her out of my fucking face. Actually, I want her out of my *life*." She ached to remember it now. How could she have been such a jerk? She was a teenager, but even teenagers could not be jerks if they set their minds to it.

Nora had grabbed her wrist with one surprisingly strong hand, and Kate's wrist with the other, and yanked them together. "You girls listen to me. You will never. Ever. Be out of each other's lives. So deal with it." She'd stalked out of the room, adding over her shoulder, "And before I see either one of you at the dinner table, this room had better be clean."

United then in irritation with Nora instead of each other, Meg and Kate had set about to dividing up the room more precisely than ever before, taking out a tape measure to mark off who got which inch of wall space, moving their dressers away from each other, even running a partition of masking tape along the wood floor, like greedy generals in land war, or toddlers in the backseat of a car. It was silly and futile, but Meg could still recall the urgency she had felt at the time to stake out her territory as *hers*. She remembered approximately once a day how she had said it: "I want her out of my *life*."

She made her way down the narrow staircase to rejoin Ellis. After the tour, they stood out in front of the houses, and Ellis stood beside Meg, and they faced the tour guide like an audience, and even if the arrangement was accidental, it felt to Meg like an intimacy. Together they were looking; together they were facing this question.

The tour guide hadn't stopped smiling at Ellis. In answer to something she explained, "And Weeksville was also home to one of the first African American newspapers, founded in 1866, called *The Freedman's Torchlight*!" She seemed so happy to share the information with them that they continued to nod and feign amazement, holding to their unspoken agreement not to burst her bubble with a brisk "We already know all this." Finally she asked, "Do you have any other questions?"

Meg was surprised—how much of a nerd could he really be!—when Ellis opened his mouth. "Well. Actually." He looked at Meg and she smiled, giving him permission for something. For everything. "Do you think there could be other Weeksville houses still around? Like, in the neighborhood? Do folks ever come bring you things or ask you to look at their houses?"

The tour guide nodded. "All. The. Time." She laughed. "I've only been working here a few months, only part-time, and I've still had a ton of people come with, like, an old map they found in their wall while the plumber was doing something, or shoes that've been hanging out in their fireplace for some reason, or you know, a Christening gown they found in the attic. Just the other day I had this old lady come in with a bunch of nineteenth-century newspapers they found stuck in the walls when they were expanding a doorway. You just walk around, and you see old wooden houses—there's one on this block that's all boarded up but that looks just like our 1900 house, really. But there's no money, you know? No money to check things out, landmark the buildings."

Meg nodded. She had been rendered mute by the whole visit, by her discomfort at the subconscious camaraderie Ellis shared with the girl; she'd spent the tour as watchful as an orphan, or the overthinking modernist heroine of Dorothy Richardson's *Pilgrimage*. She realized he'd been watching her watch the tour guide give her speech, and when Meg met Ellis's eye, something he saw on her face made him reach out and pat her shoulder, just quickly, just once, but somehow it was enough and telegraphed something to the girl, who faded back, dimming her smile to normal-professionally-friendly-because-it's-my-job wattage, and Ellis said to Meg, "Did *you* have any questions?" and it was all staged to indicate closeness that Meg had not yet earned, and her heart was exploding from it. She shook her head. She did not have any questions.

The tour guide handed Ellis her card and thanked them for visiting, urged them to visit again, to contact her anytime, to come to one of the evening events the Center hosted, treating them now like a couple. Well, was that so hard to believe? That this handsome guy might be her boyfriend? Meg thanked the tour guide with exaggerated warmth— *Threatened? By a museum employee? What! Ha!*—and the tour guide headed back up the path to the visitor's center to continue her invisible work with her invisible colleagues.

Meg and Ellis strolled around to the back of the houses, where a small replica—or maybe actual—kitchen garden had been planted. The business portion of their visit was complete. It would now be appropriate to debrief ("So! There are lots of undiscovered Weeksville houses like yours, seems like!" "Sure, it all makes sense! What a rich history our city has! Well, see you around!") and then, with some gently joking aside about the ravages of time, say goodbye and head their separate ways. But Meg felt such an urgency to stay near him that she didn't mention leaving. Neither did he. They walked the yard like performance artists or monks, slowly as could be, one miniscule step after another, as if they might actually warp the passage of time. Meg was sure she heard chickens. Were there chickens? Were they actually warping the passage of time?

Finally Ellis said, "What are we going to do?" He stopped walking and looked at her.

Meg swallowed, found her voice. "Pardon me?"

*We.* She thought he might reach out and take her hand, but of course he didn't. He turned to face the backs of the houses. She did too. They stood there looking together, and Meg thought she knew that they were seeing the same thing in the same way—not just the houses now but the houses as they had been and how they would be in the future—and the intimacy of sharing this architectural scopophilia was almost more than she could bear. At any minute her knees would buckle. What could she say to him to express what she felt, as idiotic as it was? *Take me here, now, on this historically accurate lawn of native grasses!*

"About the house," Ellis said, pragmatically. "What are my parents and I going to do about that damn house? Knowing what we know, you know?"

"Right. Yes. Absolutely," replied the librarian.

"If we know it was part of Weeksville, I mean, what is the right thing to do? Do we donate it to the Historical Center? Do we pay the city to inspect it, have it landmarked? Do we restore it historically accurately? What's our responsibility?"

"You mean, like, legally?"

Ellis shot her a look. "I mean, like, ethically."

"Oh. That. Right. I keep forgetting you're so into that."

He squinted, surveying the terrain. "These people who lived here. They took in refugees and orphans and runaway slaves. They did things we would never consider, just to help other Black folks. And white folks too, whether anyone thought about that or not. And now here I am, an ordinary guy, living an entire life that would not have been possible had they not fought for it." Meg nodded, thinking of her own freedom fighters: the suffragists, Elizabeth Cady Stanton, Erica Jong. "What's right to do? Can we really ignore it all and try to turn a profit?" He rubbed his hands over his scalp.

"I think," said Meg, then stopped. Who was she to think anything about it? It wasn't really hers, was it? She tried again. "What do you think? What's your instinct?"

Ellis shook his head miserably. "I really don't know."

They left the center together and walked down the street to where Meg had chained her bike. She felt humiliated for the thoughts she had had when leaving her beat-up bicycle there a mere hour earlier: *This neighborhood is not good. Someone is going to steal my bike.* She'd even considered popping off the seat to take with her. What was her problem? Yes, it was a valid instinct for a New Yorker who had bikes stolen in fancier neighborhoods than this, but also, here was hardly anyone even around. How had those fears gotten so ingrained?

She tried to picture the countryside superimposed over the scrubby terrain. Here she'd been obsessing over if Ellis liked her, if he would brush her arm, if he would move toward her in some way that indicated he planned to kiss her, just an overgrown girl with a crush. And meanwhile he'd been struggling over his responsibility toward his heritage, what he owed the country's tortured past, this country that a few hundred years ago would have offered him nothing, that maybe even now offered him less than she knew. Meg took off her glasses and rubbed at her face, as if she could rearrange her features, smooth out her thoughts. She put them back on and pulled her bike helmet over her hair. "Do I look *too* cool with this helmet on? Is it intimidating you?"

He smiled. "Yes."

She smiled back, leaning her unchained bicycle against her hip. "Ellis, I think you're a really good person, you know that? And not just because you like my extremely cautious fashion sense. I mean—the fact that you're so worried about all this. I feel like most people would just say, okay fuck it, let's sell to the highest bidder and let the whole mess be someone else's problem."

"That's kind of been America's M.O.," Ellis conceded.

"Exactly. And I—I know you and your family are going to figure out the right thing to do. Do what's right for you guys. And if you need any help with any of it, you know I'm here for you." Meg straddled her bike, ready to ride off and release him into his evening. Maybe he would call the tour guide at her number on the card she'd given him. Maybe he'd go home and chat with his dead wife. None of it was up to Meg, and if she were honest with herself, she didn't want it to be. She wanted him to want her. But she didn't want to tell him what to do, any more than she wanted him to tell her what to do. Maybe she'd always been this way, and it explained why, like a guy in a Hemingway novel, she never got too attached for too long.

He leaned forward, put a hand lightly on her handlebar. "Meg," he said.

"Ellis," she said.

They stared into each other's eyes for a minute, for a hundred years. *I know how much everything hurts right now,* Meg didn't say to him. *I know you know,* Ellis didn't answer back. He said, "Thanks again for all your help."

The librarian answered, "You're so very welcome. Do email me if anything else comes up," before riding off into the already dimming evening.

Down in 2E, it was exactly as if the intervening decades hadn't passed at all. "Meggie!" Mrs. Fishman greeted her, as if she'd been sent down by her parents for leaf cookies and "Wheel of Fortune," the apartment the mid-century time capsule it had always been: Mrs. Fishman herself, old ever since Meg had known her, largely unchanged by the years, only shriveled a bit, faded somewhat, like the spine of a book shelved facing the sun, so unchanged, in fact, that Meg doubted herself, doubted everything. Had it really been that long? Had it really been any time at all? Had she, Meg, really aged, grown, morphed into a gray-haired lady who was often asked by strangers, *Aren't you lonely?* and *Why the long face, can't you cheer up?* Had her pesky little brother Jamie really transformed into a handsome architect, a married man about to become a father? Had Kate really disappeared from their lives? It all seemed ridiculous and unlikely, standing there facing Mrs. Fishman in her velour sweatsuit and bedroom slippers, the smell of burnt coffee percolating out from the kitchen.

Because as soon as Meg stepped through the door, it all came surging back—the scratchy feel of that same tweed sofa (as her fingertips ran across it in 1989), the sounds of the daytime television muttering under its breath, the way she had studied the mysterious tight grins of the framed Black and white family members who continued to collect dust on the doilied end tables. The vertical blinds were drawn shut against the day's weak autumn sun; the resulting dim had comforted kid-Meg but drove now-Meg almost immediately batty, making her uncomfortable in her own skin.

"Cawfee?" Mrs. Fishman said.

Meg nodded gratefully. She had come on a whim, hadn't steeled herself for the long train ride uptown with nearly enough caffeine, now regretted it, regretted everything. Mrs. Fishman betrayed no surprise at the unprecedented, unannounced visit from her erstwhile neighbor and sometime-ward, which led Meg to wonder whether maybe the dementia hadn't already taken hold. Though the old lady seemed steady enough, holding a translucent china cup and saucer with both hands— only when she placed the cup on the confetti-formica kitchen table was Meg able to regain her sense of scale and comprehend how tiny Mrs. Fishman had become, how enormous the cup looked in her sinewy fingers. Mrs. Fishman set out serving bowls of sugar and nondairy creamer, dosed her own coffee, sat down with a sigh.

"How's life, Megelah?" So she did remember her, even regained Nora's Yiddish-lite nickname for her. Of course, duh, Meg recalled that Nora visited 2E weekly if not daily, surely she had kept her apprised of all of Meg's various disappointing life developments.

Meg studied Mrs. Fishman's face. You could tell she had been a pretty young woman, could still locate the bone structure beneath her papery skin, her dark eyes even more prominent now. She had always struck Meg as being extraordinarily *contained*—Mrs. Fishman made small movements, walked with a dancer's self-conscious posture, moved as if perpetually working not to knock anything over.

Meg remembered that she'd been a music teacher of some sort; even as a young child, she had enjoyed seeing Mrs. Fishman arriving home around the same time Meg did from after-school activities, wearing a sophisticated black coat, a sheaf of music peeking out of her handbag, take-out food from a local restaurant steaming fragrantly from a plastic bag. Mrs. Fishman—elegant, solitary, in control—had it all figured out, or so it had seemed to Meg.

"Life is good," Meg answered, sipping the pungent coffee. "I still work at the library, you know, the Brooklyn Collection. I'm working on some exciting research projects. I write for the library newsletter—"

Mrs. Fishman nodded briskly. "Of course, Rhys's Pieces! I'm a big fan."

Meg blinked. "You are?" She wasn't sure what she had expected from this encounter, but it hadn't been this. Nora had made Mrs. Fishman sound so feeble and put-upon! The Mrs. Fishman (Meg wouldn't say "feisty," wouldn't say "spry") before her said, "I love the library! I went to the most wonderful program my local branch had the other day—a talk about, what did they call it. Gentrification and the City, or was it Genteel Traditions in the City? Well, anyway, it was wonderful."

"That's great! Hey, my mother mentioned that you were thinking about a—ah—a home, that they have great programs there—"

Mrs. Fishman held up a knobby hand. Meg noticed the wedding ring was still there, riding out the years. "Yes, I'm moving out, and you want the apartment, that's why you're here."

Meg nearly choked on her coffee. "No! I mean—my parents mentioned it, but I—no, you misunderstand. I have a great place out in Brooklyn. You know, I've always lived in Brooklyn, as an adult I mean, I work there, my whole life is there. Can you imagine, a Brooklyn librarian living in another borough! Would my library card even stay valid? You know what I mean?"

The old woman laughed. "I'm sure you'll figure it out! Because listen, before we go any farther—I want the lease to stay in my name, and I want you to live here when I go. I already told your mother. I've been waiting for you to come. So that's it, we don't have to pussyfoot around it, and we can get down to a real conversation." She stood up, and Meg half-expected her to leave the apartment right then and there, to saunter into the abyss like an Upper West Side Inuit setting off on an ice floe to die. But Mrs. Fishman only went as far as the freezer, saying over her shoulder, "I know I have some of those leaf cookies from Ferrara's in here somewhere, you still like those?" She found the ice-crystal-crusted bag, dropped some onto a china plate, presented them to Meg like frozen artifacts from the cave of her childhood. "Or are you all gluten-free, sugar-free, fun-free like everyone else these days?"

"No, no, of course not. But just to be clear, Mrs. Fishman—"

"Call me Judy."

"Judy! I can't call you Judy," Meg laughed. "You're Mrs. Fishman, famous Mrs. Fishman from 2E, I can't change now! Even my mother calls you Mrs. Fishman."

Mrs. Fishman selected a pink leaf, balanced it on her saucer, where she left it to languish. "Your mother does what she wants. That is one formidable woman. You're a lot like her, you know. I always thought that about you. Even more than your sister, God rest her soul, who was the spitting image of your father."

This characterization did not ring at all true to Meg, and she was again washed with doubt. Why had she come here again? She nibbled on the edge of a green leaf, Kate's favorite. It tasted like freezer.

"Well, all I wanted to say is—I mean, I'm not here for your apartment. I just was thinking of you and felt like saying hello." Even as she said it, Meg was sizing up the apartment out of her peripheral vision— not that she wanted to live there! But it *was* a spacious two bedroom, and it was true that beneath the layered rugs—could she check? No, she couldn't check of course—the wood floors were probably in pristine condition—that behind the prissy wallpaper, the walls were probably perfect, that the bathroom still had the original pink-and-black tiles, and that decades inhabited by only a single woman had left the entire structure unscathed—but these were only the things any New Yorker noticed, especially when one had been looking at terrible rental after terrible rental, sinking deeper and deeper into depression while time lurched closer and closer toward the eviction date. Meg leaned back in the chair, which wobbled, emitting an unseemly crack sound, startling her into sitting upright again, imitating Mrs. Fishman's—Judy's—Mrs. Fishman's ballerina posture.

Mrs. Fishman shrugged. "Okay, dearie, you suit yourself. But what I was going to say—I was saying to your mother—is that I need a special kind of person to take this place. That's why I thought of you." And Mrs. Fishman looked pointedly at the portrait hanging over the table, like a perpetual dinner guest. The hand-colored photograph of the handsome young man in uniform, a slightly mocking smile curling his lips, had hung there as long as Meg could remember. There was another one, a bad reproduction from the drug store photo lab, in an oval frame on Mrs. Fishman's bedside table, or anyway there had been circa 1990 or so.

"Mr. Fishman," said Meg. She devoured the rest of her cookie in one bite and quickly ate another.

Mrs. Fishman smiled. "Poor Ricky. He was such a good boy."

Meg helped herself to a third leaf off the serving plate—a brown one, meant to approximate chocolate—chomping around the edges, the way she'd eaten them as a child, as she were regressing. She was starting to crave the warm cranberry cocktail Mrs. Fishman stored on the top of the fridge. If she stayed there too long, she'd probably start dotting her "i"s with hearts.

"Tell me," she said.

Ricky had loved Judy, Judy had loved Ricky. They'd grown up on the same block down on the Lower East Side, their fathers worked at the same factory, but their parents had forbidden their teenage romance— classic American Romeo and Juliet business—because Ricky Fishman was Jewish and Judy McDonnell was a good Protestant girl, so they'd eloped after Ricky enlisted. Judy had lived with her parents, worked at the local pharmacy, wrote sheaves of passionate love letters to her handsome young husband, secretly converted to Judaism. Mostly, she waited. When he was killed in combat, half the letters were returned, undelivered. She rented the apartment with his pension and waited some more. Nineteen years old, living on her own in 1940s Manhattan. Just a girl. Could Meg imagine? Meg could imagine, a little.

"Didn't you ever want to—you know. Go out? Go dancing? Have

a little . . . fun?" Meg drained her coffee cup, swallowing a mouthful of dirt-like grounds. She helped herself to water, looked quickly, just in a normal way, around the tidy kitchen, poured more coffee for Mrs. Fishman. Nora had always sworn that Mrs. Fishman stayed faithful to Ricky's memory, but Meg found it hard to believe. Seventy years without sex? Really? Even more than that, there was something a bit odd about the idea of the withered woman before her "staying faithful" to a husband who had never moved much past boyhood. The boy in the portrait—he could have been Mrs. Fishman's great-grandson.

Mrs. Fishman smiled mysteriously. "Oh, I've had my fun. Actually, I've gone dancing *every night.*" She lowered her voice, leaned close to Meg, the steam from the fresh cup of coffee misting her hair. Mrs. Fishman pointed to the portrait and said, "He visits me." She giggled girlishly. "Every night, I put on a record we used to play together, and Ricky visits, and he holds me close, and we dance. And then—" she pointed at Meg, then pointed toward the bedroom, "he takes me to bed." Something flickered over Mrs. Fishman's face. "Does that sound crazy? I usually don't tell people about it. They usually don't like to hear."

Meg reached out to pat Judy's hand. "It doesn't sound crazy at all. Not to me." She paused. "I hang out with Kate every night."

Mrs. Fishman nodded. "I've always wondered if she comes to you. She comes to your mother too, you know." Meg blinked. Okay, now she was certain—Judy Fishman had begun to unravel. Who wouldn't after such a life? Mrs. Fishman continued: "Poor Ricky, he just—I'm tired, you know? I'm old! I need a rest! I'm ready to go live somewhere else. I'm sure he wouldn't bother you, or you know, whoever moved in. He's only ever had eyes for me."

Meg filed away a joke to tell James later about potentially getting date-raped by an amorous ghost—now there was something you didn't see in every Craigslist apartment ad! But there it was, that was love: Mrs. Fishman had made space in her life for Ricky, even now. Meg couldn't so much as picture Ellis in her apartment, couldn't imagine finding room for his big, muscular body on her fussy little loveseat. What did it mean that she couldn't stop thinking about him, thrilled when he drew near, but couldn't envision mixing him a drink in her kitchen, sitting beside him on her leafy balcony, worried her life would seem silly to him, and dull, and small?

They moved onto earthly chit-chat. Wasn't the weather strange, hadn't the Upper West Side changed? Eventually Meg extricated herself, out of a sense of obligation, went upstairs to ring her parents' bell, found with relief that they weren't home. On the train ride home, she lost herself in a book Mrs. Fishman had lent her—poetry by soldiers—and tried not to think much about anything at all.

# 21

**A DOOR OPENS AND SHUTS** when no one is home. All the windows fly open, an unseasonable breeze gusting through the rooms. A floor creaks beneath invisible feet. In the middle of the night, an audible moaning.

It isn't enough. People kept coming and messing things up. A construction worker is the first to reenter the house after the men take their lunch break, and he notices right away an icy spot in the air. *What the . . . ?* He looks around for an open window, sees that all the windows have been opened. Which of those idiots he works with has done this? It's way too cold to leave them all up like that. But when he lumbers over to pull them shut—nothing doing, they are stuck open, all of them.

He mutters curses, tromps over to the counter where he puts down the brightly colored sports drinks they've gotten for later, when they again become thirsty. Turns around and *Fwoosh. Thud.* When he turns back to the counter, he sees all five bottles have fallen to the floor. Did he knock them over somehow? Is he losing his mind? He looks around, shudders in the cold, puts them all back on the counter. Turns to leave the room and—*Fwoosh. Thud.* The counter must be slanted. But the bottles weren't on their sides, so . . . ? He leans over to gather them, and when he stands up, his head slams into a drawer that's been yanked open. He shouts in pain, staggers. What is this, some sort of Three

Stooges routine? The hair on the back of his neck and his arms is all prickled, and he has a creepy feeling in his stomach, like he's had too much beer and then gas station taquitos.

The man is irritated now. He will get back to work and do what he needs to do and go home and have a drink, because Jesus Christ. So he goes into the small room off the kitchen where they have been working on the floor. And God damn it all, things are not much better in here! He shakes his head, unwilling to go crazy on a normal shift. They should be getting time-and-a-half in that kooky house, where things seem to shift around on their own, where paint doesn't dry the way it usually does, where nails and screws aren't enough to hold things together. Because there, in the middle of the floor, is a pried-up floorboard—not by them, they've all been out to lunch at the same diner together—and as if dug out of the floor itself, a bunch of old objects lined up in a row.

The man turns around, scooping his sports drink off the pile of bottles on the floor on his way out. Nope, no thanks. That house—it's too much for him. It's just too much.

# 22

*IT WAS SO EARLY* in the morning that the sky was still cataracted with nighttime, the street lamps just now flickering off. Meg waited a few minutes for the bus that was supposed to come before she gave up. What she needed now was to walk anyway, and if she was a few minutes late to meet Ellis, well, okay. She had to walk until she caught up with her brain, until she found herself again; she had to walk across bombed-out expanses of North Brooklyn that she usually pretended didn't exist despite their proximity to the places where she lived and worked, across where scrubby grass and pine forests had once stood; she had to walk until her blood pounded in her legs.

She was soon in a part of the neighborhood she didn't know well, where the store signs were all in Yiddish, and the men were all in suits and hats, like a sudden trip to nineteenth-century Ukraine. Here were the Hasids in black, with their wide-brimmed hats and long coats. Groups of teenaged mothers dressed to the nines—stylish dresses, patterned tights, patent leather shoes, and cascading tumbles of wig-hair—scurried around, even as early as it was, pushing buggies. She felt suddenly conspicuous, glaringly non-Jewish, shabbily and wantonly dressed (in a dress that was long, sure, but also presented her cleavage like a display case).

Brick buildings lined the narrow roads. Here was the morning chorus of storefronts opening up for the day, the metal gates rattling up. *RRRRTTTTHHHHAAAATTT!* A Kosher bakery. *RRRRTTTTHHHHAAAATTT!* A shop selling modest clothes and hats. *RRRRTTTTHHHHAAAATTT! RRRRTTTTH-HHHAAAATTT!* Up rolled the metal gates, exposing each shop's glassy scleras to the sun. A wig store; a kosher butcher's; a bookstore; the signs in English and Hebrew. A bodega, a bodega, another bodega. Meg was hungry; she longed for a bacon, egg, and cheese on a roll but doubted she would find one here. How much had to happen to make such a breakfast kosher? It had to become something else, was what had to happen. She was doomed to stay hungry.

Meg looked people in the eye as they crossed paths, something a combination of shyness and a city-dweller's sense of self-preservation usually prevented. She evaluated everyone she walked by, thinking about the neighborhood's tumultuous past. That elderly Caribbean man—would he throw a Molotov cocktail through a kosher butcher's window? That thin-lipped mom herding one, two, three, four, seven identically dressed children along the sidewalk—would she hurl rocks at a Black man's car? Who were the people who did the things that made riots? Every person Meg passed was a person, after all, someone's baby, someone's beloved. It was in groups that they became frightening, that they became fearless, that they did things you couldn't read in their eyes when they passed you on the street, holding a newspaper and a paper cup of coffee.

She crossed Eastern Parkway, which bisected the neighborhood, almost getting hit by three different cars, the normal amount for those long crosswalks. The parkway had been progressive in its time, she recalled—Olmsted and Vaux had conceived of it as an extension of their pet project Prospect Park, a scenic path for pleasure, though it hadn't actually been constructed until later: a wide street with green strips on either side for trees and benches and the encouragement of bike-riding and chess-playing, opening up that swath of inner Brooklyn to sunlight. Of course, in order to build the parkway, the city had had to bulldoze large sections of mostly Black neighborhoods, including a lot of old Weeksville, which was still in its forgotten, unexcavated awkward stage. The parkway served as a pragmatic memorial to the city's earlier mess. It was a miracle that those few houses on old Hunterfly Road had been spared, the house on Holland Avenue. Who knew what else hadn't been recognized in time, how much history had gotten bulldozed so that well-to-do Brooklynites could spend their summer weekends driving efficiently from Grand Army Plaza to the shore?

Whose city was this, anyway? Abandoned newspapers ghosted down the street, past storefronts closed behind graffiti-stained gates. It didn't belong to her, any more than it belonged to the rich people on the Upper West Side, any more than it belonged to the recent Syrian refugees scraping by in the outer boroughs, any more than it did to the Lenape Indians who had once roamed the land. Did it? She walked the desolate blocks radiating toward Holland Avenue, past vacant lots and boarded-up houses, her ears quivering from the thunderous elevated stretch of the old BMT train lines.

An old lady pushed a shopping cart past Meg, her hair towering in a Caribbean-print batik turban, her cracked ankles painfully exposed in the cold, humming an eerie song. She smelled like incense and jerk seasonings. Meg wanted to grab her and do she didn't know what. Be comforted by her. Comfort her. Eat her. Be eaten by her. What was that song? The woman looked up at Meg suddenly as their paths crossed, her irises very bright green and skewed by strabismus. Meg looked away.

Here, too, on the Caribbean side of Crown Heights, all along the avenues, shops were opening for the day. *RRRRRTTTTHHH-HAAAATTT!* A heavy metal gate rolled up at the Jamaican Grocer's. *RRRRRTTTTHHHHAAAATTT!* Another one revealed a money wire shop that advertised international calling cards colored green, yellow, black (the sign in the window read, plaintively, "Call Home"). An empty Caribbean bakery that had apparently once, a sign claimed, sold the best hardo bread off the islands; a shop selling Rasta-themed clothes and hats; a Dunkin' Donuts with a line out the door. A nail salon, a nail salon, another nail salon. A hair salon that specialized in braids, next to a hair salon that specialized in weave. A bodega, a bodega, another bodega—how they stayed in business lined up on the same block like triplets, a mystery. A restaurant that specialized in meat patties. Meg's stomach rumbled. She stopped at the corner for a two-dollar bacon, egg, and cheese on a roll, paid on her credit card because she never had cash when she needed it, ate it out of its foil bed while walking, hardly noticing when she burned her mouth on the melted American cheese. After she was done eating, she balled up the foil and threw it into an overflowing can.

Meg walked more slowly now, the greasy breakfast anchoring her to the world, like she'd eaten a gravity sandwich. She tongued the tender flap of singed skin on the roof of her mouth, a measurable pain, the kind she had learned to treasure after Kate's death.

Meg's legs thrummed from walking, but soon she was near where Ellis texted that he was, and they met on a street corner, and he was holding two cups of his sweet tea. She smiled gratefully as he handed one to her.

Meg and Ellis made their way down the deserted avenue. Ellis had texted her in the night—there was something at the house he wanted to show her, as soon as possible—and while she was thrilled to see a text from him, she was also terrified at the idea of going back into that house. She hadn't been sleeping, and she felt raw, reduced to a big walking nerve. But what, she was going to say no to Ellis? Now? After all they'd been through? Besides, it would be good for Rhys's Pieces, she told herself. She'd write a cracking yarn in there and amuse Mrs. Fishman.

So now they walked together in the dusky morning, the avenues of Crown Heights made indistinct by a fog that seemed misplaced, as if it belonged on a Pennsylvania hilltop and had taken a wrong turn somewhere. Meg noticed a police car idling at one intersection, a cop on foot a few blocks away. That was weird, wasn't it? Or anyway, it stood out to her, not the kind of thing she saw in her own neighborhood mere miles away.

That fall, police brutality had been in the air. It made her notice cops more, she realized, and look at them differently. The news vibrated with tales of boys getting shot by police—unarmed Black boys, mostly—with such startling frequency that Meg found herself shutting off the radio, closing the newspaper, unable to take in anymore, all the while berating herself for having the privilege to not think about the stories unless she wanted to, for using, maybe even abusing, that privilege. James showed his Luddite sister his social media feeds, which were crowded with the hashtag #BlackLivesMatter, heartbreaking memes of boys' last words before being shot by the police—"Mom, I'm going to college," or "I don't have a gun. Stop shooting."

This was what she was thinking about when she heard the glass shattering, which made her jump, look beseechingly at Ellis as if he could explain the noise since it was his neighborhood. It took her a beat to identify the sound—the ghost having a temper tantrum over at the house? Wait, what? No—a shop window shattering in the frigid November air.

Meg and Ellis exchanged a look. There was no one else on the block besides a couple of skinny teenagers in black hoodies, running away from the shattered front window. "Aw man, that's Sonny's," said Ellis. Then he yelled, "Hey! Hey you! What the hell do you think you're doing!" Meg put out a hand to stop him—was he crazy? This could be *dangerous*!—but he took off after the boys. When the boys, spooked, turned around, Meg saw that they were white, their sweatshirt hoods only partially covering the side-curls the Hasids wore. Ellis chased them. "Stop! STOP! I wanna talk to you! Wait!" Alarms blared from Sonny's, and Meg guessed that within a few minutes, there would be police sirens too. She watched helplessly. What was *she* supposed to do about any of this?

Ellis was fast, but the boys were faster—they turned another corner, running off silently and disappearing into the shadows like spirits. Ellis leaned forward over his knees. "Damn, Williams," he panted, "you gotta get back to the gym."

Meg trotted up to him, putting a hand on his back. "Are you crazy?" She laughed. "Are you *okay*?"

He nodded, panting, then shook his head. "I'm fucking horrified—" *pant, pant* "—that I'm so out of shape."

Sonny's alarm wailed plaintively into the air. They were all the way down the block now but saw who Meg guessed was Sonny himself run out, standing in the street and bellowing: "Who did this? Show your-self, ya cowards!" Sonny must have been in the kitchen in the back, Ellis muttered, starting the pulled pork, blackening the catfish. The kids had known he would be there. That's why they had come; it's why they had run so quickly.

In the same moment, Sonny saw Ellis standing there, sweating and panting, and police car sirens wailed up the street. Meg watched in horror as the muscular policemen—they looked like frat boys you'd see yelling at their girlfriends outside sports bars—hopped out of their car, their hands on their guns. Was this really happening? This wasn't real-ly happening. She couldn't understand it all quickly enough, couldn't comprehend how Ellis, genteel, sophisticated Ellis, knew so immedi-ately to put hands in the air. He cast her a sidelong glance, shrugged, "I'm not trying to get shot today." They were a horrible distance away from the cops, there in the indistinct light—close enough for the cops to see them but far enough away that any movement could be misread.

Meg felt a fear very different from the spooked feeling of encoun-tering ghosts in bedrooms. There was nothing eerie, nothing nebulous. There was just a hunted-animal feeling, inarticulate and pulsing in her limbs. Was this what it was to be Ellis? To not even have time to think, *but this is unfair, how can you blame me, I have advanced degrees, I have nothing in my pocket more menacing than a borrowed paperback,* to know instead, innately, *they suspect me and I have to show that I would surrender.* For an awful moment, Meg could read descriptions of the incident in the future newspapers: he was a charging bear; he was a subhuman hulk. "Your honor," the uglier cop would have said, "the six-foot-five, probably almost seven feet tall, perp lunged forward. He had his hands at his waistband. I was afraid for my life." And that would be enough, all he had to say; this, Meg thought, was what it really meant to be haunted.

Ellis called out in the chilling silence, "Hey, Sonny! Officers! Don't shoot! I'm unarmed! I saw what happened. Sonny, it's me! Ellis Wil-liams!" Ridiculous. Fucking ridiculous that he had to say it that way. That he had to move slowly and cautiously toward them, that Meg felt she should walk with him in the same surrendering way, as if it might help if they saw her along with him in solidarity—at least it was light out now, maybe even these idiots could see through their hopped-up adrenaline his camel coat, his calm face—his hands in the air, until Sonny squinted and said, "Oh shit! Hey, man! That's—you're Harmon's boy, right?" And Ellis nodded thankfully, and the cops took their hands off their guns.

"It was two boys, Sonny. Teenagers, skinny little white boys. Really," he said this to the cops, who squinted at him. Meg nodded vigorously, though the cops did not seem to register her presence.

Sonny sucked his teeth in disgust. "Makes sense."

"Does it?" One of the preadolescent cops turned on Sonny.

"They mad. They mad because that thing last week, when the windows got broke at the bar or whatever it is."

"Oh, yeah," Ellis explained to the cops in his most starchy, scientist's voice, enunciating each word like its edges might save him: "That wine bar, over by Eastern Parkway, you know? The fancy new place? It was written up in the *Times*?" The cops blinked blandly. Right, they probably read the *Post*, if anything, or watched Fox News, consuming the informational equivalent of Burger King. "Well, they had their windows smashed last week, and these teenagers got arrested. Black teenagers. They were on the security camera footage, they definitely did it," (this to Sonny, who was grumbling) "and then there was a story on the news about gentrification and racial tension in Crown Heights, and an old Black guy they interviewed said something like, 'Well, the yuppies ain't so bad, at least they ain't the Jews.'" Sonny opened his mouth and closed it again. It *had* happened, after all. They couldn't unsay what someone else had said. It had been on TV.

The shorter cop rubbed his butter-smooth face and squinted at Sonny. Sonny put his hands in the air. "But it wasn't me that said it," he said. "I guess all us old Black guys look alike to them. That's okay, I don't blame them. They all look alike to me." He chuckled at Ellis who nodded neutrally. The tween police squad consulted, started scribbling something on their pads, Meg couldn't imagine what. Tickets for the shards of glass? Eventually the cops nodded their heads, releasing them back into the flow of ordinary life, now carbonated with adrenaline. Ellis waved to Sonny, who nodded his thanks, and Ellis and Meg turned to walk down the sidewalk toward Holland Avenue.

It took them a moment to be able to speak. Finally Meg said, "That was fucking weird."

Ellis nodded. "No kidding." Then he looked at her, touched her shoulder. "Hey. Hey, I'm really sorry about that."

"You? You didn't do anything!"

"'Course I didn't. But that's not the point. I chased the boys, I was there with you. If the cops had—if something had happened—well. If something happened to you. I couldn't forgive myself."

Meg shook her head. "I don't even know what to say. That was so messed up. That they even looked at you funny, you know?"

"Yeah, well. I'm sure you've had messed-up walks, too. Right? Rachel used to say I would never know what it was like to be a woman walking down a dark street at night."

"I guess so. Yeah, I mean, of course, I've had creepy nights. I've been followed, I've been leered at, I've felt like there were places I just couldn't go. But still." Her mind was fuzzy, fizzy, unable to focus enough to move past platitudes. It was better to stop talking, then, to walk silently beside him. Her thoughts turned to the house, wondering what they would find when they got there. The front windows smashed in by antigentrifiers? The construction crew suspended near the ceiling by an angry poltergeist? Each seemed equally likely.

"I remember," said Ellis, his voice cauterizing the air between them, "this time we were at Sonny's lunch counter. Me and my dad. I was minding my own business, drinking an Orange Crush, when Professor Williams delivered unto me his Presentation on the Crown Heights Race Riots of 1991, or as it was known at that time, Last Month. I must have been about eleven I guess, and I'd asked why we hadn't been to the rental house in a while, why the streets looked different. I'd watched the riots with my parents on TV, but somehow that made it feel far away. I couldn't quite figure out why my mom was crying, why my dad was pacing around, all hectic."

Meg nodded, though she didn't remember the riots in the same visceral way—it had been another unfortunate news story, mostly swept aside as she applied for colleges or pined after a boy or whatever else teenage Meg had been wrapped up with at the time.

Ellis continued, "I remember I'd only taken a bite of my sandwich before Dad launched into his lecture, this kind of like an incantation, that I'm sure went over big in his undergraduate seminars but was so embarrassing for a kid"—and he pitched his voice to sound like a movie preacher—"'A boy! just a bit younger than you! was playing on the sidewalk. A Black boy, as it happens. His parents here from Guyana, looking for a better life. A better life for their young Black son. A hot summer night, playing on the sidewalk with his cousins. Not a care in the world. A car comes careening off the avenue, just like that. A motorcade passing by, the motorcade of a holy man to the Jews. A holy man. But one of the cars speeds through a red light to catch up, is struck, careens. Careens into the Black boy.' And I'm getting all impatient, like Jeez Dad, can you just tell me what happened?"

Meg laughed, got lost in the way Ellis told his story, could picture the speech singing its way out (people gather to hear, Sonny stops cooking, a beat cop coming in for coffee stands transfixed, and preteen Ellis sits there mortified, wishing to transform into an ice cube, praying to melt into his soda), how eventually Harmon pieced together the story—the Jewish guy kills the Black kid, gets pulled out of his car and beaten, and soon race riots erupt in the neighborhood, each feeling attacked on their home turf. Three whole days of de facto war. Three days of fire and pillaging and looting and killing and chaos. Ellis admitted his interest was piqued here, because he was eleven and now it sounded like a video game. He didn't yet know that he could die, that anyone could die. The boy who was pinned by the car, the boy who started it all, that boy didn't have a face or a name in Ellis's mind, wasn't an actual kid, was he? It all sounded pretty exciting, and he knew it probably wasn't the right response to feel a vicarious thrill curdling in his gut, like when playing a brawl *Street Fighter*, but hey, his father knew how to tell a story.

And Ellis, recounting his father's story, showed he could tell a story, too. He would have made a great teacher himself, had he not been so intent on rebelling against Harmon; Meg could see it all, felt viscerally (walking down those same streets where the riots had happened) how the memories had congealed, left keloid welts on the skin of the city. "'The people will forget,' Harmon decreed, 'but the neighborhood, the city! Will not forget! The land can't ever fully forget what it sees, never forgets the taste of children's blood.' He stops then and leans back and takes a huge bite of his sandwich, and the crowd that's gathered starts *applauding*, and I'm so mortified at this point, I'm like 'Dad. Okay. I get it. It sucked. Can we please go now?'" Ellis shook his head, laughed a little. Meg smiled at him, reached out to rub his shoulder. Was this a thing she could do now? It seemed like it was.

They turned the corner onto Holland Avenue. That newish storefront—had it been an old wooden church, burned to the ground in 1991? The traffic light ahead, added after a pile-up in 2006? The streets were still morning-quiet except for an occasional livery car racing toward the Parkway. Rush hour took place elsewhere, where the city's other life was lived.

A delivery truck puttered down Holland with a swervy slowness that suggested a lost driver checking a GPS. The logo struck Meg—something about it was familiar, though she couldn't have said how—a large, eerie eye in a diamond, more like a Masonic symbol you'd find on a dollar than like a regular truck, the words SHIPPING & RECEIVING unhelpfully arched above. She followed the truck's eye all the way down the block, shook off the creepy feeling of being watched by an inanimate object as Ellis led her toward the house.

They stood on the destroyed sidewalk and regarded the house on Holland. It was certainly the most unsettling, unsettled building Meg had ever faced in her long history of occupying their haunted city: a sagging edifice, shutterless windows like the eyes of a junkie startled in a compromising moment, a clammy chill emitting from it like actual weather. Unbidden, her mind served up the words, "with the first glimpse of the building, a sense of insufferable gloom pervaded my spirit." Who had said that? She shuddered. And—

"It's got good bones," a voice behind them boomed. They both jumped, whirled around. A portly, red-faced man in khakis waved a clipboard at them.

Ellis laughed. "Oh, shit! Man, I forgot you were coming this morning. Meg, this is our contractor. His men are having some trouble working in the house."

"No kidding," Meg said wryly.

The contractor laughed, clapped Ellis on the back. "You look like one of my guys now! Everyone's *spooked*. You oughta hear the stories they tellin' me, it's like a buncha old biddies who rode the Spook-a-Rama too many times at Coney Island. I tell 'em, it's just a house, relax, *ladies*." He shrugged at Meg, inviting her to join him—*Ladies! Get it! Because they are frightened and weak!*—horking out the hearty laugh of a Macy's Santa Claus by way of Sheepshead Bay.

"I see," Ellis answered. He looked at Meg. She raised an eyebrow, all she could muster.

They walked up the steps and into the house together. Meg braced herself at the door. The last time she'd been in this house, she'd been knocked to the floor. There was an angry presence in there, they knew that much. What was it capable of?

She tried to remind herself to breathe, to keep everything in perspective. She was probably still jumpy. Almost getting shot by twelve-year-old cops had that effect on her, apparently.

It was cold in the house, colder than the brisk November day itself, so cold that Meg looked around for an open window, a pane of broken glass. The contractor shook his head. "I've seen this before, believe me. You ain't da first." He directed his comments to Meg now, having decided she must be the mistress of the house. "It's cold, it's clammy, there's a weird wind. It's no good. Worse than roaches, worse than rotten wood, know what I mean? No good at all."

They moved loudly through the first floor, as if they might scare off whatever shouldn't be there. The contractor pushed open the door of the first floor apartment. Meg winced. He stomped through the living room, Meg and Ellis trailing behind—he walked like an elephant, but a circus elephant, the graceful kind. What was it to be a man like that, so assured, so unselfconscious, so *ordinary*? He probably went home after work and took off his boots and watched network television and thought it was wonderful. Maybe he never even thought to ask himself what life was all about. Or maybe he knew what life was all about. Maybe he was who the world had been made for. Maybe he understood everything. His favorite food was probably cheeseburgers. Meg sighed and followed him into the gloom.

But even as she braced herself for the hypothermic evil, the inchoate danger and swirling darkness that had accosted her last time they'd entered the keeping room, it seemed now, in the newborn morning, with the calm, ordinary presence of the contractor there beside them, like any other construction site. Meg was able, for a moment, to see the room as just a room. The floor was torn up, the walls stripped to studs, the air on the humid side, but to look at the room now was to render all talk of the supernatural absurd, like in the moments after orgasm when the whole idea of sex seemed unlikely and odd.

"Now look," said the contractor. "I got a crew of men sayin' that weird shit is happenin', like heavy equipment launchin' though the air, doors slammin' *and lockin'* on their own, creepy sounds and shit. It's nothing I ain't seen before. What can you do, houses in this city been through a lot of shit! I can tell 'em it's neighborhood kids pullin' pranks on 'em, no problem. We will get the job done. No problem. But you gotta help me with this, my man. Tell me what to do with all this." He gestured into the keeping room like a muscular Vanna White.

Ellis and Meg stared. There was the floorboard Meg had tripped on when they'd been there together a few days earlier. Okay. So it had been loosened, so now it gaped open, neatly placed perpendicular to the other boards, which was weird, but you could imagine it happening with the help of a very fussy squirrel with excellent manual dexterity, or perhaps an archeologically minded rat.

Then Meg saw what the contractor was talking about. Sitting quietly in a neat row, like a kids' baseball team ready to play, were dusty objects: A crumbling leather-bound book. An incomplete set of jacks. An ivory comb, a few dark strands of hair tangled around the tines. A pair of small leather shoes. A folded, ancient map. A desiccated rag doll.

"Tell 'em what they've won!" bellowed the contractor, chuckling. The contractor would go about his day's business, would eat a fast food lunch. He would watch a murder-mystery program on television. He would sleep next to his wife. But Meg and Ellis knew better. Death, death, death.

"Holy shit," answered Ellis.

Ellis stepped toward the objects, knelt before them. Meg watched him. The room was still. Still a room. A map. A book. She looked at the contractor leaning in the doorway, recently bereft of its door. She studied the structure around him, trying to envision the future the Williamses had in mind for the house—an open living space with modern fixtures and bright track lighting, some rich couple moving in and installing a million dollars' worth of wallpaper and mid-century modern furniture.

Ellis looked wearily past the contractor. "You found it in the floorboards?"

The contractor's head swiveled on his wide, red neck. "No, sir. My men found it all just like that. Laid out yesterday after lunch, neat as can be. We were in here, Jimmy tells me a hammer went flying through the air, I decide we all need a break, we go out and eat at the diner, we come back in, and we see all this shit. No one was in the house, you know. It just kinda—appeared."

Ellis sighed. 'Tell you what, man," he said. "Let me figure out what the deal is with this stuff. Maybe my father collected it for historical context." They all knew this was far-fetched, but no more far-fetched than any other explanation, including the construction workers playing erudite pranks on each other. "You and your guys take the day off. I'll call you tomorrow and let you know what my father wants to do. But there won't be any more weird shit going on. I promise."

The contractor raised his eyebrow. "If you say so." He clambered off, left them alone in the house.

"So this is what you wanted to show me?" Meg stood on one side of the artifact-line-up, spoke to Ellis across the open floorboard.

He shook his head. "Actually, no. I hadn't even seen this. I was here early yesterday, before the contractor and his guys showed up." He rubbed his face, mumbling something how fucked-up it all was—she couldn't disagree—and then moved over to the doorway that connected the keeping room to the kitchen, where the door had recently been removed. "This." Ellis knelt down, ran a fingertip over the jamb. Meg came close, leaned over, conscious of Ellis's apple-cinnamon smell. She moved her finger toward his. Only then did she see it: scratched in the wood, worn almost away by the tides of the door opening and closing, a faint dispatch: IRIS WAS HERE.

Meg wanted to believe, of course she did. But the librarian in her was detective-sharp, wary of circumstantial evidence. She straightened up, smoothed her dress. "That could have been anyone. Anyone who ever lived in the house, right?"

Ellis stood in the doorway, jammed his hands in his pockets. He looked so young there in a beam of light trickling in from the kitchen windows, dust motes swirling around him, that something in Meg shifted, reached out again to him—poor baby! He shrugged. "Anyone who lived in this house before that door was there."

"Ah, right. That *was* an old door," Meg conceded.

"The contractor asked if we wanted to keep the door—like to use the wood for something. He said it was really nice wood. Old-growth."

Meg nodded. "They don't use that in construction anymore."

"Right. Haven't for probably a hundred years."

"But who was she? That name doesn't appear in any of the census records we went through."

"Exactly."

Meg rubbed her fingers over the markings again, felt a tremor in her fingertips.

What happened next was so strange that Meg, loudmouth Meg who loved telling anyone who would listen all about the supernatural, Meg who had been wanting something especially eerie to liven up her newsletter, yes that Meg, wouldn't tell a soul about it. She couldn't bear to reconstitute it, so deeply unsettling was the encounter:

All the doors slammed shut at once. Meg and Ellis looked around, called out, but there was no answer. Of course not; they were alone in the house.

Panic simmered in Meg's throat. "Hey, what the—" She went to the front door and rattled the knob, shoved her shoulder against it. Ellis came behind her, tried to open it.

"I guess I didn't do a very good job fixing this," he said, attempting lightness. But his voice sounded strained.

Meg tore away, feeling ice wrap around her. She went back into the keeping room and stopped short, swallowing a scream.

They were back in the hole in the floor, just as neatly as they had been arranged on the floorboards: The crumbling journal. The jacks. The comb. The shoes. The map. The doll.

"Okay," said Ellis. "Did—did you move those?"

Meg shook her head, laughing, though nothing seemed funny. "Are we going crazy? Did you put something in this tea?"

The back door slammed open suddenly, letting in a noisy gust of air and leaves, and slamming shut just as quickly. Meg jumped, unable to catch her breath. It was hard for her to slow her mind, to parse what was happening. (The front door now banged open, slammed shut again.) That had always been her sanity—pinning things down into words—and now the words weren't working. What had happened before, with the cops—that had been scary, that had been real. This was not real, and therefore (the window closest to her flew open, slammed shut) why did she feel so scared? Her life had been full of things she couldn't quite explain. This was just another. Wasn't it?

But the fear was hard to release, as if it had wormed into her bone marrow, infected her blood stream. It wasn't hers to release; it belonged to someone else, somehow. When Kate had died, this had been the way the grief behaved, filling Meg's capillaries, impossible to shake. There was no relief anywhere when a feeling gripped you like this, and it was awful, awful. One wanted to be in charge. One wanted to be able to talk oneself out of unpleasantness, *All right, it's not that bad*, adults were used to telling themselves, *here, get through this and afterwards you can have a cookie, a glass of wine. Promise.* Adults were used to being in control of their emotions. But Meg's emotions had always been unruly. She had had to work so hard to tamp them down, to tame them like horses, or at least train them like interns. *No, grief, down boy down. Love and longing? No thank you, you may go now, thank you for your interest.* Her superpower had always been control.

Now she found herself out of control, trapped in this hysterical house. That house needed to calm down already! Meg closed her eyes, tried to breathe, like a teacher working to stay measured. This would not overtake her. But it would, it did. Voices pressed against her ears: her mother saying, *A woman needs a family, don't you want your own little girl?* Kate saying, *Don't forget me, Meg. Don't ignore me like you did when we were young. Don't let me die the way you did before.* Even Mrs. Fishman: *There are different ways to gain your freedom, you know.* Voices saying things their people would never say, but that a part of Meg knew they meant to. And then a little girl, louder than all the others: *I never got to be a woman. Doesn't every girl deserve to be a woman? Don't you remember what it was like to be a girl?* The girl: *Don't be so hard on me, Meg.*

Meg's eyes snapped open. A girl's voice. The girl's voice. But also— of course. Of course!

"Oh," she said to Ellis, as the house seemed to rumble around them. He blinked at her. "Of course! Remember we read about the orphan? The orphan girl who Jacob Jenkins adopted! And the smallpox that passed through—Ellis, what if the little girl died here and never wanted to leave?"

Meg gathered some hithertofore well-hidden bravery, and as Ellis cried, "No! Wait!" stepped across the threshold into—stillness. The rumble stopped. The churn quelled. As if the keeping room wanted her to stay a moment. As if someone wanted to show her these things.

Meg knelt on the floor, ignoring her knee-creaks and the debris constellating on her long black skirt. She could hear all the doors of the house slamming open and shut at once, and although Ellis gasped and muttered, "Fucking Christ, man," Meg understood it for what it was, the house embracing her somehow, stilling itself, willing her to stay, to concentrate and notice and think. Meg spread the items across the floor, first holding each in her hands, feeling electrified as when

Ellis brushed his fingers against hers. It wasn't easy to shut off her habitual monologue of doubt and dismissal—This was stupid, that was
stupid, this wasn't really real, real life was elsewhere—but somehow
you knew when you had to. You knew when it was time to open to
the world. You knew when you actually needed, in your Godless, reli-
gionless, sacrednessless life, in the world that worshipped busyness and
breathlessness and speed over thought, in the universe where reactions
were published before events had completed themselves, where reflec-
tion was something only a mirror did, you knew when you had to slow
down your pulse and *look*. Meg remembered from some submerged
place having read about a man who created miniscule, precise sculp-
tures out of grains of rice, using eyelashes as paintbrushes. The man
had reported slowing his breathing to do his work, diminishing his
pulse. This was what Meg had to do to look at the objects left for her.
This was what was needed. A Meg with a different metabolism.

Meg reached out to touch the journal, and its cover felt warm, like
touching skin. The book opened. Ellis disappeared. The house disappeared. Horse flank and farm dust, pebbles from the road and mold
from trash festering in gutters. The filtered light of sun through thickets of trees. Yeast and coffee; piano and carriage rattle. The scrawled,
spidery text. *Weeksville, 1863. Mrs. Jenkins thinks I ought to keep a
journal. It is what cultured ladies do.*

Here was the one the journal had been waiting for. Meg the reader
lost herself in the text; Meg the historian understood the context; Meg
the librarian was gentle with the onionskin pages. Meg the girl went to
the dusty farm village with the scared, tough little kid.

Meg pieced together what the journal sketchily described—"the
draft riots," she murmured to Ellis—"the Orphan asylum." And in
a few pages, "Oh God, smallpox." There weren't many pages to read.
She closed it when the entries abruptly stopped. Fingered the precious
shoes, collapsed into themselves as they were, like faces at Pompeii.
Hefted the jacks in her palm, ran a finger over the comb, stroked the
brittle hair of the doll. Unfolded the map: Brooklyn, the farmlands. A
promotional flier stuck within advertised a grand new plan to build,

of all things, a bridge, from Manhattan to there, a Brooklyn Bridge. These things: all that was left of a life.

Meg thought of all the stuff she would leave behind—how her floor-to-ceiling shelves of books would someday become nothing more than someone's problem. Who? She wouldn't admit even in her own mind that her mother had a point, but without her own family—assuming she outlived James, which she'd better damn well do out of politeness if nothing else—who would ever sift through the evidence that Meg had lived, acknowledge that Meg, too, had taken up space in the world, that a whole experience of life, Meg's own particular universe, was gone? That once, Meg was here? Who would mourn? Once Meg had thought this was her gift to the world, her greatest ambition—that no one should have to mourn her. Who had mourned this little orphan, with her scratchy diary, her few imprints on Earth?

It had been the only home the girl had had. She had shaped that room, and that room had shaped her. At this point, the room *was* her. She had nowhere else to rest.

Meg looked at the journal again, running her fingers over the inside cover, where the girl had written her name. She looked up at Ellis. "Look." He took the book in his hands.

The house went still around them.

Meg had the strangest feeling that the walls were crumbling away, but when she looked, they were still there, solid as ever. She looked at Ellis, who leaned in the doorway, patient. Meg repacked the items into the hollow in the floor, replaced the board, tapped it down.

Ellis held up his hand to her and said, "Don't laugh, okay?"

"Um, okay. Don't laugh at what."

He didn't look at her then, but said, to the room: "Iris."

He said, "Iris, listen—I want you to know that I—we are sorry. We are sorry for everything that happened to you. You can stay, okay? Stay here and rest. Do you hear me, Iris? You stay as long as you want. We'll put your room back together how you like it."

They stood silently in the room, looking around.

"Do you feel that?" Ellis asked Meg.

Meg was quiet. "Feel what?"

"Nothing. Nothing! It feels . . . normal. Like a normal, ordinary house." Ellis laughed. "This house has never felt like this before." And he was right. The house was just an ordinary house.

They walked together out of the keeping room. They stood in the ruin of the living room. It could be pieced back together. Meg could help the Williamses apply for the historical registry; they could protect the house together, renovate it in a way that respected its bones, respected the neighborhood, respected the girl and her room. Meg thought that the girl would be still then. She had the feeling that if they left her alone, the girl would be still.

"I think it's going to be okay," Meg said.

Ellis reached for her hand, drew her to face him. "I trust you."

Meg smiled. "I trust you, too."

And Meg, who didn't care about love, who didn't even believe in it; Meg, whose chest was opening like a birdcage, like a book, like a door; Meg whose spine was pressed against the doorframe, Meg wrapped her arms around his neck and kissed him, and Ellis kissed Meg, and they stood there that way for a long, long time, as Ellis rebuilt his house and moved in, as Meg made 2E her own home, as they went their separate ways, as they made a life together, as they spent the rest of their lives together, as they never saw each other again, as Iris settled back into her home and Ellis made sure her story was told, as all of these things happened at once and none of them happened at all, they stood that way for the rest of time, as the house eventually crumbled around them, as the city disappeared into the sea, as everything else ceased, and they are standing there still.

# EPILOGUE

**HOW HUMBLING** it is to see the world chug along without you. To see the city expand and contract, shuddering through its various labor pains. A bridge, another bridge, a veining of trains, appendectomies of buildings that seemed solid as the earth itself. To have lost one's hope of ever leaving a mark.

Still. To have lived. To have lived at all. To have lived at all, and to have been free, and to have had, if nothing else, some time here. To have lived at all is a lot.

How we wish mediums could really let us speak! I have to admit I've spent years watching spiritualists and sibyls make great noise. I've skulked around Crow Hill séances snorting with a schoolgirl's defensive derision. But how I wished it could work. How we wish we could coo into ears. *There there. It's all right. I'm all right. I'm here with you. Of course I am.*

One day she appears in a flush of excitement. She coaxes me from the room. Only she can do this. She promises it's worth it. I give in. Out we go, into the bluster of night. The neighborhood is quiet. In the field near the Hunterfly Road cottages, where they are building a new museum, shining under the streetlamps, is a smooth disk of ice.

We hold hands, and we skate. Slipping, sliding, laughing, huge snowflakes on her eyelashes, dusting her curls. We try figure eights and loop-the-loops and we are graceful and we are fools and we laugh and laugh.

I pulse with joy, a feeling as foreign as another language.

We glide on the ice. We skate all night. She calls out my name.

*Iris,* she calls.

I say, *I'm here.*

# BIOGRAPHICAL NOTE

**AMY SHEARN** is the author of the critically acclaimed novels *How Far Is the Ocean from Here*, chosen as a notable debut by *Poets & Writers* and a hot summer read by the *Chicago Tribune*, and *The Mermaid of Brooklyn*, which was a selection of Target's Emerging Authors program, a Hudson News Summer Reads pick, and was also published in the UK and as an audiobook. She is a senior editor at *Forge*, a fiction editor for *Joyland Magazine*, and her writing has appeared in the *New York Times*, *Slate*, *Real Simple*, and many literary publications. She earned an MFA from the University of Minnesota, has received a Promise Award grant from the Sustainable Arts Foundation, and has participated in residencies at SPACE on Ryder Farm, the Unruly Retreat, and elsewhere. Amy lives in New York City with her two children.